W9-ADU-462

A SENSE OF
ENTITLEMENT

ANNA LOAN-WILSEY

Glenview Public Library
1930 Glenview Road
Glenview, Illinois 60025

KENSINGTON BOOKS
www.kensingtonbooks.com

KENSINGTON BOOKS are published by

Kensington Publishing Corp.
119 West 40th Street
New York, NY 10018

Copyright © 2014 by Anna Loan-Wilsey

All rights reserved. No part of this book may be reproduced in any form or
by any means without the prior written consent of the Publisher, excepting
brief quotes used in reviews.

All Kensington titles, imprints, and distributed lines are available at special
quantity discounts for bulk purchases for sales promotion, premiums, fund-
raising, educational, or institutional use.

Special book excerpts or customized printings can also be created to fit spe-
cific needs. For details, write or phone the office of the Kensington Special
Sales Manager: Kensington Publishing Corp., 119 West 40th Street, New
York, NY 10018. Attn. Special Sales Department. Phone: 1-800-221-2647.

Kensington and the K logo Reg. U.S. Pat. & TM Off.

eISBN-13: 978-0-7582-7639-1
eISBN-10: 0-7582-7639-7
First Kensington Electronic Edition: July 2014

ISBN-13: 978-0-7582-7638-4
ISBN-10: 0-7582-7638-9
First Kensington Trade Paperback Printing: July 2014

10 9 8 7 6 5 4 3 2 1

Printed in the United States of America

To Kenneth George Loan, my father

*The superior man is aware of righteousness,
the inferior man is aware of advantage.*

—CONFUCIUS, 551–479 B.C.

CHAPTER 1

I was the only one on deck, or so I thought. Water dripped from the brim of my straw hat as rain splattered against my umbrella. My knuckles turned white as I clung desperately to the slippery railing. The boat lurched beneath my feet and I thanked Providence yet again that I'd forgone eating supper. Only someone as ill at ease as me would be out in this weather. As I glanced about me, the satin ribbon on my hat fluttered for a moment in the wind and then stuck to my damp cheek. I peeled it away as I took another peek beneath my umbrella. I saw no one.

"*Un, deux, trois . . .*" I began counting in French to calm my nerves.

Why had I let Sir Arthur talk me into this?

Looking back I realized, as always, I hadn't had much of a choice. But I had erroneously thought that I would enjoy myself. Six weeks in Newport, the "Queen of Resorts," with a plethora of new plant species to collect, miles of hiking along seaside cliffs, and only some light typing duties. It would be like a vacation. At least that's what Sir Arthur said. He and his wife, Lady Phillippa, had rented a cottage in Newport for the summer Season, and having a few loose ends to finish up with his manuscript, Sir Arthur suggested that I accompany them. I grew up in the Middle West. To me an ocean was a static black and white image I saw through the lens of my mother's stereoscope. I leaped at the chance to witness the vast, churning blue sea for myself. But Sir Arthur never mentioned a boat ride.

I'd never been on a boat before and had never planned to be on one. People die on boats. At least that's what my mother told me over and over when I was a child. If I ever questioned her she would remind me that her brother burned to death on the *Sultana* and my father's uncle drowned after falling out of his fishing boat on Oneida Lake in New York. I grew to know she was right. One can rarely pick up a newspaper these days without finding some tragedy that is linked to the sinking or explosion of a ship. So why in heaven's name did I have to board this vessel? Sir Arthur, of course. When Sir Arthur insists on something, it's not my place to question him. In this case, I may have if a young woman in a white Gainsborough hat hadn't impatiently prodded me twice in the back of the knees with her baby carriage, thus propelling me into the crowd and toward the gangplank. Before I could voice any protest, I was aboard and following the steward to my room. My stomach churned, either from a slight case of seasickness or from swallowing the terror I felt but couldn't show, from the moment the ship pulled away from the dock. And the trip would take almost twelve hours!

Fresh air on deck didn't help. Staying belowdecks in my berth that I shared with Miss Kyler, Lady Phillippa's lady's maid, didn't help. Strolling the length of the ornate Grand Saloon, admiring the high gilded ceilings and intricate panel carvings, didn't help. Listening to the afternoon concert on the hurricane deck didn't help. I kept my seat through the march, the schottische, and the overture, but when the orchestra struck up Faust's waltz, "Golden Wedding," I felt my stomach lurch and spent the next twenty minutes clutching a water basin in the public washroom. I skipped attending the evening concert altogether. Entering the dining room for dinner, with its scents of freshly baked bread, smoked meat, and butter, certainly didn't help. I hadn't eaten since breakfast yesterday. Even listening to Miss Kyler's cheerful banter as she described past summers in Newport with Sir Arthur and Lady Phillippa in the Gallery Saloon sipping ginger ale didn't help. Regardless of the fact that to all ostensive purposes, the *Providence* was a floating palace for all to enjoy, nothing helped. And nothing would alleviate my fears and settle my stomach until I had my feet planted firmly on dry land.

Eventually Miss Kyler bid me good night. As sleep was out of the question, I thought I would try fresh air again. So despite the late hour and the rain, which started an hour into our journey, I sought solace out on deck. I didn't find it.

". . . *quatre, cinq, six, sept, huit, neuf, dix* . . ." I continued counting.

Slam!

I jumped at the sound of the door and clenched even tighter to the railing. Before I could reproach myself for reacting so violently to the closing of the door, I heard it, over the sound of the rain spattering against the deck and the waves crashing against the sides of the boat—an audible scraping noise. I looked toward the sound to see a broad-shouldered man in a raincoat and round-crowned rubber hat, his back to me, pushing a steamer trunk along the deck. What was he doing? I wondered. Why would he have his travel trunk up on deck in the rain? Trunks were not rainproof and I visualized the effects that the rain was having on its contents: books ruined, shirts stained, hats limp and misshapen. He pushed his burden toward a gap in the railing and stopped. Why would anyone be so reckless? Surely he knew he could fall?

"Sir!" I yelled out. "Please take care!" He stepped closer to the edge. "Watch out!" I screamed to no avail. With the sound of the waves, the rain, and the distance between us, I don't think he heard me.

The boat lurched again beneath my feet. I wrapped the crook of my arm around the railing, securing myself even more as the man swayed slightly but didn't retreat from his post. Now all I could do was watch.

To my relief he gained his balance. He looked about him, as if to check for witnesses to his folly. He spotted me. We locked eyes for a moment and he scowled. Water dripped from the ends of his long, thin black mustache. A shiver went down my back that had nothing to do with the cold wind at my back. I turned my face away, appearing to gaze back out over the ocean, but watched him out of the corner of my eye. He shook his head and dismissed me with a wave of his hand as he turned back to the trunk. He crouched down and with one swift push shoved the trunk overboard. I leaned slightly over the railing, nearly losing my umbrella to the wind, and watched the trunk fall through the air and disappear into the darkness. I heard it land with a splash and imagined it bobbing up and down in the waves for a few moments before upending itself and sinking straight into the water.

What was in that trunk? I wondered. Why would anyone want to throw it overboard? My mind raced and the same thought came back to me again and again: *a dead body*. After finding one of my employers in one, I'd never been able to look at travel trunks the same way again. And now one was sinking down to the bottom of the ocean right below me. The fear of the boat, seasickness, and the anxiety from watching what might have been the disposal of yet another dead body were too much. I couldn't take it anymore. I retched over the side of the railing. With my stomach now empty, I wiped my mouth with a handkerchief, already damp from the rain, staggered back from the railing, and felt for the wall behind me. I inched along the wall. As I approached a door, it flung open, the light from within flooding the deck. A short, brawny man in his early fifties with a partially bald head, a graying dark brown mustache, deep-set eyes, and a dimpled chin stood in the hall. He was hatless yet otherwise impeccably dressed in formal evening attire and he looked vaguely familiar.

Where have I seen him before? I wondered. He recoiled as I dashed by him out of the rain.

"Excuse me," I said, but the gentleman was already preoccupied with the man from the deck, who had joined him from outside. I stepped around the corner. I stopped to catch my breath, not yet trusting my wobbly legs to carry me back to my room. Someone began to whistle Beethoven's "Ode to Joy."

"Who was that?" one of the men said, extremely vexed. I distinctly heard the sound of a hand brushing with the grain of a coat sleeve. "And stop doing that." The whistling stopped.

"Nobody, just some seasick lady who was out on deck," was the other's reply. "She's nothing to worry about."

"Nothing? The damn woman got me wet!" the first man said.

"Sorry, boss. I can find her for you." I held my breath. Little did they know how easily I was to be found. *And what then?* I wondered.

"Forget it." I let my breath out. "I want a report, man. Did you do it? Is it gone?"

"Yeah, it's gone. And trust me, no one will ever find it either."

"Good. Now let's hope that put an end to it."

"They won't be able to mistake the message, boss."

"Good, for I will not have my Season disrupted, Double-day. Whatever it takes, do it."

"Yes, sir," the man called Doubleday said. "At least that little gnat won't be bothering you again." Little gnat? Were they talking about me or someone else?

"Let's hope no one bothers me again," the gentleman said. "Understand?"

"Yes, sir!"

"Let's hope so. Now get out of here. I don't want anyone seeing us together." The whistling started again.

That was my cue. Before the men turned the corner to find me eavesdropping, I tucked my umbrella under one arm, put my handkerchief to my mouth just in case I got queasy again, picked up my skirts, and ran.

CHAPTER 2

"Bloody hell!" Sir Arthur said, handing the telegram to his wife, Lady Phillippa. She pursed her lips and pouted. "Apologies for my language, dear." Only Lady Phillippa could solicit an apology from Sir Arthur. She nodded her head in response and then turned her attention to the telegram. She scanned the contents.

I had met up with them and their other staff as soon as the boat docked in the Newport harbor. I hadn't slept at all and was still feeling shaky and nauseous, whether it was from the boat crossing the water or the shock I'd received from witnessing a man throw a trunk overboard I didn't know. I'd spent the last leg of the journey curled up against the wall in my berth. I regretted missing the sunrise that Miss Kyler assured me had been spectacular, but having dry land beneath my feet again made up for my disappointment. I was thrilled to be off the boat. Our entourage had just disembarked when a telegraph operator came through the crowd shouting, "Sir Arthur Windom-Greene! Urgent telegram for passenger, Sir Arthur Windom-Greene!"

"Oh, Arthur, this is terrible," Lady Phillippa said, handing back the telegram. "When will you have to leave?"

"Immediately."

"Are you saying you're simply going to turn around and go back to New York?"

"It's unavoidable, I'm afraid. Though I plan to take the express to Boston, not New York. I may be able to get a boat to Southampton tomorrow morning."

"But Arthur, we just got here!" If Lady Phillippa had been a child, she would've stomped her foot. "As it is, you'll be gone for two or three months. Can't you wait a few days?"

"The Viscount is ill, Phillippa. I have to go now. You could come with me?" Sir Arthur said, knowing full well what his wife's response would be.

"And miss the Season? Now you're being ridiculous. Besides, your father has a constitution like a warhorse."

"You're lucky you even got the telegram," a voice from nearby said. We all turned to see a lanky middle-aged man wearing the latest style of stiff-crowned hat the color of his brown hair and a well-tailored single-breasted square-cut suit. His clothes were incongruous with his unkempt, shaggy hair, untrimmed mustache, and purplish bruise on his left cheek.

"Excuse me?" Sir Arthur said, not even trying to hide his annoyance at being eavesdropped on. The man was oblivious to Sir Arthur's tone.

"Mark my words, the telegraph operators are going on strike this morning at eight o'clock sharp. You're lucky you arrived when you did or you wouldn't have gotten it in the first place."

"Strike?" Lady Phillippa said. "You must be mistaken, sir. This is July in Newport. There are no strikes in Newport and certainly not during the Season." The man simply shrugged.

"I guess even workers in Newport want better pay and fewer hours. Something to think about, eh, lady?" the man said, tipping his hat. As he stepped into the crowd, an elderly man in a top hat purposely tripped him with a cane, sending him stumbling into several passersby.

Why would someone do that? I wondered as the man with the cane disappeared into the crowd.

"Hey, watch where you're going," one passerby said.

"Pardon me," the shaggy-haired man said before he too mixed in with the crowd.

"Well, I never," Lady Phillippa said, completely flustered and oblivious to the intentional tripping.

"Don't worry, dear. The locals know better than to do anything to disturb the Season. Well," Sir Arthur said, gesturing to his valet to retrieve his trunks from the wagon the poor man had loaded only moments ago, "I'm off."

His wife presented a cheek, which he duly pecked with the slightest of kisses. "Say hello to your papa for me." And that was it for good-byes. Sir Arthur motioned to his valet and started to walk away.

"Sir?" I said, flabbergasted by this sudden turn in events. If Sir Arthur was to be gone for two or three months, what was to become of me? He wasn't even going to say good-bye.

"Ah, Hattie! Blast it! I'd forgotten all about you," Sir Arthur said.

Lady Phillippa eyed me. "Isn't she going with you?" his wife said.

A sudden horror struck me. My heart started pounding and I broke out in a cold sweat at the thought of accompanying Sir Arthur. If I had had trouble crossing from New York City to Newport, I couldn't imagine how I'd manage an ocean voyage.

"No," Sir Arthur said, to my utmost relief. "As much as your skills would be most helpful, Hattie, this is a private family matter. I'll have to attend to the details myself."

"Yes, I can see that is most appropriate, Arthur," his wife

said, tending to speak in my presence as if I weren't there. "But what of the girl, then?"

I first met Lady Phillippa briefly two days after I'd been in Sir Arthur's employ. She had accompanied him to Kansas City, the first and only time she had joined him on one of his research trips. She had been civil when Sir Arthur introduced me but little else. In the intervening years since then, I had worked many times for Sir Arthur at his home in Virginia, including this spring as I helped him finish his latest manuscript, and had interacted with Lady Phillippa on several occasions. As when we first met, she was always civil but withdrawn. She was a loving mother and a renowned hostess, but unlike her husband, who treated me like a trusted confidante, I was nothing but a "typewriter" to her. Hence she was more than a little surprised when Sir Arthur insisted I accompany them to Newport and, "as we were almost finished with the work," have a well-earned holiday. I had always admired Sir Arthur's generosity, but this sounded too good to be true. As I'd never seen the sea before and only heard rumors of the glorious "Queen of Resorts," I jumped at the chance. Lady Phillippa was not thrilled, but as I stayed out of her way and gave no cause for her to regret my presence, she did nothing to prevent me from going. Of course, what Sir Arthur wants, Sir Arthur gets. . . .

"You still have the manuscript to finish typing," Sir Arthur said to me in response to his wife's question. "That will take a week or two." I nodded. "And I trust you can submit it to my publisher and make any copy edits on my behalf without having to consult me?"

"Of course," I said.

"You can wire any major changes I may need to consider."

"Yes, sir."

"So that gives you about three weeks of work."

"But that only puts her into August, Arthur," Lady Phillippa said.

"We'll call it an even month then. I'll have your wages arranged to be wired when I get to New York. And of course you can stay at the cottage during that time."

"What shall I do for the last week or so, sir?" I asked.

"Take that holiday I mentioned."

"Arthur," Lady Phillippa said. "Isn't that being a bit too generous?"

Sir Arthur ignored his wife. "And after that time has expired, I grant you permission to write your own recommendation letter and sign my name."

"Arthur!" Lady Phillippa objected. "That's absurd. I know she's been helpful to you, but you can't trust—"

"Phillippa," Sir Arthur said sternly. His wife blushed at the rebuke. I'd only heard Sir Arthur speak to his wife that way once. I was mortified to be the cause of his sharp tone again. "Hattie can be trusted. You'd be wise to remember that while I'm gone." Lady Phillippa glanced at me, but I couldn't read her expression.

"Sir?" Logsdon, Sir Arthur's valet, said as he approached. "Everything's ready, sir." Sir Arthur looked at his watch. A whistle blew.

"That'll be the train. Good-bye, dear," Sir Arthur said, kissing his wife on her forehead. Drawn by a sudden cacophony of cries, calls, and squawks, I stepped away, in an effort to give the couple a moment of privacy, enthralled by a flock of gulls swooping over refuse dumped from a fishing vessel. One large dark-headed bird, pecking and flapping its wings at any others that came close, was rewarded with a fish head larger than its mouth. As it soared away with its prize, I turned back. Sir Arthur had disappeared into the crowd.

"The luggage is secured and our carriage is waiting, ma'am," Kyler said.

"Thank you, Kyler," Lady Phillippa said. Then she turned to me. "If I can trust you, Miss Davish, as my husband says, then I will have you ride with the luggage and ensure its safe arrival." Before I could respond, she turned on her heel and alighted into the carriage. Miss Kyler sent me a sympathizing glance and then pointed to the wagon where the luggage was loaded.

So much for a vacation, I thought as I watched Lady Phillippa's Rockaway drive away. I picked up my typewriter and made my way to the wagon. A man, wearing a wide-rimmed, high-crowned, drab-colored soft fur hat, pushing his way forcefully through the crowd, in his determination to get through jabbed his elbow into my shoulder, sending pain through my arm and nearly knocking me down. If my reflexes weren't to tighten my grip on my typewriter case, I surely would've dropped it. Instead, his coat had been open, and as I bent forward to gain my balance one of his brass buttons snagged on the satin trim around my sleeve.

"Oh, pardon me," he said absentmindedly as he yanked the button free. In that moment I noticed a silver shield-shaped badge on his breast pocket. It read: "Pinkerton National Detective Agency."

What was a Pinkerton detective doing in Newport? I wondered. Unless he was here for a summer holiday, I couldn't help remembering the man who had hinted about the telegraph operator strike. Could there be truth to the scruffy-haired man's rumors? Could the arrival of a Pinkerton detective hours before a rumored strike be mere coincidence? I doubted it. With the deadly conflict at the Homestead steel plant in Pennsylvania between striking workers and Pinkerton detectives a year ago, animosity between the two sides had only increased. The Pinkertons were as anti-strike as ever. Yet at the moment none of that mattered to me. I was already out of sorts after a sleepless, ill-spent night, Sir Arthur's abrupt departure, and my loss of a stable position, let alone Lady Phillippa's cool reception to the idea of my remaining in Sir Arthur's employ and thus in her household for another month. This man's rude behavior pushed me to my limit. Pinkerton detective or no, his behavior had been inexcusable.

"No, I will not pardon you, sir," I said. "You—" I looked the man in the eye, fully prepared to chastise him and take my frustrations out on him, when the man began to whistle. I stopped short, my mouth still open. It was him! The man who had thrown the trunk into the ocean. Suddenly the need to distance myself from him outweighed my desire to put him in his place.

"Hey, don't I know you?" he said.

"No, you must be mistaken," I said, looking away and waving to the driver of the wagon. The detective shrugged, began whistling "Ode to Joy" again, and continued on down the dock. I straightened my bonnet, brushed my dress, and let out a sigh of relief, but a moment too soon. The Pinkerton man turned around and looked back at me with a puzzled expression on his face. Before he could place me as his witness on the boat, I grabbed my typewriter, stepped quickly to the wagon, and climbed in next to the driver.

"Let's go," I said, watching for the man in the crowd. "Lady Phillippa wouldn't appreciate her luggage being late."

CHAPTER 3

As the sun began to rise over the gray roofs, green trees, and white church steeples of the town, I looked about me for the first time. Our wagon plodded along, finding its way slowly down Long Wharf past the boatbuilders' shops, tenement houses, run-down saloons, and sailboat moorings while navigating the heaps of discarded crates, lumber, broken oars, coils of weathered rope, and chunks of metal lying here and there on the wharf. The strong scent of decaying fish and salt water filled the air. As we joined the multitude of wagons, carriages, and carts driving back and forth to accommodate the nearly one thousand passengers who had arrived on our ship, fishermen, sailors, dockworkers, and boatbuilders walked the streets, filled the shops, and plied their trades, calling to one another over the din of seagulls cawing, carriages rattling, and boat whistles blaring. I was overwhelmed and had lost sight of Lady Phillippa's Rockaway long ago.

We then left the wharf and turned down a main thoroughfare, Thames Street. On one side, the harbor opened up revealing a shining calm blue sea punctuated by docks, wharfs, and slips. And there were boats everywhere. Steamboats, ferryboats, and fishing boats glided back and forth while rowboats and catboats wove their way through the watery alleys between colorful lobster buoys and dozens of anchored yachts with tall white sails reflecting the morning sun. It looked nothing like the choppy dark water I had crossed to get here. Across the street stretched a diversity of buildings of wood shingle, brick, and stone. Butcher shops, hardware and dry goods stores, banks, jewelers, milliners, and fish markets shared the street with homes, some a century old. Here the shades in the shop windows were still drawn, the awnings not yet unfurled. We passed market squares and parks, including one built next to a stately brick building pre-dating the founding of our country.

Eventually we left the shops and clusters of old homes and turned into a neighborhood of wide, well-manicured tree-lined streets and unseen dwellings hidden behind high, thick stone walls. It was quiet—the only sounds I heard were birds chirping, the clomping of horses, and the warm breeze rustling through the leaves. I closed my eyes, took a deep breath of the fresh, salty air, and relished the quiet, slow ride. This was more what I had anticipated thinking about visiting the "Queen of Resorts." I couldn't rid myself of the anxiety that the sudden shift in my situation created, but here, away from the bustle of town, I could try. With only Sir Arthur's manuscript to finish and submit, I'd have plenty of time to consider the events of the night and act later.

When we finally turned down Ruggles Avenue, I caught my first glimpse of the cottage Lady Phillippa and Sir Arthur had rented for the Season. Unlike the homes on Bellevue, Narragansett, and the other residential avenues that were hidden behind walls, the grounds of the Windom-Greenes' summer cottage were surrounded by a short wrought-iron fence and a well-trimmed hedge that allowed a full view of the house. I gasped at what I saw.

They call this a cottage?

An eclectic mix of stone blocks on the first story and wooden shingles on the second, the "cottage" was a sprawling two-and-a-half-story mansion with multiple chimneys, balconies, verandas, and alcoves under a massive gabled roof punctuated with dormer windows. As we approached the house, we passed Lady Phillippa's hired Rockaway heading back to the stables. The coachman tipped his hat to the wagon driver, who returned the favor. We passed the main entrance, a recessed porch ornamented by a rainbow of colorful gladiolus, and drove to the back entrance, where we were greeted by a footman, still wiping the sleep from his eyes. He and the driver unloaded the carriage as I stood there uncertain what to do next.

"You Sir Arthur's secretary?" the footman finally said, without stopping what he was doing.

"Yes," I said.

"Welcome to Fairview. We've been expecting you. Kaarina's inside. She'll show you to your room."

"Thank you . . . ?"

"The name's Johnny."

"Johnny? Not John?"

"No, why?"

Should I tell him *John* might be more appropriate in the presence of Lady Phillippa? That in Virginia Lady Phillippa managed the house in the traditional English way? No "Johnnys" or "Jimmys" allowed. *No,* I thought. Who was I to say? Maybe Lady Phillippa would be less formal in Newport. I hoped so.

"Never mind," I said. "Thank you, Johnny."

The footman shrugged, picking up as many suitcases as he could carry. "Sure."

"And thank you," I said to the wagon driver. He tipped his hat and clambered back up onto the wagon and drove away. I picked up my typewriter and as many of my hat boxes as I could carry and went in. A maid, no more than fifteen years old, with a wide smile, despite a chipped front tooth, and wisps of bright red hair escaping from beneath her cap, helped me with my boxes.

"If you'll follow me, miss," she said.

She led me up three flights of uncarpeted wooden stairs that were smooth and slippery beneath my shoes. Once I left the brightness of the day outside, my eyes took a few moments to adjust to the darkness of the stairwell. With no windows, the only light to guide us came from a lamp positioned on each landing that reflected off the highly polished white tile walls. *It's not as if I'm wearing slippers,* I thought as I held tightly to the thin railing. If I was to traverse these stairs for any length of time, I was going to have to get more sensible shoes.

"Has Lady Phillippa sent word for me?" I asked as we arrived on the uppermost floor.

The maid frowned and shook her head. "Only that I was to bring you to your room."

I nodded and followed her down a long hallway, lit by windows at either end, and into a whitewashed room, set with two wrought-iron beds with simple white linens, a dressing table with a washbasin, and a chair. And nothing else: not a framed picture of a dear parent left behind, not a cutout from a magazine taped to the wall, not a pair of old, comfortable slippers under the bed. The fire had already been banked and the wooden floor was bare. I shivered. I'd never completely dried from my foray on the ship's deck.

"If you don't mind, you'll be sharing with me, miss," the maid said, blushing. "Washroom's at the end of the hall to your left." I simply nodded. I was never one to shy away from a walk, in fact I relished long hikes, but the idea of traversing the entire length of the hall to visit the washroom was simply beyond me right now. I was exhausted. "That's your bed." The maid pointed to the one against the far wall. With no place to set up my typewriter, I left it in its case and placed it on the floor next to the bed.

"Thank you for sharing your room, Kaarina. I'm Hattie, by the way," I said, taking off my shoes.

"Of course, miss. I was so excited when Mrs. Russell told me who the new girl was. I thought it would be a kitchen maid or even a housemaid, but a secretary! I've never met a lady typewriter before. You must have lots of learning to be able to work for the master. I want to be a parlormaid myself one day. Maybe—"

"I'm going to try to get a few hours of sleep, Kaarina," I said, lying down, barely able to keep my eyes open.

"Oh, right. Sleep well, miss."

Exhausted and cold, I pulled the sheet and cotton blanket over me, not bothering to undress, and fell asleep almost instantly.

"Oh, Hattie," Lady Phillippa said, putting a letter she'd been reading on the table. "What am I going to do with you?"

I had wondered the same thing since the moment I woke up. I had slept soundly for the few hours afforded me, but I'd been woken up to Kaarina shaking me after I had missed breakfast. She had kindly brought me black coffee, toast with butter, and raspberry jam. As I hadn't eaten in almost twenty-four hours, I ate every bite. After washing up, I spent an hour in our room looking over Sir Arthur's unfinished manuscript. If I worked diligently and was uninterrupted, I would finish not in the two weeks that Sir Arthur had surmised but in a few days. What then? I would submit the manuscript, which would take a few hours at the most. Sir Arthur had given me a month of wages, but I had less than a week's worth of work. What would I do? Should I take the holiday that he suggested? It was tempting. Since beginning my career as a lady typewriter and private secretary years ago I could count the number of days I'd taken purely for leisure on my fingers. I had brought my plant press with me and could easily spend weeks hiking the island and collecting new plant specimens for my collection. But then what would Lady Phillippa say? Would she allow me to remain at Fairview while I frittered the days away bathing on the beach and adding to my plant collection? When Kaarina returned to tell me Lady Phillippa wanted to see me, I assumed my questions and musings about taking a holiday had been moot; the lady had already decided my fate.

"Ma'am?" I said, knowing full well what Lady Phillippa was talking about.

"With Sir Arthur gone, you don't have a purpose in this household now, do you?" Lady Phillippa said.

"I have a few days' work left on Sir Arthur's manuscript."

"Yes, but what then?" Lady Phillippa raised her teacup to her lips and hesitated, looking at me over the rim. I knew a rhetorical question when I heard one and stood silently awaiting her word. "Sir Arthur did mention that you'd be able to write yourself a glowing recommendation letter?"

"Yes, ma'am."

"Then I think it prudent that you do so. I'll sign it when you're through."

"Yes, ma'am."

"I wouldn't be doing you any favors if I allowed time to lag between your assignments."

"No, ma'am."

"Questions may be raised as to how you spent that time, don't you think? Especially if you are under my roof."

"Yes, ma'am."

"Good, I'm glad we have come to an understanding."

"Yes, ma'am. I will arrange to visit an employment agency this morning, if that suits you?"

Lady Phillippa picked up the letter she'd been reading when I arrived. "There'll be no need to submit to the scrutiny of an agency."

"Ma'am?" I said, suddenly not understanding her at all.

She smiled like a Cheshire cat and waved the letter in her hand. "I think I have a solution that we will both be happy with." She pointed to the letter. "This came yesterday in anticipation of our arrival. It's from Mrs. Charlotte Mayhew." Lady Phillippa said the woman's name slowly for impact, and for good reason. Sir Arthur and Lady Phillippa may have been British nobility, but Charlotte Mayhew was equivalent to American royalty. Charlotte Mayhew was the wife of one of the wealthiest men in America. Along with Mrs. Astor and Mrs. Vanderbilt, she was purported to be one of Newport society's grande dames. Her husband was one of the most influential men in the country. Mrs. Mayhew was one of the most influential women in Newport. While working for Sir Arthur and his circle of friends I'd learned that social standing, among other things, was vitally important to this wealthy class. And before we arrived, Miss Kyler and I spent many a mealtime discussing the finer points of Newport society. While other summer resorts attracted multitudes of visitors, some more hospitable, many much closer, none carried the status of Newport. Lady Phillippa, who still had two unmarried sons and hoped to find brides among the title-seeking upper classes of America, would summer nowhere else.

"And," Lady Phillippa said, hesitating for dramatic effect, "she's looking to hire you."

"Me?" I didn't know what else to say. Why did Charlotte Mayhew want to hire me? How did she even know of my existence? And before yesterday I'd been in Sir Arthur's employ. I wasn't even available. Or was she assuming that Sir Arthur would give me up simply because she asked? I had to wonder what he would have done. And I didn't like the answer that I came up with.

"Well, not you exactly," Lady Phillippa said. "But a social

secretary. The one she had got married and left her without a replacement. Can you imagine? Now she's in desperate need of help. She always plans a great number of parties, receptions, and the like. She says here that Sir Arthur is known to have employed secretaries of 'the highest quality and reputation' and would he be willing to hire her out for the Season? She's talking about you, Hattie. I know, because you've spoiled Sir Arthur. He was dissatisfied with every secretary he hired before you, and all of them were men. Now he'll only work with you."

A social secretary?

Lady Phillippa's compliments were lost in my sudden panic of thought. What did I know about being a social secretary to one of the most famous socialites in the country? I was a typewriter. What did I know about planning guest lists in high society? Granted I'm extremely well organized, efficient, discreet, and a quick learner . . .

Maybe I can do this, I thought. The few days of work I had left to do for Sir Arthur would have to be stretched into weeks of late night typing, but what a challenge, a thrill, to showcase my abilities. But would Mrs. Mayhew take me on with no experience?

"Yes, spoiled. Why else do you think he hired you back after that fiasco in Arkansas?" Lady Phillippa was saying. "And you're lucky he did too or your reputation would've been sullied by the scandal. And then again in Galena? What kind of ill luck do you have, girl? Obviously, Mrs. Mayhew knows nothing about your dealings with the murders and we're going to keep it that way, right?"

What was Lady Phillippa saying now? I had no idea my "adventures" in Eureka Springs and Galena had affected my reputation. That would be catastrophic. My reputation was all I had. What would Mrs. Mayhew think if she knew? I hoped never to find out.

"Yes, of course, ma'am," I said.

"Good! I'm inviting Mrs. Mayhew to tea this afternoon to meet you so we can get this settled."

"You do understand that I have no experience as a social secretary, Lady Phillippa?" I admitted.

"Oh, Hattie," Lady Phillippa said, waving away my concerns with her hand. "Don't worry about that. Even if you only last a week, it will mean a great deal to all of us to be able to say that you have worked for Mrs. Charlotte Mayhew."

Now I knew why Lady Phillippa was so eager to oblige Mrs. Mayhew. Lady Phillippa was taking advantage of an opportunity. Having the socialite call on her at Fairview alone was a coup, but to have Charlotte Mayhew in her debt would do wonders for Lady Phillippa's social standing. And didn't Charlotte Mayhew have a daughter the perfect age to marry one of Lady Phillippa's sons? I had thought her displeased with me. I was relieved that that wasn't so.

"Now since you're here," Lady Phillippa said, indicating for me to sit at the secretary, "you can write the invitation for me. And then you can write the necessary recommendation letter from Sir Arthur."

"Yes, ma'am." I gladly took my seat, picked up a pen, and dipped it in the inkwell.

"And Hattie, when you do come to tea, wear your most modest suit, if you would."

I looked down at my dress, made of broadcloth and dotted swiss, in pale green with beige accents to show off my eyes. I had saved up a month's pay to purchase it for my time in Newport. Miss Kyler had helped me pick it out, saying I'd need a stylish summer day dress to properly represent the Windom-Greene household. She owned an identical one in pale yellow.

"I admire you trying to look presentable and staying up with the current trends," Lady Phillippa said, "but we wouldn't want Mrs. Mayhew to think you have aspirations beyond your station."

CHAPTER 4

"Can you believe it, Lady Phillippa? A strike during the Season?"

"No, it's ridiculous. Isn't there something that can be done?"

"Gideon would do something. I know he would. But he's in New York and the irony is that because the operators are striking I can't wire him and tell him about it!"

After changing into my navy blue dress skirt and blue-striped shirtwaist as Lady Phillippa had requested, I waited to be summoned in the Servants' Hall watching the kitchen staff prepare for tea. This was a special event: Mrs. Mayhew was coming, and they wanted it to be perfect. I'd never seen a tea like it. The silver, lace-covered trays were laden with plates of thin slices of buttered bread, a small dish each of daintily cut slices of ham and tongue, little pots of preserved pineapple and gooseberries, a porcelain dish of honey in the comb, and several desserts, a cream cake, a rich, dark fruitcake, and little Dresden china cups filled with custard. Oh to be able to sample one of the cakes! The summons came a few minutes after the tea trays had arrived again, slightly less full, downstairs. I snatched up a leftover piece of fruitcake from the tray and ate it on the way. It was as good as I thought it would be. I brushed my skirt for crumbs and was poised to knock at the parlor door when I overheard Mrs. Mayhew mention the strike.

So the telegraph operators went on strike after all, I thought as I knocked. The shaggy man on the docks this morning was right.

"Come in, Miss Davish," Lady Phillippa said, only using my formal title for the third time in our acquaintance. Neither woman stood when I entered the room. Despite protocol, my eyes immediately stopped on Mrs. Mayhew the moment I entered the room. I'd seen sketches of Mrs. Mayhew in the newspaper but couldn't reconcile those with the woman sitting before me. In her late forties, with graying blond hair and draped in purple silk, everything about Mrs. Mayhew was round, her round face, her round blue eyes, and, most notably, her large bulging torso. I quickly shifted my glance to the floor. "This, Mrs. Mayhew, is Miss Hattie Davish, my husband's private secretary. But as you know, Arthur was called back to England on urgent family matters, and she is free to devote herself to another employer at this time."

Mrs. Mayhew waved me closer, took out a pair of solid gold spectacles, and regarded me with the same scrutiny as she might a prized horse, with discernment and, despite her attempts to hide it, obvious interest.

"Well, Lady Phillippa, she certainly is presentable." Lady Phillippa smiled at me encouragingly. Mrs. Mayhew picked up the recommendation letter I'd typed this morning and scanned the contents. "And she certainly comes highly recommended."

Lady Phillippa nodded. "Yes, Sir Arthur has been most pleased with her performance. He trusts her even to attend to tasks beneath his notice."

"Not too independent, I hope, Lady Phillippa?" Mrs. Mayhew said, glancing at me again.

"Oh, no, Mrs. Mayhew, simply reliable and loyal."

"And her penmanship? I can't have a secretary with poor penmanship."

"Certainly not. See for yourself, Mrs. Mayhew." Lady Phillippa handed Mrs. Mayhew a sample of my handwriting, the recommendation letter I'd written out before typing.

Mrs. Mayhew nodded her head approvingly. "Very acceptable. Yes, she should do nicely."

"To be fair, I must warn you she has no experience as a social secretary," Lady Phillippa said. "She's mainly a typewriter and takes dictation."

How little Lady Phillippa knew what I did in her husband's employ, I thought.

"Really? You should've told me first thing, Lady Phillippa," Mrs. Mayhew scolded.

"I apologize, Mrs. Mayhew, but I—"

"Don't worry. I like the look of her. She'll do," the lady said, smiling at me for the first time. "When can you part with her?"

"Whenever you prefer, Mrs. Mayhew," Lady Phillippa said, smiling, relieved and triumphant. "Name the time and she'll be at Rose Mont."

"Delightful!" Mrs. Mayhew clapped her plump hands like a little girl. "I've been ever so busy, what with the garden party coming up and Cora's ball and—"

"I don't know how you do it, Mrs. Mayhew," Lady Phillippa said.

"Well, one must do what one must, Lady Phillippa," Mrs. Mayhew said.

I had remained silent for the duration of the exchange, knowing that was what was expected of me. I'd been in many situations before where my opinions and feelings were not

considered or required by my employers. And many where I'd
been discussed as if I weren't present in the room. But I didn't
mind; besides Sir Arthur, who actually asked my thoughts on a
matter on occasion, most of my employers had been fair but of
the same kind. A servant was there to serve, not to pontificate
or add to the discussion. I was used to this. I had to be. Lady
Phillippa had every right to offer me up on a platter for her
own benefit and I had no occasion to decline the assignment.
But why would I? As Lady Phillippa had pointed out, one didn't
get a more prestigious position than being in the employ of Mrs.
Charlotte Mayhew, even for a short period of time. I would be
forever linked to one of the most powerful families in the
country. Unlike many assignments I felt obliged to take due to
Sir Arthur's intervention or recommendation, I gladly accepted this one, despite Lady Phillippa's ulterior motives. This
would be one of the most exciting assignments of my career.
So despite appearances, I was getting the better of the bargain.

"The servants take tea at five. If she wants tea today, Miss
Davish should be settled into Rose Mont by then," Mrs. Mayhew said. "I'll tell Mrs. Crankshaw to expect her."

"Yes, of course. I'll send her over in my carriage by four
thirty."

"Oh, no need. I'll send a carriage for her," Mrs. Mayhew
said.

Lady Phillippa beamed. "That's generous of you, Mrs.
Mayhew," Lady Phillippa said. Then she waved her hand at me
without looking in my direction. "You may go now, Miss
Davish."

"Ma'am," I said to Mrs. Mayhew. "My lady," I said to Lady
Phillippa, and turned my back. I kept my composure with difficulty. My heart pounded as I forced myself to walk slowly
when all I wanted to do was run. In less than an hour I had to
pack and prepare for my new assignment. The familiar thrill of
anticipation threatened to overwhelm me. What would work-

ing for Mrs. Mayhew be like? Would I be acceptable? Would I learn my new role quick enough to stay on the whole Season? Would I fit in with the existing staff? What would Sir Arthur think when he came back?

"What do you think of the concert schedule at the Casino, Mrs. Mayhew?" Lady Phillippa said before I was out the door. My mind was racing in preparation while the ladies having tea had already forgotten about me.

Oh well, I thought, my fervor slightly quenched. *At least some things will be the same.*

"You're getting off on the wrong foot here, miss. We've already begun our tea!" The housekeeper, Mrs. Crankshaw, a tall woman, taller than me, with a back as straight as a board and a tight bun of dark brown hair that did nothing to conceal deep furrows across her brow, shook her head. "Right! Now where are your things? Never mind, I will have James take them to your room when, and only when, he is finished eating. Normally, I would have time to show you to your room, make sure you are settled in, before I explained to you the rules of the house and certainly before tea, but we don't have time to do anything of that now if you expect to eat. You should be eating in your sitting room, not here among the maids, but we aren't going to interrupt our tea for you. The mistress mentioned that you were expected, which we did at half-past," she said, referring to the timepiece at her waist, "and now it is ten past the hour. Your tardiness does not become one of your level of service, I can tell you." I opened my mouth to interrupt her and defend myself, but she simply held up a hand and continued. "No more discussion. Find a place at the table and we'll see to the formalities afterward." Mrs. Crankshaw took a breath, about to begin again. I took my chance.

"I apologize for my inconvenient arrival, Mrs. Crankshaw.

I pride myself on my punctuality, but Mrs. Mayhew's carriage, as promised to Lady Phillippa, never arrived. I had to walk and came as quickly as I could."

"Sounds like her." One of the young girls at the table snickered. "She forgets everything."

"Probably can't remember her own Christian name," another added. Several girls giggled at the jest.

"Enough!" the housekeeper said, instantly silencing the maids. "I don't take well to girls who don't respect their betters." Then the housekeeper looked down her nose at me, her thick eyebrows scrunched close together. "You mean to tell me you carried your trunk"—she pointed to my typewriter case—"and other things all the way from Fairview? I don't take well to girls who embellish either."

"No, Mrs. Crankshaw," I said. "My trunk and hatboxes are still at Fairview. I'll have to arrange to have them brought here somehow."

"Then what is too important to leave behind, your powder and cold cream? I can tell you right now I don't take well to women in my staff who spend too much time on their appearance." She glanced to one of the maids, causing that woman to blush.

"It's my typewriter," I said, trying to keep my tone civil. Mrs. Crankshaw couldn't know she was calling into question the one thing in my possession that I cared most about. My livelihood had depended upon it since the day my dear, deceased father presented it to me upon my enrollment at Mrs. Chaplin's school. He must've saved for months to afford it.

"Typewriter?" the housekeeper said. "What does a social secretary need with a typewriter? You do know your position, don't you?"

I wasn't about to admit to Mrs. Crankshaw that I had no practical knowledge of my new position. "To serve Madam," I said.

"Right, very good," the housekeeper said, giving me her approval for the first time since we met. "That's why we are all here. To serve to the best of our ability."

"My thoughts exactly," I said, although I had several other thoughts running through my head as well: *What will Sir Arthur think of my taking a new position? Why didn't the carriage arrive? Did Mrs. Crankshaw always live up to her name? Why would one family build a house this enormous, this grandiose?* I'd never seen anything like it. Made of limestone, with a red tile roof, Rose Mont dwarfed even Fairview in size. With Greek Revival columns three stories high in front and over a hundred arched windows and French doors, it sprawled across almost half an acre among the several acres of mowed lawn and rose gardens that gave the house its name. And the Mayhews only lived here six weeks out of the year!

"If I wanted your thoughts, I'd ask for them," the housekeeper said in a tone much like that of an employer and not like a fellow member of the staff. "I don't take well to cheek, Miss Davish." Was there anything this woman did take well to? "Now take your place so we can all finish our tea."

A young blond-haired woman with porcelain skin and big blue eyes smiled and waved at me. I set my typewriter case down and took the chair next to her.

"I'm Britta," she said in a very strong accent, reminiscent of a Swedish maid I'd met while working for Mrs. Kennedy years ago.

"Hi, I'm Hattie."

"I will make the introductions if you don't mind, Britta," Mrs. Crankshaw said, sitting at the right side of the butler, who sat at the head of the table. Britta's cheeks flushed. She pulled at her left earlobe while concentrating on eating her cold roast beef and crumpets.

Mrs. Crankshaw proceeded to introduce me to the other people sitting at the longest servants' dining table I'd ever seen.

Besides the housekeeper and the young maids, my dining companions consisted of Mr. Davies, the gray-haired butler with bushy eyebrows and round green eyes, Monsieur Valbois, the short French chef with a pointed nose and long black drooping mustache, Issacson, Mrs. Mayhew's lady's maid, who was as blonde as Britta, slightly younger than me, and wearing a most fashionable lavender tailor-made suit, Britta, the parlormaid, James and Leonard, the footmen, both well over six feet tall and strikingly handsome in their morning livery, and the coachman, Elmer, a portly man of middle years who never looked up from his food. I wondered why the table was so large but then remembered this seating only represented the upper servants. The other servants, the additional footmen, groomsmen, laundresses, housemen, and kitchen assistant and maids, ate later. I'd never worked in a household this large. I hoped that I would soon find my place among them.

I had expected questions for me after I was introduced, but instead Mr. Davies, Mrs. Crankshaw, and Monsieur Valbois spoke to one another over the bent heads of the rest of the staff. No one else added to the discussion and few even showed interest. After the strained dinner, Mrs. Crankshaw led me up the back stairs into the Grand Hall.

"You can close your mouth now, Miss Davish," she said as I stood, slack jawed at the single most opulent room I'd ever seen. The floor was gleaming marble, carpeted in Persian rugs, the walls, hand-painted with platinum and gold leaf, were covered with fifteen-foot-tall panels depicting Greek myths, and the ceiling, soaring thirty, maybe forty feet above, was a glittering mosaic of stained glass depicting a rose garden with an immense crystal chandelier that would fill the room I shared with Kaarina at Fairview, dangling from the painted sunburst at its center. The red-carpeted marble staircase, on the other side of the room, was wide enough for a dozen people to stand side by side on its bottom step and swept up to meet the second-floor hallway, an open balcony that encircled the entire hall. And here and there tall pedestals displaying priceless objects of art, tables holding porcelain vases filled with flowers, or life-size statues of Athena or Venus dotted the room.

"Is that water I hear, Mrs. Crankshaw?" I asked.

"Yes, there is a fountain behind the stairs. Now follow me."

She led me through several smaller rooms, all with priceless paintings, gilded furniture, vases filled with fresh bouquets, mahogany moldings, Persian rugs, and priceless bric-a-brac, and yet, with the exception of the library, no apparent purpose, back to the servants' stairs and up to the second floor. I followed as she maneuvered through a series of inner hallways, opening an occasional door and commenting, "This is Mrs. Mayhew's drawing room, right?" or, "This is Mrs. Mayhew's bedroom, right?" Finally Mrs. Crankshaw opened a door and motioned for me to precede her inside.

"And this is your sitting room," Mrs. Crankshaw said, "where you would've been served your dinner, if you'd been punctual." Preoccupied with admiring my surroundings and worried I might never find my way again, I ignored the housekeeper's barb.

My sitting room? I thought. I'd never had my own sitting room before. Seems I had my own bath as well. As Mrs. Crankshaw explained, the sitting room, with its polished cherry woodwork and pale rose damask wall coverings, was part of a three-room suite consisting of sitting room, bedroom, and bath. A large oak desk covered in green leather and silver writing accessories beckoned. Instead I approached the bookshelf and scanned the titles of a variety of reference books: a current atlas of the city of Newport, the latest Social Registers of Newport, New York, Boston, and several other cities, a Newport city directory, an American and an English *Who's Who,* an *Almanach de Gotha,* and *Burke's Peerage.*

"Since Mrs. Pemberton, the former social secretary, is not

here to acquaint you with your duties, it falls to me," Mrs. Crankshaw said. I could feel my stomach clench in anticipation. "As Madam's secretary, you are expected to maintain her calendar, answer her mail, and pay her personal bills."

I breathed a sigh of relief. Mrs. Crankshaw hadn't mentioned anything that I hadn't done for other employers before. I began to relax as she approached a large white closet that took up one side of the room.

"You are to have the menus approved, which should be my job," Mrs. Crankshaw grumbled. "And mind I don't take well to those that waste Chef's time." Before I could reassure her on that measure, she continued. "You're to put together guest lists and seating arrangements while avoiding any social faux pas. You're to address all invitations by hand and deliver them personally. You're to deal directly with florists, caterers, and social entertainers." The list of duties went on and on.

Although I maintained perfect posture and didn't blink, I squeezed my perspiring hands together. Menus? Guest lists? Social faux pas? This was not going to be my typical assignment after all. I hoped Monsieur Valbois wasn't the temperamental type.

"Madam will decide if and when preprinted invitations are necessary. If you need anything that is not here, you tell me, not Madam. We have a standing order with George H. Carr, on Thames. Is that clear?"

"Yes, thank you," I said, despite being not sure at all if everything was clear.

"Right, now here's the stationery," the housekeeper said, nodding her head and opening the double doors of the closet to reveal more stationery than I'd ever seen outside of a stationery shop. Notepaper of all sizes, some inscribed with the Mayhew family crest and some simply with *ROSE MONT* embossed across the top in gold, were stacked tightly next to their accompanying envelopes. Notebooks, pads, pencils, erasers, pens, and bottles of ink were tucked into boxes neatly to one side.

"This does meet with your approval then?" Mrs. Crankshaw said, challenging me to say otherwise.

I knew she meant the duties in their entirety, but I couldn't keep my awed gaze from the contents of the closet. Organized to perfection and almost glimmering under the electric light, the stationery was just waiting for me to put it to good use.

I am up to this challenge, I thought as I smiled at Mrs. Crankshaw, who raised an eyebrow at me in response. In fact, I couldn't wait to begin.

"Yes, Mrs. Crankshaw, I think it will do me quite nicely."

But wait I would have to do.

Mrs. Crankshaw had kept me a full hour longer, first detailing her litany of rules and expectations for all female household staff and then explaining what had already been done for the upcoming garden party and ball. The musicians had been engaged, but the menus were still in dispute. I still had the invitations to complete and address, of course, but luckily for me, Mrs. Pemberton, the previous secretary, had already supplied Madam with a guest list for both. My task was to see to the minor adjustments that would need to be made to the guest list as the event approached, such as cancellations due to illness, unexpected travel, or Mrs. Mayhew's fickle opinion that a guest was "no longer suitable." I could only imagine what that could mean.

I then spent two more hours arranging for someone to retrieve my trunk and hatboxes. I had numerous exasperating conversations, going back and forth between Elmer, the coachman, and Mr. Davies, the butler. As there had been no word from Mrs. Mayhew, the coachman was unwilling to accommodate me. Only when a call came that Mr. Mayhew was arriving on the early morning steamer was Mr. Davies able to convince the coachman to pick up my things on the way to the wharf. But that meant that I would be without a change of clothes, toiletries, or a proper box for my hat until the next morning. With nothing left to do and, despite my exhaustion, no inclination for sleep, I brought out Sir Arthur's manuscript and set up my typewriter on the desk in my sitting room. I'd never used a desk that dwarfed my little typewriter. I was thrilled. I found blank paper in the closet and set to typing. Calm and composure settled over me as the steady, familiar clicking and clanking of the keys hitting paper filled my new home. After only two pages, I staggered to my feet, found my way to the bedroom, and for the second time today collapsed onto the bed fully dressed. But this time I had a smile on my face.

CHAPTER 5

I awoke to the sound of my door clicking shut. I bolted up-right in bed. My trunk! It sat at the foot of my bed. I had slept so soundly I hadn't even heard them deliver it.

I really was tired! I thought. I jumped out of bed, changed my clothes, and splashed water on my face and neck, eager to start my day. I bounded down the back stairs to the kitchen only to find the scullery maid just stoking the oven fire. I was up before the chef and breakfast was an hour away. Even Mrs. Crankshaw was still warm in her bed. Now what did I do? Mrs. Mayhew wouldn't need me until well after breakfast.

I'll go for a hike, I thought enthusiastically. A bit of fresh air would do me wonders. But then I hesitated. Did I dare leave the grounds before requesting permission from Mrs. Mayhew? No, I couldn't jeopardize my position for a hike, no matter how eager I was to see more of Newport. *So I won't leave the grounds,* I thought. With the massive estate stretching from Bellevue Avenue to the ocean cliffs, I'd have more than enough to explore in an hour. I wasn't used to reporting my comings and goings, but this household was different, or so

Mrs. Crankshaw informed me, so I found the kitchen maid Sena, who was busy boiling water for tea and coffee. She was the most senior staff member about. When I told her I would be back well before breakfast and would only be taking a stroll about the grounds, she looked at me with a furrowed brow but nodded her head slowly. She probably wasn't used to having anyone tell her their comings and goings either.

Without changing my shoes, I slipped out the servants' entrance door and immediately found myself facing an immense expanse of perfectly manicured green lawn under the sky, a jumble of puffy clouds ablaze with the pink, purple, and red of dawn. And then I was struck by the alternating rhythmic swish and boom sound of crashing water. How had I not noticed it before? I walked slowly, as if in a dream, drawn to the soothing sound of the waves. I passed through numerous rose gardens and gave them barely a second glance. I only stopped when I could go no farther. Resting my hands on the top of the stone wall separating Rose Mont from a well-worn gravel path that snaked along the top of the cliffs, I held my breath. Before me, stretching out to the distant horizon, was the vast shimmering blue ocean. Not the boat ride through Block Island Sound at night or my glimpse of Newport Harbor had prepared me for this. This was the ocean I'd dreamt of, the endless, ceaseless, unforgiving, mesmerizing sea. I couldn't take my gaze away. Seagulls glided on wind currents just above me and waves crashed against the black rocks far below while I stood there, enthralled by the beauty for I don't know how long. But when I heard someone walking toward me on the path I realized I'd been standing there too long. I regretfully pulled myself away from the scene and returned to the house.

"Where have you been?" Mrs. Crankshaw said as I entered the Servants' Hall. "Mrs. Mayhew has been ringing for you. I had to go in your place and explain your mysterious absence. She is eager for you to get started. You're lucky she's a forgiving mistress. But I can tell you, one word of this to the master and you won't last an hour longer in this house. Now get up there. She's in her sitting room. I'll send up your breakfast."

I was flustered and embarrassed to have been negligent in my duties. I should've been here. I should've waited to talk to Mrs. Mayhew before I'd gone out. I wanted to apologize to Mrs. Crankshaw; she should not have had to make excuses for me. I wanted to explain to her that it wouldn't happen again. I wanted to shake off the hypnotic sound of the waves still in my ears. But Mrs. Crankshaw wouldn't stop talking.

"Stop standing there like you'd never been chastised before. Go," Mrs. Crankshaw said, shooing me away with a wave of her arms. "She's expecting you. So go. Go!" I turned around and began climbing the winding back stairs. I'd gone two flights before I realized I had no idea where I was going. I'd been given a brief tour of the house last night, but I'd been tired and the house was so big, I quickly got lost. I considered going back down to ask Mrs. Crankshaw but decided against it. Instead I opened the first door that I came to that looked like the one that led into the house proper. I opened the door a crack and peeked out to make sure no one was about. Luckily I'd found the wide second-floor hallway I'd been led down last night. I headed in the direction of what I remembered might be Mrs. Mayhew's sitting room, peering into rooms with open doors hoping to find either Mrs. Mayhew or a housemaid who could direct me. I was unlucky to find neither. But what I saw was astounding. Room after room was as elaborately and expensively decorated as those I'd seen last night, glittering chandeliers, gilded mirrors stretching the length of the room, high-backed mahogany chairs, silk draperies. Were there no rooms with simple, comfortable décor?

"Who are you? And what are you doing in my house?" a man demanded. I twisted around to face him.

I was speechless. And not because I'd been caught by the

master of the house wandering from room to room or because he had a towel draped around his neck and was dressed in only a quarter-sleeve shirt and tights but because the man storming toward me was the gentleman I'd seen on the boat yesterday morning. He was the same man who had conspired with the Pinkerton detective to push the trunk overboard, Mr. Mayhew, one of the richest men in America!

Why?

I had no more time to wonder, as he was quickly upon me. He was merely a few feet away, with more than indignation written across his face, when I finally found the courage to speak. "Miss Hattie Davish, sir," I said, far more meekly than I'd like. "I'm Mrs. Mayhew's new secretary, sir."

"Then what are you doing here?" he demanded, pulling a monocle from his breast pocket and staring me in the eyes. I was relieved when not a flicker of recognition showed in his gaze.

"I'm lost, sir. This is the biggest house I've ever been in. I can't seem to find Madam's sitting room."

"Carry on then," he said. I stepped out of his way as he strode past me. I let out a sigh of relief as I watched him go down the hall and disappear into one of the rooms that had been closed.

"*Un, deux, trois,*" I counted, trying to collecting my composure, but my mind raced. I pulled out the pad and pencil I always carried and started a list. My hands shook as I did.

1. Why would Mr. Mayhew want a trunk thrown overboard?
2. Why would he be involved with a Pinkerton detective?
3. What was in the trunk?
4. Why did everyone think Mr. Mayhew had arrived this morning and not yesterday?

I tucked the notebook away, silently chiding myself for wasting time making a list of questions that had nothing to do with me. I was still lost and now late meeting with Mrs. Mayhew. But before I could get reoriented in this enormous house, footsteps and the sound of whistling echoed down the hall behind me. I froze.

Is that "Ode to Joy" again? Hoping I was wrong and would find a maid carrying a duster or a footman with a tray, I looked back and locked eyes with the Pinkerton detective. I instantly turned my face away and feigned interest in the elaborate swirl pattern pervading the yellow marble wall but watched him out of the corner of my eye. Whether from the distance between us or his preoccupation, he didn't give me any sign of recognition either. Instead he stopped at the same door Mr. Mayhew had entered and knocked. A moment later the detective opened the door and disappeared, leaving the door slightly ajar. Before I knew what I was doing, I'd headed straight down the hallway, walking slowly past the door the men had entered. Mr. Mayhew was speaking.

"I won't have this, Doubleday. As you can see, my time in the gymnasium has been interrupted again. The man's a menace. I assume you're aware of the telegraph operators' strike?" Doubleday mumbled a reply. "It wouldn't have happened if I'd owned the telegraph. No labor unions exist in my companies! Maybe I should speak to Gould when he comes to Charlotte's party." *George Jay Gould?* I wondered. I immediately took note to make sure he was on the guest list. "Anyway, what's the news out of Biddeford?"

"We took care of it," Doubleday said. "The mills are running with most of the workers back on the job. The union men seem to have disappeared, though." The man chuckled. "You shouldn't hear anything more from them."

"Good. Either way, I want you to double your men and at first sign of any trouble make sure their weapons are visible. I can't afford a strike or a slowdown in production. And cut wages in half if necessary." Papers rustled and then were slapped down onto a table. "By God, did you see this headline, Doubleday? More banks have failed! Nine banks in six cities! What the hell is Cleveland doing to this country?"

"It is unfortunate, sir," Doubleday said obligingly.

"Yes, it is . . . unfortunate," Mayhew scoffed. "Let's hope you don't have savings tied up in a bank."

As they spoke of business and banks I'd been reminded whom I was eavesdropping on. After all, if Mr. Gideon Mayhew wanted a trunk pushed into the ocean who was I to question him? He had his reasons and most likely a simple and innocuous explanation. Perhaps the trunk didn't even have anything in it, let alone a dead body! Had I let my imagination and previous experiences get the best of me? As I walked past the office door for the second time, I spied a chambermaid entering one of the rooms down the hall with her arms full of bed linens. She'd be able to guide me to Mrs. Mayhew's sitting room, assuming the lady was still there. I gave up on learning anything more about the trunk or why these two men had been so eager to see it disappear into the ocean and strode quickly toward where the maid had disappeared.

"Miss Davish!" Mrs. Mayhew said when I finally arrived. The chambermaid had been obliging, leading me through a maze of interconnected rooms, a shortcut she called it, and delivered me to the sitting room within minutes. I instantly recognized it from my tour last night, with its white woodwork, sea green damask wall coverings, and plush white furniture. I lamented, however, that I still didn't know how to get here again. Mrs. Mayhew was lying on an overstuffed chaise longue upholstered in pink silk, stroking the long pure white fur of a

Turkish Angora cat. The sun sprayed a medley of colors on the floor beside her as it streamed in through the stained-glass transom. "I rang hours ago," Mrs. Mayhew exaggerated as the cat leaped from her lap and crossed the room. "I've been waiting for you."

"I apologize, ma'am," I said, the cat brushing up against my leg in greeting. I knelt down to pet him and was rewarded with a purr. His fur was silky and soft. "I got lost." To my relief, Mrs. Mayhew laughed. The cat scampered back to the warm lap of his owner.

"It is the biggest house in Newport, isn't it?"

"I wouldn't doubt it, ma'am."

"I helped design it myself. Didn't I, Bonaparte?" she said, pulling the cat close and snuggling her cheek into the back of his head. "Well, we'll have to make sure that Mrs. Crankshaw gives you a proper tour so you don't lose yourself again." I couldn't tell her Mrs. Crankshaw had given me a tour but I'd been too tired and nervous to pay attention. "I'm most anxious to get started. The garden party is in a few days and I have a million letters to answer. You can sit there." She pointed to a chair next to the oak secretary piled with papers, letters, and magazines. "Hand me the first one, will you?" I took the seat but had no idea which letter in all the chaos she was referring to. My hand hovered over the pile. "Just grab one," she said. I did, an invitation that was postmarked yesterday.

"Ah," she said, glancing at the contents. "Tell her I'd be delighted." She handed it back to me. I looked about for something to write with but couldn't find a single pen or pencil in the vast array of things on the desk. I pulled the pencil from my skirt pocket and scribbled her response on the envelope. With no empty space on the desk, I set the letter on the floor and handed Mrs. Mayhew another.

"She's persistent," she said, shaking her head. "I'll give her that. But I wish Miranda would stop inviting me. I do so hate

to say no." I took the letter from her, jotted down *no* and
started a new pile on the floor.

The next was a monthly bill for flowers. *Five hundred dollars?* I had to read it twice, the sum was so alarming. I glanced
at the bouquet of pink and white hollyhocks on the center
table. These fresh blooms, and those like them in every room
I'd seen so far, including my own sitting room, cost more in a
month than I earned in a year. And yet Mrs. Mayhew barely
glanced at the bill before tossing it back at me.

"Fine," she said. "The checkbook's in the drawer. Take it
with you and write them out as I approve them. I'll sign them
later." I opened the drawer of the desk with difficulty.

"What's in here, ma'am?" I asked, pulling on the solid silver drawer handles.

"I don't know, invitations, bills, and calling cards that arrived after Mrs. Pemberton left?"

After a moment or two of pulling gently, I yanked hard
enough it nearly flew out from the desk. Papers of every size,
shape, and color had jammed the drawer and some now had
dropped on the floor. *What a disaster! I must organize this later,* I
thought as I rummaged through until I found the checkbook.

"There's fifteen thousand deposited in the bank in my account for this month. You're to keep track, you see."

"Yes, ma'am," I said. I'd never been responsible for so
much money in my life. "Here's a request for a donation to the
Children's Friend Society."

"Oh, you can get rid of that and any others like it."

"Ma'am?" I said.

"Charity requests, Miss Davish, ignore them. Gideon insists
we don't give any money to the poor. He says such people are
less fit anyway so why waste good money on them?"

What kind of man allowed his wife to spend hundreds on
flowers but not a penny on a children's charity? In all my years
working for the privileged, I'd never encountered such a cal-

lous attitude toward the less fortunate. And yet all I could say to Mrs. Mayhew was, "Yes, ma'am." I tucked the donation request in my pocket and vowed to send them something myself. It was the least I could do.

We continued in this way for several hours, the pile on the desk slowly diminishing as the stacks on the floor grew. When we were finally done, or truly when Mrs. Mayhew tired of the activity, the desk was nearly empty. I was able to quickly organize what remained.

"Ma'am?" I said as Mrs. Mayhew was drifting off to sleep. I placed the stacks from the floor onto the desk.

"We're done for today, aren't we?" she said without opening her eyes.

"Yes, ma'am, but I found a letter addressed to your husband at the bottom of the pile."

Mrs. Mayhew sat up quickly, jostling her cat awake. He mewed in protest as I handed the letter to her. The letter had been delivered days ago by post and was still unopened.

"Oh, dear. How could this have happened?" She looked up at me and frowned. "Thank goodness I have you now," she said. "This won't happen again." It wasn't a question.

"No, ma'am."

"Gideon won't be pleased." She looked around as if inspiration for the solution to the problem would be found somewhere in the room. Then she turned to me again and handed back the letter. "You must deliver this to him immediately."

"Of course, ma'am." I kept my anxiety out of my voice. The prospect of interacting with Mr. Mayhew again wasn't appealing. Whether the incident with the trunk proved to be sinister or not, Mr. Mayhew didn't strike me as a pleasant man. "If you could tell me how to get back to his office, ma'am, I'll take it to him right now."

"Oh, no, Miss Davish," Mrs. Mayhew said, glancing at the pink and gold gilded porcelain clock on the mantel. "Gideon is done with breakfast and his morning exercise. He's probably at the Reading Room by now. You'll have to give it to him there." Another room I had no idea how to find.

"I apologize for my ignorance, Mrs. Mayhew, but would you be kind enough to direct me to that room? I assure you I will learn my way around as soon as possible as not to trouble you again." To my surprise, Mrs. Mayhew laughed.

"Ha, ha, how deliciously naïve! I do like you, Miss Davish. What a funny idea, the Reading Room in this house! And to think I wouldn't be allowed to enter it. Ha, ha!" I tried not to blush as the woman laughed at my expense. "Seriously though, Miss Davish, you must acquaint yourself with the important places and people in Newport if you're to work in this house."

"Yes, ma'am." I knew how I'd spend this night—reading the books in my sitting room.

"I need to be able to rely on you."

"Yes, ma'am."

"Very well. The Reading Room, Miss Davish, is an exclusive club in town. Have Davies arrange for Elmer to take you there. Now, take those"—she motioned toward the stacks on the desk—"except the magazines, I want to read those later, and make sure the replies are in this afternoon's post or hand-delivered when appropriate."

"When would you like to sign them, ma'am?" I said, trying to calculate how I was going to personally deliver a letter to Mr. Mayhew somewhere in town while still getting several dozens of letters into this afternoon's post.

"Oh, no, I don't sign replies. You answer them for me. I rely completely on you for these things." She lay back on the chaise longue, the cat purring and content once again. "I have other things to do."

I looked about for a case or even a box I could carry everything in but saw nothing of the kind. So I gathered up the stacks of letters and papers, the checkbook, and the letter to Mr. Mayhew and held them tightly against my chest.

"Would it be possible—?" I began, hoping to make an arrangement with the coachman, but she raised her hand for silence.

"You're excused, Miss Davish," Mrs. Mayhew said, closing her eyes again.

With the stacks of papers in my hands, I retraced the way the chambermaid had led me through the house back to my own suite, only to struggle to open the door. I clutched at the knob, with no success, as three people, all nearly the same age, about twenty, ascended the grand staircase down the hall. The two women, a blonde and a brunette, each carried a tennis racquet and a simple straw hat with wide satin ribbon. They wore sporty tennis dresses, one in blue-and-white-striped denim, the other in pink broadcloth with peach-colored piping. The man was tall and lean, with a suntanned, clean-shaven face and ginger hair. He wore a black cap, black belt and white shirt, tie, and trousers, and a racquet was slung over one shoulder. The group was animated, laughing and speaking boisterously, their voices echoing off the marble walls and staircase. I tried in vain to open the sitting-room door before they saw me.

"Well, well, what do we have here?" the man said, approaching too fast. I stood my ground but knew better than to say anything. "I know all the pretty maids in this house, but I don't know you."

"She's no one I know," the dark-haired girl in pink said. "What's your name, girl?"

"Hattie Davish, miss," I said, my palms growing clammy as the man circled around me, making me step back from the door and cutting off my only escape route. "I'm Mrs. Mayhew's new secretary."

"I didn't know Mother found a new secretary," the brunette girl said again, stripping her gloves off, one finger at a time. I studied Gideon and Charlotte Mayhew's only daughter. With long dark eyelashes, high cheekbones, and a dainty chin, Miss Mayhew would be a favorite with Lady Phillippa's sons. Her companion was not so graced. The blonde had thick eyelashes and a mouth, which was scowling at the moment, too large for her face. "She sure needs one. How appalling of Mrs. Pemberton to leave so suddenly like that. You can go, miss," Miss Mayhew said, much to my relief.

I turned and tried to reach the doorknob again, but the man stepped in front of me. He brushed my cheek with the tip of his finger. With my hands full I could do nothing to stop him.

"If you'll excuse me, sir," I said, and tried to step toward the door again. He didn't move.

"You look too pretty to be a secretary." He took my hand, causing me to tighten my grip on my papers with the other, and ran his thumb across the tips of my fingers and down my palm. "But you do have the calluses to prove it." His face was close, so close I could count the faded freckles on his nose. "I like calluses on a girl." His smile was wide, but his bright blue eyes didn't blink. It took everything I had not to yank my hand away and take another step back.

"Leave the girl alone, Nick," the blond girl said. "Let her get back to work."

"What's it to you, Eugenie?" Nick said, still rubbing my callused fingertips.

"Let's go, Nick. We have to change for the concert."

"You can go, Sis. I'm having a spot of fun here." I glanced at his sister, Eugenie, silently pleading for her not to leave.

"Really, Nick," Miss Mayhew said. She grabbed Nick by the arm and pulled him away. "Mother wouldn't appreciate you toying with her new pet. That's for her to do."

"I do believe you're jealous, Cora," Nick said flirtatiously.

She playfully hit Nick with her glove. "You are incorrigible, Nick Whitwell!" Cora Mayhew said. She grabbed the cap from his head and wagged it in front of his face. He snatched it from her with one hand while pulling her toward him with the other. He snuggled into her neck, kissing her. She shrieked in delight.

"Oh, come on, you two lovebirds," Eugenie said. "I don't want to miss the concert at the Casino."

And with that the three headed down the hallway without another word or backward glance at me. I stood rooted to the spot for a moment, shaking with rage, humiliation, and fear. I'd been threatened, pushed down stairs, and poisoned, but nothing had infuriated me as much as that man's smile as he gently rubbed my fingers. I was simply another sport to him. All I wanted now was to slip into the sanctuary of my sitting room. I quickly set down the papers and opened the door but jumped as I came face-to-face with Britta, the parlormaid.

"You haven't eaten your meal, miss," she said. She held a tray with a teapot, a cup and saucer, and a plate of cold roast beef slices, bread sandwiches tied in a ribbon, stuffed tomatoes, grapes, orange slices, and a small bowl of lemon pudding. "I couldn't let it sit there all day. Would you like me to leave it, miss?"

"Yes, please, Britta," I said as I forced a smile on my face. I bent over to retrieve the papers from the floor.

"The tea's cold. Would you like a fresh pot?"

"Coffee would be nice."

"Very good, miss." I watched as the maid returned the tray to the table. In my head I was counting, *Un, deux, trois*. It didn't help. The moment she closed the door behind her, I let out my pent-up frustration by dumping all of Madam's papers and invitations into a pile on the desk. My desk now looked like Mrs. Mayhew's had.

Oh, why did I do that?

More discontented now with myself for having given in to such childish behavior than with Nick Whitwell's cavalier attitude, I closed my eyes and pictured Walter's smile, hoping the image would replace that of the rich blaggard rubbing my hand. To my surprise, it didn't make me feel better. Not wanting to question why, I opened my eyes, took stock of the mess I'd made, and set to reorganizing Madam's invitations, bills, and letters before Britta came back with the coffee.

CHAPTER 6

And to think I was going to ride in a carriage! Walking down Bellevue Avenue with the sunshine on my face was a balm for my frazzled nerves. The street was dressed in summer splendor, towering trees that draped over the high walls and thick, lush privet hedges that lined the road. Shrubs and flowers, hydrangeas, impatiens, and roses at full bloom, along with English ivy, decorated the wrought-iron gateposts and sidewalks. And the mixture of scents: The flowers, the freshly cut grass, the privet hedge, and sea salt could be bottled as Newport's own perfume. I took another deep breath of the fresh, fragrant air. I was heading in the opposite direction from the ocean and I had no time to pause, but it was glorious to be outside. I'd originally spoken to Mr. Davies, the butler, about a carriage as Madam suggested, but when I asked he informed me, not unsympathetically, that Mr. Mayhew had already driven himself into town with the trap and Elmer, the coachman, was taking Mrs. Mayhew out calling in the victoria soon. She must've forgotten again. Instead he gave me the address to the

Reading Room, about two miles straight down Bellevue Avenue, and wished me luck.

Now I couldn't imagine riding. When I had nearly run from Lady Phillippa's at Fairview to be at Rose Mont on time, I had no appreciation for the beauty around me. Now despite my haste, I still had time to take it all in. I caught glimpses of other grand houses including Mrs. Astor's Beechwood and Mrs. Vanderbilt's new Marble House. And I experienced what Miss Kyler called coaching, dozens of carriages of every shape and size, victorias, buggies, traps, dogcarts, and phaetons, parading slowly up and down the avenue carrying men and women in their finery. The idea, Miss Kyler said, was to "see and be seen." In my walk to the Reading Room, I "saw" the same barouche pulled by two white horses with a unicorn on the crest; it passed me four times.

I'd walked well over a mile when the simultaneous sounds of a loud sputtering motor, a blaring horn, and the frightened neigh of a horse made me turn around. Advancing toward me, horn honking every few seconds and careening through the coaching traffic, was a motorcar. I'd only seen them in magazines—victorias without a horse. I watched transfixed as it swerved wildly to one side, trying to avoid a couple of elderly ladies in black lace bonnets, their mouths and eyes wide open in horror, only to nearly collide with a wagon parked on the side of the road. The horse reared, deep tire treads mere inches from her footprints in the street, tossing crates into the air. As the crates smashed into the street, sending cans of peas, string beans, and peaches rolling into the oncoming traffic, the motorcar drove for several yards down the sidewalk, uprooting flowers and nearly missing a tree. Squeals of delight from the two female passengers mixed with the rumbling engine as the motorcar veered back into the street. I couldn't help but stare, my mouth gaping as it passed me. The women in the motorcar waved. Holding on to their hats and laughing with glee were

Cora Mayhew and her friend Eugenie. The driver beside them was none other than Nick Whitwell.

I rapped lightly on the door of the Reading Room, a large, wooden building with a second-story balcony, knowing as a woman I'd never be allowed to enter. The porter opened the door and frowned.

"No women allowed," he said without trying to hide his disdain for me and my gender. "Go home." He began to close the door in my face.

"Sir, I'm Mrs. Charlotte Mayhew's secretary and I have a letter for her husband that I must deliver. Is Mr. Mayhew here?" I'd hoped mentioning such an important man would at least keep the door open. I was right.

"No, Mr. Mayhew left about a half hour ago for the Casino. You may be able to find him there."

"Casino?" I said. Why hadn't I read about Newport last night? I'd shown my ignorance the second time in an hour. I vowed to correct this as soon as I could.

"You said you're Mrs. Mayhew's secretary and you don't know about the Casino? You're about as aware as a rock, aren't you?"

"I only arrived in town yesterday morning," I said in my defense. "I'm from the Middle West."

"Could've fooled me," he said. "Well, you'll be acquainted with the Casino soon enough—the Mayhews are regulars."

"Would you be so kind to direct me?" I said, trying to maintain a civil tone.

"It's down that way, miss. Now please be so kind to step off the porch! I don't want to lose my job."

The porter sent me back several blocks the way I'd come down Bellevue Avenue. I had passed the Newport Casino on my way without realizing it. It was more a sprawling complex of redbrick and wooden-shingled buildings than a single building.

I had skirted it, braving the passing traffic and the multitude of pungent piles of horse dung, to cross the street, because a man, the same shaggy-haired man who had told Sir Arthur and Lady Phillippa about the telegraph operators' strike, stood on a wooden crate, chanting, "Eight hours labor, eight hours recreation, eight hours rest," over and over. I'd avoided him, not because I didn't sympathize with his cause—some people work in deplorable conditions and need a champion—but because his aggressive tactics were off-putting. There must be a better way than shouting at random passersby?

The labor man was still there when I approached but was in deep conversation with another man as I passed under the shadow of the brick archway entrance. The music of a military band playing John Philip Sousa filled the air, drowning out their voices and everything else. Cora Mayhew and the young Whitwells had been destined for a concert. Was this it? I hadn't seen the motorcar anywhere. I hoped I didn't have to face Mr. Whitwell again.

Before I stepped into the sunlight of the expansive courtyard, with its manicured lawn tennis courts, walking paths, and prominent rounded clock tower, another porter blocked my path.

"We ask guests to wait for a break in the music before entering, miss," he whispered. I looked into the almost empty courtyard. No one was playing tennis. Only a few people strolled about. From the sound of the music, the concert was being held in the attached theater to the right. I wouldn't be interrupting anything. Obviously this was another club where I wasn't welcome.

"I'm looking for Mr. Mayhew. I have a letter I must deliver immediately. Is he here?"

"Yes, he's here. Wait here a moment, if you please." The man didn't blink at my demand for urgency. Nor did he walk any faster across the lawn.

He must be used to it, I thought.

Never a fan of Sousa, I walked back toward the entrance and waited. The shaggy man had resumed his place on the box and was chanting labor slogans again.

"Eight hours labor, eight hours recreation, eight hours sleep. An injury to one is the concern of all. We mean to uphold the dignity of labor."

Several people passed without even looking at him, but he was not deterred. Then a victoria arrived and a gentleman with two gold-banded cigars sticking out of his pocket and wearing a straw derby alighted. Once a taller man, the gentleman with gray hair and a drooping mustache, was stooped at the shoulders, and was leaning on a gold-handled cane that was otherwise meant for effect. And yet he couldn't have been more than fifty years old. As he passed, the man on the box shouted at him.

"You may walk by me without acknowledging me, Mr. Whitwell, but you won't be able to ignore me for long!"

Whitwell? I wondered. *Could he be related to Nick Whitwell?* I took a step toward the men and listened to the exchange more closely.

"Shut up and go away, Sibley, or I'll have you arrested for trespassing and harassment."

"I'm within my rights, Mr. Whitwell, as are those whom you employ. We will have what's rightfully ours whether you like it or not."

"Your kind isn't wanted here, Sibley, and won't be tolerated."

"You'll have no choice, Mr. Whitwell. By the way, have you sent any telegrams lately?"

Mr. Whitwell shook his cane at the man he called Sibley. "Stay away from my banks, Sibley, or you'll regret it!"

"You have something for me?" Mr. Mayhew said, suddenly standing next to me. I jumped. Engrossed in the argument oc-

curring right in front of me, I hadn't heard his approach. Or
was there something about the man that made me nervous?

"Yes sir, Mr. Mayhew." I handed him the letter. "Mrs. Mayhew found this on her desk this morning and insisted I deliver
it to you personally as soon as possible."

"I don't think I'm the one that's going to be doing the re-
gretting, Mr. Whitwell!" Sibley shouted at Mr. Whitwell's back.
The gentleman stormed away, leaning heavily on his cane as he
tottered toward us. Sibley resumed his slogan chanting: "We
will uphold the dignity of labor. We will uphold the dignity of
labor."

"Scum," Mr. Mayhew said under his breath before nodding his head at the approaching Mr. Whitwell. Was he speaking of Sibley or Mr. Whitwell? I couldn't tell.

"First the strike and now we can't even go to the Casino in
peace!" Mr. Whitwell said to Mr. Mayhew. "What is this place
coming to? My wife said to me only yesterday—"

"Complete piffle," Mr. Mayhew said.

"It may be, Gideon, but the man's a pest."

"I'll take care of him, Harland," Mr. Mayhew said coldly.
"He won't bother you anymore." The tone in his voice made
me want to back away. I heard him speak this way before, to
the Pinkerton detective on the ship. An image of the trunk
dropping into the water flashed through my mind.

What was in that trunk? I wouldn't be at ease around this
man until I knew for certain.

"Good, Gideon," Mr. Whitwell said, "because if I see that
man again, I won't be responsible for my actions! Havana?" He
pulled one of his cigars out and offered it to Mr. Mayhew, who
shook his head to decline. Mr. Whitwell replaced the cigar in
his pocket.

"By the way, Harland, we need to talk about the Aquidneck
National." Mr. Mayhew turned his back to me, without ac-

knowledging or thanking me, and walked with Mr. Whitwell back toward the courtyard. "We can't afford closure. What can you tell me about . . . ?"

I took my cue, grateful to be away from that hard, cold man, and headed back to Rose Mont and the dozens of invitations waiting to be addressed and delivered.

CHAPTER 7

I was up before dawn. Mrs. Mayhew's garden party was today.
I'd spent the past few days following the same routine, starting with breakfast in my sitting room while reading through
Who's Who or poring over the map of Newport. Then I'd
spend an hour or two with Mrs. Mayhew and her cat, Bonaparte, short for *Napoléon Bonaparte,* going through her mail and
rearranging the seating arrangements for the party yet again.
The rest of the morning was spent responding to her mail,
writing out checks, and writing out guest names on place
cards. Each afternoon, I would walk to Morton Park, the
southern terminus for the streetcar, ride the streetcar to Franklin
Street (to save time, Mrs. Mayhew said), and proceed down the
bustling thoroughfare of Thames Street, making last-minute
preparations for the party: ordering tents from G.H. Wilmarth &
Son, confirming the arrival time of the Steinway piano rented
from M. Steinert & Sons Co., checking the progress of Mr.
Arend Brandt, the florist, in finding the vast number of hollyhocks Madam ordered; it would be close. And of course, as
Newport had three times more millinery shops than restau-

rants, I'd visit a different one each day, including Mrs. Mayhew's favorite, Schreier's Queen Anne Millinery Establishment, planning how to spend my first month's wages. I'd seen
Mrs. Mayhew's bills. A new hat there, like the plum velvet hat
with pansies, feathers, and stiff satin bow I wanted, would indeed cost me almost a whole month's wages.

I'd spent my evenings reading and then typing up Sir
Arthur's manuscript. I had settled into a routine. I spent my
days less solitary than I was accustomed to, interacting with Mrs.
Mayhew every morning, Britta, the parlormaid, at every meal,
the shopkeepers of Thames Street, valets and housekeepers of
other grand "cottages"; even Bonaparte the cat came by every
night looking for the scraps from my dinner plate. I had little
time to myself to hike or explore beyond the streetcar route and
the homes Mrs. Mayhew had me hand-delivering calling cards,
invitations, or notes to. Yet despite all this, I had found the past
few days and my new tasks quite satisfying. The only exception
and my least favorite task to date had been to ask Mrs. Crankshaw,
at Mrs. Mayhew's insistence, if the best linen, the tablecloths, the
napkins, and the doilies with the lace and family crest embroidered with gold and silver silk thread, would be pressed and
ready for the party.

"What?" Mrs. Crankshaw had yelled at me when I asked.
"I don't take well to those that question my efficiency. What
does Madam think I'm doing down here, sitting around with
my feet up eating macaroons all day? Of course the linen is
ready."

Luckily, Mrs. Mayhew hadn't changed her mind about the
menus. I wouldn't want to have to question Monsieur Valbois
as well.

But today would be anything but routine. I'd never assisted
in a garden party and I had no idea what was in store for me.
All I knew for certain was that I was to be present at all times,
as Madam put it, "just in case." In case of what, I could only

imagine. So I took advantage of the only time I knew would be my own today and was out the door at first light, my hand lens around my neck and specimen jars in my carryall bag. I made my way across the lawn to the gravel path that followed the cliff and, having a choice, hiked southward. Again I paused as the sun rose over the ocean. I don't think I could ever tire of the sight. I hiked less than a mile, at different times passing through a stile, down a series of steps, by a rose garden that rivaled Mrs. Mayhew's, by a boathouse and through several stone archways, all the while following the path as it wound along, passing other great "cottages" on the right and sheer cliff drops on the left. And all the while I couldn't keep a smile from my face.

I collected new specimen after new specimen, some right along the path, some requiring a scramble through the brush, one I had to lie on my stomach and, cautiously leaning over, pull from the cliff face itself.

I might need a larger plant press, I thought to my delight.

With the exception of when I started my collection, I'd never added so many new species at one time, and I'd barely gone a mile from the house. I was reluctant to return, as I hadn't found a way down the cliffs to the plethora of algae and other sea plants that clung to the rocks below, but I had to get back. When I entered, Britta, the parlormaid, was descending the stairs.

"What have you been doing, Hattie?" she asked, laughing and pointing at my dress.

I glanced down. I thought I had thoroughly brushed the gravel from my bodice but instead saw hundreds of tiny seeds and burrs clinging to my skirt. I hadn't noticed them before but couldn't wait to determine if they belonged to plants new to my collection. "I took the path along the cliffs," I said.

"It looks like you missed the path and found the bushes instead," she said, smiling. "Remind me not to go walking with you! Now go change before Mrs. Crankshaw sees you." She scrunched up her nose and pushed out her lips, mimicking Mrs. Crankshaw's most sour expression. "I don't take to girls bringing home bushes on their skirts!" Britta was still laughing as I raced up the back stairs to change.

"No, Jane, Caroline Astor hasn't called on me. I don't know what it will take, but mark my words, that woman is going to acknowledge me yet! But that's not why I called. It's about Gideon. I think he's cheating on me again," I overheard Mrs. Mayhew say as I was about to enter the drawing room. Silence followed. "He spends every morning in his gymnasium." Silence. "I know he's always done that, but now he spends even more time. And"—she hesitated for dramatic effect—"he's staying in New York." More silence. "I know he's supposed to be here for the party. That's why I think there's something going on. And now who am I going to get to stand in for Gideon?" Another hesitation. "You're right. It isn't the first time; it won't be the last. I have enough to worry about without this!"

I hadn't seen Mr. Mayhew since the day I delivered the letter to the Casino. He had returned to New York late that night. It was typical for the men of Newport to return to New York after the weekend had ended, but Gideon Mayhew had left a day early. So with the matter of the trunk unresolved, I couldn't shake the unease I felt whenever his name was mentioned. Although it caused Mrs. Mayhew distress, I wasn't disappointed to hear he wasn't going to be here today. I knocked.

"Hold on a minute, Jane," Mrs. Mayhew said. "Come in." I entered the room and found Mrs. Mayhew cradling a telephone to her ear. Unlike the majority of the houses I'd worked in that had a telephone, Mrs. Mayhew didn't have only one in the hall on the first floor. So far, I'd counted three. "Oh, Davish! Good, you're here. Sit over there." I sat in the nearest chair and pulled out my notebook. "I'm certain because he wired me from New York," Mrs. Mayhew said into the telephone. A slight hesitation. "Yes, I know there's a strike going on. He wired it through Providence." Silence filled the room while Mrs. Mayhew sat listening into the telephone.

"What?" she exclaimed. "Who told you that? Your maids can't strike. Harland would dismiss them all. Oh, Jane, what would you do?" Mrs. Mayhew glanced up from stroking her cat on her lap and started when she saw me. Had she forgotten I was there? I wondered.

"Jane, my secretary's here. I'll talk to you at the party." She put the receiver down. "You won't need that," she said, pointing to my notebook. I placed the notebook on my lap but didn't close it or put my pencil away. Mrs. Mayhew said this to me every day. She had a tendency to believe her words should be memorable enough not to warrant writing anything down. I didn't disillusion her. I simply wrote everything down as she lounged with her eyes closed, which was often enough.

She handed me a copy of the afternoon's guest list with several names crossed off and replacement names scribbled in. "Take care of this, will you?"

Oh, no, I thought. *She's changed the guest list again.*

"Of course, ma'am." I waited as Mrs. Mayhew sat staring at a life-size marble statue of the Roman goddess Minerva, slowly petting Bonaparte. Was this it? I was about to stand, assuming I was excused, when she spoke again.

"As you know, throwing any party demands full cooperation from everyone," she said.

"Yes, ma'am." I knew that the party was demanding the staff to work on what would be for many their half days off.

"You are new to this house, Miss Davish, but I wonder if you've heard anything?"

If she was talking about the grumbling this morning at breakfast over the lost half day off, yes, I'd heard plenty. Britta had told me all about it, as we were wont to chat a few minutes when she brought my meals. As a new employee I hadn't expected time off yet, but I could see why they complained. Their half day was all the time they got, and if they didn't get that time off they didn't get any time. Britta even insinuated that Mrs. Mayhew purposely scheduled parties at a time she knew would keep the servants at home. I wondered whether the accusation was true or whether she simply forgot, as she had forgotten to send the carriage for me, overwhelmed with trying to run such an enormous household while keeping up with her active social calendar. Knowing the disarrayed state of her affairs between secretaries, I tended to believe the latter.

But was that what Mrs. Mayhew was asking about? Could she be referring to rumors of an affair? "I rely on you to tell me such things," she said.

"I'm not sure what you mean, ma'am," I said.

"My dear friend Jane was just now telling me that her girls aren't happy, that there's rumors going around about maids asking for more time off. Have you heard of the telegraph operators' strike? It's disrupting everything. You must've heard about it."

"Yes, ma'am, I've heard about it." I was beginning to understand what Mrs. Mayhew was asking. It had nothing to do with her husband.

"Well, Miss Davish? Have you heard any such rumors in this house?" I was chagrined that she would ask me to inform on the other staff. Luckily, I had nothing to tell.

"No, ma'am. I haven't heard any rumors of a strike among the staff."

"Of course not, who wouldn't want to work at Rose Mont? It's a privilege and they know it." Mrs. Mayhew sat back in her chair and sighed. "I won't be requiring your services until the party. After you've written the new invitations, have the coachman deliver them. That way you'll be free until the party"—my heart leaped at the words and then sank as she finished her sentence—"to help Mrs. Crankshaw in any way that she deems appropriate. This party must be a success! You know you are my eyes and ears downstairs today."

"Yes, ma'am."

"Good. I knew I could rely on you." And with that I was dismissed.

CHAPTER 8

Under a brilliant blue sky and with the ocean as a backdrop, the scene of the party was a riot of texture, color, and fragrance. I had never seen anything like it and, if Mrs. Mayhew's vision was realized, nor had anyone else. On the green expanse of sloping lawn, two dozen white canopy tents, vines curling about their posts, fluttered gently in the breeze. Under their shade, tables and chairs had been brought from inside and decorated as if they too were part of the garden, vines curled around chair and table legs while long stems of multicolored hollyhocks had been interwoven into the backs of the chairs and graced the tables in a variety of centerpieces. Enormous white wooden planters containing towering topiaries in whimsical shapes of deer, rabbits, and birds, including a peacock with real feathers, dotted the lawn. Six actual peacocks strutted about where they pleased, as did Bonaparte the cat. The last time I saw Bonaparte, he was stalking one of the unsuspecting birds under table number twelve. A wooden platform equipped with a grand piano, surrounded on three sides by white wooden trellises overflowing with violet wisteria, marked the stage where the music recital would take place. And everywhere were white rose petals, from Mrs. Mayhew's prize rose garden, strewn about so liberally that every step released their subtle scent.

Mrs. Crankshaw, when I had offered my services, had been at a loss to find something for me to do. And then Mr. Brandt, the florist, arrived. I spent most of the morning, to my delight, assisting Mr. Brandt in weaving the vines and arranging centerpieces. With the soothing sound of the ocean, the warm sun, and the fragrant flowers I couldn't have asked for a more pleasant way to spend a summer morning. And to think I'd been worrying Mrs. Crankshaw would've had me folding napkins in the Servants' Hall or doing some such dreary work. When Mr. Brandt was satisfied that all was done to his specifications, I set out to finish my own work. With the silverware, all engraved with an elaborate *M*, glinting in the sun, I set a place card above each china dessert plate, painted with climbing vines of wisteria, purchased exclusively for this party. I was almost finished when I read the name on the card again, *Mrs. Julia Grice.*

Could it be?

I had wondered from the moment I deciphered the new guest names Mrs. Mayhew had given me. Along with Mrs. Grice I'd been pleasantly surprised to read the names of Mrs. Oliver Fry and Miss Elizabeth Shaw, known to me as Miss Lucy and Miss Lizzie, the lovely elderly sisters I'd met in Eureka Springs last fall. I didn't doubt for a moment that I knew these two ladies. They were two of a kind. Besides, they only wintered in Eureka Springs and called New Haven, Connecticut, home. Yet Miss Lizzie, in our continued correspondence, had never mentioned that she and her sister would be in Newport. I couldn't wait to see them.

I finished setting out the place cards. As I began to double-check my work with the names on the seating map in my hand, Mrs. Mayhew arrived outside to survey the progress.

Maids and footmen alike had been pressed into service decorating and setting up the tables under the direction of Mr. Davies. Ignoring Mrs. Mayhew, I rechecked Miss Lizzie's and Miss Lucy's place cards. The name that came next was Mrs. Julia Grice. As with every time I'd seen the name, it brought Walter to mind. Could it be a relation? But here I was seating Mrs. Grice next to Miss Lizzie. The coincidence struck me as extraordinary, but before I had time to think of it further Mrs. Mayhew, clenching down on her bottom lip, left Davies and headed straight for me. Her expression told me I had done something wrong, but as I glanced at the place markers I was satisfied that she wouldn't find fault with my effort. Mrs. Mayhew stopped short of me and went to the center table, right in front of the stage, and ripped one of the place markers in half. I glanced at the name on the seating chart I held and read *Gideon Mayhew.*

"Davish! Davies!" Mrs. Mayhew yelled. The butler and I rushed to her side, exchanging glances. "Mr. Mayhew will not be attending this afternoon's recital." I had wondered when she would make the news public. Suddenly the woman turned to me. "Davish, what am I to do?"

"I believe Mr. James Gordon Bennett has arrived from New York," I said, as if I'd done this my whole life. Part of my new tasks was to scan the "Cottage Arrivals for the Week" column listed daily in the *Mercury* newspaper.

"Really? Wonderful, Davish! Do invite him in Gideon's stead. I knew I could rely on you."

"Thank you, ma'am."

"By the way, what was in that envelope you delivered to Mr. Mayhew the other day, Davish?"

"I have no idea, ma'am," I said, trying to keep my indignity out of my voice. The suggestion that I would ever open anything I was not instructed to was an affront I had difficulty ignoring, even from Mrs. Charlotte Mayhew.

"Of course you don't," Mrs. Mayhew said, sighing. "Well, whatever it was prompted my husband to go back to New York early. And now he's planning to stay there!"

Why would she think the letter had anything to do with it? The letter appeared to me to have been addressed in a man's hand, not a woman's. Maybe she was simply using it as an excuse.

"He's known about this for weeks and he promised that he would attend. I even invited Maestro Jacobi because he favors him. Is it too much to ask?" Davies and I remained silent, both knowing a rhetorical question when we heard one. Without another word, she walked away.

"She's quite disappointed," I said as Mr. Davies straightened some nearby silverware.

"Yes, she does seem rather"—the butler hesitated, obviously searching for the most appropriate word—"put out."

"Mr. Mayhew's snub of his wife's party definitely qualifies as a reason to feel put out," I said.

"I'm sure the master had his reasons," Davies said, defending his employer while shaking his head.

"She's put out by more than her husband snubbing the party, if you ask me," the footman James said as he walked past carrying a tray of crystal goblets. "Where's Mrs. Astor? We're still not good enough for that great lady?"

"James!" Mr. Davies scolded. "Yours is not the place to comment. Now put the goblets over there."

"Isn't the music delightful?" Britta said, standing next to me. With our duties temporarily at a lull, several of the maids and I crowded at the end of the third-floor hallway. With the window cracked open, we listened to the music and peered down at the party scene below. The musicians had begun only a few minutes ago. Earlier, people had mingled on the lawn, sipping champagne and eating the picnic fare: salmon croquettes, lobster mayonnaise sandwiches cut into leaf shapes, minced ham roll sandwiches in purple silk ribbons, a variety of custards, cakes, fruits, ices, and cheese. Lady Phillippa was there, as were the two girls I'd met in the hall yesterday, Cora Mayhew and her friend Eugenie Whitwell. I had spied Miss Lizzie and Miss Lucy almost immediately. Except for the fact that Miss Lucy was thinner and Miss Lizzie was more plump, the two elderly sisters looked exactly the same as I remembered them.

Now that everyone was seated I could get a good look at the woman named Mrs. Grice seated with them. Dressed in an expensive but simple gray and white lawn dress and wide-brimmed straw hat with white egret feathers, she sat ramrod straight, barely moving except her head and thin neck a bit from side to side when the necessity arose. She appeared to be in her early sixties, and her well-coiffed hair was silver, her skin pale and surprisingly smooth but for deep wrinkles at the corners of her mouth—a permanent scowl on her face. *Not an easily approachable woman,* I thought. And then she smiled at something Miss Lizzie said. It transformed the woman's proud, haughty demeanor and I couldn't deny the resemblance to Walter. Could one of his relatives be in Newport? Wasn't his family from St. Louis? Maybe he had an aunt or distant cousin from out east. But why was she sitting with Miss Lizzie and Miss Lucy?

Crash!

Something below us, a tray of glassware from the sound of it, had smashed to the ground. The music stopped. Britta and the other housemaids bolted down the stairs, knowing they were responsible for cleaning up what was now lying in pieces on the floor. I stayed where I was and watched Mrs. Mayhew signal for the music to continue as Nick Whitwell, a glass of champagne in his hand, staggered into view. He threw the glass, sending it shattering to the ground, and then grabbed someone else's glass at the nearest table. Crossing the lawn, he continued drinking from or tipping over every glass within his reach, creating havoc and general disapproval as he went. Cora and Eugenie, as one, leaped up and confronted Nick. He tossed his straw hat at them. It sailed past the girls and landed in the custard on a young gentleman's plate. The man laughed, but the girls, both glaring at Nick, grabbed him, each taking an arm. As they steered him to his seat at Mrs. Mayhew's table, I could see the front of him for the first time. His tie was undone and a streak of spilt red wine darkened the front of his white shirt and tan waistcoat. I shivered. It looked like blood.

Eugenie and Cora pushed Nick into his seat next to a middle-aged couple. If I hadn't remembered their names from the seating chart, their furious expressions and resemblance to the drunken man would've told me they were Mr. and Mrs. Harland Whitwell, Nick's parents. I'd recognized Mr. Whitwell from the Newport Casino a few days ago; he'd arrived with five of his gold-banded Cuban cigars and now only had two. I hadn't known until now that he was related to the rude young man who had accosted me in the hallway. I was beginning to realize that Newport's high society consisted of a small but elite inner circle. I looked again at Mrs. Julia Grice. *Could it be—?*

"Hattie," Britta called from the stairwell. "Mrs. Crankshaw is looking for you." I immediately descended the stairs and found the housekeeper in her office off the Servants' Hall.

"Right!" she said when she saw me. "This urgent telegram arrived a few minutes ago for one of the guests, but all of the footmen are serving. I want you to give it to Mr. Davies. I'd do it, but I found the maids loitering and I have to keep an eye on them. I don't take well to loitering."

"Of course," I said, glancing at the name on the envelope, *Harland Whitwell.* "But isn't there a telegraph operators' strike going on?"

"You ask too many questions, Miss Davish, but yes, that's

why this can't wait until after the party. It was wired to Providence and then delivered by post. It's two days old already. Now go!"

I ran upstairs and found Mr. Davies coordinating the serving of the second dessert course, fruit ices served on a bed of frozen calendula petals, and gave him the telegraph. I watched from the buffet table as the butler found Mr. Whitwell and stood by waiting to deliver the note. Mr. Whitwell was arguing with his son. I couldn't hear the words, but the father's face was red and tiny beads of spittle clung to the corners of his mouth. He was furious. His wife, Mrs. Jane Whitwell, a plain, round-faced woman in her mid-fifties, who looked slightly ridiculous in her very expensive but very youthful pink and white lawn dress of puffy sleeves, flouncing lace, rosebuds, and wide silk bows, placed her hand on his arm, gently restraining him. Suddenly Nick leaped up.

"To hell with you then!" he shouted.

He pushed his way through the tables, knocking over a serving table, and staggered across the lawn toward the ocean. He kicked at one of the peacocks, sending the bird skittering away. I was glad that Bonaparte was nowhere to be seen. Cora and Eugenie stood to follow. Mrs. Mayhew caught Cora's eye and shook her head. Cora and then Eugenie sat down again, both following Nick's progress with their eyes. Mrs. Mayhew turned back to face the music. Mr. Davies, as if nothing had happened, leaned over and offered Mr. Whitwell the telegram. After reading the telegram, Mr. Whitwell shook his head, said something to his wife, and threw his napkin onto the table. He took his leave of Mrs. Mayhew, who, quite put out by yet another disruption, ripped the skin from her bottom lip with her teeth as she took his hand. Mr. Whitwell whispered something in her ear, patting her gently on the back. She nodded and smiled as they parted. He dashed by me, as fast as a man needing the use of a cane can dash, as he left.

Not having to guess the nature of the argument between father and son, I wondered what was in the telegram. First Sir Arthur, then Mr. Mayhew, and now Mr. Whitwell. They had all received news that prompted immediate departures. Sir Arthur had urgent family business in England. From what Lady Phillippa had said, Sir Arthur's father, the Viscount, was gravely ill. But what about Mr. Mayhew and Mr. Whitwell? As they were self-made men of industry and banking, respectively, I could assume business had called them away. Or was there something to Mrs. Mayhew's suspicions? Mr. Mayhew had arrived a day earlier than she knew and then left a day earlier than she'd planned. And I hadn't forgotten about the incident with the trunk. I shook my head, annoyed with myself. Obviously my mind was too idle as I stood here waiting for Mrs. Mayhew's word. I needed to find something more constructive to do than speculate about the lives of the people I worked for and their friends. If only I could go work on Sir Arthur's manuscript. A few hours of typing would straighten me out.

"Miss Davish." Mr. Davies saying my name pulled me out of my own thoughts.

"Yes," I said.

"Mrs. Mayhew would like to see you when the music is done."

"Yes, of course." Mr. Davies went back to his duties while I waited where I was. Biding my time, I tapped my foot to the beat of the jaunty waltz the musicians began to play. Instantly I was taken back to my early childhood, before my mother's death, when she would play Irish jigs on the old fiddle she brought with her on the boat. My father would dance, or at least attempt to, making us both laugh by his uncoordinated, flailing moves. Looking back, I realized that after her death my father never allowed music in our house. Thus I never learned to play piano like other girls. I'd used my dexterous fingers to learn to type instead. *What happened to her fiddle?* I wondered.

"Miss Davish," Davies hissed. Startled out of my reverie, I realized the music had stopped and people were politely applauding. Everyone stood and formed little groups on the lawn.

"Thank you, Mr. Davies," I said. "Seems I too was caught up in the music." He nodded as I passed and made my way to Mrs. Mayhew's side.

"You asked for me, ma'am?" I said.

"Davish, there are some ladies here who—"

"Hattie, dear!" Miss Lizzie cried. She wrapped her arms around me and kissed me on both cheeks. My face flushed with embarrassment. I adored Miss Lizzie and was happy to see her, but such a display of affection wasn't appropriate in front of Mrs. Mayhew. From her expression, Mrs. Mayhew was as surprised as I was.

"Oh, let the girl breathe, Lizzie," Miss Lucy chided.

"We're just so happy to see you," Miss Lizzie said. "Aren't we, Lucy?"

"You know each other?" Mrs. Mayhew asked.

"Oh, yes. Hattie discovered who killed our dear leader, Mother Trevelyan, last fall." An awkward silence ensued. Murder wasn't a polite topic of conversation at a garden party.

"Oh, ah, yes, well. I had heard about that. I didn't realize that the secretary in question was my own Miss Davish," Mrs. Mayhew said. She stole a quick glance at me, her expression unreadable, before turning back to the elderly sisters. "How awful for you ladies."

"Yes, but Davish bore the brunt of it," Miss Lucy said. She looked me up and down. "Still worn-out, I see. I've seen old boots on a military man look better. Don't you ever sleep, Davish?" I smiled. They hadn't changed a bit.

"We had no idea you would be here, dear," Miss Lizzie said. "But then I saw you standing over there in the doorway. Your last letter said you were still working with Arthur on his book."

"As you can see, she's working for me now," Mrs. Mayhew said. "I quite rely on her, you know." The old ladies nodded their approval. I tried not to blush at the compliment, but inside I reveled in the praise. "Lady Phillippa is here if you'd like to inquire about Sir Arthur. I do believe he had to rush off to England on urgent business."

"That would explain him giving you up, Davish," Miss Lucy said. "Can't think of any other reason."

"You gave us a delightful surprise," Miss Lizzie said. "Now we get to return the favor. Julia, dear, there's someone we'd like you to meet." This last comment was directed at the woman wearing the wide-brimmed hat with egret feathers who had been sitting with them. I coveted the older woman's hat but not her attitude. The music and fine food had done nothing to relax her pinched mouth.

"Miss Hattie Davish, may I present you to Mrs. Julia Grice," Miss Lizzie said. "Dr. Grice's mother." My heart raced, my breath became rapid and shallow, and my fingers began to tingle.

Is Walter here as well?

Without thinking, I glanced about me, looking for him, and was rewarded not by a sighting of Walter but with a frown from his mother. Of course he wasn't here. I would've seen his name on the guest list. I returned my attention to the woman in front of me.

How extraordinary, I thought, to meet Walter's mother not in Eureka Springs or St. Louis but in Newport. Quickly I grew self-conscious as the woman waited silently, staring at me. Was she expecting me to speak first? What should I say to Walter's mother? First impressions were so important.

"I'm pleased to make your acquaintance, ma'am," I said, trying to keep the tremor from my voice.

"Hmm, yes, well," Mrs. Grice said. There was no easy smile for me.

"I trust Dr. Grice is well?" I asked.

"Yes, Walter is quite well, thank you."

I didn't know what else to say. As on many occasions before, Miss Lizzie and Miss Lucy saved me from my predicament.

"Mrs. Grice is our guest at Moffat Cottage, dear. We met this winter while she was visiting Dr. Grice in Eureka and we invited her to visit us this summer."

"But don't be looking over our shoulders for the good doctor," Miss Lucy said perceptively. "Dr. Grice was too busy to join her." I had to consciously not let my disappointment show.

"And how do you come to know my son?" Mrs. Grice said. It almost sounded like an accusation.

What could I say? That I'd met him during a saloon smashing? That he'd carried me through the streets of Eureka Springs when I'd been unconscious after a fall? That he left her side at Christmastime and traveled across the country when he thought I needed him? That he was joining me for an early morning rendezvous when we discovered a dead man? That every letter he'd ever sent was preciously preserved in a locked box that traveled with me everywhere? What could I say but, "We met in Eureka Springs. At the same time as I met Miss Shaw and Mrs. Fry."

"And he was sweet on her too, wasn't he, dear?" Miss Lizzie said.

My cheeks burned with embarrassment as Mrs. Grice's eyes flared open and she pursed her lips even tighter.

"I don't think so. A servant?" Mrs. Grice declared indignantly.

"But Julia, dear," Miss Lizzie said, confusion registering on her face.

"Lovely party, Charlotte," Miss Lucy said, suddenly changing the subject.

Mrs. Mayhew looked at Julia Grice and then at me. Mrs. Mayhew's countenance was tranquil, all but her lower lip, which she was biting again, a sure sign of her indignation.

"Thank you, Miss Lucy, but I would have Mrs. Grice know that Miss Davish is not a simple servant. She is an extremely capable social secretary who comes highly recommended. She has worked in the best of households and I can say with confidence that only the best work for me." Whether she was simply defending her choice in staff or whether she actually believed what she was saying, I silently thanked Mrs. Mayhew for her confidence in me. I could see now why Mr. Davies and Mrs. Crankshaw would not hear a negative word about their mistress. She'd earned their loyalty. I only hoped I could live up to her ideal. "And I believe she could easily find many an eligible bachelor who could be sweet on her. Even my own Cora's fiancé, Nicholas, mentioned her charms."

I shivered at the thought of Nick Whitwell talking of me to his future mother-in-law. Which charms had he mentioned? My callused fingers? My helplessness? My fear? He was not one I'd considered eligible for anything but being a drunken brute.

"I meant no disrespect to you, Mrs. Mayhew," Mrs. Grice said, smiling. How lovely her face was when she smiled. *Just like Walter,* I thought. She glanced my way, hesitating, wanting to say something to me, but instead frowned slightly, then added, "Thank you for a lovely afternoon." Mrs. Mayhew nodded.

"Yes, lovely party, dear," Miss Lizzie said, nervously picking up three bonbons in the candy basket on the table next to her.

She popped one into her mouth. "And such a beautiful house. I do so love the peacocks."

"Thank you. You're excused, Miss Davish," Mrs. Mayhew said.

"Thank you, ma'am," I said, nodding my farewells to the other women. I was relieved to be able to return to the house and the typing I had to do. As I retreated toward the house, the women continued chatting mindlessly about the delightful view, the ingenious colored gelatin molds the ice cream was served in, the lovely weather.

"Wherever did you find so many hollyhocks?" I heard Mrs. Grice ask.

Could my first meeting with Walter's mother have gone worse? I didn't think so. I'd warned Walter from the start that we were unevenly matched. How I wished he were here! When I reached the house, I looked back. The cluster of women I'd left had broken up. Mrs. Mayhew was mingling with the other guests; Mrs. Grice had moved on and was speaking with Mrs. Jane Whitwell while a rotund naval captain in full dress uniform had captured Miss Lizzie's and Miss Lucy's attention. Miss Lucy caught my eye. I gave her my bravest smile and she winked. I went to my work with a lighter heart and a pledge to write Walter that night.

CHAPTER 9

"Come with us, Hattie," Britta said.

With dinner over, I was typing at the large desk in my sitting room making progress on Sir Arthur's manuscript when Britta, Sena the kitchen maid, and James the footman interrupted me.

"Mrs. Mayhew has given permission for some of us to have a few hours off tonight, since we missed our time off this afternoon. We're going to the Forty Steps."

I'd read about the Forty Steps but hadn't had the opportunity to see them yet. In my efforts to acquaint myself with my new surroundings, beyond the atlas and city directory, I'd read a tourist guidebook, *In and Around Newport 1892*, I found among the books in my room. It mentioned the Forty Steps as a "well-known" place that had recently been improved for seeing the "rocks below." With no other description, I'd been intrigued. With a possible way down from the cliffs to the rocks and their associated plant species beckoning, I couldn't resist.

"Thank you, Britta," I said, slipping my rubber overshoes

into a bag along with a few specimen jars and my plant press. "I'd love to join you."

We were joined downstairs by a few more maids I'd barely met and one of the groomsmen. As we walked, Sena, a girl of sixteen with fuzzy brown hair, small green eyes, and a bulbous nose, who until this moment had spoken but a few words to me, suddenly began emulating Mrs. Crankshaw by talking fast and asking me questions. Sena skipped along as she did.

"What is that contraption you're carrying? And why do you leave the house so early in the morning? I heard you're not from New York or Newport. Where do you live? Where did you get that smart-looking hat? Why are you carrying rubber overshoes? Do you plan to go down on the rocks? I heard that you found a dead body."

With that last comment, the entire company halted in their tracks and stared at Sena.

"Sena!" Britta said.

"Hush, girl," the groomsman said.

"What?" Sena said. "I overheard some ladies talking today at the party and they said that Hattie had found a dead body. I only wanted to know if it was true."

"It's not polite to ask so many questions, Sena," James, the footman, said.

"It's all right," I said. "I think by now even Mrs. Mayhew knows." As everyone seemed to know about Mrs. Trevelyan, being the public figure that she was, I told a simple version of my misadventures in Eureka Springs. To Sena's delight, I retold how I found my murdered employer in a trunk and became involved in investigating the death of the late hatchet-wielding temperance leader, as we walked toward the Forty Steps. However, I kept the other incidences to myself. No one needed to know, and I didn't want reminding, that Mrs. Trevelyan was the first of three dead bodies I'd found.

And then we were there, the Forty Steps, a broad section of

the Cliff Walk at the end of Narragansett Avenue from which a steep wooden staircase jutted out from the cliff and descended exactly forty steps down to the crashing waves and rocks below. We heard the conviviality before we saw the dozens of others we joined in the fresh evening air. Someone was strumming a banjo and voices were raised in laughter and the occasional song. Judging by the older, simpler style of hats and dresses, the crowd consisted mostly of servants on their night off. The conversations I overheard as I parted from Britta and the others and wove my way toward the steps confirmed it.

"Your missus does what?" one woman in her thirties asked her younger companion.

"She dons an apron, snaps on white gloves, and follows me around all day."

"Well, I've never heard of such a thing. I can't imagine what Mrs. Flagg must say to that?"

"Oh, she's quite put out. The missus acts like we don't even have a housekeeper."

"Well, if I were Mrs. Flagg, I wouldn't stay there. They're not the only high-society family in Newport."

"Mrs. Flagg nothing," the younger girl said. "Us maids have had our fill too. It ain't right, a rich lady like that checking floors and mantelpieces with her gloved finger." I wondered who the controlling mistress was but moved on.

"Ah, Mr. Whitwell's all right," a footman, judging by his height and handsome face, was saying to a group of maids. "He even offered me one of those Cuban cigars when my sister's boy was born. But the missus, what's with the flouncy collars?" The maids giggled.

"I think Mrs. Whitwell is trying to stay young," one of the maids suggested. "But she does look rather silly."

"I like her dresses," the youngest of the group said.

"You would, Biddy. You're only fifteen."

"She's certainly rich enough to wear whatever she wants," another said. All heads nodded in agreement.

"Did you hear about Nick Whitwell?" the footman said, whispering behind his hand. The girls leaned forward. "I heard from Clara, our kitchen maid, who has a brother who works there, that Mr. Nick got expelled from the Reading Room."

"Really?" one of the maids said. "Why?"

The footman took a few steps toward the girls, so that I could barely hear him. "Because he was caught, eh . . . taking a bit of fresh air, if you catch my meaning, and aiming it right off the porch!" The girls squealed with delight at this shocking bit of gossip.

I smiled at their innocence and waved when I saw Miss Kyler, Lady Phillippa's maid, near the top of the steps. *Maybe she can tell me something about Sir Arthur,* I thought, making my way toward her. Before I reached her, someone shouted above the din of the waves mixed with the music, the call of seagulls, and the hum of dozens of voices.

"We will uphold the dignity of labor! We will uphold the dignity of labor!"

The music stopped. The crowd hushed as I turned to see who had called out. There, in the middle of the merrymakers, standing on a small boulder, was Sibley, the man I'd seen standing outside the Newport Casino arguing with Mr. Whitwell some days before. Sibley was now addressing his fellow workers.

"Listen, fellow laborers. Remember 'an injury to one is the concern of all!' " he said. "It's us or them and if it were up to them I wouldn't even be talking to you."

"Then shut up!" someone yelled.

"Then they would win. No, sir, I won't rest until you have your rights."

"Then don't. But the rest of us would all like to relax right now." We all looked to see who had shouted back. It was

James, familiarly putting his arm around Britta's shoulders. She was smiling and relaxed into his embrace. "I'll agree we work too much. But do we have to talk about how we work too much as well?"

"That's my point," Sibley said. "Talking about working too much isn't enough. We must join together and do something about it."

"And what would that be?" another man asked.

"Strike!" Sibley said, smashing his fist into the palm of his other hand. Several people laughed or dismissed him with a wave of their hands. Most turned their backs and went back to talking with their friends. The banjo player began another tune. But a few people, including Sena, the groomsman, and several others, stayed listening.

"Like the telegraph operators?" a young woman asked.

"Exactly," Sibley said.

"But they're striking against a company, not a family," Sena said. "Isn't it disloyal and ungrateful for household staff to even think about striking? Working for the Mayhews is a desirable position. I'm the envy of many a maid. Why would I put my position and future at risk for a few extra hours off a week?"

"It's not disloyal to want a full day off a week. It's immoral of your 'family' to deny you. But you're right. You work for some of the richest people in this country. You do have a prestigious position. So think of the message you would be sending to other maids if you demanded your rights! You could do so much good for your fellow workers. If you stood up to your 'family' it would give courage to the more unfortunate to do the same."

From the number of people who'd turned their backs on him, Sibley's impassioned speech was falling mostly on deaf ears. But then why had Mrs. Mayhew asked me about discontent in her own staff? What had prompted the rumors? Perhaps more people were listening and sympathetic to his cause than was apparent. Certainly the maid with the controlling mistress had voiced grievances.

"No, thank you, sir," Sena said. "I worked hard to get where I am and I'm not about to jeopardize my position." With that she spun away, pulling the two other maids and the groomsman with her. Someone had brought out an accordion and now joined the banjo player. Before long, everyone had moved away from the labor man but me. I wondered why I was still there. I too started to walk away.

"I've seen you before," he said, stopping my retreat, "at the Newport Casino a few days ago."

I was startled that he remembered. "Yes, you and Mr. Whitwell were having words."

The man laughed. "That's one way of putting it." He shoved out his hand. "Lester Sibley, at your service."

"Hattie Davish," I said, taking his hand before realizing it might not be a good idea to be seen fraternizing with him.

"I like you, Hattie Davish."

"You just met me, Mr. Sibley," I said, now suspicious of his intent.

"Doesn't matter. I can tell an honest laborer when I see one. What line of work are you in, Hattie Davish?"

"I'm Mrs. Charlotte Mayhew's social secretary."

"So are you treated fairly, Hattie Davish? Or do you work at all hours, always at the beck and call of Mrs. Mayhew?"

"Long and unusual hours are the nature of the job, Mr. Sibley," I said.

"Are cramped, cold, dreary living quarters part of the nature of the job too?"

"I have a spacious suite of rooms, Mr. Sibley."

"And what about your private life, Hattie Davish? Can you do as you like, even in the little time you do have off?"

"Yes, I believe I can." I was tiring of this line of questioning. Like Sena, I had worked hard to attain my position. I was

respected, well treated, and enjoyed challenging, satisfying work.
What more could I ask for? I was content. Why shouldn't he be?
But Mr. Sibley wasn't about to give up.

"Did you know that one dinner party at Marble House or
Rose Mont costs over a thousand dollars? One dinner party.
What do you make in a year, Hattie Davish?"

"That, Mr. Sibley, is none of your concern," I said, doing
nothing to hide my irritation. "I understand there are people
in need of a voice such as yours, but I am not one of them."

"Whether you know it or not, Hattie Davish, you are one
of them. My voice, my message, my cause, is fair rights for all,
and that includes maids, butlers, clerks, and social secretaries."

"I'm grateful for my position, Mr. Sibley. I have been poor
and I have been lonely."

After my father died, I was an orphan with no siblings, no
close living relatives, and less than twenty dollars at my disposal. The doctors who attended, though I would say "killed,"
my father had taken almost all we had. I was no longer able to
live in my childhood home, and all I could afford was a tiny
basement room at Mrs. Coombs' Boardinghouse that flooded
during spring rainstorms. Luckily, my father had paid my tu-
ition at Mrs. Chaplin's school in full. I never wanted to imagine where I would be now if not for my typewriter, my
training, and the opportunities given to me by the likes of Sir
Arthur and Mrs. Mayhew.

"So," I said, "despite the limitations or demands placed
upon me, I prefer my current full and interesting life. Once I
could never have imagined standing on the top of a cliff, looking out over the ocean, listening to banjo and accordion music
while discussing labor strife with a man such as yourself."

Lester Sibley nodded his head. "If only I could persuade
you that you could have even more. Here, at least take this."
He reached into his pocket. "Damn, I forgot."

"Forgot what, Mr. Sibley?"

"Excuse my language, but I forgot that all my pamphlets are lying on the bottom of the ocean. Don't you see, Hattie Davish, that they don't want you to realize you deserve more? And they'll stop at nothing to prevent it." I had no idea what he was talking about, but his comments about his pamphlets called up the image of the steamer trunk bobbing in the water before it disappeared beneath the waves.

"Were you in a shipwreck, sir?" I asked.

"No, no, kind lady," Lester Sibley said, smiling crookedly. "No, on the trip over from New York my travel trunk, containing all of my literature, was stolen from my room. As it was nowhere to be found when we arrived, I can only assume someone sent it overboard. Like I said, 'they' will stop at nothing to keep me from spreading the word. Did I say something funny?"

I had involuntarily laughed out loud in my relief and embarrassment. Here I had been imagining the worst, a trunk hiding a dead body, whereas the only thing Mr. Mayhew and the Pinkerton detective were guilty of was ridding the world of more labor propaganda pamphlets. Although I still didn't approve of Mr. Mayhew stooping to theft in the night, I felt foolish for assigning to him such evil doings. But how did I explain my reaction to the poor man's misfortune? I looked about me quickly. People were dancing, laughing, drinking from bottles and flasks, tapping their toes, and clapping their hands to the rapid beat of the music. The accordion player had a monkey on his shoulder clapping tiny cymbals together. The animal even wore a little fez.

"No, no, I apologize, Mr. Sibley. I merely caught a glimpse of the monkey. He's quite amusing."

"Yes, of course," Sibley said, not appearing to understand at all. "Back to what I was saying, Miss Davish. Our movement seeks to—" The last thing I wanted was for him to return to the previous conversation.

"It's been interesting talking to you, Mr. Sibley, but if you'll excuse me, I haven't been down the steps yet." I took several steps away, hoping he wouldn't follow me.

"Of course," he said, realizing I wasn't going to be swayed to his cause tonight. I gratefully headed toward the cliff-side staircase as he headed to a group of people congregated around the accordion player.

Relieved to be free of the labor man's attention, I grabbed the railing at the top of the stairs and walked several steps down. And then I froze. I'd made the mistake of looking down through the empty space between the steps. Beneath my feet, at least twenty feet below, was nothing but slimy, black rock and swirling water.

I don't think I can go down there, I thought, my palms sweating as I imagined myself losing my balance and slipping into the turbulent waves below.

I dropped to a sitting position, my heart racing, but I couldn't keep my eyes off the water. I began to inch my way backward up to the top. But then, as I nearly reached the top, the waves slipped away from the rocks for a moment, revealing several red algae plants, their fronds gently flowing with the current. As the waves crashed again, I heard giggling above me. I glanced up at two young girls, probably maids, waiting at the top of the steps. In my seated position, my skirts were blocking their way. And they were giggling at me.

Rightfully so, I thought, suddenly feeling ridiculous. I'd been down staircases before. Why was this one so different? I stood up, let the girls pass, and watched as they held on to their straw bonnets while carelessly skipping down the steps. I peered down again to watch the algae beckoning me from below. If young girls could do it, so could I, I thought. Besides, I had to have that plant. I secured my hat against the breeze, took a deep breath, and grabbed the rail once again.

"Let her go!"

I spun my head around at the second shout of the night. Instantly the music stopped and the only sounds were those of the waves crashing below and the clattering cymbals of the monkey, who didn't know to stop. I followed the stares of the hushed crowd toward the cause of the commotion. I should've known. It was Lester Sibley! His hat had fallen off and he held Britta in his arms. She was squirming in his embrace, trying to release herself, but the labor man was reluctant to let her go.

"Can't you see she was dancing with me, footman?" Sibley said as James hovered nearby.

"She wants to dance with me now," James said. James tried to pull Britta away, but Sibley would not let go of Britta's arm. She began to cry. I could see from where I stood the red welt already rising on her arm.

"Let her go now!" James shouted.

"I'm sorry," Lester Sibley said, releasing Britta, who fumbled into a group of gaping girls. "I didn't mean—" Without allowing the labor man to finish his apology, James yanked his fist back and swung at the man, landing a hard blow right in Lester Sibley's face. Sibley staggered back, holding his hand to his nose as blood streamed down his chin and dripped onto his white shirt. James lunged for the man again. Britta and a few other girls nearby screamed. Several men snatched the footman's raised arm and pulled him in the opposite direction.

"No fair, Chase," one of the men told James as he resisted the hold on his arms. "You've got a foot on the man."

"Serves him right for preaching about unions and strikes when we're all trying to have a good time," someone added.

"He's only trying to help us," another said.

The accordion player began a jaunty tune, but no one was listening. Instead voices rose above the song as arguments about Sibley and his cause broke out among the previously merry group.

Our group from Rose Mont had closed ranks around

Britta. Sena put her arm around Britta and, followed by the other girls and the groomsman, led her away up Narragansett Avenue. Britta glanced back once, her eyes as red as the welt on her arm, just as James jerked free of the men restraining him and stormed away down the Cliff Walk. He quickly disappeared around the bend.

What was that all about? *Mr. Sibley sure has a knack for stirring up trouble wherever he goes,* I thought, looking about for the cause of the commotion. Mr. Sibley was nowhere to be seen.

CHAPTER 10

B *oom!*
"What was that?" Sena exclaimed. I'd caught up with Britta, Sena, and the others from Rose Mont. We'd just turned onto Bellevue when the explosion went off.

"Look at that!" Britta exclaimed, pointing north toward Touro Park. Over the trees, thick lines of smoke curled up into the night sky, blurring the stars.

With unspoken assent, we picked up our skirts and ran. Others quickly joined us, their eyes captivated by the eerie glow ahead. We were all destined for the site of the explosion, two similarly squat brick buildings, on opposite corners of Green Street.

A grotesque tableau of Dante's hell, I thought, watching transfixed by the walls of red flame flashing against the dark sky.

From the relative safety of the sidewalk across the street I could feel the blistering heat press against my skin. Massive columns of black smoke billowed above the buildings, with small tendrils drifting into the street, weaving their way through the crowd. And rising above it all was the cacophony of chaos, pounding in my head. The fire roared like wind during a storm on the Plains. Police and firemen, who had arrived before us, shouted at one another over the clanging of bells. Panes of windows, already partially broken by the blast, shattered to the ground. One large piece landed a few feet away, the gold-stenciled letters *LOAN* still intact. Skittish horses bucked and neighed as carriages arrived on the scene. And then came a rumble and crash as a roof collapsed and the sound of gushing water spraying from the hose carriages onto the flames. I wanted nothing more than to hold my hands over my ears, but instead I shielded my eyes from the blaze with one hand and held a handkerchief over my mouth with the other; the metallic taste and smell of the smoke had begun to fill my mouth and lungs.

And yet I, like everyone else spellbound by the scene, stayed, wondering what caused the fire. Was it a gas leak? Or electric wires that got too hot? Or a faulty furnace with the coals left burning? But what about the explosion? Fires were an all too common occurrence; explosions were not.

With the infusion of water came clouds of blinding smoke and then the signs etched above the doors of the burning buildings gradually became legible: NEWPORT SAVINGS BANK and AQUIDNECK NATIONAL BANK.

Thank goodness! They weren't homes where the residents had moments ago been peacefully sleeping in their beds or sipping sherry in their parlors as I feared. Most likely the banks were empty and no one was hurt. From the exterior, the savings bank appeared to have suffered the more extensive damage: Part of a wall had collapsed, the windows were all blown out, and the roof had collapsed and was still aflame inside. The national bank had lost some of its windows and had partial damage to its roof. The explosion had obviously originated in the former building and had spread to the latter. A fireman wearing a black rubber coat, tall rubber boots, and a leather fire helmet walked past. He pushed the helmet back from his forehead with his forearm, leaving a long smear of black ash across his brow.

"What happened?" I asked.

"Don't know yet, but we think it was intentional." Before I could ask more, he was gone.

Intentional, I thought. Who would do such a thing? Then I saw Mr. Doubleday, the Pinkerton detective, standing among the crowd several yards away. I couldn't hear him, but his lips were puckered as if whistling. What was he doing here? He was probably a curious bystander, but something in his stance made me uneasy. And then out of the smoke Lester Sibley, holding a bloody handkerchief to his nose, walked past the detective. Mr. Doubleday grabbed ahold of the labor man's collar and nearly yanked the smaller man off his feet. Sibley shouted and with his free hand attempted to free himself, but to no avail. The detective was both taller and stronger. I maneuvered closer, careful to keep several people between us but close enough to hear what Sibley and Doubleday were saying.

"I told you it would get ugly if you didn't shut your mouth and leave Newport," Doubleday said.

"What are you talking about?" Lester Sibley said.

The bigger man gestured toward the burning buildings with his chin.

"What? I didn't have anything to do with this!" Sibley proclaimed. "I'm not an anarchist. I simply want fair treatment for workers. Why would I burn down a bank?"

"I don't know. It seems like something a radical like you would do."

"I'm telling you I didn't have anything to do with this!"

"Maybe, maybe not."

"What are you saying?"

"I'm saying, Mr. Sibley, that if you don't stop your inflammatory talk and leave Newport on the next boat or train, you may find yourself in a load of trouble." Doubleday snatched

Sibley's hat off his head and threw it to the ground. With one deliberate stomp of his foot the detective flattened the stiff-crowned hat. "A load of trouble!"

"You can't threaten me. I know my rights. I was nowhere near this place when the explosion happened." Suddenly Lester Sibley caught sight of me. "Ask her. She can tell you where I was tonight." Mortified that both men were looking at me, one with pleading eyes, the other with a suspicious stare, I turned my back on both of them and walked as fast as I could through the crowd and away from the grim scene. I didn't look back.

I couldn't sleep. I normally didn't sleep well, but tonight I couldn't think of anything besides Lester Sibley. My thoughts bounced back and forth between the unanswered questions surrounding the man and self-reprimands for my cowardice toward him. Why did I fail to come to the man's aid when I could've vouched for his whereabouts? Doubleday was threatening Mr. Sibley and I did nothing to help. I was ashamed of myself. I hadn't even had the guts to write Walter as I'd planned. I was restless, with a growing pang of guilt in the pit of my stomach. *Tomorrow,* I thought. Tomorrow I would track down the labor man as soon as I had a moment free to make amends.

But to get through tonight, I typed up the list of questions in my head:

1. What had caused the explosion?
2. Was it intentional? If so, why?
3. Why did Detective Doubleday think Lester Sibley was responsible?
4. Why did Detective Doubleday threaten Lester Sibley?
5. What was Doubleday to gain if the labor man left?
6. Why had a simple dance resulted in blows between James and Lester Sibley?

7. What will Walter's mother tell him about our meeting this afternoon?

Then I laid out my new plant and seed specimens on the desk in my sitting room. I studied their details under my hand lens and using James L. Bennett's *Plants of Rhode Island,* which I'd borrowed from Mrs. Mayhew's library, identified the species names for the newest additions to my collection. One by one I preserved my specimens in my plant press. Normally the task filled me with joy and satisfaction, but tonight I felt empty. I'd let someone down. For some reason my thoughts returned to Walter and my meeting with his mother.

Had I let him down as well? His mother didn't approve of me, but Walter never minded the gap between us. Or did he? Was I blinded by my fondness for him? I'd once explained to Walter that I could never be more than what I was. It didn't seem to bother him. So why was I suddenly doubting his affections? Because his mother was unimpressed? If Walter no longer had faith in me, would I still have faith in myself? And Sir Arthur? What if he no longer valued me? Was I worthless because someone like Julia Grice said so?

"No," I said out loud to the empty room. When had I stopped looking to myself for strength and pride? When had I let the opinion of others dictate my worth? I admitted I'd wronged Lester Sibley by not staying and corroborating his story, and tomorrow I would right that wrong. But that was no reason to let my mind spiral out of control, into a state of depression and doubt.

"Buck up, Davish," I told myself. "You've got work to do."

I settled down in front of my typewriter, slipped in a blank sheet of paper, and, feeling the cool touch of the keys beneath my fingertips, began on another page of Sir Arthur's manuscript. I hadn't typed half the page before my eyelids drooped and I staggered off to bed.

★   ★   ★

I didn't rise early enough for a hike. And when I did awaken, my courage from the night before was dimmed by sunlight. A sense of loneliness almost overwhelmed me.

"Good morning, Britta," I said overenthusiastically when she arrived with my breakfast, I was so grateful to see her. She smiled halfheartedly, her normally cheerful countenance clouded, as she placed the tray on the table and sat opposite me.

"Is everything all right?" I asked, pouring us coffee. She sighed but didn't answer my question.

"You missed a lively discussion downstairs this morning."

"Was it about the incidence at the Forty Steps?" I asked. She took a quick gulp of her coffee and tugged at her left ear. I knew I'd said the wrong thing. "I'm sorry if I'm prying."

"No, Hattie. It's okay. Actually, all the fuss this morning was about the fire last night. Only a few of us saw it and the rest of the staff were jealous. Someone had a comment or question about everything."

"Like what?"

"Oh, everything, like, 'Did they say what caused the fire?' 'Mrs. Post's chambermaid said a bomb exploded!' 'Was anyone hurt?' 'How many buildings burned down?' 'I'm glad my money's not in either one of those banks.' 'I can't believe I went back along the Cliff Walk and missed everything!' "

Britta and I both laughed at her imitation of the younger maids.

"Of course, even though we were there, none of us know much about what happened either," she said, shrugging. I nodded, picturing Detective Doubleday yanking Lester Sibley by the collar. What was that about?

"You're right," I said, remembering what the fireman had told me. "We probably don't know the half of it."

"I glanced at the papers before Miss Issacson brought them up to Mrs. Mayhew. They didn't seem to know much more

than we do," she said, piling the dishes of my half-eaten breakfast onto a tray without comment. Britta was already used to
my eating habits. I'd finished the broiled tomatoes and brandy
peaches but couldn't face the poached egg on anchovy toast.
"Hope it's not true about bad things happening in threes."

"What do you mean?" I said.

"Well, first the telegraph operators went on strike and then
this fire. Hope nothing else happens."

I'd never been superstitious and rejected the rule of three
outright, but Britta's comment put me in a pensive mood. Yesterday I would've thought that the travel trunk incident was
the first in a string of unfortunate events, the strike, the altercation at the Forty Steps, the fire, my meeting with Walter's
mother, my abandonment of Lester Sibley, but I now knew
better. And yet?

"I hope so too, Britta. I hope so too."

CHAPTER 11

M rs. Mayhew called for me after breakfast and I spent several hours working, updating Mrs. Mayhew's calendar, sorting letters, invitations, and calling cards, and creating a seating chart for the supper at Mrs. Mayhew's upcoming ball. Her lavish garden party had ended only yesterday afternoon and yet she had scheduled another lavish entertainment in just three days' time. *Astounding!* I thought. *With so many parties, luncheons, concerts, and lectures to plan and attend, how can they call these weeks in Newport a holiday?* I'd be exhausted.

As I made suggested changes to the guest list, Mrs. Mayhew, lounging on her chaise longue and stroking a serene and contented Bonaparte, pored through dozens of invitation samples that had arrived from the stationery store this morning.

"What do you think of this one?" she asked, holding up a plain white card with a simple green border. Before I could respond, she held up another with an elaborate floral design. "Or this one?" Again she didn't wait for a response.

"You were at the fire last night, weren't you?" she said, without looking up. Her question surprised me. Was that recrimination in her voice or was she merely trying to confirm a fact?

"Yes, ma'am, I was."

"There are rumors about it already, but I don't know what to believe." I waited, my pen drying as I stopped my writing, giving her my full attention. "I heard mention of a bomb."

How did that rumor get started? And how had Mrs. Mayhew heard of it so soon? Britta said the newspaper hadn't provided any details. Although many thought the telephone was a poor substitute for a personal visit, I knew Mrs. Mayhew didn't always share that opinion. The telephone was a lightning-quick lifeline of gossip. Had she already had at least one telephone conversation this morning?

"I wouldn't know, ma'am," I said.

"I heard you could feel the ground shake a mile away." Yes, because she rarely, if ever, interacted with the staff who witnessed the blaze, she had definitely been on her telephone.

"Some of the housemaids and I did feel something when we were walking back from the Forty Steps."

"That's more than a mile. Jane was right then. It could've been a bomb. What with all the strike talk and now this, one would think that anarchists have made it to Newport. This is a disaster. What will become of the Season with this chaos and destruction? What will they do next? Dig up the greens at the Country Club? Ransack the Casino? Pour tar on Bailey's Beach? Appear unannounced at my ball?"

I didn't want to contradict her, but her equating bombing a bank, doing thousands of dollars in damage, disrupting commerce, and potentially endangering human lives with someone arriving uninvited at her party was a grotesque line of thinking. Besides, she was getting herself worked up for nothing.

"It could've been a gas leak or an old boiler exploding," I said.

"Of course, you are right. I knew I could rely on your lev-

elheadedness, Davish. Oh, thank goodness. I hate to think that
Mrs. Post might postpone her luncheon because of this. What
does it have to do with us, anyway?" She smiled and began
flipping through the invitation samples again. "Are you finished with the guest list?"

After the conversation with Mrs. Mayhew, I was relieved to
get away from Rose Mont, even just to deliver another letter, this
time a spontaneous invitation to tea to Mrs. Harland Whitwell. I
had no doubt Mrs. Mayhew intended to interrogate her friend
about the fire. I'd learned from Britta at breakfast that Jane's husband, Harland Whitwell, was a co-founder of the Aquidneck
National Bank. Fortunately, that building had only suffered
minor structural damages and was rumored to be ready to open
for business in a few days, again something I learned thirdhand
from Britta.

The invitation had to be delivered immediately, never mind
that Mrs. Mayhew had promised me another carriage ride that
didn't materialize or that she gave me no indication as to where
Jane Whitwell lived. My job was to know these things, and after
days of reading the Newport books I was now prepared. A few
days ago I confused the Reading Room, the exclusive all-
gentlemen's club, with a physical room somewhere in the vast-
ness of Rose Mont. Now I not only knew where the round
stone tower called the Old Stone Mill was (in Touro Park at
the top of Mill Street), but I also could quote its history and
the varied theories as to who constructed it and why. I favored
the one that claimed the tower was a windmill built by Bene-
dict Arnold, the first governor of Rhode Island and great-
grandfather to the famous Revolutionary War general. I felt
confident, and admittedly a bit proud, that I could easily find
my way around Newport, with or without a carriage. Ironically, my efforts were unnecessary in this case, as Mrs. Whitwell
lived in a "cottage" named Glen Park less than half a mile

straight down Bellevue Avenue. I hoped future deliveries or tasks would be more of a challenge.

And so I found myself walking around to the back of Glen Park and under an umbrella of wisteria vines meant to hide the servants' entrance from the windows above. A kitchen maid let me in.

"What do you want?" Mrs. Whitwell's housekeeper asked after I'd been left standing in the kitchen for several minutes.

"I have an invitation for Mrs. Whitwell," I said. "I'm Mrs. Mayhew's social secretary."

"Well, give it to me then, and I'll see that she gets it."

"I'm afraid, Mrs. . . . ?" I said.

"Johnville," the housekeeper said.

"I'm afraid, Mrs. Johnville, that Mrs. Mayhew requested I deliver it personally and return with a response." I shrugged my shoulders to indicate that I knew this was a breach in protocol.

"Oh, all right. Follow me." She led me up the back stairs and pushed through a door into a hall. Stretching away into the distance, the hall, like a sketch I'd once seen in *Harper's* of a gallery in the Metropolitan Museum of Art, was lined with a plush red carpet and dozens of portraits, landscapes, and still-life paintings in elaborately carved gold-leaf frames hung from red silk ropes on the walls. Rose Mont wasn't the only extravagant home in Newport, I thought as I glanced at each painting as we passed. Mrs. Johnville looked straight ahead, not giving the paintings a single glance.

Halfway down the hall, we approached one of several closed doors with open etched-glass transoms. The housekeeper was poised to knock when a shriek pierced the silence of the hallway. Mrs. Johnville forced open the door, but the room was empty. She looked back at me.

"Where did that—?" Before she could finish, someone screamed.

"Haaarlaaaand!"

I followed Mrs. Johnville as she dashed down the hall and was confronted by Nick Whitwell rushing toward us. He didn't stop.

"Oh!" Mrs. Johnville said, smacking her elbow against the wall attempting to get out of the young man's way.

Nick Whitwell said nothing as he raced by, but for one brief moment our eyes met. I dropped my eyes, trying to avoid his piercing gaze, and noticed a conspicuous bulge under his waistcoat. Before I had time to consider why he was running in his own house or where he was going or what he could be hiding, someone screamed again.

"Noooooooo!"

Mrs. Johnville ran and stopped abruptly in an open doorway a few yards down the hall. I hesitated a moment, watching the retreating figure of Nick Whitwell before I joined her.

Oh God, not again!

Mahogany bookshelves, their leather-bound books sticking out spine down or tipped over like dominoes, lined the walls and an enormous oak desk stood prominently in the middle of the room. The door of a small metal safe hung open, nothing but a gold cigar box labeled *Partagás* left inside. Overturned books, ledgers, and papers littered the desk while many more were strewn about on the floor. And sprawled amidst them on a well-worn Persian carpet of red, green, and gold was Harland Whitwell, his wife kneeling at his side, blocking most of the view of the man with her body.

"Harland, Harland, Harland," she repeated over and over as she rocked back and forth over her husband.

She clutched one of his hands to her chest. Her husband held something, a letter, pamphlet, or leaflet, in the fist of his other hand. I stepped closer and nearly tripped on Mr. Whitwell's cane, lying abandoned on the floor. I tiptoed over the cane and peered over the distressed woman's shoulder.

Oh God, has it happened again?

I turned away, cursing my curiosity, my ill luck, Mrs. Mayhew's penchant for gossip, and anything else I could think of to blame for bringing me here at this moment. I took a deep breath and closed my eyes tightly. It was too late. His bright starched white shirt and waistcoat flashed before my closed eyelids. And there in the middle of his chest, like a rose on the white field of a family crest, was a blossom of splattered red blood. I opened my eyes and gazed down at the man again. A cigar, identical to the one I'd seen him offer Mr. Mayhew at the Casino, jutted from Mr. Whitwell's waistcoat pocket. Speckles of blood clung to the shiny gold wrapper.

Poor Mr. Whitwell, I thought. *He'll never smoke a Havana cigar again.*

CHAPTER 12

"Is he dead?" Mrs. Johnville whispered from behind me. I hadn't heard her approach.

"I don't know, but I can find out," I said. The other times I'd found a dead body, Walter had felt at the person's wrist for a pulse. I didn't expect to find one.

I knelt down next to Mr. Whitwell. His wife was on his other side, watching my every move. I placed two fingers on the man's wrist like I'd seen Walter do. I couldn't feel a pulse. I didn't need Walter to tell me what that meant.

"I'm so sorry, Mrs. Whitwell," I said.

The grieving woman pulled her bulky husband onto her lap, cradling him like a child. The white ruffle frill on the yoke of her girlish day dress touched the wound, turning the trim red.

"No, no, no," she repeated.

Unable to comfort her, I decided the next best thing was to look about me for any indication as to who might've killed the man. My first thought was to look at what he clutched in his hand. I knew better than to try to pry it out of his hand but instead peered down into the crumpled paper hoping I could read something that would give me a clue.

. . . *higher wages, shorter hours . . . for a day's work* was all I could read, but it was enough. This looked like a labor union propaganda pamphlet. But Lester Sibley had said he'd lost them all when the Pinkerton detective threw the trunk overboard. How had Harland Whitwell acquired one? And why was he clutching it when he died? Was he trying to tell us something?

"I called the police," Mrs. Johnville said. I hadn't realized that she had left.

"Johnville!" Mrs. Whitwell's head shot up to glare at her housekeeper. Her shout startled us both, as Mrs. Whitwell had not said anything coherent in the last few minutes. "Who asked you to call the police?"

"Um . . ." Mrs. Johnville floundered for the words. "No one, ma'am, but . . ." She hesitated to state the obvious.

"If your husband's been murdered, Mrs. Whitwell . . . ," I started to say, not sure how I was going to convince her to involve the police.

"If?" Mrs. Whitwell said. "Of course he's been murdered! Poor Harland. Weeks!" she screeched for the butler. "Weeks!" She suddenly yanked her husband's tie and pulled at the pearl buttons of his waistcoat. "We have to get him out of those bloody clothes! He'd hate for anyone to see him like this."

I put my hand over hers. "We should wait for the police, Mrs. Whitwell," I said, drawing her hand away. "And then you can clean him up. Mrs. Johnville, don't you think it would be a good idea to get Mrs. Whitwell a cup of coffee or tea or something?"

"Yes, of course," the housekeeper said, dashing away.

"Why don't you sit down, Mrs. Whitwell, and wait for your coffee?" I said, putting my arm around the grieving woman and slowly guiding her to her feet and to a chair away from the body on the floor. I looked about for something to cover the man up with so his wife didn't have to keep looking at him but had trouble finding anything. I did notice, however, several papers with the *Aquidneck National Bank* letterhead. One correspondence caught my eye, the telegram that had arrived for Harland Whitwell during the garden party. The words *foreclosure* and *bankruptcy* leaped off the page. I opened several drawers in the desk. They brimmed with papers of all sorts. Receipts with the names of local merchants I recognized, memoranda on the stationery of several businesses whose names I didn't recognize, letters from several charities, and personal correspondence. A few had *ROSE MONT* embossed across the top. It was all well organized into stacks with staples and large paper clips. I found what I was looking for in a bottom drawer, a stack of clean white handkerchiefs with a simple *HW* stitched into the middle in brown silk thread. I pulled three from the pile and laid one gently over the dead man's face and another over the bloody wound. I gave Mrs. Whitwell the other.

Mrs. Johnville came in, followed by a footman carrying a silver coffee service. The footman immediately left, leaving Mrs. Johnville to pour the coffee. She put in three cubes of sugar and several tablespoons of milk. She handed it to Mrs. Whitwell, whose hands were trembling. She put the cup to her lips and drank the entire contents without stop. She handed the cup back and Mrs. Johnville poured more. Over the rim of the second cup, first Mrs. Whitwell looked at her husband's dead body, blood already seeping through the handkerchief on his chest, and then her gaze found me.

"Who are you?" she asked.

"I beg your pardon, ma'am," I said. "I'm Hattie Davish, Mrs. Mayhew's secretary."

"That's right. I saw you at the garden party, didn't I?"

"Yes, ma'am."

"What are you doing here?"

I picked up the invitation I'd dropped on the floor at first sight of the dead man.

"I came delivering this," I said, handing her the envelope. "It's an invitation to tea from Mrs. Mayhew." Even as I said them, the words sounded inane.

Jane Whitwell tried to open the envelope, but her hands were shaking too much. She handed it back to me. "Keep it. I've no use for it now," she said.

We all stood in silence a moment until a knock on the door woke us from our reverie.

"The police, ma'am," the butler announced. Two men came into the room, both wearing blue policemen's uniforms. The two rows of brass buttons on their jackets glittered under the electric chandelier. One was young, barely in his early twenties, clean shaven with straw yellow hair. He still wore his hat, a dark blue flat cap with a visor, gold braid, and brass metal hat badge. He was too far away for me to read what it said. The second man was in his early fifties, graying hair on his head and in his long, twisted mustache, and was well over six feet tall. An imposing figure, he dwarfed everyone else in the room. He politely held his hat in his hands, a long silver fishhook jutting out through the fabric. He walked over to Mrs. Whitwell, barely looking at the dead body on the floor.

"I am so sorry, Mrs. Whitwell," he said. "Everyone knew your husband to be a kind, hardworking, charitable man. He will be missed."

"Thank you," Mrs. Whitwell said, dabbing her eyes with her handkerchief. She still stared down at her husband.

"Now, I'm Chief of Police Sam Preble and I'm going to be personally investigating this heinous crime against your husband. He was a valued member of this community and deserves nothing less." Mrs. Whitwell nodded her approval. "That's Sergeant

Ballard," he said, indicating the young man standing still and silent by the door. "He's going to be assisting me. Show some respect, Ballard," Preble said. The young officer quickly took off his hat.

"Now, I don't want to trouble you too much, ma'am," Chief Preble said. "I know this is a difficult time for you and your family, but I do have a few questions I have to ask you."

"Of course," Mrs. Whitwell said.

"Did you find your husband dead, ma'am?"

"No," she said. "I mean yes. Oh, I don't know."

"Take your time, Mrs. Whitwell," Chief Preble said.

"I mean to say that I found Harland like that on the floor." She pointed to her dead husband. "I came by to see if he was all right." A sob caught in her throat. She held the handkerchief up to her mouth.

"Please continue if you can, Mrs. Whitwell," the police chief said. Mrs. Whitwell nodded. "Why did you think he was not all right, ma'am?"

"Harland usually spends a couple of hours in the morning working in here. I'd come by to see if he'd learned anything new about the fire last night. Anything that might've eased his mind. He'd been distraught before going to bed, pacing, mumbling to himself, wringing his hands. And there he was."

"Dead?" the policeman said in almost a whisper.

"No, he wasn't dead, at least not at first."

A glint of hope shone from the policeman's eyes. "Did Mr. Whitwell say anything to you?"

"Yes, he said, 'Sibley.' " Mrs. Whitwell looked up from her dead husband and regarded the police chief for the first time. "Does that mean anything to you?"

Chief Preble's eyes widened. So did mine.

"Yes, ma'am, it does. Lester Sibley is a man with a great capacity for trouble. A labor man we're holding on the suspicion of arson. We believe he may have been involved in the bank fires last night."

"Chief Preble?" I said, no longer able to remain quiet.

"Yes? And you are?"

"Miss Hattie Davish, social secretary to Mrs. Charlotte Mayhew. I was here delivering an invitation to Mrs. Whitwell when the housekeeper and I came across Mrs. Whitwell here with her husband."

"And?"

"And I think you would be interested to note what Mr. Whitwell is holding in his hand."

Chief Preble stepped over and looked at the dead man for the first time. He lifted the handkerchief with his little finger and peeked at the man's face for a moment before letting the handkerchief drop. He carefully removed the handkerchief covering Mr. Whitwell's chest and examined the wound before looking at the pamphlet in the man's hand. Unlike me, Chief Preble had no qualms about prying the paper out of the man's grip. The chief smoothed the pamphlet out on the floor, reading.

"What is it?" Mrs. Whitwell said.

"Besides the usual rhetoric, it calls for a strike at several banks, one of which is in Newport."

"Why would he be holding that?" Mrs. Whitwell said. "What does that have to do with anything?" With each word her voice rose in pitch to the point of hysteria.

Chief Preble showed Mrs. Whitwell the pamphlet. "Doesn't your husband own controlling shares in all of these banks, Mrs. Whitwell?"

"Maybe; I don't know. Harland's a prominent banker, I know that much, but he never talked about work with me. But even if he did, what does that have to do with his murder?"

"Ma'am, this pamphlet was authored by Lester Sibley."

"Then Harland was trying to tell me who killed him, wasn't he?"

"I don't know, ma'am," Chief Preble said, avoiding Mrs. Whitwell's gaze and her questions by slowly folding the pamphlet in half and then in quarters. He stuffed it into his jacket pocket. "It may seem that way but—"

"Chief Preble, I want you to arrest this Lester Sibley immediately!" Mrs. Whitwell said.

"I would, ma'am, but you see—"

"That man murdered my husband! If you don't arrest him this instant, I'll see that you never work again."

"Mrs. Whitwell, I can't arrest Lester Sibley for the murder of your husband."

"Why not?" she demanded.

"Because he didn't kill your husband."

"How dare you tell me you know who did and didn't kill Harland. Harland himself told me."

"That may be, ma'am, but Lester Sibley couldn't be the murderer."

"And why not?"

"Because, Mrs. Whitwell, as I said before, we brought Lester Sibley in for questioning about the fires. The man's been locked up since last night."

CHAPTER 13

Preble had more questions, but as Mrs. Whitwell was growing more and more agitated, Mrs. Whitwell's lady's maid was summoned and escorted Mrs. Whitwell to her bedroom. The policeman then asked Mrs. Johnville to call a doctor. That left Chief Preble, Sergeant Ballard, the dead Mr. Whitwell, and me. Chief Preble began examining the dead man's body in earnest.

Without looking up, the chief said, "Tell me who you are again?"

"Mrs. Charlotte Mayhew's social secretary, Miss Hattie Davish."

"And you came here, purely by coincidence, and found Mrs. Whitwell with her husband's dead body?"

"Yes. I came to deliver an invitation to Mrs. Whitwell from Mrs. Mayhew. Mrs. Johnville, the housekeeper, and I heard a scream and traced it to Mr. Whitwell's office. We found Mrs. Whitwell in here with her husband."

"Do you know the Whitwells?"

"Only by sight. I've never spoken to either of them until today."

"Good," the policeman said, bending over Mr. Whitwell so close to examine the wound, he could've rested his chin on the dead man's chest. The chief leaned back and looked at me. "You might be able to give me some objective insight."

"I'll help any way I can."

"Good. Ballard," he said to his sergeant, "contact the coroner's office. We need to get an autopsy done right away. Tell him suspected close-range bullet wound. There's stippling on the skin. Now," he said to me, searching the surrounding area for something, "being an outsider, tell me everything you know about the Whitwells. Wait, what's this?" He picked up a small piece of bent metal. "Ballard!" he shouted. "Found an empty cartridge case. Tell the coroner definitely gunshot wound. Okay, Miss Davish, about the Whitwells?"

"I don't know them at all, sir," I said, staring at the light from the chandelier above reflecting off the warped piece of metal in the policeman's palm. It was smaller than the size of my thumb and yet the bullet from it had killed Harland Whitwell. I took a deep breath before continuing. "I'm sure I can't tell you anything you don't already know."

"Tell me anyway."

I told him everything I knew, about the friendship and the snippets of telephone conversations I'd heard between Mrs. Mayhew and Mrs. Whitwell, about the argument I'd witnessed between Lester Sibley and Mr. Whitwell, the partial conversation I'd heard between Mr. Mayhew and Mr. Whitwell, and the argument between Mr. Whitwell and his son, Nick.

"And as you mentioned, Mr. Whitwell is somehow connected to the national bank that was involved in the fire last night," I said. "I noticed while I was looking for something to cover the man's face that there is a great deal of correspondence about the bank in his desk."

Chief Preble stood and went over to the desk. He pulled out several drawers, glancing at their contents. I stood and pulled open a drawer and retrieved the telegram I'd noticed earlier and handed it to the policeman.

His eyes widened as he read. "Wow! What a coincidence. Who would've guessed? I better keep this as evidence. So what more can you tell me about Nick Whitwell?"

I was surprised by the chief's line of questioning and hesitated to reveal the incident at Rose Mont when I first encountered Nick. "He's engaged to marry Cora Mayhew. He drives a motorcar recklessly. And he stirred up quite a commotion at Mrs. Mayhew's garden party yesterday."

"And your impression of Nick Whitwell? Be completely honest with me, Miss Davish," the chief said sternly. "I know you work for Mrs. Mayhew, but this is a murder investigation. I won't be telling your employer anything, so be honest with me."

"Nick Whitwell appears to be an unprincipled rogue," I said.

The officer laughed. "I thought you didn't know any of the Whitwells?"

"I don't," I said, sharper than I intended. I didn't like being accused of lying.

"Then you're perceptive, Miss Davish. That's exactly how I'd describe the miscreant."

"Why do you want to know about Nick Whitwell?" I asked.

"Since Lester Sibley, the most obvious suspect in the case, was under lock and key, I have to wonder who else could've done this. Nick Whitwell rises to the top of my list."

"You think Nick killed his own father?" An image of Nick running away with something hidden under his waistcoat flashed through my mind. Could it have been a gun he was hiding?

"The argument you witnessed between father and son was

one of many over the past few months. I've even been called on two occasions where they were disrupting the peace, once at the Casino and once at Bailey's Beach. The fights must've been something for these rich folks to involve the police. You, in your line of work, probably know how they like to keep things among themselves." I certainly did. "I blame it all on the son, since Harland Whitwell was known as a sturdy, gracious fellow." *Truly?* I wondered. I pictured the two times I'd seen Harland Whitwell. Neither time would I have described him as gracious.

"So the next question is, what were they fighting about? Money, probably. Usually is. But was it serious enough that Nick would actually kill his father for it?"

"Would he inherit?" I asked.

"Most likely. We'll look into it. Ah, they're here to take the body." Accompanied by Sergeant Ballard, the butler, and Mrs. Johnville, two men carrying a stretcher between them came into the room. They lifted Mr. Whitwell onto the stretcher.

"When you're done, I want a full report," Chief Preble told them as the two men from the coroner's office carried Mr. Whitwell away feetfirst.

"I have to tell you, Chief Preble," I said after they carried the stretcher away, leaving only me, the policeman, and the housekeeper in the room, "Mrs. Johnville and I saw Nick right before we found Mrs. Whitwell and her husband in the office."

"That's right, Officer," the housekeeper added as the policeman spun around to stare at me.

"Where?" he demanded.

"Right out there in the hallway," I said. "He was running in the opposite direction."

"Was he coming from the office?"

"I don't know, but he did have something hidden under his waistcoat."

I didn't have to voice my speculation about the gun. The policeman's face told me he knew what I was thinking. "Are you sure?"

I nodded.

"Okay, but let's keep this to ourselves for now. Okay, Miss Davish, Mrs. Johnville?" We nodded in unison. What else was there to say? "Where is Mrs. Whitwell?" he asked the butler, who had returned.

"She's in her bedroom. Dr. Guthridge is with her now."

"Lead me to her," the policeman told the butler.

After the two men left the room, Mrs. Johnville hesitated, staring down at the bloodstained carpet.

"Who would do such a thing?" she said.

"I don't know," I said, answering her rhetorical question.

"He was such a decent man, a reasonable employer. I can't imagine who could've done this."

"He had no obvious enemies then? No one he might've wronged? No one he might've argued with over business or politics or . . . ?"

The housekeeper shook her head. "No, nothing, except of course the usual quarrels with . . ."

"With his son?" I said, finishing her thought. I remembered the argument between the two I'd seen just yesterday. She frowned but nodded slightly. I waited, but she said no more about it.

"And then there's the pamphlet," she said cryptically.

"What about it?" I asked.

"I know how Mr. Whitwell came to have it," she whispered.

"You do?"

"That man they were talking about has been passing out those pamphlets at all the cottages in town. I don't know why. He is not not going to get any of us to strike. So why bother?"

"And he came by Glen Park when?"

"A few weeks ago. Only me and a few others were in the house at the time, getting it ready for the Whitwells' arrival. I couldn't get him out of my doorway. The man wouldn't take no for an answer, so I took some pamphlets, to make him leave. As soon as he was gone, I threw them away."

"If you threw them away, then why do you think you know how Mr. Whitwell got one?"

"Because I saw one of the pamphlets on the table after breakfast the next day. When I threw it in the trash, I noticed that the stack the man gave me was gone. Someone had taken them out of the bin. I'd wondered why anyone would want to do that. I think now someone gave them to Mr. Whitwell or"—she hesitated— "he found out who had them." *And he's dead now because of it?* I wondered. From the look on her face, Mrs. Johnville held the same thought.

"I must be going," the housekeeper said abruptly.

I was torn. What was I to do now? I should follow Mrs. Johnville downstairs and return to Rose Mont. But what I wanted to do was go with Chief Preble to Mrs. Whitwell's bedroom. Would he implicate her son in the crime? Or would the chief refrain from mentioning his suspicions? Either way, I knew my duty was to Mrs. Mayhew. My curiosity was not to be satisfied today.

As I followed the housekeeper down the hall toward the servants' door, the butler and policemen had paused to speak to two housemaids, with red puffy eyes, draping crape over a mirror on the wall. The two men began climbing the grand staircase, hand-carved from sandstone and marble with a balustrade supported by dolphins and mermaids, when Chief Preble called, "Miss Davish?"

"Yes," I said, turning to face the man on the stairs.

"Did you deliver your invitation?"

"No, she didn't want it," I said. *Why would that be any con-*

cern of his? I wondered. The invitation to tea was moot now with everything that had happened.

"Do you want to face Mrs. Mayhew with less than what she expects?" I chuckled to myself. Chief Preble was giving me an excuse to accompany him. He obviously knew Mrs. Mayhew's invitation was prompted by her desire for gossip about last night's fires. My employer, knowing I'd been witness to this tragedy, would want nothing less than a full, titillating report.

"Thank you, Chief," I said, excusing myself from the housekeeper and quickly joining the men as they ascended the stairs. "I wouldn't want to be remiss in my duty." The butler scowled at me but said nothing.

When we entered Mrs. Whitwell's bedroom, a soothing mix of white furniture and blue fabrics, silks on the bed, damask on the wall, her lady's maid, a housemaid, a nurse, and Dr. Guthridge were in attendance. I purposely avoided looking at the medical kit, with its shiny metal instruments the physician had laid out on a dressing table. I couldn't look at the doctor either as he attended to Mrs. Whitwell, lying on her bed, propped up with almost a dozen white lace-covered pillows. Despite knowing Walter, I still held deep resentment and fear toward physicians. In my mind, they killed my father. Instead I stood quietly out of the way and focused on the back of Chief Preble's head.

"Can I talk to her?" the policeman asked the doctor.

"I've given her a sedative, but she's awake," the doctor said, stepping back from the bed.

"Mrs. Whitwell?" the policeman said.

"What do you want?" she sighed, her eyes closed. "Have you arrested that Sibley man yet?"

"No, ma'am. But I do have a few questions. Did your husband own a handgun?"

"He belonged to the shooting club," she said vaguely. "Clay birds or something."

"Yes, ma'am. But I'm asking about a handgun, possibly a derringer, not a shotgun."

"You mean like the small silver, pearl-handled one he had?"

"Yes, can you tell me about it?"

"Everyone in the shooting club has one. It's just a token, engraved with their name on it when they join. But why do you ask? That little thing couldn't kill my husband."

"At very close range, I'm afraid it can be very deadly. Where does he keep it, ma'am?"

"What?" Mrs. Whitwell said drowsily.

"The gun, ma'am. Where did your husband keep the gun?"

"In the safe. Is that all?"

But the safe was empty, I thought. Could that have been what Nick was hiding under his waistcoat? If so, where was it now? Did Nicholas Whitwell kill his father?

As if the policeman had read my thoughts, he said, "Almost, but I need to ask you about your son, Nicholas." Jane Whitwell's eyes shot open and she lunged up from the bed.

"Oh my God, is Nick okay? Where's my son?" The doctor rushed over and quickly injected something into her arm. The sight of the long needle sent my head reeling. Nausea rose in my throat as I groped for the back of a chair to keep myself steady.

The doctor and nurse eased Mrs. Whitwell back to her pillows.

"I'm sure your son is fine, Mrs. Whitwell, but we don't know where he is. I was hoping you might know."

"What time is it?" she asked.

"Half-past ten, ma'am," Mrs. Whitwell's lady's maid said, consulting the clock on the marble mantel.

"Then he and Eugenie are at the Casino playing tennis or on their way to Bailey's Beach."

"Thank you, Mrs. Whitwell. We'll leave you in peace now."

"Why do you want to know where Nick is?" she asked almost as an afterthought.

"We would just like to ask him some questions." The policeman tipped his hat. "Good day, Mrs. Whitwell." He turned to leave, with me following closely behind. Without the policeman there, I didn't want to have to explain my presence.

"No," Mrs. Whitwell said from her bed.

"Excuse me, ma'am?" the policeman said, stopping in the doorway.

"I said no."

"No, to what, ma'am?"

"You will not ask my son any questions."

"But—"

"No!" Mrs. Whitwell said, cutting the policeman off.

"You must rest now, Mrs. Whitwell," the doctor said. "You mustn't tax yourself." His patient ignored him.

"You're to arrest Lester Sibley, Chief Preble. And do nothing else. Do you understand me? You are not to question my son, my daughter, my servants, my friends, Harland's business associates, no one. This investigation ends now."

The room fell silent. I've known people who expected their directives to be taken as law, but Chief Preble was the law. How could Mrs. Whitwell speak to him like that? And what did she expect him to do, arrest a man who was innocent of the crime? Chief Preble had already explained to her that Lester Sibley couldn't have killed her husband. Someone else had. To find the killer, the chief had to investigate.

"Very well, ma'am," Chief Preble said, frowning. "If that's how you feel, I won't bother you again." He tipped his hat again and disappeared through the door.

I was stunned. This was preposterous! How could he let her get away with this? She obviously realized that the police suspected her son and she was covering for him. But if he was guilty, her son had murdered her husband!

I handed the lady's maid the invitation without explanation, raced after Chief Preble, and caught up with him in the hall. "Chief," I said, "how could you do this? How could you drop a murder investigation simply because Mrs. Whitwell's afraid her son is involved?"

"You know who the Whitwells are."

"Yes, but . . ."

The policeman shrugged. "I have a job to keep, Miss Davish. And speaking of keeping one's job, I'd get back to Rose Mont, if I were you." I stood speechless as the head of Newport's police force walked away.

CHAPTER 14

"Mrs. Mayhew has been ringing for you for ten minutes!" Mrs. Crankshaw said when I arrived. Mrs. Mayhew was probably anticipating the answer to her invitation. She was in for a surprise, I thought. But instead the surprise was for me.

"Finally! I've seen a can of spilt molasses move faster than you, Davish!" Miss Lucy said when I knocked and entered the drawing room.

"Now, Lucy, dear," Miss Lizzie said. "The girl has had a shock and had to walk from Glen Park, besides." What was Miss Lizzie talking about? Surely they couldn't know about Mr. Whitwell already?

"I've been ringing for you," Mrs. Mayhew said. "Wherever have you been?"

"I was at Glen Park, ma'am," I said. "As you requested."

"I *know* that," she said. "What took you so long to come back? As Miss Lucy said, we've been waiting. Now tell us everything."

"You know?" I asked.

"That Harland Whitwell was found with a hole in his chest a child could stick their hand through?" Miss Lucy said, eliciting a grimace from Mrs. Mayhew for her gruesome analogy. "Yes, we know."

"But how? It happened less than an hour ago. How did you even have time to come from Moffat Cottage?"

"It's the modern age, dear," Miss Lizzie said. "We all have telephones."

"And luckily in this case," Miss Lucy said, "the servants weren't shy to use them!"

"Yes," Miss Lizzie said, "our cook is Jane Whitwell's housekeeper's second cousin, twice removed." So Mrs. Johnville, somewhere between telephoning for the police and the doctor, found time to call her cousin to gossip. Amazing! "And she mentioned that you were involved, dear, so of course we came right over. You don't mind, do you, Charlotte?"

"Of course not, Miss Lizzie." Charlotte Mayhew waved her hand impatiently. "Now, Davish, speak!"

I recited slowly what I knew the three ladies were expecting, a detailed account from the moment I arrived at Glen Park to Mrs. Whitwell's dismissal of the police.

"Well, of course Jane's not going to want the police spreading rumors that Nick killed Harland," Miss Lucy said. "As long as she believes this labor man, Lester Sibley, did it, she can deny any wrongdoing in the family."

"What do you think, Charlotte?" Miss Lizzie asked. "Isn't your Cora engaged to the boy?"

"Yes, but as long as there's no proof Nick did anything, it actually makes the engagement more desirable. Gideon's always been concerned that Harland would cut Nick out. Now Nick will inherit after all." I couldn't believe what I was hearing. Yet I knew to keep silent and to keep my opinion of their callous discussion from showing on my face. "And of course, it wouldn't do well for her place in society if the police can prove Nick did it. This way, she'll have everyone's sympathy, instead of their derision."

A slight rap at the door stopped the conversation. Mr. Davies, the butler, stepped into the room.

"There's a telephone call for you, ma'am."

"Whoever it is, tell them to call back, Davies," she said, annoyed at the interruption.

"It's Mrs. Whitwell, ma'am. She said it was—" Before the butler could finish, Mrs. Mayhew was up out of her seat and out the door. Mr. Davies followed, closing the door behind him.

"Well," Miss Lucy said. "I wouldn't think Jane would be in any condition for making telephone calls. I mean, using the telephone before your husband's even in the ground is a bit crass, don't you think?"

"But do you truly think the police won't investigate any further?" Miss Lizzie asked.

"She's Jane Whitwell, Lizzie," Miss Lucy said as if this were all the explanation needed. Miss Lizzie shrugged and nodded her understanding.

"How are you, Hattie, dear?" Miss Lizzie said, noticing me for the first time since I told my story. "Do sit down."

"The girl's fine, Lizzie. It's not like this is the first dead body she's come across," her sister said.

"That's true," Miss Lizzie said, still looking at me in expectation.

"I'm fine, Miss Lizzie," I said. "Thank you." To my surprise, I had no need to prevaricate. I was fine. Seeing Mrs. Whitwell's grief was more disturbing than seeing her husband dead on the floor.

"It's happening anyway!" Charlotte Mayhew said as she uncharacteristically burst through the door.

"What's happening?" the two elderly sisters asked simultaneously.

"That was Jane. She's hysterical. Her husband hasn't been dead two hours and the rumors are rampant."

"About Nicholas?" Miss Lizzie asked.

"Yes, and other terrible things. Thompson, Harland's lawyer, has been there, from New York. He was to meet with Harland just this morning. Jane said he insinuated that Harland's financial affairs are not in order as Jane supposed. And then Jane overheard Mrs. Johnville chastising a housemaid who said she and some of the other girls won't work in a house run by a murderer. And the worst of it all, Jane's already received four hand-delivered declines to her dinner party next week!"

"But the woman's in mourning," Miss Lucy said. "She'd have to cancel the party anyway."

"Yes, but the proper thing to do would've been to wait for the cancellation and then send condolence cards instead. Those declines were a message."

Those declines were probably more of an attempt of the invitees to learn what was going on, precisely as the three ladies in front of me were doing, by sending a personal messenger to the house, then commenting on Jane Whitwell's decline from society.

"She can't let this go on," Mrs. Mayhew said. "It's bad enough that someone murdered her husband. Now her place in society is at stake."

"What about the police then?" I asked. "They could investigate and spare Mrs. Whitwell the unnecessary speculation."

"Never," Mrs. Mayhew said.

"Then Davish here can do it," Miss Lucy blurted out.

"Miss Lucy!" I cried, shocked and disappointed she would suggest such a thing. I cringed as my outburst drew all eyes to me.

"What do you mean, Miss Lucy?" Charlotte Mayhew said, still watching me.

"What I mean is that Davish here has proven to be quite the detective. She discovered the culprit in the murder of our temperance coalition leader, Mother Trevelyan, last fall."

"Really?" Mrs. Mayhew said, turning to the elderly sisters.

"She also cleared Sir Arthur Windom-Greene's name in a murder charge this past Christmas," Miss Lizzie said.

"I do rely upon her," Mrs. Mayhew said thoughtfully, as if she'd forgotten I was in the room. "But she's a secretary!"

"Yes, your secretary, dear," Miss Lizzie said.

"So?"

"So," Miss Lucy said. "You say you rely upon Davish in other ways?"

"Yes," Mrs. Mayhew said suspiciously.

"So rely upon her now to investigate Harland Whitwell's death for you, instead of the police. She'll find out the truth and Nick will be cleared of all suspicion." I wondered how Miss Lucy could be so sure Nick Whitwell wasn't involved.

"And why would I do that? I need her working here with me, not gallivanting all over Newport playing detective. My ball is in two days, Miss Lucy. Two days!"

"Because if Davish plays detective, she would report to you, and only you. Only you, Charlotte, will know the truth." Mrs. Mayhew's eyes lit up in understanding. "You wouldn't have to worry about the success of your ball, Charlotte. You'd be the most sought-out woman in Newport." With that last sentence Miss Lucy sealed my fate. I didn't like it one bit.

"Of course I'll still rely on you to sort my correspondences, send replies, attend to the bills, and remain diligent about updating the guest list," Mrs. Mayhew said, spelling out the terms of my new role, "and you will remain available for hand deliveries." To me nothing had changed except now she wanted me to add snooping into her neighbor's tragedy for her own personal edification to my duties. "As to the 'investigation,' I want a full report every morning immediately after Issacson brings in my breakfast; I'll read it along with the newspapers. And above all I'm relying on you to conduct yourself in a proper and discreet manner. There's no use hav-

ing information if everyone else knows it too!" Out of the
corner of my eye, I could see Miss Lucy purse her lips.

"Of course, Mrs. Mayhew," I said, trying to keep the disappointment out of my voice. How was it that I kept getting into
situations like this? I'm a typewriter, a secretary. Who would've
thought I'd be probing into the personal life and death of Harland Whitwell? If J. P. Morgan asked for financial advice or Mrs.
Caroline Astor invited me to tea I wouldn't be more surprised.

Just one more challenge, Hattie, I told myself. "I will do my
best, ma'am."

"Best? Of course you'll do your best. I expect nothing less.
In fact, I expect you to solve the crime."

"But Mrs. Mayhew—"

"But nothing, Miss Davish, I'm relying on you to find me
the answer." She held a finger up to punctuate her point. "And
you will be the reason Caroline Astor will leave her calling
card at Rose Mont. I'll see the inside of her ballroom yet!"

"Yes, ma'am," I said, though I still couldn't grasp the signif-
icance of Mrs. Astor's calling at Rose Mont. Charlotte Mayhew was one of the richest, most influential women in the
country. Why would she pine after a calling card like a disappointed schoolgirl? I wanted to ask but knew better.

Maybe Miss Lucy will know, I thought.

"Now I want you to go speak to Jane; even I know she's
the first person you need to speak to. Here." She scribbled
something down on the stationery with *ROSE MONT* embossed across the top, folded it in half, and handed it to me.
"This will get Jane talking to you. Now off you go."

"Yes, ma'am," I said, and excused myself from the three
ladies' company. Miss Lucy was still pursing her lips in displea-
sure when I left the room. Why was she upset? I wondered.
She was the one who suggested I take on this ridiculous role.

I was opening the door to the back stairs when I heard
footsteps fast approaching. *Not Nick again,* I thought. I held my

breath, fearing the worst, but let out a sigh of relief when I turned to see Miss Lizzie, waving her arms at me. She stopped, stooped over, trying to catch her breath.

"Lucy wanted me to . . . ," she said, wheezing and panting between each word, "to ask you to come to tea." I had to contain a laugh. Not at the sight of Miss Lizzie, several pounds heavier than she'd been in Eureka Springs, holding her hand to her heaving chest, but at the invitation. I should've known Miss Lucy had an ulterior motive. She hadn't convinced Mrs. Mayhew to allow me to investigate for Mrs. Mayhew's benefit or for Mrs. Whitwell. Miss Lucy had every intention of getting the gossip firsthand for herself.

"Are you all right, Miss Lizzie?" I said, placing my hand gently on the suffering woman's shoulder. I realized my mistake and quickly took my hand away.

"Yes . . . thank you . . . dear. I'll be fine . . . especially if I can bring . . . Lucy good news?"

"Yes, of course. I can't guarantee when I'll be there, but I'll come to Moffat Cottage as soon as I can."

Miss Lizzie smiled at my acquiescence but then quickly frowned. "Be careful, dear."

"Of course, Miss Lizzie."

"At least there aren't any . . . stairs here," she said in jest as she caught her breath. She smiled, squinting her eyes at me, and then slowly walked back toward the drawing room. She was referring to the incident in Eureka Springs that left me scraped, bruised, and bedridden.

Yes, I thought ironically, *there aren't any stairs here, only cliffs that drop abruptly seventy feet down to the jagged rocks and an endless ocean below.* I shuddered at the thought of how many people had found their end at the bottom of those cliffs. But Miss Lizzie needn't worry, I thought, watching her retreating figure. Miss Lucy and Mrs. Mayhew had ensured that I wouldn't be going anywhere near the cliffs today.

CHAPTER 15

"So Charlotte thinks that you can help?" Mrs. Jane Whitwell said.

I didn't know what Mrs. Mayhew had written, but her note had indeed won me a personal interview with the new widow. But Jane Whitwell's eyelids were drooping and her words were slightly slurred. The effects of the sedative the doctor had given her still had a hold. She was lounging on a white wicker chaise longue in her orangery, dressed in a simple black crape gown, a stark contrast from the light-colored frilly, blousy dresses she preferred.

She's lost more than a husband today, I thought sadly.

I took a deep breath of the sweet citric scent. Any other time I would've been thrilled to be invited into this sanctuary. Sun streamed through the lattice windows, at least twenty feet tall, which marked the entire southern wall of the room. Potted lemon, orange, and palmetto trees were interspersed with marble statues of Poseidon on the sandstone floor. And in the middle, a red marble fountain, accented by bronze figures of dolphins, sea nymphs, and seahorses, bubbled with water, the rhythmic echo of the splashing water soothing. No wonder why Jane Whitwell chose this haven in which to grieve.

"Yes, since the police called off their investigation Mrs. Mayhew thinks it's prudent that a discreet inquiry be conducted, to not only discover your husband's killer but to exonerate anyone wrongly suspected." I couldn't come right out and mention her son's name, but even through her drug-induced haze I think she took my meaning.

"But why you? Aren't you Charlotte's social secretary?"

"Yes, and as such I would be most discreet. More so than a professional detective, I can assure you."

"But do you have any experience with . . . ?" She couldn't bring herself to mention the word *murder*.

"Yes, I have had some experience in cases like this." *Unfortunately*, I thought but didn't say. "Do you remember the death of Mrs. Edwina Trevelyan, the temperance leader? She was murdered during the American Women's Temperance Coalition's annual convention in Eureka Springs, Arkansas, last fall. It was in all the national papers."

"Yes, I think I do remember hearing about that. I met Mother Trevelyan once at a temperance fund-raiser in New York several years ago. Quite the zealot if I remember."

"I was her secretary at the time of her death and aided in her murder investigation."

Mrs. Whitwell lifted her head off her pillow with obvious effort and stared at me. Her gaze wavered; her head bobbed slightly as if it were loosely attached. "Really?" she said finally. "That was you?" She obviously had read the exaggerated accounts of my role in a newspaper.

"Yes, ma'am. That was me."

"Well, then, by all means, find that Lester Sibley and prove he killed my husband."

"I will do my best to find your husband's killer, ma'am," I

said, careful not to promise anything beyond that. "To start, may I ask you a few questions?"

"Yes," she said, resting her head back again.

I pulled out the notebook I'd brought with me. "I won't ask you about how you found your husband. I was there when you explained it to the police. But could you tell me, ma'am, if your husband's office is normally neat and organized or was the disarray not unusual?"

"No, Harland was an exacting, orderly man. I was shocked by the condition of the room, especially his desk."

I nodded. I had assumed as much, since the contents of his drawers were well organized. I glanced at the first set of questions on my list:

1. Why was Mr. Whitwell's desk neat, but the office was in such disarray?
2. Was someone looking for something? Did they find it?
3. Did Mr. Whitwell catch them in the act?

I wrote *maybe* next to question number three and read the next set of questions:

4. Or had Harland Whitwell confronted a staff member about having Lester Sibley's leaflets?
5. Is that how he came to have one?
6. Why was he holding it in his death grip? A message about his killer?
7. Did anyone hear the gunshot?
8. Why was Nick Whitwell running away from his father's office? Did he kill his father?

"To your knowledge, had your husband ever met Lester Sibley in your home?"

"No, not that I know of. Why would he?" Her question was sharp and full of recrimination.

"That's what I'm trying to find out, Mrs. Whitwell," I said softly, wishing I had answers that might bring her comfort.

"Of course, continue," she said, waving her handkerchief about distractedly.

"Do you happen to know how your husband came to have the labor leaflet?"

"No, I have no idea how that rubbish got into our house, unless Sibley brought it with him." Mrs. Johnville's explanation seemed most likely then. I glanced back at my list.

"Did you hear a gunshot go off?"

"No, I didn't." That didn't surprise me. In a house this size, with the need to use call buttons and bells to summon someone, I could imagine no one hearing it. "But then again, maybe I did."

"Ma'am?"

"I did hear something as I walked down the hall. I remember wondering why anyone would be uncorking champagne at this hour. I remember hoping . . ." She stopped and turned her head toward the pillow. She began to cry quietly. I sat with her in silence for several moments. "Harland had been upset so much lately," she said through her tears. "I remember hoping that there was a reason to celebrate." She wiped her eyes with a handkerchief. "Could that have been the gun going off?" I nodded. "Then if I'd only arrived earlier . . ." She sighed deeply, her shoulders shaking, at the thought.

"You might have been hurt as well."

"Oh! I'd never thought of that."

I looked at my list again. "I apologize for asking this, Mrs. Whitwell, but you would know better than anyone."

"What?" She sighed. She was growing weary of my questions.

"Do you know of any reason why someone would want to kill your husband?"

"No. No," Jane Whitwell said, tears streaming freely down her face. "Oh, Harland."

If only I could walk away from this now, I thought. I hated myself for prying into this poor woman's sorrow simply to satisfy some rich lady's thirst for gossip. Yet my job depended on it. I sat with Mrs. Whitwell in silence for a few moments while she gathered herself together again.

"I'm sorry to intrude on your grief, ma'am," I said, sincerely sorry to be asked to do this, "but I have one last question." She took a deep breath, the release more like a sob than a sigh, and dabbed at her eyes again.

"If it will help," she said.

"From what I've read about your husband, he was one of the most successful bankers in the country. He even owned the Aquidneck National Bank here in Newport."

"Yes, my husband is, I mean was, a prominent banker, Miss Davish. What does this have to do with his murder?"

"Do you know of any financial trouble Mr. Whitwell was having?" I remembered the telegram I noticed on his desk. The word *bankruptcy* had leaped off the page.

"No. Besides the fire last night, I don't know of any trouble in that quarter. You must know Harland was worth millions." Then why was one of his banks going bankrupt?

"Ma'am, would you mind if I had a look through your husband's desk? I may find some indication as to who did this."

Springing up into a sitting position, which I didn't think she was capable of, Mrs. Whitwell issued an emphatic, "No."

"I can't stand the thought of seeing that room again," she said. "Not while I still have the image of Harland lying there, bleeding into the carpet."

I was about to explain that I could search the room alone when she collapsed back onto the chaise longue and burst into another fit of sobbing. I quickly thanked her for speaking to me and excused myself.

I'd gone into this investigation because I'd been ordered to by my employer, but as I listened to the retreating wails of the grieving widow I grew more determined to find closure for this woman. No one should have to suffer a death without knowing the cause. I'd experienced that with my father. To this day I don't know what caused my father's death. The lack of closure has haunted me for years. The physicians attending him blamed his occupation as a hatter, but I blamed the physicians, and when my father only got worse, taking calomel and their blue pills, my conviction grew stronger. As a teenager, I was forced to watch as my beloved father went slowly mad and died under the doctors' care. I might never know what they did to him. But as I strode from the bright, warm orangery into the dark, back servants' stairwell I vowed that I would discover what had happened to Harland Whitwell.

"As you can see, I'm very busy," the bank manager said without looking up.

On my way to the police station where I hoped Lester Sibley was still in police custody, I passed the banks that were set on fire last night. One bank was almost completely destroyed and still smoldering. The Aquidneck National Bank had fared better, and despite its being closed for business, the door was ajar. I stopped. Could someone inside be able to shed some light on Mr. Whitwell's finances? Ideally I'd be able to contact his accountants in New York. But even if I could send a telegram, which the strike made impossible, who was I that they would respond? I decided it was worth a try, pushed the door open, and stepped into a pool of natural light; a column of sunshine filled with tiny floating ash particles was streaming straight down from a hole in the roof.

From the outside, with its board-covered windows, the bank had appeared quiet and deserted, so I was astounded by the flurry of activity I encountered inside. Clerks, secretaries and maids alike worked together, sweeping up piles of cinder and ash, scrubbing down walls, desks, and lamps and picking up, sorting, and stacking piles and piles and piles of papers. I admired how much they'd accomplished in less than twenty-four hours. Unhindered, I made my way across the stone floor, sidestepping papers, piles of ash, and pieces of charred roofing tile. In an office marked MANAGER I'd found a man wearing spectacles and a waistcoat that didn't button over his rotund stomach, filing envelopes into the labeled pigeonholes of a large oak office desk.

"Sir," I said, "I'm sorry to distract you from your task after such a calamity, but I wondered if I could speak to you for a moment?"

"Please, can't you see we are not open for business today!" he said. I walked over to the desk and picked up a stack of envelopes. That got his attention. "What are you doing with those?"

"If I file these for you, will you grant me a minute of your time, Mr. . . . ?"

"Mr. Niederhauser."

"Mr. Niederhauser, my name is Hattie Davish, and I am Mrs. Gideon Mayhew's social secretary. I am on an errand for the lady and have but one question to ask you."

"Well, if Mrs. Mayhew sent you," he said, reluctantly stepping aside.

I went to my task directly. The envelopes were all labeled with names of clients. Several had singe marks. I worked quickly in silence until I came to *Harland Whitwell*. I turned with the envelope in my hand.

"Have you heard the news, Mr. Niederhauser, of Harland Whitwell's death?"

The man nodded. "Yes, it's horrible, isn't it? But bad news has a way of coming in threes, doesn't it?" I shrugged. Wasn't that what Britta said this morning? It must be comforting to believe that after three unhappy events bad luck had run its course. Somehow I doubted it.

"The telegraph operators' strike was unprecedented here in

Newport. Who would've known then that I'd now be trying to salvage what was left of my failing, burned-down bank?" Mr. Niederhauser said. "And now one of the co-founders of the bank has been murdered. It makes you think."

So the telegram I saw about the bank on Mr. Whitwell's desk was true. The bank had gone or was going bankrupt. But with the country's current financial situation I wasn't as surprised as I should've been. I'd read about bank closures across the country in the newspaper every week.

"Do you think they are connected?" I asked as I went back to the filing. The man pulled his chin hard between his thumb and finger.

"I don't know. Like someone had it in for the bank, maybe?"

"Or someone had it in for Harland Whitwell?"

"No, quite the opposite, I'd think. Mr. Whitwell was a fair employer, an honest partner, a good family man. He founded the Whitwell Charitable Foundation, for goodness' sake. In fact, I still can't believe someone actually murdered him."

"Do you know Lester Sibley?" I asked.

"Is he a client?"

"I don't know, but I don't think so."

"No, the name doesn't sound familiar."

"He's a labor organizer," I said.

"Is he that guy that's been standing on his soapbox outside the Casino?"

"Most likely," I said, having seen him doing exactly that the day he argued with Mr. Whitwell.

"No, a man like that wouldn't even get through these doors. Why?"

"Because Mr. Whitwell was found clutching a labor union propaganda leaflet when he died."

"I don't wonder. That Sibley guy, if that's his name, had a whole gang of people passing those out a few weeks ago, be-

fore the Season started. I think he was trying to rile the local
townspeople before the summer residents arrived. May have
worked too. Some blame him for the telegraph operators'
strike. Mr. Whitwell was furious when he found out some of
the leaflets targeted the bank. Sibley even had the nerve to
hand one to me!"

If Sibley was passing out pamphlets a few weeks ago, what
was in the trunk the Pinkerton detective pushed overboard?
Replenishment? If so, the bank manager was right; Whitwell
could've gotten the pamphlet weeks ago.

"Did you read it?"

"No, just tossed it in the garbage where it belongs. Like I
said, Mr. Whitwell was furious, almost fired a few of my best
clerks merely for reading it. Boy, has that been a headache. I
guess bad news comes in fours after all!"

Didn't Mr. Niederhauser realize this appalling behavior of
Mr. Whitwell's contradicted the impression he and most people
had of him? Could the bank's financial straits have soured Mr.
Whitwell's normally generous spirit? Or had the arguments
with Sibley transferred to the banker's employees? Could one of
those employees have killed him?

"Thank you for your help, Mr. Niederhauser," I said as I
finished the filing. "I wish you luck in getting the bank back in
order."

"Thank you for that," he said, jutting his chin toward the
desk. "As a clerk, I always hated that task." I turned to leave.
"By the way, what was the question you wanted to ask me?"

"You've already answered it for me, Mr. Niederhauser," I
said, and before he had a chance to realize how much he had
revealed about the connection between the bank's demise and
that of Mr. Whitwell I left.

CHAPTER 16

The police station was a two-and-a-half-story redbrick
building on Market Square with tall ground-floor windows and a large outdoor clock. When I inquired after Lester
Sibley, the attending police officer, the same Sergeant Ballard
who had accompanied Chief Preble to the scene of Harland
Whitwell's murder, furrowed his brow.

"Popular prisoner," the policeman said. "You're the second
person to want to see our guy in the past fifteen minutes." As
the jailhouse a few blocks up Marlborough Street incarcerated
convicted long-term criminals, Lester Sibley was the only man
being temporarily housed here. Before I could inquire after
the other visitor the policeman said, "Follow me."

"You won't get away with this, labor man!" someone
shouted as the officer escorted me upstairs to the holding area.

"Hey!" Sergeant Ballard, reaching the top of the stairs first,
rushed out of view. "Let him go!" the policeman yelled. I hur-
ried to follow.

A tall man in a braided straw hat with a wide black ribbon

band was reaching through the bars of the holding cell, choking Lester Sibley around the neck.

"Stop!" I cried.

Sergeant Ballard yanked the man back. It was Nick Whitwell.

"Don't touch me!" Nick said, shoving the policeman away.

"You must leave now, Mr. Whitwell," Ballard said.

Nick, his face flush with anger and maybe something more, pointed his finger at Sibley. "Don't think you and your kind aren't responsible for this."

Lester Sibley held his hands to his throat and shrugged his shoulders. "I don't know what you're talking about," he said, his voice strained and thin.

"Please, Mr. Whitwell," Ballard said, indicating the stairwell with his raised nightstick. "I don't want to arrest you for assault and battery."

Nick laughed. "You can't arrest me," he sneered. "I'm a Whitwell." He poked the policeman in the chest. "And you're nobody."

"Please leave, *sir*," Ballard said, stressing the last word. "I will detain you if I must."

"And then what?"

"I will have to notify Chief Preble and your mother, sir, of your misconduct."

Nick flinched at the mention of his mother. "You won't get away with this, Sibley," the young man said as he turned toward the door. "You again?" he said to me as I tried to step out of his way. He grabbed my chin and stared into my eyes. "Be careful, secretary." His breath reeked of wine. He glanced at Lester Sibley in the holding cell for a moment before returning his attentions to me. "There are some dangerous elements out there." He chuckled under his breath before releasing me. He disappeared through the door and bounded down the stairs. I let out the breath I'd been holding.

May I never see that man again, I thought, trying to keep my composure.

"Mr. Sibley," I said, approaching the holding cell. Still mindful that I'd deserted the man when he'd asked for my help, I'd been dreading this interview. And now after witnessing Nick Whitwell choke the man, I questioned what I was doing here at all. Mr. Sibley was sitting on a wooden bench, with a hand around his throat, only his latest injury. A purplish bruise circled one eye, his lips were swollen, cracked, and bleeding, and his soot-covered clothes smelled of smoke, yet Lester Sibley's eyes were clear and defiant.

Could this be my fault? I wondered, remembering Detective Doubleday's threats. Or had Nick confronted him earlier as well?

"Is he all right?" I asked the officer.

"Yeah, he came in a little roughed up." *A little?* I felt sick to my stomach. If only I'd spoken up, this man might not be sitting here in this horrendous condition. He might not have been attacked by Nick Whitwell. What could I possibly say now? An apology would not be enough.

"Miss Davish, isn't it?" Mr. Sibley's calm but strained voice pulled me from my reflections.

"Yes, it is."

"What are you doing here?"

"First," I said, hesitating. "First, I would like to apologize for not speaking up on your behalf last night with Detective Doubleday. I'm truly sorry."

To my surprise, Sibley rolled his eyes, shook his head, and dismissed me with a wave of his hand. "Don't worry about it," he said. "Doubleday's had it in for me since he got here. Nothing you could've said would have stopped him from doing this." He pointed to his face. "Besides," he said, chuckling, which sounded more like a gargle, "in my line of work, I'm used to needing thick skin. As you just saw." He jutted his chin toward the door. "I'm not very popular." I was astonished by his nonchalant attitude but relieved by his forgiveness. I couldn't imagine my work requiring such risks.

"So what's the second reason you're here?" he asked.

"Oh, of course," I said. Caught up with Mr. Sibley's plight, I'd almost forgotten my official reason for visiting. "I've been requested by my employer to look into the death of Harland Whitwell."

"What?" The man leaped to his feet and crossed the cell in two large steps. "Harland Whitwell is dead?"

"You didn't know?" I asked.

"No, when did this happen?"

"This morning."

"What did he die of? Did his horse finally get sick of its small ration of oats and kick him in the head? Did he choke on the bone of some roasted rare and expensive bird he had a fancy for?"

"The police believe he was murdered, Mr. Sibley," I said, not refraining from expressing the distaste I had for his callous reaction. "He was shot in the chest."

"Oh," Sibley said, suitably chastened. "So why are you here talking to me again?"

"Because one of your labor pamphlets was clutched in the dead man's hands."

"You must be joking! Could it be that Harland Whitwell finally felt remorse for all the hardship he placed on his workers for no good reason?"

"Your name was on the dying man's breath, Mr. Sibley," I said.

"What? Why?"

"I was hoping you'd answer that."

"Answer what?"

"Why Mr. Whitwell's last thought was of you?"

"Oh my God, what are you implying?"

"Mrs. Whitwell believes you killed her husband."

"So that's why Nick Whitwell was here. He thinks I killed his father." I nodded. "And how could I have done that? I was here all night!"

"Yes, I know. Chief Preble told Mrs. Whitwell as well. Mrs. Whitwell and her son remain unconvinced."

"They're trying to stop me. That's all this is. You saw it with your own eyes. I'm getting too close to success and they know it. Well, they can choke me, kick me, knock me around, but they won't stop me. I won't let them intimidate me. I'll continue with my little 'nuisance' campaign until every worker on this island gets what they deserve. Or at least until every rich summering 'robber baron' gets what he deserves."

"Who is he, Mr. Sibley? Nick Whitwell, Harland Whitwell?"

"No, you know, all the 'summer residents.' All those high-society rich folks who think that it's okay to pay their workers next to nothing for twelve to sixteen hours of work a day while squandering millions on homes they only live in six weeks out of the year. They think they can come to Newport, leave the entire laboring world behind, and play all summer. Did you know that one of Newport's 'summer residents' once spent sixty-seven hundred dollars on a dress?" It didn't surprise me now, though it would've shocked me only a few days ago. Having paid dozens of Mrs. Mayhew's bills, I was all too familiar with such extravagance. "But they can't give their maids a full day off?"

"Is that why you came here, Mr. Sibley? Instead of organizing the mills or the factories or the coal mines? You came here to disrupt people's summer holiday?"

"Yes, in a way. The people I represent or hope to represent don't get the choice of a summer vacation. Like you. Miss Davish, when was the last time you had more than one day of leisure? Have you ever had a proper vacation? Do you even know what it's like?"

He was trying to make this personal. And he was right. I hadn't had more than a full day off in years. Even the holiday I was supposed to enjoy here in Newport had been canceled. Yes, he had a point, but he was risking his health and safety to make it. Why?

"How I spend my time is irrelevant, Mr. Sibley."

"That's my point. You don't have any time. It all belongs to the likes of Mrs. Mayhew."

"Are the Mayhews on your list of 'robber barons' whose vacation you wish to disrupt?" I said, trying not to sound as flustered as I felt. Lester Sibley nodded.

"Yes, the Whitwells, the Vanderbilts, the Astors, the McAllisters, the Posts, the Havemeyers, the Mayhews, all of them. And you'll thank me for it!" he declared.

I doubt it, I thought, my sympathy for him waning. Instead I said, "Did you or did you not visit Mr. Whitwell recently, Mr. Sibley?"

"No. The last time I saw the man was outside the Casino. You were there."

"Then how did he get one of your pamphlets?"

"I've been giving them out all over town, before I ran out of them, that is. I might've even given them to his household staff before the man arrived."

"Might have or did?"

"I did and I'd do it again."

"So besides the fact you were hoping to agitate his maids and footmen—"

"And bank employees," Lester Sibley interjected.

"So it *was* you that spoke to his bank employees? The bank manager thought it might be."

"Only the clerks, but yes, before the Season started."

"When exactly?"

"Early June."

"Can you think of any other reason, besides your being a nuisance, why Harland Whitwell would be thinking of you when he died?" I asked. "Why Jane and Nick Whitwell are vehement that you killed him?"

"No," he said. Unfortunately, neither could I.

I walked downstairs hoping to speak with Chief Preble before I left. He hadn't been there when I'd arrived earlier.

"Miss Davish, isn't it?" he said, remembering me from this morning. I nodded. "Well, what can I do for you?" He was winding a long piece of fishing line around his hand.

"I wanted to inform you of my newest duties for Mrs. Mayhew," I said, having no idea how the policeman would take the news of my meddling in police affairs. I'd had varying reactions from policemen in the past to my involvement in their investigations or lack thereof.

Preble tilted his head to the side and smirked. "Now why would you feel the need to do that?"

"Because it involves investigating Harland Whitwell's death," I said. I expected Chief Preble to leap from his chair or drop his fishing line, but he didn't move a muscle. "Go on," he said simply.

"Mrs. Whitwell is concerned about her place in society as rumors spread of her son, Nick, being involved. There have also been insinuations of financial trouble. Mrs. Mayhew has assigned me the task of uncovering what I can about the truth behind these rumors." I left unspoken my impression that Mrs. Mayhew was more interested in receiving a calling card from Caroline Astor than the truth.

"So they want to circumvent us while still, supposedly, learning the truth?"

"Yes, I believe so," I said.

"So they can either deny the truth or cover it up completely," he said. He wasn't posing a possibility; he knew.

I suddenly felt uncomfortable being here. If that was indeed Mrs. Mayhew and Mrs. Whitwell's intention, then even my presence here, let alone this conversation, was a violation of Mrs. Mayhew's trust. She hadn't explicitly forbidden me to speak to the police, but now I realized it was implied. However, I was here, the damage was done, so I might as well get as much information from the policeman as I could. This might be our last polite conversation.

"I don't know about covering it up," I said, "but I do know that Mrs. Whitwell is still convinced that Lester Sibley was the culprit."

Preble was shaking his head. "Impossible. I told her that."

"Yes, I know. I've even been to speak with Mr. Sibley. He obviously couldn't have done it and, frankly, I don't see he had much of a motive. Killing Mr. Whitwell doesn't help the workers' cause any."

"No, I agree."

"But Nick Whitwell is a different story, isn't he?" I asked. "He has violent tendencies and, as we said before, he often argued with his father."

"Yes, Whitwell Junior is definitely different. We've been aware of his dubious activities for years. We've never had sufficient cause to do anything about it, though."

"Until now?"

"No, young lady, not even now. Remember we're talking about the Whitwells here. Unless we can prove, without a shadow of a doubt, that Nicholas Whitwell killed his father in cold blood, we can't do anything."

What if I could prove it? I wondered. I'd kept secrets for my employers before and was well-known for my discretion, but I'd never been faced with such a moral dilemma in my work before. What if I did uncover the murderer but was honor bound not to tell anyone but Mrs. Mayhew? Would I be able to convince her to inform the police? I'd hope so.

"Could you tell me about these dubious activities of Nick Whitwell?" I asked.

"Sure, they're no secret," the chief said, slipping the ball of fishing line into his breast pocket. The hook was still there in his hat. "The kid has a penchant for pretty girls, gaming tables, and what we around here like to call 'expensive escapades,' like the time he took target practice at a herd of sheep outside of town. His father had to pay thousands of dollars to satisfy and silence the farmer. And with this new toy of his, you know, the motorcar, he's run down fences, flower beds, even someone's pet poodle."

"Until his encounter with Mr. Sibley upstairs," I said, "I had no idea how reckless he could be." I shivered as I recalled my personal encounter with him. At the time I'd been frustrated and annoyed. Knowing what I did now, I should've been afraid. "So there was plenty of acrimony between father and son?"

"Yes, the kid had no consideration for his father's position and Harland Whitwell was definitely someone who cared what people thought of him. He couldn't stand that his son was so blatantly disrespectful. He only wanted Nick in Newport with them so they could contain the damage. Goodness knows what he'd get up to if left alone in New York. And then there was the money."

"Was there other financial trouble, besides the bank?" I asked. I told Preble about my conversation with the bank manager, Mr. Niederhauser, confirming what we had known already; that the bank, Mr. Whitwell's bank, was going bankrupt.

"In this horrible financial climate, with news every day of factories closing, banks closing, people striking, farms going under, men jumping off bridges or cutting their own throats, who knows? Could one of the richest men in America be on the brink of financial ruin? Your guess is as good as mine, Miss Davish. I'm just glad I have a job." *Me too,* I thought.

"Could there be some connection between Whitwell's death and the bank fires?" I asked.

"I haven't got the full report yet, but I know the fires at the banks were intentional. Anarchists have set bombs before to make a statement. Remember the Haymarket massacre in Chicago?" he said. I did. A violent confrontation between labor demonstrators and police turned deadly when someone threw a bomb into the throng of riot police. "But I've never seen anything like it in Newport, though. At first it didn't make sense. When I spoke to Sibley, he indicated that a clerk strike was imminent at several banks in town, including the two set on fire last night." *Imminent?* That wasn't the impression I got from the bank manager.

"Do you think someone purposely set fire to the banks to prevent a strike?"

"Or to destroy evidence of what that strike would've done to the financial health of those institutions."

"Could Harland Whitwell have been having severe personal financial problems?" I said. "I would think the loss of one bank wouldn't be that damaging to such a wealthy man. But several, all at the same time?"

Preble nodded. "Maybe. And his son's disregard for his father's predicament might've been the cause of the rows," the chief said.

"But is it a motive for murder?" The policeman shrugged. "Can you tell me anything about a Pinkerton detective named Doubleday?" I asked, taking the policeman by surprise.

"Silas Doubleday? Why do you ask?"

I told him about seeing Doubleday push the trunk full of propaganda pamphlets overboard on the ship. I also explained how I'd seen him fighting with Lester Sibley at the scene of the fires. What I didn't mention was the connection between the detective and my employer's husband, Gideon Mayhew.

"Well, we actually spoke to Mr. Doubleday last night," the

chief said, "but only as a witness to the scene. I asked him what brought him to Newport, since we rarely have trouble that would involve Pinkertons. He gave me some story about keeping the labor wheels greased. I assumed he was involved in stifling the bank clerk strike."

"Could he have set the fire?"

"Even without knowing who's employing him, I'd bet a fire would do much more financial damage than a strike. No, I think he would've stopped it some other, quieter way. Like what he did with the steamer trunk." It made sense. Whoever he was working for, most likely Gideon Mayhew, wanted life and business to run smoothly and not be violently disrupted like with the destruction of the bank.

"So you don't know who set the fire?" I asked.

"We've got Lester Sibley in custody for a start, but like you, I'm continuing to investigate all the possibilities." He smiled, his way of personally and professionally sanctioning my role in the investigation of Harland Whitwell's murder. I felt relieved that he approved.

"Thank you so much, Chief Preble, for your help," I said.

"Better your job than mine, Miss Davish. I'd wish you good luck, but I think you're going to need more than that." He was smiling as he put out his hand, but a chill ran down my spine as I shook it.

What have I gotten myself into?

CHAPTER 17

Where is Britta? I wondered.

It wasn't until Bonaparte's insistent scratching and mewing at my door that I stopped typing my report for Mrs. Mayhew and realized Britta had never arrived with my dinner. The cat came at the same time every night. I looked at my watch, eight fifteen. His stomach must be set to a timepiece.

"I'm sorry, kitty," I said, opening the door for the cat. "No scraps tonight." Bonaparte rubbed against my leg, unconvinced.

She'd never been late before. What could've happened? I had to find out. I left Bonaparte to his own devices and headed downstairs. The staff was sitting down to their dinner when I arrived. Britta was among them, but her face was flush and she was pulling at her ear. Something more than forgetting my dinner was on her mind.

"You forgot Miss Davish's dinner?" Mrs. Crankshaw scolded when I explained my presence. "Britta, you know I don't take to well to forgetfulness."

"She's as bad as Mrs. Mayhew," Annie the chambermaid

said, giggling. "But with Britta it's love, not old age." Britta leaped up, tears in her eyes.

"Did I miss something?" I whispered to her as she darted past me. She shook her head violently.

"Yeah," Annie said after Britta was gone. "We were teasing Britta about last night. We think she's got a beau she ain't telling us about." I pictured the events of last night: the crowd at the Forty Steps, Britta dancing with lots of different men, Lester Sibley's comments about her beauty, the confrontation between Sibley and James. In all the events of the night I couldn't imagine how the others had surmised an attachment. Maybe I'd missed something. If I hadn't been talking to Lester Sibley . . .

"Well, I don't, you gossip!" Britta exclaimed as she reentered with a tray. I saw her eyes quickly dart around the table. They rested on the downturned head of James for a split second before moving back to Annie. "And I'd appreciate you not saying such things again."

"I was just teasing," Annie said, sounding hurt.

"You know I don't take well to teasing, Annie," Mrs. Crankshaw said. "What you're saying is dangerous. Britta could lose her position if she was caught out secretly with a man."

"Honestly?" I asked, searching Britta's face for a reaction. Her eyes were defiant, but she was biting her lip. Was there truth to the gossip after all?

"Of course," Miss Issacson said. "Mrs. Mayhew is particular about this."

"No, she's not particular. She's like every lady of her stature," Mrs. Crankshaw said. "Few society employers will tolerate their servants secretly courting, and you can almost forget about being a married servant. I knew a girl once, a scullery maid, who was secretly married. Before she resigned, her husband became ill and they had nothing to live on, so she needed to keep the job. The master of the house found out and summarily dismissed her without references. They both ended up in a county workhouse." At this Britta turned on her heel, crying. She dashed out of the hall and up the stairs.

"What's wrong with her?" Annie said.

"Can't you see you upset her?" James said. "You and your big mouth."

"I was just teasing," Annie said again.

"Hush," Mrs. Crankshaw said, silencing the room. "Britta is bringing you dinner, Miss Davish."

"Yes," I said, ignoring Mrs. Crankshaw's dismissal. My dinner might get cold, but Britta needed a few moments alone and I had to find out the truth of this. "But what if you do want to step out with someone?"

"Then you get permission," Mrs. Crankshaw said.

"Oh," I said. I'd stepped out with Walter without asking permission. What would Sir Arthur say? Would he dismiss me summarily like the scullery maid because I was blissfully ignorant of protocol? I hadn't seen Walter since Christmas, but we corresponded on a regular basis. Should I tell Mrs. Mayhew? Should I write Sir Arthur?

Before I could decide what to do, James made a guttural noise in his throat. "Permission," he said, spitting the word out venomously. "It's degrading."

"It's required," Mrs. Crankshaw said matter-of-factly.

"No wonder those maids in Milwaukee went on strike. We're not even treated like real people," James said.

"What maids in Milwaukee?" Annie asked.

"I read about it—"

"Right! Now that's enough. I'll have no talk of strike at the table," Mrs. Crankshaw said.

"Yes, please," Mr. Davies said, "we've had enough disruptive conversation already tonight."

"What's disruptive about talking about maids in Milwaukee?" James said.

"I don't care if they're Mrs. Vanderbilt's maids at Marble

House," Mrs. Crankshaw said. "We will not have strike talk at this table."

"But, Mrs. Crankshaw, it's not like we're talking about *us* striking," James said.

"Enough," Mrs. Crankshaw said, slamming her fist into the table, rattling dishes and plates. Mr. Davies raised his eyebrows, but he said nothing. "I don't take well to words of strike in this house. What is this world coming to?"

Everyone bent their heads over their bowls, ignoring me and focusing on finishing their meal in silence. I watched James for a few moments before I left the hall. Why had he been so angry about having to ask permission to court? And then there was the altercation at the Forty Steps. What else was he angry about? And why had he brought up the strike in Milwaukee? He and Lester Sibley were obviously not on friendly terms, but they seemed to have something in common. Was James disgruntled with his lot in life? Did he believe he deserved more free time, higher wages? Mrs. Mayhew did suspect someone in her household of strike talk. Was James a union sympathizer? If so, he might have more to do with Lester Sibley and the events of the last two days than I thought.

What a day, I thought as a wave of depression and sadness swept over me. Murder, attempted murder, Britta's distress, strike talk downstairs. I took a bite of the graham biscuit from the dinner I'd found waiting for me and sat down at my typewriter. With the first clack of the keys I started to feel better. The familiar scratch of Bonaparte at my door even made me laugh. Disappointed earlier, he wasn't one to give up on his nighttime scraps. I stood up and walked over to open the door. A streak of white fur flew past me.

Now why did he do that? I wondered. Bonaparte usually liked to linger in the doorway, rubbing against my leg. I started to close the door.

"Oh, James," Britta's voice said pleadingly. "What are we going to do?"

If the tone of her voice hadn't frozen me in place, the fact that she was talking to a man right outside my room would have. I'd thought she'd left.

"Don't worry about it, Britta," James said. "No one is going to find out."

"But what if they do?"

"No one will, trust me."

"And what about that labor strike guy, what was his name, Lester?"

"What about him?"

"Well, first you're talking to him like you're old chums and next you're punching him in the mouth."

"The first was all business; you know that."

"And the fight?"

"You know about that too."

"Well, I'm worried, James."

"Don't. Sibley wants this too badly to say anything."

"Wants what? A strike? It's too dangerous, James. We shouldn't even be talking about it."

Strike? So the rumors were true. Mrs. Mayhew and Mrs. Whitwell had both mentioned talk of the Newport servants going on strike. It would be chaos. It would be an abrupt end, at least for a while, of afternoon recitals, garden teas, costume balls, and dinner parties. But then again, maybe that was the point. But what was Britta worried Sibley would talk about?

". . . just follow the plan and we'll get through this Season without anyone the wiser," James was saying. I'd missed his answer about joining the strike.

"And then?" Britta asked. Silence followed as James obviously fought to find the answer.

"Let's get through the next few weeks first," he said.

A moment or two later I heard receding footsteps and then all was quiet on the other side of the door. Bonaparte had already found the cutlet I'd left for him and had curled up on top of my bookcase.

Oh, to have that peace of mind! I thought, listening to him purr. I returned to my typing, the only way I knew how to achieve peace of mind, and finished my report. But it didn't help. I put a blank sheet of paper into my typewriter the moment I was finished. I started a list:

1. Why was James talking to Britta outside my room?
2. Was Annie's gossip close to the truth? Did Britta have a beau? James, perhaps?
3. What was she afraid Lester Sibley would say?
4. What does Lester Sibley have to do with Britta and James?
5. Is James going to try organizing a strike at Rose Mont?
6. Has Lester Sibley been successful in organizing a servants' strike throughout Newport, or is he targeting certain houses?
7. What is the plan James proposed he and Britta follow? Are others involved?
8. Does any of this have anything to do with Harland Whitwell's death?

Satisfied that the last question was truly the only one that concerned me, I ripped out the paper and replaced it with a new one:

1. Who killed Harland Whitwell?

I paused. So far, I'd found little reason for anyone to kill Harland Whitwell. By most accounts, he was well liked. My list of suspects was strikingly small. Lester Sibley, although the only suspect in Mrs. Whitwell's mind, couldn't have done it. And even if he hadn't been in police custody, what motive did he have? What about Nicholas Whitwell? Granted, I didn't have a fondness for the man, but I couldn't think why, beyond simple father-son dislike, he would kill his father. However, if Nick benefited financially from his father's death, that might be a motive. I added to my list:

2. Who benefited from Harland Whitwell's death? Nick? Jane Whitwell? Eugenie Whitwell? Bank partners?
3. Who are Harland Whitwell's bank partners?
4. Was the burning of the bank related to Whitwell's death? If so, how?
5. Could a disgruntled bank employee have burned the bank or killed Whitwell, or both?
6. Could a disgruntled servant have done either or both?

Could a member of the Glen Park staff have killed Mr. Whitwell? Mrs. Johnville had insinuated as much. And after listening to the conversation between Britta and James I knew a servant strike at Glen Park was within the realm of possibility. What if one of Mr. Whitwell's staff had already approached him? What if that servant was dismissed? Could that be a motive for murder? I jotted down a quick list of people to speak to tomorrow, straightened the papers on my desk, put Bonaparte out to find his way back to Mrs. Mayhew, and prepared for bed. As I finally laid my head on the pillow, I tried to push all thoughts of Harland Whitwell's murder out of my head. I let my mind wander from thoughts of Walter, to the encounter I'd had with his mother, to the dinner conversation about courtship. As I fell asleep my mind came back to the same question about Nick Whitwell again and again: Why would Cora Mayhew want to marry a man like that?

CHAPTER 18

"My, you are thorough, Miss Davish," Charlotte Mayhew said after reading my report. "I knew I could rely on you."

I had risen early, as usual, and had gone for a hike along Ocean Drive. The southernmost part of the island, less inhabited by people and "cottages," was home to the currently quiet Spouting Rock, a large cavity in the rocks that after a storm interacts with the waves to produce a fountain of water spraying fifty feet or more in the air, as well as to calm, shallow inlets, rocky headlands, sandy beaches, and wild vegetation. Hoping to find new plant specimens to add to my collection, I brought my small plant press along. I wasn't disappointed. In fact, it was exhilarating. I hadn't enough time to collect and press all the new plants I saw. Species I'd only read about jutted up between rocks, sprawled across dunes, or clumped in hedge-like clusters along the road. I planned to come back soon. But Mrs. Mayhew had been expecting me the moment her coffee was delivered.

"Thank you, ma'am," I said as I finished addressing an envelope to *Commander Converse* for Mrs. Mayhew's ball. As was protocol, each of the gentlemen invited to the ball received an envelope with the name of the lady he would be escorting in to dinner. I'd had to write and rewrite several as Mrs. Mayhew changed her mind. I'd noticed several officers from Fort Adams and the Naval War College had most recently accepted. "I regret I haven't learned a great deal."

"If you keep at it like this," she said, waving the report in her hand, "I'm sure you will in time. Now when you're finished with those, I would like you to type up a copy of this report and hand-deliver it, along with my condolence card and an invitation, to Mrs. Whitwell. After church, of course."

"Ma'am?" I said. The idea of delivering a report that contradicted the lady's own insinuations, while placing the possible blame for her husband's murder on her son, was not appealing. But I wasn't in a position to argue or even question Mrs. Mayhew's motives.

"Yes?" Mrs. Mayhew said, her tone almost challenging me to question her.

"Would you like to include a personal note?"

"Yes, thank you, Davish," she said, smiling and reaching out her hands for a piece of stationery and a pen. "What a good idea."

Less than thirty minutes later, armed with a stack of gold-trimmed oversized envelopes, I stepped into the hot sun, blinking as my eyes adjusted to its brilliance. There wasn't a cloud in the sky and my hat, with its short brim, did little to shade my face. Yet I didn't mind. I was to spend a good portion of my day "hand-delivering" invitations to Mrs. Mayhew's ball. And after spending yesterday indoors in the presence of a dead man, his widow, and the police, I relished the excuse to stroll the streets, admiring the gardens lining the estate walls and taking in the fresh seaside air. The "cottages" I'd been living in were beyond any luxury I'd ever experienced, but I found the rooms cold and forbidding.

Mr. Davies had actually arranged a carriage for my use this afternoon, to go to Fort Adams and the Naval War College, but I was on my own this morning. So I consulted my map several times and realized that over the course of the day I would see most of Newport. My first stop was Mass at St. Mary's, a fifty-year-old red stone church with a prominent steeple on William Street. After Mass, fortified with the peace the service brought me, I made my way back to Glen Park, the Whitwell residence, for a visit I wasn't looking forward to. As black crape with white ribbons hung from the doorknob indicating a house in mourning, I knocked instead of ringing the bell at the servants' entrance as I had yesterday. Had it only been a day since I'd rushed in to find Mrs. Whitwell wailing over her dead husband's body? I looked up at the ceiling of interwoven wisteria vines; a few of the remaining purple flowers hung down. The leaves rustled in the wind and blew a few blossoms down on my head. I loved wisteria, but now the scent made me think of death.

I'm so tired of this, I thought. Before a tear had a chance to well up in my eye, I brushed the blossoms from my hat and shoulder and knocked on the door again. A housemaid I'd never seen before answered the door.

"Is your mistress in?" I asked.

"No, she isn't."

"She isn't?" I couldn't imagine where a widow of one day would be other than secluded in her home, deep in mourning. "Did she go to church this morning?"

"I don't know where she went. Come back later," the maid said, closing the door.

How strange, I thought. *Where could Mrs. Whitwell be?*

I left Glen Park and strolled through Newport's neighborhoods, often crisscrossing Bellevue Avenue, now catching a glance at the ocean, now crossing streets full of parading carriages. Continuing my role as Mrs. Mayhew's "personal carrier," delivering the latest round of invitations, I called at cottages with names like Angelsea, Seaview, Chateau-sur-Mer, Honeysuckle Lodge, Roselawn, Ochre Court, Belcourt, Resthaven, Chepstow, Kingscote, Stoneleigh, Cave Cliff, Cliff Lawn, Rock Cliff, and Land's End. With my stack of golden-trimmed envelopes in hand I had an excuse to enter through gates, step beyond walls, and get a glimpse of the breathtaking grounds and gardens hidden behind them. Long stone walkways stretched away to the ocean under trellises dripping with wisteria and Virginia creeper. Fern gardens blanketed the ground beneath gigantic shade trees. Fanciful arboretums had rows of trees pruned into geometric shapes or the shapes of animals. Ponds of every shape and size were stocked with darting goldfish and adorned with giant lily pads and spouting fountains. Rainbow-colored flower beds were carefully laid out in complex geometric patterns and accented by statuary.

Only my professional discipline kept me from dallying among so many exotic plants. Three times I stepped away from a path to look more closely at a flower or plant, twice to admire a new variation of rose and once to see the finest specimen of a *Dahlia pinnata* I'd ever seen. After seeing such cultivated beauty, I was looking forward to hiking back to Ocean Drive to deliver the few remaining invitations and seeing again the wilder side of Newport's splendor. However, that would have to wait. I had yet to deliver Miss Lizzie and Miss Lucy's invitation at Moffat Cottage and, knowing Miss Lucy, I knew I would be there awhile.

Despite the extraordinary walk through the beautiful estates, my stomach churned at the thought of calling on Miss Lizzie and Miss Lucy. Not on account of them, of course, but from the likelihood of another encounter with Mrs. Grice,

Walter's mother. I dreaded having to face her again. With thoughts of humiliation and rejection running through my mind, I didn't notice the crowd down the street until I was only a few blocks away. It was a picket line! Though fewer than a dozen picketers carried placards saying: SOLIDARITY and AN INJURY TO ONE IS THE CONCERN OF ALL, their boisterous chanting of their slogans over and over had drawn a crowd of three times that. They marched in front of the Ocean House Hotel. And among them was Lester Sibley. When had the police released him? I wondered.

"What's going on?" I asked one of the bystanders, a woman in a stylish straw hat with a large projecting front brim, trimmed in silk orchids.

"Looks like the telegraph at Ocean House is running again. Someone must have quit the strike." *Mrs. Mayhew and her set will be happy to hear that,* I thought.

As I drew nearer, I noticed the Pinkerton detective Silas Doubleday force Lester Sibley away from his group, pushing him to the side of the street. Suddenly a jarring engine roar came from behind me. I twisted around as a motorcar, Nick Whitwell's motorcar, careened by me heading straight for the pair of arguing men. Did they see it? Of course no one could miss the grating sound.

"Watch out!" someone yelled.

Doubleday and Sibley jerked around and leaped out of the way moments before the car careened across the spot where they'd been standing. It swerved toward them, two wheels scraping along the sidewalk, missing their feet by inches. The crowd, no longer paying any attention to the picketers, scrambled in every direction. Many barely avoided being run down by the deadly contraption before it raced away. But one person capitalized on the commotion. The minute he'd stepped out of the line of the car, Silas Doubleday drew out a short, thick billy club and began swinging it at anyone still holding a placard.

Making contact with arms and legs and heads, Doubleday single-handedly ended the picketing. Beaten and battered, the picketers, if they were able, dropped their placards and scattered, leaving their fallen comrades behind.

"And let that be the end of it!" Doubleday shouted as he casually placed his club on his belt and strode away, whistling "Ode to Joy."

Doesn't the man know another tune? I thought peevishly.

Several people, myself included, hastened over to those who still lay on the ground. One man was moaning, bent over his leg, his trousers ripped where the club had connected with his shin. Another lay unconscious but without any obvious injury. When two men tried to lift him, however, he screamed in pain. Lester Sibley lay motionless on the ground. I knelt by his side and placed my hand on his wrist as I had seen Walter do so many times. I felt Sibley's pulse and breathed a sigh of relief when he opened his eyes at the feel of my touch.

"Are you all right, Mr. Sibley?" I asked.

"I will be," he said as he struggled to sit up. I helped him into a sitting position. "What happened?" *Oh, no,* I thought. *He's taken a blow to his head and doesn't remember anything.*

"I believe you've been hit on the head," I said. If he didn't remember anything, I wasn't going to be the one to bring up the Pinkerton man's attack.

"No, I remember Doubleday hitting me," he said, rubbing the back of his head and wincing as he touched a sensitive spot. "Bastard," he added under his breath. "No, I was talking about that motorcar. It was out of control." He hadn't realized, as those of us in the crowd had, that either he or Detective Doubleday was the motorcar's target. "I didn't even know someone in town had one of those things."

I didn't tell him Nick Whitwell owned the motorcar. This time the driver was hidden under an odd combination of a mackintosh coat, yellow and green plaid woolen scarf, round-crowned rubber hat, and goggles. But whom was he kidding? Nick had already tried once to injure and maybe even kill Sibley. The disguise wasn't fooling anyone.

"I'd never seen one before. Who would've guessed I'd get so close!" He chuckled.

"Could you be stirring up so much trouble and resentment that people want to kill you, Mr. Sibley?" I asked.

He stared at me in wonder. And then to my astonishment he smiled. "Well, I certainly hope so," he said. "You saw what happened at the jail. Why?"

"Because I believe the driver was trying to hit you," I said.

Lester nodded as if giving approval. "Then I'm doing my job, Miss Davish. I'm doing my job."

"That may be how you feel, Mr. Sibley, but it would seem that Detective Doubleday has put an end to your work here."

"What do you mean?" he said. How could it not be obvious to him? Maybe the blow to his head was more serious than it looked.

"Look around you, Mr. Sibley," I said, indicating the abandoned placards and the injured men lying nearby. "No one is likely to join a picket line here or, when the word gets out, anywhere in Newport again."

Lester Sibley struggled to his feet, brushing off my attempt to help him.

"Oh, on the contrary, Miss Davish. This incident, like the one in the jail, proves I'm getting close to success. No, a bump on the head and a threat from some out-of-control car isn't enough to stop Lester Sibley from demanding the rights that all working people deserve!"

I was afraid he was going to say that.

CHAPTER 19

"Davish!" Miss Lucy said when the maid escorted me to the front parlor.

What a difference! I thought. Compared to any room in Rose Mont or Glen Park, excluding the servants' quarters, the parlor of Moffat Cottage was small. Yet here among friends, in this room with its painted cream white walls accented with green and gold fleur-de-lis, its simple walnut furniture, its plush velvet green pillows and damask drapes, I could rest on the settee or touch the simple glass bowl filled with nuts without apprehension. Here I wasn't a talking piece of statuary.

"I don't think I'll be happier seeing the back of Saint Peter after walking through the pearly gates!" Miss Lucy said.

The old lady licked her lips and grinned from ear to ear. I knew Miss Lucy was fond of me, but I wasn't kidding myself that I personally was the source of her joy. Miss Lucy knew for a fact that I came bearing news. I'd debated the ethics of telling the elderly ladies what I'd found out for Mrs. Mayhew regarding Harland Whitwell's death. Mrs. Mayhew was under the impression that she alone was getting a report. If I told the

Shaw sisters everything I'd told Mrs. Mayhew, I'd be violating her trust. Yet I knew Miss Lucy, at least, would not take no for an answer. I decided to tell them no more than they probably already knew.

"You've been remiss in visiting," she said, wagging her finger playfully at me. "I thought you agreed to come for tea yesterday. I was afraid I was going to have to call on Charlotte again if we hadn't heard from you."

"I'm sorry, Miss Lucy," I said. "I couldn't get away until now. You got my note?"

"Yes, yes. At least you're here now. Sit down, Davish."

"Where is Miss Lizzie?" I said, sitting on the settee opposite. I didn't dare mention Mrs. Grice.

"Here I am, dear," Miss Lizzie said, entering the room. She was carrying a plate of brown bread and licking something orange colored off her fingers. "You missed Julia, Hattie. She went out again as soon as we returned from church. My, this marmalade is messy." I was relieved to hear Walter's mother was out. Suddenly Miss Lizzie clapped her hands, sticky fingers and all. "Oh, Lucy, dear, did you tell Hattie about—?"

"Lizzie!" Miss Lucy said, sharply interrupting her sister and effectively stifling the other woman's enthusiasm.

"But shouldn't . . . ?" Miss Lizzie said, glancing quickly back and forth between me and her sister.

"Do sit down, Lizzie, so Davish can get on with her news." They exchanged a glance I couldn't interpret the meaning of.

Miss Lizzie had taken a large bite of bread, but her face was red. Miss Lucy had definitely prevented her sister from telling me something. What didn't Miss Lucy want me to know?

"Hattie, dear, do you have news?" Miss Lizzie said, her overly eager tone ringing false as she sank into the nearest chair.

"Yes, she was about to tell us what she's learned about Harland Whitwell's death," Miss Lizzie's sister said sternly.

"I was?" I said, distracted by the sisters' odd behavior. "I simply came by at your request and of course to deliver this invitation to Mrs. Mayhew's ball." I handed the envelope to Miss Lucy, since Miss Lizzie's fingers were covered in sticky jam. Miss Lucy snatched it from me and scowled.

"You know darn well, Davish, that I came up with the idea of you looking into Whitwell's death."

"Oh, don't sound so annoyed, Lucy," Miss Lizzie said, herself sounding peevish. "Maybe there's nothing to tell. Is there, Hattie dear?" Now what had created the sudden quarrel between the two? What had I missed? I hoped I wasn't the cause. Maybe it would lessen tensions if they heard what I had to tell them.

"Well? Is there something to tell?" Miss Lucy's face lit up with anticipation.

"If you remember, Mrs. Mayhew was adamant that I not share what I learn with others," I said.

"Poppycock!" Miss Lucy declared.

"Lucy!" her sister admonished. "Hattie's just doing her job, after all. The one you arranged for her, if my memory serves me well."

"Of course, but I never meant for her to exclude me!"

"If it makes you feel any better, Miss Lucy, there isn't much to tell about Mr. Whitwell's death yet," I said.

Miss Lucy scowled again.

"Of course not, dear," Miss Lizzie said, reaching over with her plate. "Try one, Hattie? It's real New England brown bread."

"Don't distract her, Lizzie," her sister said, hoping I might tell her something after all. "Let Davish speak. Well?"

"I can tell you Lester Sibley couldn't have killed Harland Whitwell."

"We knew that already, Davish!" Miss Lucy said, throwing her hands up in exasperation. "Tell me something I don't know."

"Could you tell me something, Miss Lucy?" I said. The lady, taken aback by my question, stared at me blinking for a moment or two.

"What?" Miss Lucy said, a mixture of annoyance and curiosity in her tone.

"Why is it so important to Mrs. Mayhew to have Mrs. Astor leave a calling card? It's just a calling card."

"Oh, Davish, don't be so naïve," Miss Lucy snorted. "There's no such thing as 'just a calling card.'"

"What Lucy is trying to say, dear," Miss Lizzie said, "is that in polite society an established matron must call on you first before you can claim an acquaintance with her. Therefore, regardless of how much money Gideon Mayhew has or how large Rose Mont is, Charlotte will never be a member of the Four Hundred until Mrs. Astor acknowledges her by leaving her calling card."

"The Four Hundred?" I asked.

"It's how they refer to the exclusive inner circle of high society. Some people will do anything to be a member."

"Such as use the murder of a friend's husband to advance their own agenda?"

"There are strict rules in society, Davish, and here in Newport, Caroline Astor makes them. Charlotte Mayhew knows that," Miss Lucy said. "She, along with many others, has been trying for years to break into Mrs. Astor's inner circle. Some spend tens of thousands year after year, renting cottages and giving parties, trying to climb the social ladder, only to be snubbed. Most leave Newport when either their money or their patience runs out. As they say, 'Few are bidden and many devoured.' If having you solve Harland Whitwell's murder will pique Mrs. Astor's curiosity enough to call on Charlotte, then so be it."

"Are you members of this Four Hundred?" I asked.

Miss Lucy slapped her knee and cackled while her sister, her mouth full of bread, simply smiled and shook her head.

"No, dear, we're too old for all that," Miss Lizzie said. "And even if we weren't, we aren't nearly rich enough for the likes of Mrs. Astor. Besides, like Charlotte Mayhew, we come from humble beginnings and are considered 'new' money. Only 'old'-money families dance at Beechwood."

Charlotte Mayhew humble? I thought but kept my doubts to myself.

"New money, indeed," Miss Lucy said, her hand still at her chest, trying to slow her breathing down. "My husband made his fortune making bricks! Now, no more equivocating like a politician caught with his hand in the ballot box, tell us about Harland Whitwell!" I'd hoped she'd forgotten, but I should've known better. "So who killed him?"

"Truth is I've found little reason why anyone would want to kill Harland Whitwell."

"Besides his son, you mean, dear," Miss Lizzie said, smashing the bits of crumb on her plate with a fork.

"Yes," her sister said. "Have you learned anything more about Nick? Everyone knows about the nasty father-and-son quarrels."

I'd shared so much of the investigation into Mrs. Trevelyan's death with these two ladies, I was ill at ease withholding what I knew. But how did I tell them something of what I'd learned without betraying Mrs. Mayhew's trust? And then it occurred to me.

"Yes, actually," I said. Miss Lucy was suddenly at the edge of her chair. Miss Lizzie set the plate on her lap. "I think I saw him try to run Lester Sibley down with his car." As this had nothing to do with Harland Whitwell's death, I felt free to share. I hoped it would be enough to deflect any more questions about the murder.

"Really?" Miss Lucy said. "When?"

"As I was walking here, only a few minutes ago."

"But how can you be certain it was Nick Whitwell, dear?" Miss Lizzie asked.

"Who else has a motorcar in Newport?" Miss Lucy said. "Or anywhere else for that matter? We've heard about them, of course, but Nicholas Whitwell is the only one we know to actually own one."

"True," Miss Lizzie said, nodding.

"And we've all seen him driving that thing around," Miss Lucy said. "He's more reckless than a tornado at a picnic. Are you certain he tried to run the labor man down?"

"Either him or a Pinkerton detective named Silas Doubleday. He and Sibley were having an argument and the car aimed right for them."

"Now why would Nick Whitwell want to kill Lester Sibley or this Doubleday fellow?" Miss Lizzie said.

"I don't know about Doubleday," I said. "But like his mother, Nick Whitwell may believe Lester Sibley killed his father."

"But we all know Sibley was in jail and couldn't have done it," Miss Lucy said.

"Maybe the family is trying to deflect the blame," Miss Lizzie said. Miss Lucy and I stared at Miss Lizzie. She had picked up the bowl of nuts from the table and was cracking them between her teeth.

"What are you talking about, Lizzie?" her sister asked. "And use the nutcracker, will you? You look like a giant squirrel in sea green silk."

"Oh, I don't know," Miss Lizzie said, reaching for the silver nutcracker on the table. "I thought maybe Jane and Nick knew something we don't."

"About Lester Sibley?" I asked.

"Yes, dear," she said. "They know as well as we do, the man couldn't have done it. So why are they clinging to the idea?"

"Could he have done something else to get on the family's wrong side?" I said. "Something they're taking this opportunity to punish him for?" It made sense. Sibley was stirring up discontent and thoughts of strike at Glen Park and at Whitwell's bank. I'd witnessed an altercation between Whitwell and Sibley at the Newport Casino. Was that what this was about? Was the family trying to chastise Sibley for his harassment? "Or could they simply want to use Lester Sibley as a way to deflect blame from Whitwell's true killer?" I said, thinking out loud.

"Now you're talking, Davish," Miss Lucy said. "Jane and Nick Whitwell must know who killed Harland. I'm sure of it." Miss Lucy clambered out of her chair and indicated for me to do the same. She shooed me toward the door. "Now go find out who it was!"

CHAPTER 20

As I passed Glen Park on my way to Ocean Avenue to deliver the last of the invitations, I took the opportunity to call on Mrs. Whitwell again, hoping this time she'd be home. When I rang the bell, the housemaid who'd answered before opened the door. This time I introduced myself and inquired after the housekeeper. Mrs. Johnville and most of the staff had yet to return from church, the maid said. I was disappointed and expected the door to close on me for a second time. I turned to leave.

"You still want to talk to Mrs. Whitwell?" the maid asked.

"Yes, of course, but—" I said, shrugging.

"Madam's in. Follow me."

What luck. The maid led me upstairs to a tall, gilded chair in the hall and asked me to wait while she spoke to Mrs. Whitwell. I stared at the swathe of black crape that hung from what I knew was a four-foot-wide gilded mirror opposite me. I was only a few steps from Mr. Whitwell's office. I lamented that no one had properly searched the room. When I'd been in there, I'd noticed a few correspondences, including the one about the bank, but hadn't had time or the inclination to do a thorough search. As someone whose livelihood depended in part on the vast amount of correspondence my employers received, I knew I could learn more from the dead man's papers. Did I dare?

Tick, tick, tick. I glanced around me. The hall was empty. The gentle ticking of a grandfather clock about halfway down reverberating off the marble walls was the only sound. I stood hesitantly, still questioning what I was about to do, and then tiptoed toward the office. *Tap, tap, tick, tick, tap.* The sound of my footsteps echoed loud in my ears. Given the miles I had to travel today, I'd worn my walking boots, but now I wished I'd worn my slippers. I heard another noise, the far-off closing of a door perhaps, and halted, still on my tiptoes. My heart was beating fast and my breath was shallow. I listened intently, but all was still again. I waited another moment or two before proceeding. I put my hand on the brass doorknob and felt the embossed *W* press against my sweaty palm. Why was I sneaking about like a thief? Before I could question my actions again, I opened the office door and slipped inside. I looked around the room and thought of the last time I'd seen it. Images flashed through my mind: the crumpled pamphlet clenched in the dead man's hand, the loose curl that hung down the nape of Mrs. Whitwell's neck as she rocked over the dead body of her husband, the pink peony hand-painted on the china coffee cup, the blood speckles on everything, the cigar, the carpet, the desk.

"What am I doing?" I said out loud.

I had absolutely no excuse for my presence in this room, none. If I was found here, I would be expelled from the house or worse. I could lose my position, my reputation. Whatever possessed me to come in here in the first place? What did I expect to find? No evidence I found in this room would shield me from the repercussions of unauthorized prying into Harland Whitwell's personal papers. I heard footsteps above me on the stairwell and immediately turned my back on the room, closed the door behind me, and returned to my chair as fast as I could. The maid appeared in the hall just as I sat down.

"Mrs. Whitwell will see you now," the maid said when she approached me, her eyebrow cocked in question. She glanced down the hall and then back at me. "What you doing, miss?" she said. She'd seen or heard me leave my chair.

"Those columns are made of solid marble, aren't they?" I said, pointing to the architectural wonder at the base of the stairs.

The maid smiled, satisfied. "If you think that's something, you should see the Gold Room. It ain't called that for nothing," she said. "Now if you'll follow me."

Jane Whitwell looked up from staring at the floor when we entered. I was shocked by the change in her. When I'd left her yesterday, she'd been composed, almost resolved. Now the woman before me looked wretched. She barely raised her head. Her eyes were puffy and red. Her cheeks were streaked with tears. Her hair was tousled, long strands of hair fell loose from her bun, and spots of something dark and dry blemished her sleeve. Was that mud maybe or dried blood? She lifted a handkerchief to her face as her shoulders shook with a stifled sob. I wondered, if she was so indisposed and upset, why would she agree to see me?

"Mrs. Mayhew's secretary, ma'am," the maid announced.

"I am terribly sorry to intrude on your grief, Mrs. Whitwell," I said, watching the maid exit the room. "Maybe I should go and return another time."

"He didn't do it, did he?" she said.

"Who didn't do what, ma'am?"

"That labor man, Sibley."

"No, ma'am. Lester Sibley was in the custody of the police when . . ." I couldn't bring myself to finish.

"I tried to kill him, you know," she said. My immediate thought was that she meant her husband. But why would she confess to me? I shook my head, knowing that made little sense.

"Whom did you try to kill, ma'am?" I said as gently as possible.

"Sibley, who else?" she snapped.

"You were driving Mr. Nicholas's car?" I was stunned. The thought had never entered my mind that the mother, and not the son, was driving the car.

"Of course," she said. "Who do you think . . . ?" Her voice trailed away as her eyes opened wide. "Oh my God!"

She flung herself across the back of the settee and wept hysterically. I stood there completely at a loss as to what to do. *Should I say something assuring? Should I leave? How do I spare us both the embarrassment?* I reminded myself why I was here. I hoped that if I acted in as professional a manner as possible she would forgive my witnessing her breakdown.

"Ma'am, I know you are grieving the loss of your husband, and I'm truly sorry. You had a right to suspect Lester Sibley, as that was the easiest conclusion based on the evidence before us. But we all know Lester Sibley didn't kill your husband."

"I tried to run the man down in the street," she said without looking up. "And now everyone will think that Nick . . ."

"Yes, but no one was harmed. . . ." I hesitated, hoping she was listening. "So no one need know that the incident was anything but a new driver letting the motorcar get away from him or . . . her."

She lifted her head and looked at me. "An accident, you mean?" I nodded. She took a deep breath. "But Nick?"

"Is well-known for his"—I had to think of the right word—"adventuresome driving. No one will think it was anything more than that, assuming they recognized Mr. Whitwell's motorcar in the first place."

She nodded, appeased with my scenario. She dabbed her eyes with her handkerchief. "Why are you here, Miss Davish?" she said, regaining her composure and some of her haughtiness. I was reassured that she was again herself and I could proceed with my intentions.

"As you know, I was instructed by Mrs. Mayhew to find the truth about the death of your husband."

"Yes," she said.

"I have done so in good faith but have found little to suggest who might've killed him."

"What have you found?"

I didn't have the heart to tell her that her son was my, and the police's, number one suspect. "All that I've uncovered so far is in this report." I handed it to her. "It is an exact duplicate to the one I gave Mrs. Mayhew. She instructed me to keep you well informed."

"That is kind of Charlotte," Mrs. Whitwell said, setting the report down next to her on the settee. "Will that be all, Miss Davish?" Her dismissal frustrated me. I hadn't had an opportunity to ask her what I'd come here to ask.

"To be honest, ma'am, no. I would ask a favor."

"Yes?"

"May I speak to Mr. Whitwell's secretary? I assume he is still in his employ?"

"Nelson? Why would you wish to speak to him? You think Harland's business had something to do with his murder?"

"Possibly, yes," I said.

"Well, it won't do speaking with Nelson. He's in New York. Harland keeps him there to keep an eye on things while he's in Newport. You can't wire him with the telegraph operators still striking." She didn't offer the use of her telephone, so I didn't ask.

"I believe the Ocean House telegraph is available again," I said.

"It's about time! Is that why those people were picketing?"
I nodded. "It doesn't matter. It won't do contacting Nelson.
Besides, I can't imagine what you'd learn from Nelson that a
good look at what's in Harland's office wouldn't tell you."

A thrill ran through me. This was more than I'd hoped for.
I had to keep the enthusiasm out of my voice. "Would you
permit me to look through Mr. Whitwell's papers?" I held my
breath.

Mrs. Whitwell sighed heavily and shook her head. I was
prepared for a denial. "If Charlotte can trust you to be discreet,
I guess so can I." It took everything I had not to smile in triumph. "But," she said, pointing her finger at me, "anything
you learn, you must keep between us." My hopes deflated as I
knew I couldn't keep her promise. My first loyalty was to Mrs.
Mayhew. "No police," Jane Whitwell said. "And don't expect
me to step one foot into that room. As soon as you're done, it's
to be locked forever."

I allowed my hopes to rise again. "And Mrs. Mayhew?
May I share anything we learn with her?"

"Oh, of course, that was implied. Charlotte hired you to
help me after all."

"Thank you, ma'am. I'll go straight to it, if that's all right
with you?" She nodded and I turned toward the door.

"Miss Davish?" she said, causing me to face her again.
"You will be discreet about the motorcar incident?"

What was one more secret to keep? I thought.

"Of course, ma'am."

She nodded and dismissed me with a wave as she turned to
push the call button for the maid. I opened the door and
nearly ran to Harland Whitwell's office.

CHAPTER 21

"What are you doing?"
I looked up from the letter I was reading and found the Whitwells' butler standing in the doorway, his hand still on the knob. I glanced back at the letter in my hand and then nearly smiled when I looked down at Mr. Whitwell's desk, covered with tidy piles. I'd unconsciously organized the documents I'd perused.

It had to be done eventually, I thought. To the butler I said, "I'm sorting through Mr. Whitwell's papers per Mrs. Whitwell's request."

"Oh, you're the secretary from yesterday," he said.

I nodded. "Yes, we haven't been introduced. I'm Miss Hattie Davish, Mr. . . . ?"

"It's Weeks, Miss Davish. Aren't you Mrs. Mayhew's secretary?"

"Yes, I've been requested by Mrs. Mayhew to assist Mrs. Whitwell in this since she doesn't have her own secretary and Mr. Nelson is in New York."

The butler let go of the doorknob and his frown lessened a bit. "Might I assist?"

"Thank you, but I'm almost finished."

Sadly, it was true. I'd entered the office over an hour ago with such high expectations. Ignoring the image I had of Mrs. Whitwell cradling the dead body of her husband on the rug beneath my feet, I picked up all the papers scattered on the floor, including three with blood splatters on them, and went to work. Using my long years of practice ascertaining the most pertinent information from a document with a mere glance, I scanned every piece of paper, every ledger, every book, in the room for some clue as to why this man was killed. Besides the labor union pamphlet that the police now had, I'd found several pieces of correspondence to Mr. Whitwell from Lester Sibley, all along the same vein, demanding certain rights for those who were in Mr. Whitwell's employ. I also found a few letters from several prominent Newport residents, including Mr. Gideon Mayhew, discussing Lester Sibley. From those letters I surmised Lester Sibley was nothing more than a nuisance to these businessmen, albeit one they wished to get rid of. I'd known all along that the hand of Lester Sibley couldn't have held the gun that killed Whitwell, but Sibley could've been involved in some other way. Yet I'd found nothing that would suggest Lester Sibley was in any way connected with Harland Whitwell's death. I wasn't surprised, but I was still disappointed. I'd also found nothing more connecting Nick to his father's death. True, I had found a stack of unpaid, overdue bills, amounting to a staggering sum of $19,322. Almost all related to some expense or expenditure incurred by the younger Whitwell, but I'd already known that money was a source of contention between them.

Could Nick have killed his father for the money? I wondered.

What I had found, however, was evidence that not only

was the Aquidneck National Bank going bankrupt, but so too were several other banks in New York and New England that Mr. Whitwell owned. As these banks failed, so dwindled the Whitwell fortune. I'd read articles in the paper almost daily discussing the current financial situation of the country, especially concerning the possible repeal of the Sherman Silver Purchase Act. And below in the same column had been announcements of bank closures and factory strikes. Could Harland Whitwell have been a victim of the country's dire financial stress? The news was shocking and I had to read the string of letters he'd received recently from his attorneys in full to be sure. Harland Whitwell, one of the richest men in America, was on the verge of complete financial ruin! Did Mrs. Whitwell know? She said her husband didn't speak to her about business. Did Nick know? If Harland didn't tell his son, it would explain why he fought so bitterly over funds he didn't have. I'd heard of men making poor investments and ending up in a poorhouse. I never thought that could happen to someone like Harland Whitwell. Who would be next, J. P. Morgan? The absurdity of the idea made the reality all the more disturbing. What would the family do now? Unfortunately, despite everything I'd uncovered about Harland's financial state, none of it had anything to do with his death.

Or did it?

"Mr. Weeks," I said. "Maybe you can help. I'm wondering if you could answer a few questions."

"If I can," he said.

"Is this safe always left open?" I pointed to a small decorative combination safe, lined with satin, sitting on the desk.

"Usually, yes."

"Why? What's the point of a safe if it's left open?"

"Mr. Whitwell rarely kept anything of value in this room."

"But Mrs. Whitwell said he kept a gun in the safe."

"No, his shotgun is locked in a cabinet in the stables."

"What about his token derringer? The one from his shooting club?"

"Oh, he kept that locked up in the safe in the basement."

"There's a safe downstairs?"

"Two in fact, for the silver. The everyday pieces are kept in the safe in the butler's pantry. In the basement is where we keep the large and seldom-used silver. That's the one Mr. Whitwell preferred. It's located in the wine cellar, which"—the butler smiled to himself and rolled on the balls of his feet—"itself is extremely secure."

"Can you show it to me?"

After three flights down the back stairs, we walked across the large empty laundry room, quiet on this Sunday, to a small door unobtrusively tucked away in a dark alcove in the corner.

"By the way," I said. "I didn't see any ashtrays in Mr. Whitwell's office. Did he smoke his cigars somewhere else?"

"No, Miss Davish, the master didn't smoke."

"But—"

"I know; there were cigars in his pocket when . . . He simply liked to give them away. He always kept a few on hand." Mr. Weeks sighed. "Who would do such a thing to such a man?"

I had no answer for him. "I wish I knew, Mr. Weeks. I wish I knew."

Mr. Weeks pulled out his keys and opened the door for me. I stepped by him into complete darkness. After the lingering damp that never left the laundry room, the coolness in this room raised bumps on my skin. The smell of dust mingled with a slight sweet scent of Madeira.

Where am I? I wondered. *The Whitwell family's wine cellar?* Mr. Weeks confirmed my suspicion when he turned up the lamp bracketed to the wall above the open door of an empty dumbwaiter. The dull light glinted off of hundreds of bottles, of every shape and color, poking out from their racks.

"Over here," the butler said, pointing to a large unmarked steel door mounted into the wall.

"Can you open it for me?"

Mr. Weeks looked dubious.

"What are you looking for: the gun?"

"I'm looking for something that might help me figure out who killed Mr. Whitwell," I said.

"As far as I know, there's nothing but silver in there right now. I don't think the master's been down here yet this Season."

"Then where is Mr. Whitwell's gun? Please, Mr. Weeks."

The butler shrugged his shoulders and then began spinning the lock. "Step back if you would, Miss Davish," he said as he cracked open the safe. It opened with a loud click and he pulled the large door back.

"What are those?" I asked, immediately stepping forward again. Surrounded by black cases containing the family's silver, three white envelopes, in stark contrast, nearly glowed in the dim lighting. There was no sign of the gun.

"I have no idea," Mr. Weeks said. "They weren't there yesterday morning when I came to get some grapefruit spoons for breakfast."

"May I?" I asked even as I reached for the envelopes.

Two were addressed, in typed print, to *Mr. Harland Whitwell, Fifth Avenue, New York, New York.* The third was handwritten and addressed to *My dear Jane.* Why would these letters be locked in the safe? What could they possibly say that warranted being locked away? And who put them there? Certainly not Mr. Whitwell; they weren't there until after his death. Mrs. Whitwell then?

I opened the first envelope and pulled out a three-page document, an insurance policy. I scanned the contents. Harland Whitwell had taken out insurance on his own life for $1 million less than three months ago. Mr. Whitwell's well-timed, foresighted measure protected his family from ruin. They might never again live at the standards they were accustomed to, but they certainly wouldn't have to face the poorhouse.

I opened the second typed letter. It held several documents: more insurance policies, but for the Aquidneck National Bank, including one signed by James H. Barney Jr. & Co., Fire Insurance agents, a firm located on Thames Street, here in Newport.

"How convenient," I said, a hint of suspicion forming in my mind. "I wonder . . ."

"What is convenient, Miss Davish?" the butler asked. I flinched at his question. I hadn't realized I'd spoken out loud and I certainly didn't want to voice my growing suspicion. Instead I ignored his question and held out the handwritten letter addressed to the lady of the house.

"Mr. Weeks, is this Mr. Whitwell's hand?" The butler nodded. "Could Mrs. Whitwell have put this in here?"

"Yes, of course. The mistress knew the combination, but I haven't known Mrs. Whitwell to ever visit the wine cellar, let alone go into the safe."

"Who else knows the combination?"

"Besides myself and Mrs. Whitwell, Mr. Whitwell and of course, Mr.—" He stopped, taking a sudden sharp inhale of breath.

"What is it, Mr. Weeks?"

"Master Nicholas. He was down here yesterday. I didn't know it at the time, but it must've been about when we found Mr. Whitwell, well . . . found him dead. Why would—?"

I cut him off. "How do you know when anyone comes in here? I'm assuming members of the Whitwell family have a key?"

The butler took a few steps and with the wave of two fingers beckoned me to follow him out of the wine cellar. When we were back in the laundry, he closed the door and pointed to the wall at what looked like a small push button. "No one knows of this, not even the family, except the master. It's our little secret," he said, whispering.

I nodded.

"Whenever anyone enters the wine cellar, this sends a signal to me in the butler's pantry. It's to prevent unauthorized pilfering of the wine. Too many people have keys for my taste."

"So you came down here yesterday morning to find Nick Whitwell in your wine cellar, after his father's death, not before?"

"Yes. He didn't give any explanation of course, though he was extremely jumpy and irritated to be found there by me. I thought it strange that he grabbed a bottle of whiskey on the way out, but I didn't give it another thought. Master Nicholas is well acquainted with the contents of the cellar, if you know what I mean."

I nodded. "Why was it strange that he took a bottle of whiskey with him then?"

"Because Master Nicholas never drinks whiskey, only wine."

Chapter 22

"How dare you! You're dismissed!" Jane Whitwell said as I stood poised to knock on the drawing-room door.

"What? No, wait. But ma'am?" a woman's voice pleaded.

"I want you out of my house this minute."

"But ma'am, where am I to go?"

"I don't know and frankly I don't care."

"But ma'am, other maids, all over the country, are striking and walking out. I only asked for an extra evening a month off," the girl said.

"And I only want my dear husband back," Mrs. Whitwell snapped.

"May I get a reference, ma'am?"

"A reference? A heartless, selfish girl like you? You don't deserve a reference."

"But I won't be able to get another position without it," the girl nearly sobbed.

"You should've thought of that before you came in here with your demands, the day after my dear husband was found murdered. Now get out of my sight!"

The door burst open and the housemaid I'd met earlier flew past me. She was sobbing, almost on the verge of hysteria. I stared at her hasty retreat sympathizing with her plight yet inwardly grateful that it was she and not I who had lost her position. I couldn't imagine what I would do if I were cast out without a reference as she had been. I turned toward the door, these ominous thoughts in my head, and hesitated. Should I wait to approach Mrs. Whitwell with my findings? I'd been speculating on the contents of the handwritten letter, with all that I'd learned from Mr. Whitwell's office and the contents of the safe—the unpaid bills, the life insurance policy, the fire insurance policy, the bank failures—and I didn't think she was prepared for my conclusion. *No, I'd be wise to wait,* I thought, and turned from the door.

"Whoever is hovering outside my door, come in or go away," she said. Although she had given me an option, her tone demanded I show myself. I stepped into the room.

"Mrs. Whitwell, ma'am?" I said.

She was staring out of the window, mindlessly brushing her hand through the large white silk tassel holding the drapery back. "What do you want?" she asked when she saw me.

I held up the envelopes. "I have something I think you should see," I said. "Weeks and I found these in the safe downstairs in the wine cellar." I handed her the insurance policies first. She took them but never took her eyes off of me.

"Life insurance and fire insurance on the bank," I said, explaining. "You'll want to have your husband's lawyer look at them straightaway." She nodded and set them in her lap. "And then there's this." I offered her the last envelope. She took the letter and looked at it. "As you can see, it's addressed to you, ma'am."

"What is it?"

I took a deep breath and voiced what I'd been thinking

since I found the letter. "I believe it's your husband's suicide note."

The moment I said it I felt the air leave the room. Mrs. Whitwell looked deliberately up at me, her countenance hardened into stone, her eyes menacing.

"How dare you!" Jane Whitwell said quietly. I wasn't fooled by her apparent calm. Her lips trembled as she pressed them together. She squeezed her hands in her lap until her knuckles turned white. This woman was about to explode. "Leave me at once."

"Yes, ma'am," I said, as eager to leave her as she was to see me go. "And I am sorry."

"I don't need your pity, secretary. Now go! And don't think I won't tell Charlotte of your impertinence," she said. She fumbled with the letter, her hands shaking, dropping it to the floor. She snatched up and was ripping and tearing at the letter, clumsily trying to open it, before I was barely out of the room.

I was sorry. Sorry to be witness to her pathetic attempt to read the last words her husband would ever write. Sorry to be the bearer of such hurtful news. Sorry anyone should have to feel such desperation and sorrow. But it wasn't my fault. I knew she wouldn't take well to my presumption, but I hadn't expected her threat. Would she demand my dismissal as she had the maid's? Would Mrs. Mayhew concede to her friend's demand? What would Sir Arthur think? Would he scorn me simply on one woman's angry impulse? Why hadn't I simply waited to give her the letter? Even as I asked myself this, I knew it wouldn't have mattered. Jane Whitwell, in her grief and denial, would've lashed out at me at any time. What I'd delivered was very unwelcome news.

"Oh, Harland!" Jane Whitwell sobbed. I hadn't made it halfway to the back stairs when I heard her cry.

I was right then, I thought. Harland Whitwell had committed suicide. Nick must've tried to conceal the fact by locking up the suicide note and the insurance policies he'd found left in plain sight. Why else would Nick have been upset by Mr. Weeks seeing him in the wine cellar? Had Nick also upset the office and placed Lester Sibley's pamphlet in his father's hand? Or had the elder Whitwell planned the whole thing in order to spare himself the shame and humiliation of bankruptcy while at the same time ridding Newport of the labor man? But where was the gun? Had Nick carried that away too? And how much did Mrs. Whitwell really know? Much to my chagrin, I was no longer in a position to find out. I had discovered the truth behind Harland Whitwell's death, but I despised loose ends.

"Davish!" Mrs. Whitwell shrieked a moment later. I cringed but turned to face whatever wrath the grieving woman would mete out.

"Ma'am?" I said, ducking my head as I cautiously opened the door. No vase smashed the wall next to me, so I stepped in.

"How did you know?" She was standing, staring out the window, the letter loosely held in her hand. I followed her gaze. Two gray pigeons sat perched on a marble statue of Aphrodite in the garden preening each other. I had to look away and was relieved Mrs. Whitwell kept her back to me. I wasn't prepared to face the anguish and disillusionment in her eyes.

"It was more like a guess, ma'am," I said honestly. "I was having difficulty determining why anyone, besides your son perhaps, would want to kill your husband." I expected her to twist around and confront me at the mention of Nick, but she never moved.

"And?" she said.

"And when I learned that your husband was on the verge of bankruptcy, even your son had no motive. You should take comfort, ma'am, in the fact that your husband was well thought of by everyone." *With the exception of Lester Sibley,* a thought I kept to myself.

"Thank you," she said in an emotionless monotone. "Please continue."

"And then I discovered the letter and the insurance policies, and the fact that your son had hidden them. It all suggested that Mr. Whitwell may have taken his own life. Unfortunately, I read about such things happening in the paper every day."

Jane Whitwell finally turned to look at me. "But why implicate that labor man?"

"One reason is that life insurance doesn't pay survivors of someone who has committed suicide," I said.

"How would you know?"

"I read the policy, ma'am. The one I believe your son left in the safe for you to find along with the note. As to why Lester Sibley was implicated?" I said, answering her previous question. "You'll have to ask your son."

"You think Nick orchestrated this whole thing? That he discovered his father's body and this note . . ." She glanced at the letter in her hand and hesitated before continuing. "And made it look like someone had ambushed Harland? Nick threw the papers about, overturned the books, put the pamphlet in Harland's dead hand?"

"Or Mr. Whitwell did it himself and asked Nick to help." I thought this more likely unless Nick, whose behavior suggested otherwise, knew about his family's impending financial crisis. "The gun is still missing."

She nodded, sighing. "Yes, I think you're right. And to think I suspected Nick," she said under her breath. Her head shot up as if in surprise. Had she not meant to say it out loud? "You will ignore that last comment, Miss Davish," she said.

"Of course, ma'am," I said. She stared at me for several moments. I stood as still as possible, knowing from experience, she was wondering if she could trust me. I had my answer when she continued.

"I saw him come out of his father's office right before . . . So of course I thought . . . They've been fighting so much lately."

"Yes, ma'am," I said.

"And then I was so relieved to know that that Sibley man was the obvious culprit. But then the police said he couldn't have done it. I was so worried about Nick. I thought Sibley had to have done it. It didn't make sense." She looked down at the letter dangling in her hand for the third time. "And now it does, doesn't it, Miss Davish?"

"Yes, ma'am, it does," I said.

She continued without looking at me. "Harland was a good man, Miss Davish, a family man. Unlike others I won't name, I've never had reason to suspect him of straying. He loved me and the children very much. Yes, he worked hard, very hard, but always because he was concerned for my and our children's welfare. He would've done anything to make sure we were taken care of, even . . ." Her voice trailed away for a moment. We left the words *given his life* unsaid between us. "Harland never discussed business with me, thank goodness, but a wife has a way of knowing when things aren't going well. He's been so tense, so short with everyone, especially Nick, I feared for him when the bank workers threatened to strike. And then the bank burned!"

She put a handkerchief to her mouth, willing herself not to cry. I didn't have the heart to tell her that I thought her husband might have been involved with the bank fire, hoping to recoup his losses by collecting the insurance. But something must've gone wrong. His bank barely burned. It might have been what drove him to suicide.

"But this," Jane Whitwell said, lifting the suicide note up for the first time. "I never imagined any of this."

"No, ma'am. No one ever could."

We stood in strained silence for several moments. What else was left to say? I'd discovered the truth of Harland Whitwell's death. When my second report to Mrs. Mayhew was done, so too were my investigative duties. It would be a relief, if only I could tactfully leave Jane Whitwell to her grief.

"Can I get Mrs. Johnville or Mr. Weeks for you, ma'am?" I asked.

She nodded, tears in her eyes. "Ask Johnville to send up some iced tea."

"Yes, ma'am," I said, and turned to leave.

"Davish," she said, again calling me back.

"Ma'am?"

"You can be certain I will hold you to your promise," she said, holding up the letter and waving it slightly. "Except for Charlotte, who already knows all my secrets, you are not to tell a soul about the truth of Mr. Whitwell's . . . death." I envisioned more uncomfortable teas at Moffat Cottage while I artfully dodged every question Miss Lucy plied me with. "I don't have to tell you what will happen if you disappoint me."

"Yes, Mrs. Whitwell," I said, trying to keep the exasperation from my voice. When had my livelihood suddenly dangled from a tenuous string? I had another secret of Mrs. Whitwell's to keep and I didn't even work for her.

CHAPTER 23

Upon returning to Rose Mont, I saw Mrs. Crankshaw and Lester Sibley having a conversation in the driveway near the house. From Mrs. Crankshaw's stern expression and crossed arms, she wasn't "taking well" to what Lester Sibley was saying. Mrs. Crankshaw spied me and gestured to Sibley to stop talking. I smiled as I passed.

"Miss Davish," Lester Sibley said to me, tipping his new brown derby.

"Mr. Sibley," I said.

"Hurry up or you'll be late for dinner," Mrs. Crankshaw said to me. I knew better than to suggest the same for her. I'd headed around the corner to the servants' entrance when Mrs. Crankshaw said, "That was close, Lester. I told you you should never have come here. I think we can trust the girl to be discreet, at least that's what they all say about her, but if anyone else sees you . . ."

Upon hearing Mrs. Crankshaw's first kind words about me, I inwardly promised not to disappoint her. I wouldn't tell anyone about seeing her with Lester Sibley. But why was she

talking to the labor man? She was the first one to halt any
union or strike talk, idle or otherwise.

"Now get out of here," Mrs. Crankshaw said to Sibley.

"But Thelma," he said.

"Go! Oh, no!"

I peeked around the corner at the simultaneous sounds of
Mrs. Crankshaw's exclamation and the crunching of a horse
cantering up the gravel drive. Lester Sibley had hesitated too
long. Mr. Gideon Mayhew's trap was pulling up to the house.
The housekeeper spun away from Sibley and darted past me
into the house, but I knew, as Mrs. Crankshaw did, that Mr.
Mayhew had seen her with the labor union man.

"What the devil?" Gideon Mayhew said as he leaped from
his carriage and stood watching, as Lester Sibley ran down the
drive and disappeared on the other side of the wall. "Close the
gate, Elmer!" Mr. Mayhew snapped. "By God, if that man ever
comes onto my property again . . ." Without finishing his threat,
the master of the house bounded up his stairs, fist clenched.

"Yes, sir," the coachman said, not knowing if he'd been
heard. "Right away, Mr. Mayhew."

As I came into the Servants' Hall to challenge Mrs. Crankshaw about Lester Sibley, a bell was clanging over and over, Mr.
Mayhew making his fury known. Mrs. Crankshaw frowned as
she stared at the bell swinging violently from side to side. Mr.
Davies entered the room, causing everyone already seated at
the table for dinner to stand.

"The master would like a word, Mrs. Crankshaw," he said
without preamble. "Immediately." For the first time since I'd
known her she held her tongue and merely nodded.

"I've already brought up your dinner," Britta said to me.

"Thank you, Britta."

As I turned to leave, Mr. Davies stopped me with a clear-
ing of his throat. "Ah, Miss Davish, that," the butler said, pointing to the insistent bell, "is Mrs. Mayhew wanting to see you."

I sighed. I thought the bell had been Mr. Mayhew ringing for Mrs. Crankshaw. Could Mrs. Mayhew have heard from Mrs. Whitwell already in the short time it took me to walk from Glen Park to Rose Mont? Or had she simply assumed I'd be at dinner and wanted an immediate update? Either way, relief flooded through me knowing I was to face Mrs. Mayhew and not her husband.

I followed Mrs. Crankshaw out of the Servants' Hall, staring at her back, as stiff as her starched navy blue collar, as we walked.

"But the master wants to see you first," Davies said. I froze. *Me? Mr. Mayhew wanted to see me?* Mrs. Crankshaw swirled around to gape at me. I'd never seen her so pale. Did she see the same look on my face?

"Why?" I wondered out loud.

"I'm not one to question the master, Miss Davish. I'll send a maid up to inform Mrs. Mayhew you will be delayed. Now out with you both."

I followed Mrs. Crankshaw out of the room, her shoulders sagging, her head bowed. I should've felt anxious for her, but all I could do was focus on me. Why would Mr. Mayhew want to see me? Had Mrs. Whitwell changed her mind and demanded my dismissal? If so, why wasn't it Mrs. Mayhew I was seeing? Or could this have something to do with the truth I'd learned about Harland Whitwell, both his financial ruin and his suicide? Gideon Mayhew might wish to extract a promise of secrecy from me as well. But what about Lester Sibley's visit? Could it be a coincidence that Mrs. Crankshaw and I were both to be given an audience with the master of the house, an honor I would gladly do without?

"Why was Lester Sibley here, Mrs. Crankshaw?" I whispered as we climbed the stairs, her in front and me behind.

"I don't take kindly to girls who don't mind their own business," was her tart reply. I watched her back stiffen again and resigned to walking into Mr. Mayhew's study uninformed. I grew strength from the knowledge that I'd done nothing wrong. Nothing but what I had been told to do. *Surely I won't be dismissed for doing my job?*

"Come in," Gideon Mayhew said when Mrs. Crankshaw tapped lightly on the door.

"Sir, you asked to see us?" she said, her voice level and calm.

He was writing in a ledger and didn't look as we came in. "Close the door," he said. Being the closest, I obliged. As soon as the door was closed, he slammed the ledger shut and stood up from behind his desk, glaring at me. "What were you doing speaking to that miscreant in my own driveway?" he demanded. I didn't know what to say. I hadn't spoken to Sibley beyond responding to his greeting, but I didn't dare contradict the man standing in front of me.

Mrs. Crankshaw saved me from the dilemma. "Sir, if I may beg your pardon, but Miss Davish was merely returning to the house as Mr. Sibley was leaving. I alone had a conversation with the vile man."

Mayhew glanced at me, Mrs. Crankshaw's description of Lester Sibley momentarily placating his anger. "Is this true, Miss Davish?"

"Yes, sir, we only exchanged greetings as I passed Mrs. Crankshaw and Mr. Sibley."

He nodded, appearing appeased. I began breathing again.

"What about you, Mrs. Crankshaw? Why did you speak to him?"

"The man's a pest, sir. On more than one occasion I've caught him preaching to the staff about better wages, shorter hours, about going on strike to get what we deserve. Frankly, sir, he makes honest workers unhappy with their work."

"Yes. That's it, isn't it? The servants of Rose Mont are a select few and should covet their positions, not complain. And what does Sibley believe you deserve? You already get higher wages and more privileges than any other house in Newport provides. What more could you want?"

We both understood this was a rhetorical question and stayed silent.

"He's dangerous, this man. Like you said, Mrs. Crankshaw, he enjoys stirring up trouble. That's why he must never step foot on my property again. I forbid you or any of the staff to converse with this man again."

"Yes, sir," the housekeeper and I said in unison. "Of course, sir," Mrs. Crankshaw added.

"Good, now answer my question." I could see Mrs. Crankshaw's shoulders tighten. "Why were you speaking to that man almost at my front door?"

"He'd come to the front door, to make trouble, sir," she said. "I asked him to step down into the drive."

"But then why not leave it at that? Why not simply slam the door in his face?" Gideon Mayhew was no fool. He knew Mrs. Crankshaw wasn't telling him everything.

"I wanted to tell him once and for all, we were not interested in his brand of talk," she said.

"Who's been listening to him?"

"Sir?" Mrs. Crankshaw said. "I don't know what you mean."

"If you were so adamant to talk to the man that you stepped down with him into the drive, someone in this household must be taking the man seriously. Whom are you protecting, Mrs. Crankshaw?"

"James, sir, your first footman," she said to my astonishment and without hesitation. I expected her to deny that anyone was taking Sibley seriously. Instead she offered up James like a roast goose on a platter. Did Mrs. Crankshaw know more about James's feelings than I did? Did it matter? I'd heard James speak of Lester Sibley, but was he considering striking in

earnest? I hoped not. I'd witnessed firsthand at the Whitwells'
how devastating that could be. Either way, I knew Mrs. Crankshaw was withholding something from Mr. Mayhew. From
what I'd overheard from their conversation, Mrs. Crankshaw
wasn't simply telling a stranger he was unwelcome. She knew
Mr. Sibley. She'd called him Lester and he had called her
Thelma! I hadn't even known Mrs. Crankshaw's Christian
name.

"You may be dismissed," Mr. Mayhew said. "Please send
the footman up to me, Mrs. Crankshaw. I'd like to speak with
him myself."

"Right, sir, of course," she said as we both gratefully left
the room.

"That was close," she muttered under her breath.

"Mrs. Crankshaw," I started, wanting to thank her for defending me, to ask her about James, but she stopped me.

"Not another word! Go attend Mrs. Mayhew. She's been
waiting all this time."

I nodded. I wouldn't get any more out of Mrs. Crankshaw
tonight, or ever.

"Suicide!" Charlotte Mayhew gasped, putting a hand over
her mouth. I'd given her a brief account of all I'd learned
today, culminating with finding Harland Whitwell's suicide
letter. "Are you sure?"

"Yes, Mrs. Mayhew. It's undeniable. I beg your pardon,
ma'am, but Mrs. Whitwell was most adamant that this information remain a secret. No one but Jane, you, and I are to ever
know."

My employer bit her lip while nodding her head vigorously. "Of course, of course, and yet . . . ," she said. "Nick
knows too, doesn't he?"

"Yes, we assume he does, though Mrs. Whitwell hasn't spoken to him since his father's death. He's been elusive."

"Rightfully so. For a while there, rumors were rampant he killed his father." How rumors could be considered rampant in little over twenty-four hours I didn't know. "But now we'll simply have to put a stop to all that, shouldn't we?"

"If his suicide is to remain secret, how are you going to stop the rumors?"

Charlotte Mayhew giggled. "Oh, Miss Davish, you are refreshingly naïve." I bristled at the idea but kept any emotion from appearing on my face. Mrs. Mayhew thought she was giving me a compliment. "I'll simply spread the word that I know the truth but won't say what it is. Everyone will stop speculating about Nick and start gossiping about what I know. If that doesn't get Mrs. Astor to call, I don't know what will." She clapped her hands and giggled.

This time I couldn't keep the shock from my face. "You actually start rumors? Why?"

She laughed at me again. "Why else do you think I agreed to let you snoop around like this?"

"Yes, ma'am," was all I could think to say. In her own way, Mrs. Mayhew was being both noble and selfish, deflecting the unwanted attention to where it was wanted. But what if Mrs. Astor did call, expecting to be told what happened to Harland Whitwell? What then? Would Mrs. Mayhew disregard her friend's request to keep her husband's suicide secret? Would Mrs. Mayhew put her social standing before her friendship with Jane Whitwell? I didn't want to know.

And I'd helped her do this, I thought.

I hadn't expected to like every task I was required to do. And I've never expected to understand the reason. I honored my promises. I did my job. She wanted the truth and I uncovered it for her. I should have felt proud if I'd succeeded, in my first position as a social secretary, in aiding in my mistress's advance in that society. Her rise would reflect well on me and everyone in Mrs. Mayhew's employ. I even suspected that Jane

Whitwell, who might suffer for her friend's aspirations, if given the same choice would make the same decision. If her own friend wouldn't fault her, why did I feel tainted and disappointed by Mrs. Mayhew's ambition?

Stay professional. This has nothing to do with you, I reassured myself.

"I'll have my full typewritten report for you in the morning," I said.

"Good, thank you. You may go." I nodded, grateful to take my leave. "Oh, and Davish," Mrs. Mayhew said as I stood in the doorway.

"Yes, ma'am?"

"The ball is tomorrow night. I'll be relying on you."

"Of course, ma'am," I said. I turned and nearly bumped into the white satin waistcoat of Mr. Mayhew standing in the doorway. "Excuse me," I said, without looking the man in the eye.

"Watch where you're going!" he barked at me. "Charlotte, I've fired the housekeeper." This he said to his wife the moment he pushed past me into the room. Standing only a few steps outside in the hall, I heard everything.

"What?!" his wife cried. Why had he fired Mrs. Crankshaw? I thought he had believed her story about Lester Sibley. Obviously he hadn't.

"And one of the footmen, James, I think his name is."

"Gideon, tell me you're joking."

"Of course I'm not joking. Have you ever known me to joke?"

"No, you're right. You're definitely not known for your sense of humor." I wasn't surprised to hear this. Had I ever even seen the man smile? "Then what's the meaning of this, you firing Mrs. Crankshaw and the footman?"

"They're involved with that Sibley man in some way."

"But the ball is tomorrow night, Gideon. Tomorrow night!

And I'm expecting the Astors to be there. What are we going to do?"

"I don't care. I won't have any of my servants cavorting with a well-known troublemaker like Sibley."

"But—"

"It's not up for discussion and we will not speak of it again."

"But the ball, Gideon! How am I to throw the event of the year without a housekeeper and with one less footman? If anything, I need extra help."

"Do whatever you need to do, Charlotte. I only came here to inform you of the situation. Good night."

I flew down the hallway, frantically grabbing at locked doors as I went. If Gideon Mayhew caught me eavesdropping in the hallway, I'd be summarily dismissed, like Mrs. Crankshaw, like James. I'd be thrown out without a reference. I'd be homeless. Would Sir Arthur take me back? I'd hope so, but I didn't want to find out. I twisted the knob of yet another door as I strained to look over my shoulder, watching for signs of Mr. Mayhew. I saw the black, highly polished tip of Mr. Mayhew's shoe touch the brass threshold of the door. *Click!* The latch released and I threw myself through the open crack of the door. I pushed the door closed and pressed my back against it, my ear nearly touching the painted oak door. And I listened. His footsteps grew louder as he approached my hiding place. Had he seen me? I held my breath as he walked up to the door and then passed by. I stayed there, pressed against the door of the unused guest room, panting with fear and relief, long after the sound of his steps receded into silence. I lifted my hand, noticing the stinging for the first time. Scrapes and partial imprints of flowers burned red in the palm of my hand. Rose Mont's elaborately embossed brass doorknobs weren't meant to be wrenched and twisted that hard. I let my breathing return to normal before opening the door and returning to the hall. I swiftly made my way to the sanctity of my sitting room.

I dropped into the chair facing my typewriter and let out a long sigh of relief.

That was too close, I thought, vowing to never eavesdrop again. I'd been lucky this time. Mrs. Crankshaw and James hadn't been. I hadn't been fond of Mrs. Crankshaw, but I was horrified that she'd been dismissed for merely having a conversation with Lester Sibley. Or was there more to her relationship with the labor man than I knew? Had her vehement rejection of the striking and the labor movement in general been a ruse? And what about James? Had he been involved with planning a strike or had he been a victim of Crankshaw's attempt to keep her position? Or had Mr. Mayhew simply passed judgment on them both, regardless of the truth, because he could.

From now on, I thought, as I began to type up Mrs. Mayhew's report, I would avoid Lester Sibley, avoid Gideon Mayhew, say no more and do no more than was necessary, and count the days until this Season in Newport was over.

CHAPTER 24

Ding, ding, ding, ding!

I returned from an early morning hike around Almy Pond, refreshed and satisfied to have gotten both an hour of fresh air and two more new specimens for my plant collection, American beachgrass and high-tide bush, before breakfast. I was confident, with the Whitwell business behind me, that I could tackle any task Mrs. Mayhew might ask of me today. Yet the moment I stepped back in the house from my hike I was overwhelmed by the frenzy of people skittering this way and that, the clattering of plates, pots, and pans, the overlapping of shouting voices, and the insistent ring of bells. And every person I passed gawked at me.

Why are they looking at me like that?

"Will someone go see what that's all about, *s'il vous plaît?*" Monsieur Valbois, the cook, shouted. "How am I expected to cook lobster soufflé for a hundred people if those blasted bells keep ringing?"

"Hattie! You're still here," Sena said when I stepped into

the kitchen. She stopped kneading the dough on the slab in front of her. Everyone stopped, for a brief moment, to look at me. What was going on?

"Of course I'm still here," I said. "Why would you think otherwise?"

"Well . . . ," Sena said, shrugging, "since you went up with Mrs. Crankshaw last night and no one had seen you since, we all thought . . . well . . . ?"

"Thought what?" I asked.

"That you too had been fired last night."

"No, no," I said, realizing why everyone had regarded me as if a ghost walked among them. "No, I was fortunate."

She nodded. "We worried when Ethel came down with your untouched breakfast tray," Sena said.

"I hadn't realized I'd missed breakfast." No wonder I was hungry, I thought.

"Here." Sena handed me a freshly baked roll from a basket on the table.

"Who's Ethel, by the way?" I said, relishing the hot bread. "Where's Britta?"

"Britta didn't come down for breakfast," Sena said, putting her hand to the side of her mouth as if to prevent others from hearing. "But Ethel, she's one of the upstairs chambermaids, said she passed Britta on the back stairs. Her eyes were red and puffy, as if she'd been crying. Now what do you think she's upset for?"

Ding, ding, ding, ding! the bell chimed again.

"Je vous en prie," Valbois pleaded. "Will someone please go see what they want in the dining room?"

"I'll go," I said, taking the chance to escape having to explain the cause of Britta's tears. After hearing them together, I had little doubt deep affection existed between James and Britta that no one else knew about.

"Merci, mademoiselle," the cook said, immediately returning to his soufflés.

I found my way to the dining room by following an endless line of footmen delivering tray after tray of silver, plates, and glasses.

Oh my goodness! I thought as I nearly shielded my eyes from the brilliance. By far the gaudiest room I'd seen so far, the dining room was awash in light. I could almost see myself in the highly polished parquet wood floor as sunlight, from the windows that stretched up to the ceiling, bounced off the high pink marble walls, the solid bronze dining chairs, the tall gilded mirrors hung above the fireplaces, the silver and glass on the sideboard, and the myriad of gilded bronze capitals. At night, the reflection from three-foot silver candelabra on the dining table would easily light the enormous room. Yet in all the shining opulence I was instantly drawn to the dining-room table, a grand oak table that easily sat eighteen, devoid of anything but an enormous mound of white linen, ripped or cut into hundreds, maybe thousands, of pieces. Bits of lace and thread had flown about when the linen was cut and were scattered across the table and floor. I bent down and picked up a piece that had fallen near the doorway. Of the family crest only a bit of orange shield with part of the ram's head was left.

Who would do such a thing? I wondered as yet another footman shuffled past me into the room.

"Davish! Thank God!" Mrs. Mayhew said when she saw me. She pointed to the table. "What am I to do?"

"Ma'am?"

She stomped over to the table and picked up a few pieces of linen, letting them flutter back into the pile. "It's all here, every last piece of linen in the house: the bed sheets, tablecloths, doilies, napkins, handkerchiefs, everything. Do you realize what this means? We have a ball tonight and have no table linens!"

"What happened?" I asked. Yet I knew before Mrs. May-hew gave me the answer—Mrs. Crankshaw. As housekeeper, she was in charge of the linens of the house. In her anger over being dismissed, she must've spent a good portion of the night ripping, tearing, and cutting the linen, leaving it here for all to see.

"Mrs. Crankshaw, of course," Mrs. Mayhew said. "But what are we going to do?" By now I'd grown accustomed to Mrs. Mayhew's reliance on me in matters in which I had little or no experience, so why not add housekeeping to my ré-sumé?

"Could you buy more linen?" I suggested.

"You think I haven't thought of that, Davish? You think I wouldn't have already done that if enough linen could be bought in Newport?" *I'm only trying to help,* I thought. "And before you say it, we don't have time to have it sent from New York or Boston." I didn't contradict her, but of course I knew it wouldn't arrive in time from New York.

"Dix, neuf, huit . . ." I began counting backward in French under my breath, calming my nerves and my mind, and had an idea. "What about borrowing table linens from Mrs. Whitwell?"

Mrs. Mayhew opened her mouth to voice an objection but stopped herself.

"She is in mourning, after all," Mrs. Mayhew said. "I know she has some good linen without her crest on it and she won't be able to use her good linen for months. And she wouldn't dare tell anyone, knowing what I know. Yes, Davish, it just may work."

I immediately regretted making the suggestion. I'd thought they were friends; so why did I feel party to blackmail? Social climbing trumped friendship again. I'd never understand it, so I nodded and said without emotion, "I'll tell Mr. Davies."

"Good," Mrs. Mayhew said, watching the footmen at their tasks. "And then come right back. I've got work for you to do."

★   ★   ★

"This came for you, Miss Davish," Mr. Davies said, handing me a letter, written in Miss Lizzie's hand, as we all sat down to eat. With Mrs. Mayhew short staffed, I'd worked side by side with the others all day: stuffing hundreds of yellow zinnias into a wire mesh to create a wall of blossoms; folding hundreds of linens Mrs. Whitwell graciously provided; even helping to push back the carpets in the ballroom. Thus I'd forgone having tea by myself in my sitting room. And with Mrs. Crankshaw gone no one, not even Davies, protested. Not having my letter opener, I carefully tore the envelope by hand.

Expect a surprise! But don't tell Lucy I told you.

That was it. That's all it said. Why not tell me more? And why not tell Miss Lucy? Frustrated, I tossed the note onto the table and took a long sip of my coffee. The elderly Miss Shaw might have good intentions, but I hate surprises. Life is unpredictable enough without having others purposely spring the unexpected upon you. I was exhausted, my back hurt in places I'd never felt before, and now all I could do was worry about Miss Lizzie's "surprise." I picked the note up and read it again.

What could it possibly be? I wondered. Thankfully, I didn't have much time to wonder further. I was to present myself when tea was over. The clock on the mantel chimed five and I took one last gulp of coffee before heading back to work. What Mrs. Mayhew wanted of me now I could only guess. *I just hope it can be done sitting down,* I thought, putting my hand to my aching back. Issacson was putting the last flourishes to the lady's hair with diamond-and-pearl-encrusted gold hairpins when I arrived.

"You wanted to see me, ma'am?" I said.

Mrs. Mayhew swiveled around in her chair, brandishing a card in her hand, almost hitting Issacson in the nose. "It came, Davish! It came!" She jumped out of her chair with more vigor than I would have thought possible, waving the card in the air. Was she dancing a jig?

"Ma'am?" I said, trying not to laugh. She thrust the card in my face, so close I could barely read the print, *Mrs. Astor, Newport.*

"She's coming to the ball. I'm in, Davish. I'm in!"

"Congratulations, ma'am."

"Thank you," she said, sitting back down to let Issacson fix the hair that had loosened during her enthusiastic display. "And thank you for your help. You've done wonders. I knew I could rely on you!"

"Thank you, ma'am," I said as Miss Issacson raised her eyebrows in question. Women usually told their lady's maids everything. Had Mrs. Mayhew kept Jane Whitwell's secret after all? I hoped so.

"I would like to reward you. I want you in the hall tonight. You can hand out the envelopes to the gentlemen and issue all the ladies their dance cards."

"Ma'am?" I said, wishing after such a physically exhaustive day to be rewarded by a quiet evening alone in my room, not several more hours on my feet.

"Aren't you glad, Davish?" she said, pouting. I'd obviously not kept my disappointment from showing on my face. "I'm breaking protocol for you. I normally have the first footman do it. You will get to see all the excitement. You'll get to see all the beautiful gowns everyone will be wearing. You'll get to see my moment of triumph."

"Thank you, ma'am. That's kind of you."

Appeased, she smiled. "And Davish, if you don't have something appropriate to wear, I'll have Mr. Morris at the House of Redfern bring a few dresses over that you can choose from."

House of Redfern? I'd only dreamt of wearing such a dress.

My exhaustion evaporated instantly at the idea. "Thank you, ma'am. That's very generous of you. Thank you so much."

"I'll call them, shall I?" Miss Issacson offered, knowing of Mrs. Mayhew's occasional lapses in memory. I nodded gratefully to the lady's maid.

"Can't have you looking anything but your best when Mrs. Astor appears, now can we?" Mrs. Mayhew said, smiling and obviously pleased with herself. I smiled right back.

CHAPTER 25

We made a curious line as guests arrived. Mr. Davies opened the door, Mr. and Mrs. Mayhew, in their finest, greeted their guests, and I, stationed not far away, issued the necessities of the ball: to each gentleman the envelope containing the name of the lady he would escort to dinner and to each lady her monogrammed dance case and card. Mrs. Mayhew had been right. I delighted in seeing the ladies' finery I only knew from magazines. I handed dance cards to women in China silk dresses of every color and pattern adorned with pearls, beads, ecru lace, ribbons, silk flowers, and the occasional extravagantly large puffed sleeves. And all were wearing jewels: emeralds, rubies, sapphires, and diamonds that glittered under the glow of the electric chandelier, draped around their necks, dangling from their ears, encircling their fingers, and protruding from their hair. I relished being part of it, wearing my own Redfern silk dress of delicate fawn strewn with tiny rosebuds. I felt confident and presentable, and with soft, smooth silk against my skin I'd never been so comfortable in a dress.

Good thing too! I thought. For people I'd only read about in newspapers took a card or envelope from my hand. People with names such as Vanderbilt, Belmont, Bennett, Oelrichs, as well as the Grand Duke Alexis of Russia and French author Paul Bourget attended Mrs. Mayhew's ball. Even Mrs. Caroline Astor, nearly dripping with diamonds from head to waist and whose presence marked a new societal height for Mrs. Mayhew, acknowledged me with a slight tip of her head.

When I wasn't handing a card or envelope to some grand lady or duke, I stole glances into the ballroom, tapped my foot to the music, and watched the dancing. It reminded me of last Christmas when Walter and I danced at the Christmas entertainment in Galena.

Ah, Walter, I thought. *I wonder where you are now?*

I was snapped out of my reverie by the gasps of several ladies standing nearby. I followed their gaze and laid my eyes on Nicholas Whitwell. He was supposed to be in mourning. He shouldn't be here. The whispers of gossiping ladies surrounded me.

"What is he doing here?"

"Shouldn't he be home with his mother and sister?"

"I heard he hasn't stepped a foot in Glen Park since the murder."

"At least Eugenie has some sense of propriety. She's been properly closeted in her room for days."

"I've never known someone to be so blatantly defiant of good manners."

"He's young and carefree. How can we expect him to seclude himself?"

"At least he's wearing the proper mourning clothes."

Mr. Mayhew frowned but shook his hand. Mrs. Mayhew avoided acknowledging the young man and searched the room for someone or something to rescue her from committing a faux pas. Her rescuer came in the form of Cora, her daughter and Nicholas Whitwell's fiancée.

"Nick!" Cora said, taking his arm and pulling him to the side. They stood only a few feet away. "You shouldn't be here."

"You too, Cora?" Nick said, slightly slurring his words. A strong aroma of fruity liquor emanated from the young man. "My mother may insist on deep mourning, but I'm not going to miss the ball of the summer because my father's dead."

"You've been drinking, Nick," Cora said.

"Hey now, where's your dance card? I want a waltz."

"I don't have one."

Nick's eyes suddenly darted toward me. He sneered as if I were the source of his problems. "You! You little bitch! Why didn't you give Cora her card?" he demanded. Except for the loud inhalation of gasps around me, the room went quiet. I was stunned. I'd never been spoken to like that before.

"Nick!" Cora cried.

Throwing off Cora's hold, he stumbled toward me, his eyes bloodshot and spittle collecting in the corner of his mouth. I stepped back, recoiling from him, as Cora grasped his arm. He didn't stop. Instead, as she clung to his arm he pulled her toward me, her ballroom slippers sliding along the polished marble floor.

"Stop! It's not her fault, Nick. Stop!" Several men, mostly in navy dress uniforms, rushed to Cora's aid, restraining her fiancé's advance. One even mumbled an apology to me.

"You fool! I'm not dancing, out of respect for you and your family, Nick. Now I think you should go."

"Go? I just got here," he said, shoving his way out of the circle of men that had surrounded him. "I want to dance." Cora followed on his heels and the two disappeared into the crowd. I was catching my breath, not knowing what I felt more of, humiliation or indignation, when Miss Lizzie and Miss Lucy arrived, with their surprise.

Oh, no, not now! I thought.

"And Gideon, dear," I heard Miss Lizzie say, "may I present

Mrs. Julia Grice of St. Louis, who is staying with us for the summer." I handed yet another woman her dance card before turning to look at the newest arrivals. Mrs. Grice was beaming. "And may I present her son," Miss Lizzie said, "Dr. Walter Grice, who is visiting us for a short while from Eureka Springs, Arkansas."

Walter!

My heart soared. He was here, in Newport, and looking more handsome than any other man I'd ever laid eyes on. I wanted to drop the tray of dance cards and envelopes and throw myself into his arms. And then my heart sank. With his mother's arm in his, Walter no longer looked like the gentleman doctor from a small town in Arkansas. Here was a true gentleman, a man who looked comfortable among the richest of Newport, a man who belonged among the best of Mrs. Mayhew's guests, not one who should be wasting his time with the girl handing out dance cards, no matter how fashionable her dress. I suddenly dreaded the impending meeting. Although they hadn't seen me yet, the party was only a few yards away. I resisted every urge in my body to run.

"Davish?" Miss Lucy said, spying me. She had walked away from the group and had been peeking into the ballroom. "What on earth are you doing passing out dance cards? Charlotte said you would be joining the party, not holding the tray. I know she lost her housekeeper, but my word! That's like preparing a ten-course dinner only to eat nothing of it but the crumbs others brushed to the floor. Did I tell you we're losing our butler? He's gone and joined the navy!" I barely listened to Miss Lucy as I watched Walter across the room. He was chatting with Gideon Mayhew.

At the sound of my name Walter stopped listening to his host and looked around. He must not have seen me, for he went right back to his conversation. But Miss Lizzie saw whom her sister was talking to.

"Hattie, dear!" Miss Lizzie said, coming toward me with outstretched arms. More than a few guests gaped at us when she kissed my cheek. She pointed down the hall. "Are you surprised?"

"Yes, Miss Lizzie," I said, handing a dance case and card to a debutante dressed in yellow and pink, with wide, unblinking eyes. She timidly took the card from my hand and then quickly stepped away. "I'm . . . stunned. Does Dr. Grice know I'm here?"

"No," Miss Lizzie said gleefully, "and I can't wait to see the look on his face when he does! And you're in such a lovely dress too!"

What will he think, seeing me like this? Seeing me for the servant I am? I wondered. I'd told him once that we had no future together, but he'd made me believe otherwise. *Will I now have to face reality? Will he?* Unlike Miss Lizzie, I'd give anything not to see the look on his face when he saw me. I feared that my doubts would be reflected in his eyes. I didn't have to guess what Mrs. Grice's countenance would hold.

"Walter, dear," Miss Lizzie called. "There's someone here whom I'd like you to see."

Walter nodded, excused himself from the Mayhews, and with his mother on his arm turned toward me. "Hattie?" he said. Surprise, delight and confusion all flashed across his face. "I mean, Miss Davish. I didn't know you would be in Newport. You look . . . lovely." His eyes sparkled and he was beaming at me. I could tell he wanted to reach out and take my hand, but his mother's arm restrained him. Maybe it could work between us after all, I thought. I smiled back. "What brings you here?"

Before I could answer, Mrs. Grice interrupted. "She works for the Mayhews, Walter. What other reason would bring a servant girl to Newport?"

"Mother, she's not—" Walter said.

"I'd like to see the dancing, Walter," his mother said, stopping Walter from defending me. "Please escort me to the ballroom."

"Julia," Miss Lucy chided under her breath. "I know from Lady Phillippa that Davish came to Newport with Sir Arthur Windom-Greene and is Mrs. Mayhew's social secretary, not a simple servant."

"Can you deny, Lucinda, that she is a working girl nonetheless?" Miss Lucy hesitated. "Of course you can't deny it. That's all I'm saying," Mrs. Grice said, her words implying a great deal more than she said.

"What I can tell you," Miss Lucy said cryptically, "is that Davish here is more than she seems. Much more." Miss Lizzie was nodding furiously.

"Oh?"

"Yes, dear," Miss Lizzie said. "Davish has solved murders."

Miss Lucy glared at her sister for stealing her thunder. "She's currently investigating Harland Whitwell's death," Miss Lucy declared.

"So I've heard," the lady said, unimpressed. "Does Mrs. Mayhew know her secretary is snooping around in other people's business? I'd dismiss her immediately for such impertinence."

"She's doing her mistress's bidding," Miss Lucy said, satisfied with the look of disbelief on Mrs. Grice's face.

"It makes no difference. Walter, I'd like to go in now."

During this entire exchange I'd been spoken of as if I weren't standing among them. It didn't matter. During the entire exchange, I couldn't take my eyes from Walter. I exalted to see the unchanged affection in those beautiful blue eyes, but his increasingly grave countenance, as he listened to his mother dismiss me, stifled my joy.

"Yes, of course, Mother. If you'll excuse me, Miss Davish," he said to me, bowing slightly. His mother smiled up at Walter and never gave me a second glance.

"Of course, Dr. Grice," I said, my heart breaking as he walked away. "You should join them," I said to the elder sisters.

"Trying to get rid of us, Davish?" Miss Lucy said. "You still have some news you promised to tell us."

"Not here and now, dear," Miss Lizzie said. "We'll have Hattie over tomorrow and we'll invite Walter."

"Is he not staying with you?" I asked, trying to avoid promising to tell them something I was honor bound not to reveal.

"No, the young man insisted on staying at the Ocean House. Julia was quite put out by it. Maybe that would explain her coolness tonight. She's normally quite a pleasant companion."

I didn't have the heart to tell Miss Lizzie that Mrs. Grice's disposition had nothing to do with Walter's choice of residence. Simply put, Mrs. Grice had plans for her son and she wanted there to be no mistake that they didn't include me.

"Well, let's go, Lizzie. I see Gwendolyn Kirkland and I'm dying to hear what happened between her daughter and the Count."

I watched as the elder sisters entered the fray of guests, an amalgam of people dancing, drinking, laughing, lounging, flirting, and gossiping. I handed over my last dance card and lingered by the doorway, hoping for one more glance of Walter, but I couldn't find him in the crowded room. I did see Mrs. Grice, though, and did nothing to stop tears from welling up in my eyes as Walter's mother, with a smile on her face, scrutinized every eligible girl who passed nearby. I was right. Mrs. Grice had brought her son to Newport not to oblige his romantic whims with his secretary sweetheart but to marry him into one of the hundreds of respectable families summering here. She knew her son was a treasure, a welcome addition to any Newport family. If it were up to her, I'd never see Walter again.

"Eight hours for work, eight hours for sleep, eight hours for what we will!"

Someone was shouting, almost screaming, to be heard over the music and raised voices. Suddenly many voices were shouting, but the labor slogan repeating over and over was all that was coherent.

"What is going on?" Mrs. Mayhew said, looking around the hall for answers. She looked at me and then to her husband. "Gideon?" He was already on his way toward the door.

"Sibley!" Mr. Mayhew swore as he passed me and disappeared into the ballroom. Mrs. Mayhew followed and I suddenly found myself alone in the entrance hall. The music stopped, the musicians peering down from their balcony to see what the commotion was all about. I dared to get closer, entering the room and inching slowly along the wall. Everyone's attention was drawn to the middle of the room where Lester Sibley had made his way. People had instinctively given him a wide berth, so that he stood alone in a wide circle. He held his hat in one hand and raised his other in a fist in the air.

"Eight hours for work, eight hours for sleep, eight hours for what we will!" he said, quiet and deliberate. "What do you say to that, ladies and gentlemen of Newport?"

As I wondered where Mr. Mayhew had gone, Nick Whitwell dashed into the circle.

"You killed my father!" he shouted, lunging for the labor man. Lester Sibley, taken aback by the sudden violence, was stunned as he and Nick crashed to the floor. Nick, despite his intoxication, landed several blows until he was hauled off Sibley by several men. Cora flittered around them as they dragged Nick by the arms and plopped him into a gilded bronze chair against the far wall.

Lester Sibley sat up, swaying slightly, blood streaming from his nose, again. "I didn't have anything to do with your father's death!" he shouted. "I only want what's right."

"And what's right?" someone asked from the crowd. "Anarchy?"

Sibley ignored the jeer and searched the crowd for sympathetic faces. "You all here are enjoying yourselves only because others have done all the work for you."

"But they get paid to do so," someone else said.

"Yes, but do they have time to enjoy the fruits of their labors? Like Hattie there," he said, pointing to me.

I cowered against the wall, horrified that suddenly all eyes were on me. Why had I entered the room in the first place? Why couldn't I have been satisfied with hearing what was going on from a distance? Satisfying my curiosity was becoming hazardous. If I could've run from the room, I would have, but the congregation of chairs against the wall and the crush of people nearby prevented an easy retreat. Instead I dropped my eyes and stared at the floor. I couldn't bear the expressions on everyone's faces. I couldn't bear to see Walter's face right now.

"I can guarantee she's been up since before sunrise and hasn't stopped working since. Is that fair, is that right?"

"I'm sure she's well paid and has nothing to complain about," Mrs. Grice said. Though I couldn't see anything but the pink satin slippers of the woman in front of me, I knew who had said it.

"Yes, she's being paid, but when is she supposed to enjoy spending those wages?" Lester Sibley said. "As I said, eight hours for work, eight hours for sleep, eight hours for what we will!"

"Is that true?" a lady near me asked. "You've been working since dawn?" I stole a glance at her. The woman, with clear blue eyes and silver hair adorned with two emerald haircombs, held her hand to her heart and frowned. She was genuinely surprised and concerned. Fortunately, I was saved from answering when Silas Doubleday, the Pinkerton detective, pushed his way through the crowd and grabbed Lester Sibley.

"Let's go, Sibley. You're trespassing!" He yanked the labor man's arm behind him and a sickening crackle echoed through the hall. Sibley cried out in pain as the detective mercilessly shoved him toward the door. Several women gasped as they scrambled to get out of the detective and the criminal's way. I looked about for Mr. Mayhew. His wife had one hand on his arm and the other covering her open mouth. A look of shock, disgust, and indignation was etched on her face. Gideon Mayhew, his countenance an unreadable mask, watched passively as the detective removed the trespasser from their midst.

As they passed me, I heard the detective stop his incessant whistling and whisper, "I warned you. You're going to regret this, labor man. You're going to wish you'd never come to Newport. No, you're going to wish you'd never been born." A moment more and the men were gone and the music began again.

I followed. I couldn't leave the ballroom fast enough. I couldn't even spare one last glimpse of Walter, though I was desperate to. Between Nick Whitwell's verbal attack, Mrs. Grice's dismissal, and Lester Sibley's exploitation of me, the evening had been a disaster. I needed to put as much distance between me and the events of the evening as possible. But would morning be any better? Mrs. Mayhew must be mortified that I'd been in the ballroom and I could only hope that Lester Sibley's actions distracted Mr. Mayhew from dwelling on mine. I was in a precarious position. I might even lose my place in the Mayhew household.

Yet I had another reason. I had to see what Detective Doubleday was going to do with Lester Sibley. I'd seen the detective beat the labor man before. If Doubleday had hurt him, maybe even broken his arm, with all eyes upon him, I feared what he might

do to him now that no one was watching. I followed as they
went down the back stairs and out into the garden. I hid behind a tree and watched the retreating figures, mere shadows in
the bright moonlight. As the detective dragged his captive
down the drive, someone stepped out of the hedge near the
gate.

Mrs. Crankshaw. She spit at them. Which one was she aiming for? I wondered.

"Thelma," Lester Sibley pleaded. "You have to help me."

"And that's for getting me dismissed," she said, spitting at
him again. "I warned you not to cause trouble. I warned you not
to come to Newport. But oh, no, you had to anyway, didn't you?
You and your God-given rights, Lester. Now look at what
you've done."

"But Thelma, our cause is just. I'm only demanding what
we're all entitled to."

"You preach better hours, better wages, do you, Lester?
What about me? What about my rights? I have no position
now. How am I going to eat, Lester? What about me!" She spit
at him again.

"Now, now," Doubleday said. "Back away, woman. You've
said your piece."

"Where are you taking him? What are you going to do
with him?"

"What we do with all miscreants like him that don't know
when to leave," was the cryptic reply as the detective shoved
Sibley in the back through the gate, eliciting another cry from
the injured man. The two disappeared behind the wall, the detective's whistled rendition of "Ode to Joy" drowned out by
the clatter of wheels and horseshoes as a carriage drove by.

"It will be better than he deserves!" Mrs. Crankshaw
shouted to the darkness. I waited, wondering what the housekeeper would do. Finally, she turned away from the gate and
crossed the lawn toward the Cliff Walk.

What will happen to him? I wondered, looking back at the now empty gate. I shuddered to think what Doubleday deemed appropriate punishment. I had to do something. I fled the shadows of the tree, ran down the drive and through the gate. I looked about me as I reached the road and stopped short. The street was empty and quiet. Not a carriage or a cart was in sight. And there was no sign of Detective Doubleday or Lester Sibley.

CHAPTER 26

"I thought you said you would take care of him, Double-day," Gideon Mayhew said.

"I did. At least I thought I did. I beat the man senseless, for God's sake. Who was to know he would have the brass to come back?" the Pinkerton detective said.

I'd slept little last night and as soon as I thought it proper donned my hiking costume and boots and, with several collecting jars in my bag, headed to the Forty Steps. It was the first opportunity I'd had to return to collect some interesting red algae that I had seen on the rocks. I was highly rewarded for braving the stairs; my bag now held several specimens of three different species. I was reaching for a particularly large sample of a brownish-colored species I hadn't come across before when I heard the two men speak. They stood on the steps directly above me. If one looked down he'd see me. So I remained as I was, crouched over a depression in the rock, hoping to go undetected. My stockings and the hem of my skirt were soaking wet with the constant waves washing across the rocks and over my boots. It was an awkward position but not as awkward as if they discovered me listening in on their secret rendezvous.

"Brass? The man was in my house, Doubleday, in my home! My guests were disturbed, my wife was livid, and the whole evening now has a terrible taint to it. Mrs. Mayhew will never forgive me for allowing her party to turn into a spectacle. She asked me to sleep in my dressing room last night, Doubleday."

"I apologize, sir. What would you have me do?" If Mayhew hadn't named his companion, I would never have suspected Doubleday from the detective's deferential tone.

"Do? You took the man out last night. The question I have for you is what have you done?"

"What you told me to, Mr. Mayhew. Exactly what you told me to."

"Somehow I doubt that."

"Sir, I think I've been—"

"Enough. I don't want to hear any more of your excuses. I told you to take care of the situation and you failed."

"But, Mr. Mayhew—" I heard anger rising in the detective's voice.

"Good day, Doubleday. I don't need your services anymore."

"But sir—"

"I said good day to you, man. Have the decency to leave when you're told to."

From the clamor and banging above me, Doubleday was stomping back up the stairs, no whistle on his lips today.

I waited for Mr. Mayhew to leave. My feet were soaked now, and my back, especially after the toils of yesterday, ached anew. After several more interminable minutes, I heard the snap of his watch close and listened as he slowly ascended the stairs.

I breathed a sigh of relief when I was finally able to scrabble from underneath the stairs, straightening my back and sitting on something smooth and dry. *But I got my algae!* I thought, stuffing the specimen in a jar. I waited a few more minutes, watching the gulls dart across the water, one skimming so close to the waves, its white belly got wet. And all the while I contemplated the meaning of the conversation I wasn't meant to overhear. I pulled out my pencil and notebook, wet along one edge.

1. What had Doubleday done with Lester Sibley?
2. What had Mr. Mayhew wanted him to do with Lester Sibley?
3. How had Doubleday failed?
4. Would I ever find out the labor man's fate?
5. Did it matter?

With Mrs. Mayhew more than displeased with me, what mattered now was returning to Rose Mont to discover my own fate. Mr. Sibley might be on the next ship out of Newport. I prayed I wouldn't be aboard it with him.

"Davish!" Miss Lucy said when I arrived at Mrs. Mayhew's drawing room. "What an evening that was. Buffalo Bill's Wild West show had nothing over last night's entertainment!"

Mrs. Mayhew glanced sideways at Miss Lucy and grimaced.

"Good morning, Hattie, dear," Miss Lizzie said.

"Ahem," Mrs. Mayhew said, placing her fingers lightly on her chest. "If you would be so obliging, Miss Lucy, Miss Lizzie, I would like to speak to Miss Davish alone."

"Don't worry, Charlotte," Miss Lucy said. "We don't mind what you have to say to Davish. We're all friends here."

Mrs. Mayhew sighed. "Oh, very well. Miss Davish, you disappoint me."

"Yes, ma'am," I said, bracing myself for what she would say next.

"Now, Charlotte dear," Miss Lizzie said. "Hattie had no way of knowing that man was going to single her out."

"Please, Miss Lizzie," Mrs. Mayhew said. "We've already been over this and now"—she indicated me with a swirl of her hand—"Miss Davish needs to know what I've decided." I suddenly felt hopeful. If the elder sisters had discussed my predicament with Mrs. Mayhew before I'd arrived, they might have pleaded for leniency. I might not be dismissed after all.

"Of course, Charlotte, dear, please continue."

"Thank you," Mrs. Mayhew said, barely hiding her annoyance. "As I said before, Miss Davish, you disappointed me. I rely on you; you know that. But you embarrassed me in front of all my guests."

"Yes, Mrs. Mayhew. I am truly sorry. I should never have entered the ballroom."

"That's right. If you'd stayed at your post, that man would never have been able to use you against me."

"You were looking for Dr. Grice, weren't you, dear?" Miss Lizzie said, winking at me.

"Lizzie!" her sister chided. "Let Charlotte finish."

"Thank you, Miss Lucy. Is this true, Miss Davish?"

I didn't know what was worse, admitting that I'd gone into the room to see what all the commotion was about or to catch a glimpse of Mrs. Grice's gentleman doctor son. If I was being honest, I'd have to admit to both, which is what I did.

"So you were not only spying on one of my guests, but you were ignoring your duties to watch my party turn to ruin?"

"What? What are you talking about, ruin? It was a splendid party," Miss Lucy said, surprised. "First you convince Mrs. Astor to make an appearance and then Lester Sibley makes his own unannounced visit. No one will talk of anything else for weeks, maybe for years! Everyone will no doubt start calling to find out how the whole thing ends."

Mrs. Mayhew, who was frowning when Miss Lucy began, turned slightly. "What do you mean?"

"Everyone's dying to know what happened to Lester Sibley, the man who may have murdered Harland Whitwell. I know I am."

Mrs. Mayhew shot a glance at me. I tried not to blink. She had nothing to fault me for on that account. I hadn't revealed the truth to anyone, not even Miss Lucy. "It was your husband's servant that escorted the labor man away, correct?" Miss Lucy asked.

Mrs. Mayhew opened her mouth to say something but nodded hesitantly instead. Did Mrs. Mayhew even know who Detective Doubleday was? I doubted it.

"Then only you or your husband can tell the rest of us his fate." I cringed at Miss Lucy's choice of words. Not only did I recall the conversation this morning, but it reinforced the fact that my fate was yet to be determined. "Only you know. So of course, everyone will come here to find out, as I admit we did."

"Yes, that is true. As long as I'm not pitied for such a disruption," Charlotte Mayhew said.

"Pitied? From the whispering I heard last night and this morning, you're the envy of Newport." Why that would be I couldn't guess, but the idea pleased Mrs. Mayhew. A fleeting smile passed across her lip. "By the way," Miss Lucy said, "since we are on the subject . . . what did happen to that man?"

"Ah, Miss Lucy," Mrs. Mayhew said, glancing at me, "I think we must attend to the matter at hand first, don't you?"

"Yes, of course," Miss Lucy said. "Davish must be quaking like a leaf in a windstorm wondering what's to become of her."

"Yes, dear," Miss Lizzie said, "please tell Hattie she hasn't been dismissed."

Oh thank goodness! I thought, trying not to let the relief show on my face.

"I'm getting to that, Miss Lizzie," Mrs. Mayhew said, biting her bottom lip, annoyed again. "No, Miss Davish, because of that louse of a husband of mine, I'm far too short-handed to dismiss you. Gideon has gone back to New York without a care for how I'm to get on without a housekeeper and a first footman. Or so he says." Miss Lizzie and Miss Lucy looked at each other, Miss Lucy's eyebrow rising at the revelation.

"Whatever do you mean, Charlotte?" Miss Lucy said, feigning innocent concern.

"I'm getting to that, Miss Lucy," Charlotte snapped. "I have to admit, Miss Davish, you have been invaluable to me, so I am going to overlook this indiscretion. But a breach of promise must be rectified; you must make it up to me. I will be interviewing housekeepers this morning and therefore will not need your *secretarial services*." My concern rose again at the stress Mrs. Mayhew placed on the last two words of her sentence.

"Ma'am?"

"Instead, if you want to stay in my good graces, you will indulge me and attend to a 'personal' matter. And no one is to know about it." Whatever she was requesting sounded dubious, maybe even criminal, but I still had no idea what she meant.

"Ma'am?" I said again.

"Oh, Davish," Miss Lucy said, "don't be so obtuse. The lady is asking you to snoop around for her again."

"Mrs. Mayhew, is that right?" I asked.

"Yes, Miss Lucy is right, though I would've put it a different way. I would like you to do some more 'investigating' for me." Why couldn't she want three hundred copies of tomorrow's menu typed up for her by morning? Being a typewriter was so much simpler.

"Of course, ma'am, if I can help."

"Yes, well, my husband has a yacht, the *Invictus*. It's moored in the bay. I would like you to board the boat and tell me what you find. You don't need to worry about the crew. They're not living onboard at this time."

A boat? My palms grew damp, my heart pounded, and I suddenly found it difficult to breathe.

"But m-m-ma'am . . . ," I stammered.

"What's wrong with you, Davish?" Miss Lucy said. "You look like a mouse in a snake hole."

"I'm not . . . fond of boats," I explained. "I can't swim."

"Well, it's just a short ride out and the yacht is anchored and isn't going anywhere anytime soon," Mrs. Mayhew said. "I have to know, Miss Davish."

"Know what, ma'am? Will I be looking for something in particular?"

"Yes, I want to know if anyone's been living on it."

"You suspect Gideon isn't in New York but is living on his yacht?" Miss Lucy exclaimed, nearly leaping from her chair in excitement.

"I suspect Gideon's mistress may be," Mrs. Mayhew said. The two elderly sisters gasped. Miss Lucy opened her mouth to say something but snapped it shut when Mrs. Mayhew glared at all three of us, daring us to say another word. "I'm relying on you, Davish," she said to me. "I have to know."

"Of course, ma'am," I said.

"And when you get back," Mrs. Mayhew said, as if she hadn't just asked me to spy on her husband, "we'll pay the bills and go through invitations that have come in the morning's mail."

Oh, dear!

After what should've been a pleasant mile walk from one side of the island to the other, I walked along the harbor and found the dock not far from the Lime Rock Lighthouse, a whitewashed stone house and light tower, home to Ida Lewis, a lightkeeper of some renown, two hundred yards offshore. As I looked out over the harbor, from Brenton Cove near Fort Adams to the west and to Goat Island and the wharfs to the east, anchored yachts of all sizes, some with sails flapping lightly in the warm breeze, dotted the calm, blue bay as far as I could see. Within sight of the lighthouse, several docks of varying length and size, with tethered dinghies floating alongside, jutted out into the water. During the entire walk, I fretted over the impending task, attempting to prepare myself, telling myself that I had nothing to fear from a boat tied to a dock. Had I known I'd have to ride one out to the yacht in the harbor, I never would've asked Mr. Davies for detailed directions to the dock. I would've said I never found it. But I had.

Just like the Forty Steps, Davish! I told myself. *You can do this.*

I took a deep breath, straightened my hat, and took a step onto the dock. A jolt of panic shot through me. It wasn't like the Forty Steps at all. This moved! I groped for a hold that wasn't there as the dock, despite the calm water, moved slightly from side to side beneath my feet. I staggered to a mooring post and clung on until I caught my balance.

This is ridiculous, I thought. I had a job to do. Mrs. Mayhew was depending on me to accomplish this for her. She had been lenient in her punishment of my behavior last night and I didn't want to do anything to jeopardize my precarious position. I had to walk down this dock. I had to ride a dinghy. I had to board the yacht. I had to search the private belongings of one of the richest men in America. Even to me it sounded crazy, vastly inappropriate, and . . . dangerous?

How did I keep getting myself into situations like this? Thank goodness the man himself was miles away in New York City. But what if Silas Doubleday was about? He appeared everywhere trouble began. Could he be watching me? Suddenly the thought of being discovered overcame my fear. The faster I finished this task, the less likely I'd be discovered, I rationalized.

I took step after quick step down the dock until I came to the first dinghy. I looked about me for someone to row the boat before I lost my nerve. That would be asking just too much, I thought, glancing at the sun-bleached oars. A man, in a well-worn round leather sailor's hat, was coiling a thick, wet line of rope.

"Can I help you?" the boatman asked.

"Yes, I need a ride out to Mr. Mayhew's yacht, *Invictus*."

"Who are you?"

Absorbed with overcoming my fear, I'd forgotten that I might be challenged. As Mrs. Mayhew's secretary, I had no reason to be here. And what if a woman was on the boat right now? What would I say to her? Why hadn't I thought of this sooner?

"I'm Mr. Mayhew's secretary," I said, hoping that was explanation enough. I regretted misrepresenting myself in the first place. I didn't want to have to add to the lie.

"Ah, Mr. Mayhew forgot something, did he?"

"Yes, that's it," I said. The man nodded and with barely a glance, leaped into the rowboat. It rocked wildly beneath his feet.

I can't get in that, I thought. *I can't do it.*

As I took a step back, he held his hand out to me. "Come on, now. It's only a little dinghy, and I ain't gonna bite ya." My panic must have shown on my face. "Come on, now." His smile was reassuring and his rough, calloused hand looked strong.

I took a deep breath, brushed imaginary dust from my sleeve, grabbed the man's hand, and stepped aboard. "Aah!" I gasped as I nearly fell, the whole boat lurching beneath my feet.

The boatman guided me to the bench. I grabbed hold of

the sides of the boat and focused on its bottom as he sat down and shoved us away from the dock with an oar. "Landlubber, eh?"

"What?" I said, concentrating on my grip as the boat glided through the water.

"Not fond of boats, are ya?"

"No, sorry," I said, looking up and attempting to smile. I immediately regretted it as a wave of nausea threatened to make me sick. I focused on the floor of the boat again.

"Well, sit tight and I'll have you out to the *Invictus* in a few minutes."

I took his advice and tightened my grip. After barely a minute had elapsed, though I admit it felt like more, we were gliding through watery alleyways between dozens of yachts, most of which towered over our little boat, often sending us into shadow. The only sound was the slapping of water as the oars broke through, the cry of seagulls overhead, and my ragged breath.

Maybe this isn't so bad. I calmed my breathing and even dared to loosen my grip as moment after peaceful moment slipped by without incident. When I finally looked up it was to stare into a wall of white completely filling my view. We'd pulled up next to one of the largest yachts in the harbor.

"Here we are, the *Invictus*," the boatman said. With three towering masts, the yacht was over two hundred feet long. Without another word, he threw a small anchor overboard the dinghy and helped me to board the yacht.

Once onboard I grabbed the railing, expecting the need to steady myself. The yacht barely moved. Soon I was treading lightly through the parlor, the dining room, several bedrooms, the kitchen, and even an engine room, all lavishly appointed in brass, marble, and mahogany, looking for any signs that a woman was living aboard. I discovered a small area dedicated to a rowing machine, chest weights, medicine ball, and striking bag where Mr. Mayhew could maintain his daily exercise routines. Yet after what seemed an eternity but was probably less than ten minutes I'd covered the entire ship and found almost nothing. The beds were made, though one was slightly rumpled. The kitchen was spotless, not a single crumb on the table or unwashed teacup in the sink. The wastebaskets were empty. In the bathroom, I found no hint of occupation, no dirty shaving mug, no bottle of perfume or its scent; even the cake of Colgate's Cashmere Bouquet Soap was still in its paper. I had found a pair of men's patent-leather dress shoes, a couple of nautical books, *Patterson's Illustrated Nautical Dictionary* and the New York Yacht Club's *Code of Yachting Signals,* and two thick pamphlets, *Why the Purchase Clause of the Act of July 14, 1890 (Called Sherman Law) Should Be Repealed* and *Newport Shooting Club: Directory and Club Rules,* strewn about on a table, but absolutely nothing to indicate that a woman had been aboard. I was relieved that I would finally have something positive to report to Mrs. Mayhew.

"Didn't find what you were looking for?" the waiting boatman asked when I appeared back up on deck.

"On the contrary," I said. "He'll be pleased that I didn't find anything." The man knitted his brow but said nothing more. He helped me back into the rowboat and we made our way back to the dock. Back on land, I took several deep breaths, but my hands and knees were still shaking.

"Now that wasn't so bad, was it?" the boatman said, laughing.

I managed a weak smile. "I'm Hattie Davish, by the way."

"Call me Mack."

"Thank you for your help, Mack."

"Sure," he said as he tied the boat to the dock. "Anything for a pretty lady. Even if you are a landlubber."

Relieved to be back on land and with good news to report, I was in high spirits. I nearly skipped down the sidewalk. As I returned along the harbor, I noticed the cloudless sky, the sparkling sunshine on the water, the strong mingling scents of salt, fish, and hydrangea in the air. I felt buoyant and hopeful. I'd conquered my fear of boats, albeit for a short time. I'd kept my position despite disappointing Mrs. Mayhew. Maybe I could even convince Mrs. Grice I was worthy of her son. With such thoughts on my mind, I followed a narrow lane that led down to the water, promisingly overgrown with bramble and brush. I was rewarded with a sighting of three-foot-tall flowering yellow thistle! Without hesitation, I waded into the shrubs, acquiring more of the beggar's-tick seeds on my dress and stockings than I'd encountered on an earlier hike. The plant was everywhere! But an hour of picking off the sticky seeds would be worth it to add yellow thistle to my collection. Glad to be wearing my gloves, I knelt down to pull the plant from its roots. It didn't budge, more firmly rooted than I would've thought. The prickly, spiny leaves scratched my bare arms as I pulled harder and harder. Finally I stood up and yanked the plant with all my strength. As I succeeded, jerking the thistle loose from its earthy home, I lost my balance. I stumbled several feet before falling backward into the brush. I grimaced, anticipating the pain when my back would hit the ground, but something had broken my fall. I sat up and twisted around to see what it was.

"Aaaaahhhh!" I screamed, leaping away. Beneath me wasn't the ant mound or a pile of plant litter I'd expected, but the body of a man with a bloody hole in the middle of his chest.

CHAPTER 27

Who was it? I wondered. His face was hidden beneath the brush. I had to know. I knelt down beside him and pushed the branches away. Lester Sibley! I scrambled out of the bushes as fast as I could and I ran to the top of the lane, down the street, and straight toward the police station. I wanted desperately to return to Rose Mont and never think of Lester Sibley again, but I knew it wouldn't be that simple.

No, that's not right, I thought. What I really wanted to do was go to the Ocean House and find Walter. He'd been there for me at other difficult times. I wanted to draw strength from his professional calm. I wanted to feel his arms around me, hear him tell me everything would be all right. But I didn't. Despite refusing to defy the wishes of the likes of Jane and Nicholas Whitwell, Sam Preble was Newport's chief of police. I had to tell him what had happened. I continued along the bay toward the police station. I never made it that far.

"Chief Preble!" I yelled. The policeman, his cap pushed far back from his forehead, was standing on a dock dangling fishing line tied to a branch into the water. The line suddenly went taut and he jerked it back. "Chief Preble!" I yelled again. He looked up at the sound of his name. He grimaced, loosening his grip on the line as I ran toward him.

"Miss Davish?" Out of breath, I bent over as soon as I reached the dock. He quickly closed the distance between us. "Now take a deep breath and tell me what the trouble is."

"Down the lane . . . he's dead," I said, trying to catch my breath.

"You've found another dead body?"

"Not another body, Chief Preble. Lester Sibley's! And he has a bullet hole in him like Harland Whitwell." With the implications left unspoken the policeman led me to a patrol wagon parked nearby, leaped in, took the reins, and then offered his arm to help me in. Flicking the reins, starting the horses trotting, he said, "I'll have to stop at the station first and then you can take me to him, Miss Davish."

After Chief Preble relayed orders to his officers at the police station, I led him back to the stand of bushes and pointed. "He's in there," I said.

"However did you find him?" the policeman asked, alighting from the wagon. I opted to stay right where I was. I had no desire to see Lester Sibley's dead body again.

"I was plant collecting. I'd found a specimen of yellow thistle among the bushes and stumbled upon him by accident." I had no intention of telling Chief Preble the real reason I'd been in the vicinity was to trespass on Mr. Mayhew's yacht.

"Did you move anything? See anything else unusual?"

"No." I watched as Chief Preble waded into the bushes, pushing branches away to get a better view of the dead man's body. He put his fingers on Lester Sibley's wrist. Then he pushed the man onto his side, placed him on his back again, opened his coat, moved his head back and forth, and examined his scalp with his fingers.

"Well, it's obvious the cause of death is the bullet wound,

though both of his arms appear to be broken and he's been beaten around the face."

Lester Sibley's death couldn't have been a suicide like Harland Whitwell's then. No one could kill himself with two broken arms.

"I'm no medical examiner, but I'll bet you this man's been dead quite a while, probably killed late last night. We'll get him to the coroner and have an autopsy done." He examined the wound as he had Harland Whitwell's, so close I thought he'd get blood on his nose. "Without the bullet, I can't say it's from the same gun, but the wound looks similar." I nodded blankly, hoping my involvement was almost done. I was beginning to shake. "I'll have the men look around the bushes for the gun and any empty cartridges.

"Ah, Miss Davish," the policeman said, looking up from his work. "I'm sorry you had to be a part of this." He stood, approached the wagon, and pulled a plain navy blue wool blanket from the back. "Here, wrap this around you." The day was warm and fair, but I was shivering. I was glad when he drew it around my shoulders.

"We'll wait here until the others arrive and I'll have someone take you back to Rose Mont." I nodded, pulling the blanket tighter around me. We sat in silence for several minutes before Chief Preble said, "I hear Sibley was found trespassing at the Mayhew ball last night?"

"Yes, you could say that," I said. The policeman looked at me sharply, raising an eyebrow in question.

"Would you care to elaborate, Miss Davish?"

"Lester Sibley didn't simply trespass, Chief Preble. He stormed the room, chanting labor slogans. He disrupted the whole evening."

"You were there?"

"Yes, I was," I said, hoping I wouldn't need to elaborate.

"So how did the man get in?"

I hadn't thought to wonder about this before but instantly knew the answer. "He couldn't have come through the front. I was in the hall; I would've seen him. He must've come from the back portico, probably taking the Cliff Walk and then coming up the lawn."

"Yes, that makes sense. The cottage residents still resist the idea that the Cliff Walk is public, especially Mr. Mayhew. He once placed a wall across it to prevent anyone from walking across his property. The wall came down, of course, since an old city charter guarantees that the Cliff Walk is open to all, but he still thinks it's his personal path. If he had any security set up last night, he probably wouldn't have thought to post anyone in the back."

"There was a Pinkerton detective there, a Mr. Silas Doubleday," I said.

"Yes, I know about him. He's the one that roughed up the strikers picketing the other day."

I nodded, relieved the policeman knew about that. "Mr. Doubleday escorted Lester Sibley off the property," I said. "He probably broke his arms." I told him about the detective's threats and rough handling of Mr. Sibley the night before.

He nodded. "I'll talk to him, find out where he was, when he last saw Sibley."

"Do you think he could've killed him?" I asked.

Chief Preble snorted. "I can think of many people who might've wanted Lester Sibley dead. The man was causing a real fuss in town." He shook his head, looking down at the bushes where the dead man lay. "I told him to leave town, to stop stirring up trouble. He obviously didn't listen."

We heard horses approaching and soon a patrol wagon, with two more policemen, arrived.

"The body is over there," Chief Preble said.

As Chief Preble explained what he wanted the new arrivals to do, I sat in the wagon, staring out over the harbor, absently watching as two men in matching white caps struggled to raise the sails on a nearby yacht. What should I do? I wondered. I had information that might be relevant to Lester Sibley's death. Should I tell Chief Preble despite my promises to keep them secret? Could there be a connection between Harland Whitwell's death and the murder of Lester Sibley? Only a few people knew Harland Whitwell took his own life. Could someone have blamed Lester Sibley for Harland Whitwell's death and have unknowingly killed him for a murder he didn't commit? Or at least wanted it to appear they were related in some way?

Nicholas Whitwell, I thought. He knew the truth behind his father's death. In fact, he hid the suicide note and likely staged the death scene to incriminate Lester Sibley. Nicholas might still have his father's gun. Could he have killed the labor man? And what about Eugenie? I hadn't seen her since her father's death. Had she been told her father committed suicide? If not, could she have attacked Lester Sibley? Could Jane Whitwell have done it?

Chief Preble walked over to the wagon. "I think you left this," he said gently. He placed the uprooted yellow thistle on my lap. I nodded my thanks. "Collins, take this wagon and give Miss Davish a ride back to Rose Mont." Looking at the hard-won thistle, already wilting in the sun, I decided I knew too much not to tell Chief Preble something. This was my chance.

"Chief Preble," I said, taking a deep breath. I was about to walk a fine line between honesty and betrayal.

"Yes?"

"I need to tell you that I saw someone try to run Lester Sibley down in a motorcar."

"A motorcar? There are only two motorcars on the entire island and one of them belongs to the visiting sultan."

"And the other belongs to Nicholas Whitwell," I said. I knew he wasn't driving that day, but Chief Preble didn't.

Maybe this would be the incentive he needed to include the Whitwells in his investigation without my revealing any secrets.

"I know what you're insinuating, Miss Davish."

"Nicholas Whitwell had an altercation with Lester Sibley at the ball as well. He accused Sibley of killing his father. And his father's gun is still unaccounted for."

"I think we shouldn't jump to conclusions, Miss Davish," the policeman said.

"Do you think it's a coincidence that Lester Sibley has a bullet wound in his chest like Harland Whitwell did? Possibly from the same gun?"

"We'll talk again. Now go back and rest."

I nodded, knowing I'd said all I could without compromising myself. I was relieved, as the officer snapped the reins, to be leaving the ugly scene. Now I didn't have to think about it anymore.

But riding back in silence with Officer Collins, all I could do was think about it. Luckily the ride took only a few minutes, and after thanking the policeman I went straight up to my rooms. I purposely avoided the Servants' Hall; I didn't want anyone to know I was back yet. I wanted time to press my yellow thistle and to type up what was swirling around in my mind, a list of suspects. I listed eight people and these were only those who I knew had a possible, albeit sometimes a far-fetched, reason to want the labor man dead:

1. Nicholas Whitwell—hated Lester Sibley, blamed him for his father's death
2. Silas Doubleday—last person known to see Sibley alive, obvious dislike between them
3. Gideon Mayhew—considered the man a pest, furious over his trespassing on his party

4. Mrs. Crankshaw—blamed Lester for the loss of her position
5. James—blamed him for the loss of his position, came to blows with him
6. Charlotte Mayhew—similar reasons as her husband
7. Jane Whitwell—similar reasons as her son
8. Eugenie Whitwell—similar reasons as her brother and mother

With that accomplished I sat back and took a deep breath. I realized I hadn't taken my hat off. I unpinned it and tossed it on the bed. I stood, went over to the dressing table, and poured water from the pitcher into the basin to splash on my face.

Why does this keep happening to me? I wondered. At least I had good news to report to Mrs. Mayhew. I took another deep breath, dabbed my face dry with a towel, and brushed my skirt.

"Ow!" Something pricked my fingers. Beggar's-tick seeds. I was covered in them. I hadn't time to pick them off now, so I changed out of my dress into my brown suit and went to report to Mrs. Mayhew. She was dressed for a luncheon and was just pinning her hat on.

"Well, I am relieved to hear that, Miss Davish," Mrs. Mayhew said when I told her I'd found nothing aboard her husband's yacht. "I knew you wouldn't let me down."

"Thank you, ma'am."

"Are you that terrified of boats, Miss Davish? You're as pale as cold cream, and you're shaking."

I was terrified of boats, but the shock of finding Lester Sibley had to be written on my face. Obviously refreshing myself before coming down hadn't helped. Should I tell Mrs. Mayhew what had happened? Chief Preble hadn't instructed me either way. And why not? With the way rumors and news traveled in this town, she would know soon anyway.

"I'm sorry, Mrs. Mayhew, but I had an unfortunate incident from which I'm still not quite recovered."

"What happened?"

"Lester Sibley, ma'am—"

"Did that horrible little man bother you?" she interrupted, shaking her head. "Don't give it another thought, Davish. As soon as Mr. Mayhew returns from New York, I'm going to speak to him about ridding us all from this pest of a creature. If the police won't deal with him, my husband will."

"Mrs. Mayhew, Lester Sibley's dead."

She stopped her ranting and stared at me. "Dead? What do you mean?"

"That's the incident to which I referred, ma'am. I found Lester Sibley dead in a thicket of bushes as I returned from my task at the yacht."

"What were you doing in the bushes?"

Of all the questions she could've asked, I hadn't expected this one to be the first. "I was collecting a specimen of yellow thistle, ma'am. I'm an amateur plant collector."

"And how do you know he was dead and not merely drunk or sleeping?"

"He had a bullet wound in the middle of his chest."

CHAPTER 28

"A bullet wound in his chest?" Miss Lucy said incredulously.

"Oh, dear," Miss Lizzie said. "Just like Harland Whitwell."

"Just like Harland Whitwell," her sister affirmed. "What did the police say?"

After my conversation with Mrs. Mayhew, I was dismissed for the rest of the day and decided to accept Miss Lizzie and Miss Lucy's offer for tea. To Miss Lucy's delight and my relief, I was able to answer their questions without restraint. So far, when Mr. Whitwell was mentioned I'd been able to redirect the conversation back to Lester Sibley.

"They took him to the coroner for an autopsy. When I tried to speculate about suspects, Chief Preble was quick to remind me that he will investigate the murder, one step at a time."

"So he didn't tell you anything," Miss Lucy grumbled.

"No, except that he believed there were many people unhappy with Lester Sibley," I said.

"I'm worried about you, Hattie, dear. Finding another man dead like that. It reminds me of—"

"My goodness," Miss Lucy said, cutting her sister off. "This makes three men you've found shot in the chest. Isn't that right, Davish?"

"Lucy!" Miss Lizzie chided. "Be honest, Hattie dear. How are you doing?"

"That's what I want to know," a man's voice boomed. We all turned and watched Walter stride into the room. He rushed to my side, bent his knee, and kissed my hand. I clutched his hand and gazed longingly into his eyes. "Oh, Hattie," he said, "whatever am I to do with you?"

"Get up off the floor, Walter," his mother said as she entered the room.

I released Walter's hand as Walter and I stood simultaneously. "Mrs. Grice," I said, bowing my head slightly.

"I'll take two sugars, please, Miss Lucy," Walter's mother said, ignoring me and sitting as far from me as possible.

"Mother, Miss Davish has had the most terrible shock," Walter said, indicating for me to sit.

"Then she should be attended to by a physician, not courted as a lover."

"Julia, dear," Miss Lizzie said, handing the lady her tea, "Hattie has come straight from discovering another dead body."

Disgust flashed across Julia Grice's face.

Miss Lucy, on the other hand, pinched her lips and jutted out her bony shoulders. "Oh, Julia," Miss Lucy huffed. "Hattie finds a man shot and left in the bushes and you'd think we told you we'd found a mouse in the larder. This is real news." The old lady's eyes gleamed. "And besides the police, we're the first to know."

"I don't think murder is appropriate conversation for tea,"

Julia Grice said. Miss Lizzie nearly spit out the strawberry and coconut cream cake she'd been eating.

"Not appropriate?" Miss Lucy snickered, her teacup clanking hard as she nearly dropped it back onto the saucer. "You must be joking! This has been one of the best conversations I've had in months!"

"And I don't think it's appropriate to have tea with the maid or secretary or whatever she is," Mrs. Grice said, ignoring the elderly sisters' reactions. "Do you?" She never looked at me once.

"What has come over you, Julia, dear?" Miss Lizzie said, genuinely puzzled.

It was no surprise to me. I stood up again. I didn't want to be in Julia Grice's company any longer than she wanted to be in mine. "Thank you for the tea, Miss Lucy, Miss Lizzie, but I think Mrs. Grice is right. It's time I returned to Rose Mont."

"You're not going anywhere, Davish," Miss Lucy commanded. "We're not done with you yet. I don't know if it's the same gun that killed Harland Whitwell or what you were doing in the blasted bushes in the first place, though I bet I can guess, and I haven't asked what more you've learned about Harland and—"

"Lucy, dear, Hattie's right. She should rest."

"Yes," Walter said, latching on to what Miss Lizzie said and standing. "Miss Davish, as your onetime physician, I recommend that you rest as much as possible. You may still yet suffer ill effects from the shock."

"I'm fine, Dr. Grice," I said, knowing even as I said it he expected and hoped for this reply.

"I've heard that before," he said, smiling. "Let me escort you back."

"Walter, the girl said she is fine," his mother said.

"Don't listen to her, Julia," Miss Lucy said, grumbling once again. "Davish is notorious about not looking after herself. I

doubt the girl's had a full night's sleep since we saw her last."
At least that much was true, I thought.

"She's a grown woman. She can find her own way back to
Rose Mont."

"Nonsense, Mother. She needs my attention."

"I'm sure she doesn't!" his mother exclaimed even as Walter offered me his arm and began walking me from the room.

"Don't forget to report, I mean, come right back, Dr.
Grice," Miss Lucy said, still hoping to learn more about my
morning's adventures.

"I promise to tell you everything, almost," Walter said,
winking. Miss Lucy beamed.

"Return promptly, Walter. Remember the delightful girl
you're to escort to the polo match this afternoon."

Walter frowned. I tried to focus on the way his arm felt beneath my hand. Soon it would be someone else's hand there.

"Yes, Mother," Walter said. "I'll be back in time."

"Good. You wouldn't want to disappoint anyone," she said,
determined to have the last word.

"I must apologize for my mother's behavior," Walter said.
We'd walked several blocks in uncomfortable silence before he
finally spoke. "She's usually quite a pleasant person."

"She has a point, Walter," I said. "Seeing you at the ball reminded me how I've been deceiving myself. I'm a working
girl, a servant even to some, and you're one of them." Walter
stopped walking and, putting his hands on my shoulders,
turned me toward him.

"Stop, Hattie. Just stop. My mother's wrong and you're
wrong if you agree with her. I care about you and I know you
feel the same way. Let's forget all about us and them and enjoy
the fact that we're here, in Newport, together. Agreed?" I nodded. How could I not agree to anything he said with that
smile? "Good."

He pulled me against his chest for a moment, kissing the top of my head. Too soon he released me, the familiar scent of his cologne lingering in my hair. "Who would've known?" he said, searching my face for answers. "I had no idea you'd even be here. According to your last letter, you were in Virginia with Sir Arthur."

"I didn't know either until the last moment. I came here with Sir Arthur, but he had to leave for England almost as soon as we arrived. Lady Phillippa found me a position with Mrs. Mayhew."

"And how are you doing at Rose Mont?"

"I'm lucky to still have a position. With all the labor strife going on, I've known three people in the last day alone who've lost their jobs. And I have a brand-new Redfern evening gown," I added as an attempted jest.

"That doesn't answer my question," Walter said. He wanted to know whether I was happy, whether I was content in my work. I didn't want to say, but if I couldn't tell Walter whom could I tell? I started walking again.

"To be honest, my stay in Newport has been unprecedented," I said. "No, actually it's been reminiscent of working for Mrs. Trevelyan in Eureka Springs."

"But Mrs. Trevelyan was—"

"Exactly. At first I was quite content. As Mrs. Mayhew's social secretary, I'm challenged, respected, and I've learned skills that I can call upon in the future. I have a lovely suite of rooms and an excuse to frequent the millinery shops almost daily." Walter smiled at my confession. "But since Harland Whitwell died, I've done little of what I'm qualified to do. Instead I've found myself snooping into others' personal lives in order to satisfy my employer's social ambitions."

"I'm sorry to hear that," Walter said, laying his hand in mine.

"Me too. Other than her misplaced ambition, Mrs. Mayhew has been frank and reasonable. And doing her bidding has allowed me to hike and explore a great deal. I've been up every morning hiking on the Cliff Walk or down by the ocean. I've sampled some marvelous plants for my collection." I looked up at him. "And I've gotten to see you again."

"So not a total loss then?" he said, grinning.

"No, not a total loss." Even as I said it, I pictured him escorting someone else from Newport society to the polo match or to the next concert at the Casino. We arrived at Rose Mont. I dropped my arm. "I'll say good-bye here." Walter frowned.

"Why?"

"Mrs. Mayhew's guests don't come in through the back door."

"Yes, of course. But promise me you'll get some rest? You've had a great shock finding that man this morning."

"I'll try," was all I could say. "Good-bye, Walter. It was wonderful to see you."

"You say it like one of us is leaving. I didn't come all the way across the country to only stay a few days. I'll be here until the horse show in September, as will the Mayhews. So we're not going anywhere."

"Of course," I said, unable to look him in the eye. He might as well be in Arkansas. Mrs. Mayhew would never approve of my seeing Walter. She "relied on me" too much. And once his mother arranged his schedule, Dr. Walter Grice would be as unavailable to me as Master Nicholas Whitwell or Mr. Oliver Belmont.

Walter took my hand and kissed it, as I looked about to see that we weren't being watched. "Until next time, my fair secretary," he said lightly. He had no idea what Newport was like. He had no idea there wouldn't be a next time.

CHAPTER 29

"Excuse me, Miss Davish. How are you holding up?" After saying good-bye to Walter, I'd fled back into the grand house, trying to hold back tears. When I opened the back door, I literally nearly ran into Chief Preble. He'd been standing just inside the door studying a small pocket notebook in his hand. He mistook my distress over Walter for the shock of finding Lester Sibley. I quickly wiped the tears from my eyes with a handkerchief.

"Fine, Chief Preble. Thank you. Were you able to go back for your fish?"

"No, better luck next time," he said, patting the hook on his cap. "No, I've been talking to the staff about the house-keeper and footman. From what I gather, they were discharged because of their dealings with Lester Sibley." I nodded. "I was just going up to request assistance from Mrs. Mayhew. I have a few more questions for her as well."

"Do you think she knows something?" I had placed Mrs. Mayhew on my suspect list but hadn't truly thought she was involved. But now?

"I don't know," the policeman said. "Let's go find out."

"Us?" I said.

"Since you're her secretary, I think she may be kinder to me in your presence."

"If you think it will help," I said reluctantly. I wanted nothing more to do with death and murder but felt obligated to this policeman who had been congenial to me when others weren't.

"Yes. Mr. Davies said we should find her in her sitting room," he said, indicating the stairs. "After you." We climbed the stairs in silence.

"By the way," the policeman said as we approached Mrs. Mayhew's sitting room. "Ballard found one empty bullet cartridge in the bushes near where you found the body. It's a .41 caliber, just like the one we found in Whitwell's office."

"Is it from the same gun then?"

"We can't say for certain, but if it isn't, it came from one just like it."

"And all the members of the shooting club have one just like it," I said.

The policeman nodded. "Not very helpful, huh?" He stepped aside, indicating for me to enter before him. "After you, Miss Davish."

Mrs. Mayhew was lying on her chaise longue as usual, Bonaparte purring in her lap. "Are you feeling better, ma'am?" I asked. She'd complained of a headache earlier.

"Yes, thank you, Davish, but who is this?"

"Chief Samuel Preble, Mrs. Mayhew," the officer answered, removing his hat. "I apologize for intruding upon you this way, but I hoped I could have a few minutes of your time."

"Is this about that labor man, what was his name again?"

"Lester Sibley," I said.

"Yes, Lester Sibley," Mrs. Mayhew said. "What could I possibly be able to tell you about Lester Sibley, Chief Preble?"

"Actually, I was hoping to speak to you about your former housekeeper, Mrs. Crankshaw, and former footman, James," the policeman said.

Mrs. Mayhew bolted upright, sending Bonaparte bounding off her lap. "Why do you need to know about them?" she demanded. "They didn't murder anybody."

"It is my understanding, Mrs. Mayhew," the policeman said as Bonaparte rubbed against his leg, "that they were both dismissed from their positions in this household because of their association with the murder victim."

"And you think one of them may have killed him?" she asked, her eyes wide in disbelief.

"We are following every possible lead, ma'am," he said, though I knew that not to be true. The police were only following leads that didn't include the "cottage" families. "It's possible neither had anything to do with this death. But then again, they may have valuable information about the man that may lead us to his killer."

"Yes, I see. Well, I'm afraid I can be of no assistance to you. My husband was the one who discharged the servants and I have no idea what's become of them."

"Does either of them have family in the area?" Chief Preble asked.

"I wouldn't know," Mrs. Mayhew said. "I'm sure the servants' files are kept downstairs somewhere. You may find the information you seek there."

"Then I have your permission to look, ma'am?"

"Yes, if it will help."

"Thank you, Mrs. Mayhew."

"May I also interview your staff? Someone may know where they may have gone."

"No, I think that would be too disruptive. Maybe Davish can ask around, but I won't have my staff's work interrupted. Will that be all, Chief Preble? I have a headache."

"Yes, thank you, ma'am," Chief Preble said, trying to hide his disappointment. I too was disappointed. Did she know something or didn't she?

"Miss Davish, a moment if you please," Mrs. Mayhew said as I turned to follow the policeman out the door.

"Yes, ma'am?"

"My calendar is in desperate need of updating; I'm afraid I may have already missed Mrs. Moewis's lecture on architecture at 'Rough Point' this afternoon. But I will excuse this lapse if you will do what you must to rid me of this man's embarrassing presence. I don't want that policeman or any policeman in my house one moment longer than necessary. It's over there on the desk. You can work on it this evening. I'd like to know where I'm going first thing tomorrow morning."

"Yes, ma'am," I said, picturing the stack of invitations and announcements to dances, boating parties, lectures, luncheons, recitals, polo matches, and more that Mrs. Mayhew had received but ignored until now. I would be up late again tonight. Mrs. Mayhew lay back down in her chaise longue, closed her eyes, and began petting Bonaparte, again curled up in her lap.

"That will be all," Mrs. Mayhew said, mistaking my hesitation for awaiting her dismissal.

"Yes, ma'am."

I found Chief Preble in Mrs. Crankshaw's former office delving through desk drawers filled with files on every person who had ever worked at Rose Mont.

"Odd thing, Miss Davish," he said. "The file on you only has a recommendation letter in it from a Lady Phillippa Windom-Greene."

"Yes, I was working for her husband, Sir Arthur Windom-Greene, when he was called away to England on short notice. My employment here was sudden and unforeseen. If you need more information, I would recommend contacting Lady

Phillippa. Sir Arthur has a more complete employment file for me back in Virginia."

"No need, you're not a suspect," he said, chuckling.

"I'm relieved to hear it," I said, startled that he would even jest about such a thing. "Are you finding what you need for James and Mrs. Crankshaw?"

"Not much that will help. Neither has family on the island or nearby. They both came with the Mayhews from their household in New York. Wait a minute," the officer said, peering closer at the form in his hand. "Says here that Mrs. Crankshaw's closest kin is a sister who lives in Queens. It might be a coincidence, but the sister's name is Margaret Sibley."

"Sibley?" I exclaimed. "Lester Sibley may have been Mrs. Crankshaw's brother-in-law?" It would explain her familiar behavior toward him.

"Could be a coincidence, but I doubt it. All the more reason I need to track this woman down."

"And James?" I asked.

"Who knows? The man could be anywhere." The policeman shook his head and replaced the files into the cabinet. "Well, I guess this concludes my inquiries at Rose Mont," he said, slamming the drawer closed.

"Mrs. Mayhew has given me permission to speak to the other members of the staff. If I find out anything of use, I'll be sure to let you know."

"I'd appreciate that, Miss Davish, but don't expect much. I'm sure you're quite capable as a secretary, but you're not trained in interrogating suspects. You have no experience conducting a murder investigation."

You have no idea, I thought. Instead, I said, "But if I can glean valuable information from my fellows?"

"I'll be all ears."

After seeing Chief Preble out, I systematically spoke to every staff member in the house, starting with Mr. Davies and ending with Biddy the scullery maid. My inquiries took me to every part of this enormous house as I tracked down the chambermaids, kitchen maids, footmen, and housemen. I found myself in rooms I'd never seen before: the kitchen, the larder, the billiard room, the music room, Miss Cora's bedroom, Mr. Mayhew's dressing room, Mr. Mayhew's gymnasium, and several guest bedrooms. Unfortunately, the answer was always the same. No one knew where James or Mrs. Crankshaw was. I wouldn't give up, though, until I'd talked to Britta. Their relationship was more familiar than you'd typically find between parlormaid and footman. She might know where James was. But where was she? No one knew that either. Was the house that big that one could lose track of a parlormaid? I was heading outside to start my inquiries anew with the groomsmen, groundskeepers, and other outdoor staff when I ran into Britta returning from an errand outside.

"Britta!" I said as she scampered by me. "Can I have a moment?"

"Oh, Hattie, I need to get upstairs. I'm running behind," she said, donning her apron.

"I wondered if you happen to know where James is?"

Britta took a sharp inhale of breath and reached for her left ear. "How did you know?" she whispered. "You're not going to tell anyone, are you?"

I was taken aback by her reaction but attempted to appease her fears by shaking my head.

How did I know what?

"The police are looking for him," I said, only adding to Britta's distress. "They want to speak to him about Lester Sibley's murder."

"Oh, Hattie, he's done nothing wrong," the maid nearly shrieked as she grabbed my arm. "You've got to believe me!"

"Britta, if you know where he is, tell me and I'll go speak to him. The police may never have to be involved."

She nodded, removed her hand, and fumbled with her apron strings. "He's at the Aquidneck Hotel on Pelham, a block from the Old Stone Mill." I wrote down her directions in my notebook. "But please, Hattie, you've got to believe me. He only spoke to that labor man. He never intended to act, despite what Mr. Mayhew thinks. And he certainly didn't kill anyone." Britta threw her hands to her face and began to sob, confirming my suspicions about the pair.

I placed my hand lightly on her shoulder. "If he's innocent, than there's nothing to cry about," I said.

"He is innocent, Hattie," she said, still crying softly.

"Then you get upstairs and do your job and I'll get over to the Aquidneck Hotel and do mine."

Britta wiped her tears with the trim of her apron, attempted a smile, and then ran up the stairs. As I watched her go, I wondered when had my job become questioning murder suspects?

CHAPTER 30

"Miss Davish?" James said, leaning on the open hotel room door. He was a mess. His hair was disheveled and fell into his eyes. His shirt was wrinkled and wet where he'd tried blotting a coffee stain. His eyes were bloodshot and bleary. His breath was stale with a lingering stench of old whiskey. What would Mrs. Mayhew say of her handsome first footman now? "How did you find me?"

"Britta told me where you were," I said.

"Oh, Britta, my girl, why would you do a thing like that?" he said, turning his head and speaking into the back of the door.

"The police are looking for you, James, and she is worried about you," I said.

"Why are the police looking for me?"

"Haven't you heard about Lester Sibley?"

"What's there to know? The man talks to me for a few minutes about the rights of workers and I lose the best positions I've ever had. I only spoke to the man. Sure, I thought about what he said. He made a lot of sense. But is that cause enough to discharge me?"

"James," I said. "Lester Sibley has been murdered."

"What? Murdered? When?"

"His body was discovered this morning."

"But what does that have to do with me?" he asked, and then his eyes widened as realization set in. "The police think I did it?" He started to shake his head violently. "I didn't kill anybody. I didn't do anything wrong."

"I promised Britta that I would speak to you first, before the police found you. If you can provide an alibi for the time between when Lester Sibley was last seen alive and this morning, the police will leave you alone."

"An alibi? What's that? What do you mean?"

"Where were you last night?"

"I was at Buckley's Saloon and then I came here."

"Did anyone see you return to the hotel last night?"

"The desk clerk."

"And did you stay here all night?"

"Yeah, I haven't even left to get the paper."

"But can anyone verify that, James?" I didn't expect an affirmative, but he hesitated. Maybe someone had spent the night with him after all. "James, if you know of someone who can prove you were here all night and all morning as you say, then the police will know you're innocent."

"Yes, someone was here with me."

"Who?"

He hesitated again and I knew whom he was protecting.

"It was Britta, wasn't it?" I asked.

He nodded. "She spent the night here and stayed until breakfast. I told her she should go, that she was risking her job too, but she wouldn't be separated from me."

"And then she came back a little while ago to check on

you, didn't she?" Britta hadn't been out running errands when I'd seen her. She'd been here.

"Yes. How did you know?" he said. I didn't answer.

"She's risking more than her position if she's caught spending time here, James. You know that, don't you?" I couldn't resist warning him about Britta's reputation for Britta's sake.

"You don't understand, Miss Davish. We risked more by living together at Rose Mont. If we'd been discovered, both of us would've been booted."

"You were courting under Mr. Mayhew's roof?"

"Not courting, Miss Davish," he said sheepishly. "Britta and I are married. The Mayhews don't allow for married servants, but to work at Rose Mont . . . It's an honor, it's prestigious, and we couldn't turn down the chance to work for one of the grandest houses in America."

"But you risked being discharged without references," I said, dismayed. I couldn't comprehend how someone would willingly put themselves in such a dangerous position.

"It was worth the risk," he said.

"And you still think so, having lost that position?" I said, still baffled.

"What's important now is that Britta's position is safe. I'll find something. Not as a footman, of course, but I can work with my hands."

"Assuming you can shake all suspicion from you," I said.

"I didn't kill the man. Yes, my association with him lost me my position, but that's not enough to kill a man."

"Isn't it? You were willing to risk a great deal to obtain that position and Lester Sibley cost you what you valued so highly," I said, not believing it but wanting to know what he'd say.

"I didn't kill him. What more can I say? How else can I prove that I'm innocent?" He absentmindedly brushed his hands through his hair. He picked out a tiny feather left behind from his pillow. It gave me an idea.

"May I see the clothes you were wearing last night?"

He looked at me with furrowed brow. "Why?"

"You said you wanted to prove your innocence. May I see them?" I said, holding my hand out.

He disappeared into his room and produced the gray wool coat and trousers of a cheap sack suit, and a white cotton shirt. "Not quite the livery of a high-society house, huh?" he said as I began my thorough checking of his clothes.

"Your stockings too, if I may."

He left again for a moment and returned with a pair of black stockings. "What are you looking for?" he asked.

"Beggar's-tick seeds."

"Why?"

"Because Lester Sibley's body was found in overgrown bushes with beggar's-tick plants everywhere. When I found his body, I got the seeds stuck to my skirt and stockings. The killer will have gotten them on his or her clothes as well."

I finished examining every inch, and besides the faint smell of whiskey the clothes were innocuous, not a single beggar's-tick seed.

"So you believe me?" James said.

"Yes, James, I do. And I believe the police will too."

"You did say you needed a butler?" I said.

I'd accompanied James to the police station and listened as he explained his situation to Chief Preble. I added my theory about the beggar's-tick seeds. On my way back to Rose Mont, I stopped by Moffat Cottage to see the elderly Shaw sisters and explain my proposal.

"Yes, dear," Miss Lizzie said, a strawberry stain on the lace collar of her dress, "but isn't he a suspect in a murder?"

"He won't be for long," I said. "I'm certain the police will clear him of any suspicion."

"Well, he won't come with a reference, that's for certain," Miss Lucy said.

"Yes, but you know Mrs. Mayhew would've recommended him if the situation had been different."

"That's true, Lucy," Miss Lizzie said. "Charlotte did say the only reason why Gideon discharged the housekeeper and this James Chase fellow was because of Lester Sibley."

"And now Lester Sibley is dead, Lizzie," Miss Lucy said. "And what would Charlotte say of us hiring her first footman?"

"I think it's a splendid idea," Miss Lizzie said, sitting back and smiling. "You did say he's married, didn't you, Hattie, dear?"

"What does that have to do with Charlotte objecting?" her sister asked.

"Hattie?" Miss Lizzie said, ignoring her sister.

"Yes, to Mrs. Mayhew's parlormaid," I said. "But the Mayhews don't allow for married servants."

"Exactly. See, Lucy, we're doing everyone, including Charlotte, a favor."

"How so?"

"This way, Mr. Chase works for us, Charlotte gets to keep her parlormaid, and the pair get to stay close and in service. Like I said, a splendid plan." Miss Lizzie clapped her hands.

"Yes, it does seem like you've thought of everything, Davish," Miss Lucy said. "He's not an intemperate man, is he?"

Miss Lucy was wrong. I hadn't thought of everything. How could I be so irresponsible? This morning James smelled of whiskey and showed signs of intoxication, though he'd always been sober at Rose Mont. How could I have forgotten, after everything that happened in Eureka Springs, that this would be a concern for the sisters? In trying to help Britta, I'd overlooked the obvious. I grappled for a response.

Miss Lizzie saved me the effort. "The man wouldn't have lasted two days at Rose Mont if he was anything but conscientious and proper."

"And if he does on occasion imbibe," I added to cover my

mistake, "who better than you ladies to save him from its evil?" This comment elicited serious nods from both ladies.

"You're right, Davish," Miss Lucy said. "It's our duty to see Mr. Chase respectably employed and thus we can ensure he stays a faithful and sober husband."

"And you will have a first-rate butler," I said.

"That's true, Lucy, dear," Miss Lizzie said. "The Mayhews only hire the best."

"It's settled then," Miss Lucy said, "as long as the police clear him, of course."

"Of course," I said, pleased with such a positive outcome. I couldn't wait to tell Britta what I'd done.

"The police clear whom?" Mrs. Grice said as she entered the room. She was smiling until she saw me. "Are you back again?"

"Hattie has found us a replacement for Mr. Grady. Isn't that kind of her?"

"If you mention butler and police in the same conversation, how can you say he's suitable?" Mrs. Grice said, sitting down and smoothing the folds of her dress in her lap.

"Where is Walter?" Miss Lucy asked, ignoring Julia Grice's comment about the butler.

Mrs. Grice answered Miss Lucy but stared at me. "Oh, didn't I tell you?" Her eyes sparkled as she clasped her hands before her. I'd seen Walter's eyes light up like that. It didn't bode well for me. "He's escorting Eugenie Whitwell to see *A Trip to Chinatown* at the Casino's theater."

I suddenly felt nauseous picturing Walter with Eugenie Whitwell. Moreover, he was probably in the company of her brother, Nick, and Cora Mayhew as well.

"Isn't it too soon for the girl to be out in public? Her father hasn't even been buried yet. I heard they've sent the body to New York. They're having the funeral there in a few days.

Surely the girl should stay in mourning at least until then?" Miss Lucy said.

"Yes, dear, it's most inappropriate," Miss Lizzie said.

Julia Grice frowned. "I thought it was quite the coup myself," she said. "Is Miss Whitwell not one of the richest heiresses in Newport?" Oh, how I wanted to tell her that Eugenie Whitwell would not be inheriting anything but debt, but I held my tongue. "Can a mother not want the best for her child?"

What about what your child wants?

"Yes, yes, of course," Miss Lucy said. "Her father was quite rich. I'm not arguing that she's not quite a catch for Dr. Grice, Julia, but that young people today don't seem to show the respect to their elders that they used to. When my father died, I didn't go into society for months."

"Yes, well, things are changing, Miss Lucy," Mrs. Grice said, slowly shaking her head. "Whether we like it or not. I simply thought Walter should take advantage of it."

I couldn't sit and listen to Walter's mother any longer. "If you'll excuse me," I said, standing, "I must be getting back."

The two sisters nodded their farewell.

"We'll speak again, Davish," Miss Lucy said. She was still itching to get all the gossip, which the arrival of Mrs. Grice had brought to a halt.

I left the room, relieved to be out of the ungracious woman's presence. But before I had taken two steps down the hall, I heard Miss Lizzie raise her voice and say, "Yes, Julia, dear, I couldn't agree with you more. Things are changing. Who knows what will happen next? Today a child attends a play days after her father's death; tomorrow a gentleman doctor falls for a lady typewriter."

Thank you, Miss Lizzie! I thought, smiling. And I was still smiling when I arrived at Rose Mont a quarter of an hour later.

CHAPTER 31

I wasn't smiling when I heard the foursome return. I'd gone to bed at lights-out like the rest of the staff, having spent the remainder of the day and evening in my sitting room sorting through stacks of invitations to luncheons, teas, dinner parties, balls, recitals, and lectures and updating Mrs. Mayhew's calendar, but as usual I couldn't sleep. I'd borrowed a lantern from the Servants' Hall and crept out of the house, hoping a few minutes of fresh air would help. I'd crossed the lawn and stood on the Cliff Walk path, taking deep inhales of the salty air, listening to the crash of the waves. After a few minutes, I heard raucous laughter and saw the swaying points of light from two lanterns coming toward me.

Who would be on the Cliff Walk at night? I wondered. Not wishing to be seen outside after dark, I blew out my light and stepped off the path. But my precaution was for naught. As I stepped off the path, the party veered toward the house.

"Who's there?" a man shouted. I'd only met him a few times, but I knew Nicholas Whitwell's voice. Was Walter with him? I wondered. I wasn't sure I wanted to know. The group stepped closer, confirming my suspicions.

"Miss Davish?" Walter said, holding up his lantern high to see. "Is that you?"

"Yes, Dr. Grice," I said, stepping into their circle of light.

"What are you doing out here?" Cora asked. "Does my mother know you're not in your bed at this hour of the night?"

Nicholas Whitwell laughed. "Could say the same about you," he said, laughing again. He was wearing a bandage on his right cheek.

When did he injure himself? I wondered. And how?

"Oh, Nick," his sister, Eugenie, said. Although she was inappropriately out in society, she was appropriately dressed in black.

"You haven't answered my question, girl," Cora said to me again.

Walter frowned. "Still not sleeping well, Miss Davish?" he said. I shook my head.

"You know this girl?" Eugenie asked, looking up at Walter.

"Yes," Walter said without elaborating.

Eugenie slipped her hand from Walter's arm and folded her arms across her chest. "How?" she said, pouting.

"Oh, Eugenie," her brother whined, "you can be such a bore. She's a secretary who once worked for those old busybody ladies Mrs. Grice is staying with."

Isn't everyone here a busybody? I thought.

"Besides, the man's a doctor. He knows about sleeping potions and stuff." Although the details were quite right, I was amazed that of all people, Nick Whitwell not only knew my history but also came to my defense. I wasn't at all sure I liked the idea of either.

"Oh," Eugenie said, placing her hand on Walter's arm again. "That's all right then."

I looked away. Being in Walter's presence, like this, was almost unbearable.

"You're right, Dr. Grice," I said, hardening my heart and straightening my shoulders. "I couldn't sleep and thought the night air would help."

"Oh, that's right," Cora said. "You saw Nick's father as well as that nasty labor man." I nodded. "Well, I certainly wouldn't be able to sleep after seeing two dead bodies," Cora said, shuddering. Nick dropped his head and kicked the ground absentmindedly. "I'm sorry, Nick," she said, lightly touching her hand to his cheek. "I shouldn't have brought it up."

"It's okay," Nick said, putting his arm around her. "The old man's dead. That's the way it is."

"Well, Miss Davish," Cora said, "I won't tell my mother, this time. Do see that it doesn't happen again. Come on, Nick. I'm cold."

Eugenie took a few steps to follow, but Walter stood his ground. "Walter?" Eugenie said. "Walter?" I cringed at Miss Whitwell's use of Walter's Christian name. Did they know each other more intimately than I'd thought? This time he removed Eugenie's hand from his arm. "What are you doing?" she said.

"I will bid you good night here, Miss Whitwell," Walter said. "I trust your brother will see you safely home?" Nick smiled and winked at Walter.

What was that about? I wondered until Nick turned and leered at me.

"Sure, Walt," he said. "Come along, Eugenie."

"Well, I never . . . ," his sister huffed. "Good night and good riddance, Dr. Grice." She swung her face away and stormed across the dark lawn, followed by her brother and Cora Mayhew.

"You're not going to win any favors for doing that, Dr. Grice," I said.

"With Miss Whitwell or with my mother?" Walter said.

"Either."

"I only went out tonight to appease Mother, but it seems one wrong step and the evening's good has been undone."

"It would seem so," I said.

"That's what I love about you, Hattie," Walter said, reaching for my hand. "You're so . . ."

I took a step back and shook my head. "Please, don't do this."

"What are you talking about?"

"This," I said, pointing back and forth from him to me. "I once told you we didn't live in the same world. The past two nights only prove it. I'm a girl who works for a living, Walter. You're a gentleman who would hire the likes of me, not court her."

"Hattie," Walter said, concern rising in his voice. "What are you saying? I told you I escorted Miss Whitwell to please my mother, that's all."

"But your mother objects to you even consorting with me, let alone . . ." I couldn't bring myself to voice my previous hopes for the future. I could see that it didn't matter now, maybe it never did. "Don't you see you could never escort me to Bailey's Beach or to the Casino, even if your mother didn't object?" I understood the logic, but my heart objected to every word I said. "Good night, Dr. Grice."

I meant to run across the lawn fleeing Walter Grice's presence as Eugenie Whitwell had, though for very different reasons, but even as I stepped away Walter grabbed my hand and pulled me to him. His arms encircled and restrained me.

"You're not getting away that easy," he whispered in my ear as tears streaked down my cheeks. "Oh, Hattie, don't cry," he said, looking down into my eyes. "I love you."

I buried my face into his chest, desperately wanting to believe him and stay in his arms forever but unable to face his ardent gaze or the truth that I couldn't do either.

★ ★ ★

"And did you see the bandage on his face?" Leonard, the newly promoted footman, said, busy polishing a spoon.

I peeked into the Servants' Hall before putting the lantern away. The table was laid with at least fifty pieces of silver: forks, spoons, knives, trays, teapots, sugar bowls, creamers, waste bowls, pitchers, urns, and candlesticks. Several others, including Miss Issacson and Monsieur Valbois, were drinking coffee and loitering about gossiping.

This would never have happened if Mrs. Crankshaw were still here, I thought.

After Walter escorted me back to the house, his arm around my waist and kissing me good night, I'd slept better than I had in weeks, but I'd forgotten to return the lantern. The first thought in my head upon waking this morning was the exact question I heard as I approached the Servants' Hall after breakfast. Why was Nick Whitwell wearing a bandage? I'd seen him at the ball. He was uninjured then. I hadn't thought to ask Walter last night if Nick had explained it. What had happened between the ball and the time he arrived to escort Miss Cora last night?

Lester Sibley was murdered, I thought.

"How did you see that?" Annie the chambermaid was asking as I passed the Hall again. I slowed down to listen.

"I answered the door when he came to escort Miss Mayhew," Leonard said.

"Did Miss Cora ask him about it?" Miss Issacson said.

"Of course she did."

"What did he say?" Annie said.

"Said he fell down after the ball, scraped his cheek on the driveway," Leonard said, laughing.

"Ha! Right he did," Annie said. "And Miss Cora believed him?" Did the chambermaid know something? I would have to talk to her alone later.

"Yeah," the footman said. "She's going to marry him, isn't she?"

"Good morning, Miss Davish," Davies, the butler, said as he passed by me.

"Good morning, Mr. Davies." Did he know I was listening at the door? I hoped not. I took a few steps down the hallway. As soon as he disappeared into the Servants' Hall, I backed up again. The conversation had come to an abrupt end.

"Who's going to marry whom?" I heard Davies ask.

"No one, Mr. Davies," Leonard said.

"All right then, everybody, get back to your work."

"Any news on a housekeeper, Mr. Davies?" Valbois asked.

"Yes, the missus hired one yesterday. She will be joining us sometime this morning."

"Bon," Valbois said loudly, then lowered his voice. "Any news on Mrs. Crankshaw?" I stepped closer to the open doorway to hear. I peeked in again to see the butler shake his head. The cook shrugged his shoulders, set his cup down, and stood. He disappeared into the kitchen.

"Any news on James, Mr. Davies?" Leonard said. I saw Britta coming down the hall carrying a tray. She half smiled to me in greeting. I decided to follow behind her.

"Yes, actually," Mr. Davies said as Britta and I entered the Hall. Mr. Davies looked right at me. "Rumor has it James has been hired by those two old sisters, Mrs. Fry and Miss Shaw, at Moffat Cottage."

"What's this, Mr. Davies?" Britta said. "What did you say about James?"

I realized I hadn't had a chance to tell her the good news yesterday. I'd returned late and had been preoccupied with organizing and updating Mrs. Mayhew's calendar. Britta must not have visited James last night or he would've told her. That Mr. Davies already knew was proof again that Newport's rumor mill was the swiftest I'd ever experienced.

The butler repeated himself. Britta followed Mr. Davies's gaze to look at me. "Is this true?"

I looked for permission from Mr. Davies to answer. He nodded.

"Yes, I was there when the Shaw sisters made the decision."

"We all know that Mr. Grady has enlisted in the navy," Davies said. "The elderly sisters were in need of a good manservant."

"But Mr. Mayhew discharged him without a reference, didn't he?" Leonard said.

"Yeah, and what about the police?" Annie said. "Don't they think James killed that labor man?"

Clank, clank, clank. The silver tray clattered when Britta dumped it onto the table. "Oh, Annie, you're awful," she said, and then fled the room, crying.

"What's gotten into her?" Leonard said.

"I don't know," Mr. Davies said, looking at the door where Britta had disappeared. "She's normally such a steady, reliable worker."

"All the more reason we need a new housekeeper," Mrs. Mayhew's lady's maid said.

"Yes, Miss Issacson, I couldn't agree with you more," Mr. Davies said, shaking his head as he strolled to his pantry. "Now off with you all," he said without turning around.

I stopped Annie in the hallway as we both left the Hall. "Do you have a minute?" I asked.

"Sure, Miss Davish, what is it?"

"I happened to overhear you talking about Mr. Whitwell's bandaged face."

She nodded. "Yeah, isn't that something?"

"Yes, it is, but what makes you think so?"

The maid furrowed her brow and frowned at me. "Isn't it

obvious? He's lying. He didn't get that by falling down in the driveway."

"And how do you think he got it?"

"I think that Lester Sibley clipped him one before he was killed," she said. I was astonished. How did she know about the connection between the two men, let alone make the ready assumption that Nick Whitwell killed Lester Sibley? She must've heard what happened at the ball.

"And why do you think Mr. Whitwell killed Lester Sibley?"

"Because I saw them."

"Wh-h-hat?" I said, stammering. This wasn't the response I'd expected. "When? Where?"

"Since I wasn't needed during the ball the other night, Mrs. Mayhew gave me permission to spend the evening with my folks. They live on Extension Street."

"And you saw Mr. Whitwell and Mr. Sibley when?"

"Well after dark. My father gave me money for cab fare. We were driving down Bellevue and I saw them. Mr. Whitwell had Lester Sibley's arm behind him, pushing him along." I realized that she might have mistaken who actually was with Lester Sibley.

"How do you know it was Mr. Whitwell? Did you get a good look at his face?"

"No, didn't have to. I heard how he threatened him at the ball, and then Sibley ends up dead and Mr. Whitwell has a bandage on his cheek. Isn't it obvious? Mr. Whitwell was dragging the union man to his death."

"Thank you, Annie."

"Sure," she said, turning away. She turned back again. "You're the one who found the guy, huh?"

"Yes, unfortunately," I said.

She nodded. "He was shot, like Mr. Whitwell, wasn't he?"

"Yes, unfortunately."

"I'm glad we know Mr. Whitwell did it," she said.

"Why's that?"

"Because if he's going around shooting people, at least I know I won't be next."

"And why's that, Annie?" I couldn't follow her logic at all.

"Because I'm nobody but a chambermaid. He doesn't have cause to kill me. Gotta go," she said, running up the stairs.

I didn't have the heart to tell her that if it had been the murderer she'd seen and they found out, she would indeed be next on the list. As Annie disappeared upstairs, I glanced down to see the laundress climbing up the stairs toward me.

"Delia," I said. "What luck to cross your path."

"Lucky for me or for you?"

"For me. I wondered if you've come across any beggar's-tick seeds on the laundry sent down yesterday, after the ball?"

"What are they?" she said, scowling.

"Prickly seeds that stick to everything. I went hiking the other day and spent half my evening picking them out of my skirt."

"Lord help me if I did then," Delia said. "I wouldn't have the time." She began to walk away.

"So you haven't seen any then? Not even a few on a sleeve or a collar?"

"No," she said, "now if you'll excuse me, I'm running late already."

"Of course," I said, amazed that the woman hadn't even asked why I wanted to know. "I heard there's a new house-keeper coming today!" I shouted at her back congenially.

"Now that's music to my ears," Delia called back.

Now to find the old one, I told myself, and bounded upstairs to change.

CHAPTER 32

After meeting with Mrs. Mayhew, updated calendar in
hand, and seeing her off to Mrs. Edith Wharton's breakfast party, I began my search for Mrs. Crankshaw. As an unemployed housekeeper, she would be anxious for similar work. I
pored over the *Situation Wanted* advertisements in the local
newspapers from the past two days. I read one for a "competent chambermaid, the best Newport and New York references," "a young man as coachman; first-class city and country
reference, disengaged on account of family going to Europe,"
several for first-class French cooks, and even one for "an experienced Englishman: expert at silver, salads, etc., thorough
valet, competent as butler, luncheons and dinners attended.
Good references," but no one who fit Mrs. Crankshaw's situation. With no luck from the newspapers, I headed out to visit
the employment agencies.

I visited two of the agencies with no luck. The plate next
to this second-story office door read: *Peck's Employment Agency
for Governesses & Domestic Servants*. I hoped I'd find a trail of
her here. There was only one agency left. I entered the plain,

whitewashed office and approached the woman reading behind the only desk. She was tall, thin, with a thick bun of pale
yellow hair piled on top of her head. She wore a simple white
shirtwaist with puffy sleeves and a plain navy blue, three-pleat
skirt. Spectacles stood on the end of her nose as she chewed
the end of her pencil.

"Good morning!" the woman said, smiling. She pushed up
the spectacles, took the pencil out of her mouth, and began
tapping it on her cheek. "My, aren't you a sight for sore eyes."

"Good morning," I said, surprised by her exuberant greeting. "Mrs. Peck?" I made a guess.

"Oh, yes," she said, pushing herself back from the desk and
standing. She examined me from head to toe as she rounded
the desk. "Well groomed, intelligent countenance, respectful
manner. Yes, I can find an excellent position for you." She
clapped her hands together. "Too bad the Mayhews already
hired Mrs. Ethel Broadbank. I think you'd make them an excellent housekeeper."

"Oh, I'm sorry," I said. "I'm—"

"Not a housekeeper," Mrs. Peck said, interrupting me.
"No, I should've guessed you were more cultured than that. A
governess, then?" I shook my head. "A lady's maid?"

"I'm not here looking for work."

"Oh, you're not?"

"No, in fact, I already have a position in the Mayhew
household. I'm Mrs. Mayhew's social secretary."

"I knew it," Mrs. Peck said. "I can always spot a professional girl when I see one."

"Thank you," I said, quite flattered.

"Too bad, though, I would've made a substantial commis-
sion. Well, what can I do for you, eh . . . I didn't get your
name."

"Hattie Davish."

"Yes, well, Miss Davish, since you aren't here to hire my

services, and are therefore obviously here on behalf of Mrs. Mayhew, what can I do for you?" I didn't correct Mrs. Peck. In some ways I was working on Mrs. Mayhew's behalf. The more I discovered, the less likely the police would interview anyone at Rose Mont again.

"I'm here to inquire about Mrs. Mayhew's former house-keeper, Mrs. Crankshaw," I said.

"Ah, Thelma Crankshaw, yes, well . . . actually, if you'd been here an hour ago . . ."

"She was here?"

"Yes, the delirious creature came in thinking I could help her."

"But you couldn't?"

"Oh, dear me, no," Mrs. Peck said, shaking her head.

"Do you at least know where I can find her?"

"Yes, let me get her file." She walked across the room to a row of black metal cabinets and bent down to retrieve a file from the bottom drawer of the last one. The drawer was marked *Hopeless*. "Yes, here it is. She's staying at the Perry House Hotel, room three-seventeen."

"Thank you, Mrs. Peck," I said. "May I ask a question?"

"Of course," the employment woman said, slipping the file back into the drawer and closing it with her foot.

"Why is that drawer labeled *Hopeless*?"

"Because, Miss Davish, there are certain individuals I cannot and will never be able to find employment for."

"And Mrs. Crankshaw is such a person?" I was shocked. "I grant you she's gruff and strict with her staff, but she must've been an excellent housekeeper. She worked for the Mayhews for seven years."

"Yes, all of that is true," Mrs. Peck said, sitting back down behind her desk. "But Mrs. Crankshaw is as well-known for her temper as she is for her work. Now she's been tainted by her association with strikers and was dismissed without a refer-

ence from her employer of seven years. And this time, from
what I hear, her temper got the best of her. She burned her
bridges, or should I say sliced up her lady's linen, when she left.
No potential employer is going to risk taking a vengeful
troublemaker such as Thelma Crankshaw on. I told her that
in no uncertain terms when she came in. I do think she was
quite upset by it, but it's the truth. How could I tell her otherwise?"

I pitied Mrs. Crankshaw and shuddered at the thought of
being in her position. Without the possibility of employment,
what would she do? Where would she go? How could this
woman sit there with so little compassion? Didn't she know
that single women with little or no family, women like Mrs.
Crankshaw, women like me, might be destitute without work?

"So as I say, Miss Davish," she said, pointing to the filing
drawer, "she's hopeless." Mrs. Peck suddenly smiled broadly.
Her odd reaction, after proclaiming the tragic end to someone's
life in service, startled me. "But you, on the other hand—"

"Thank you for your help, Mrs. Peck," I said, having the
urge to distance myself from this woman.

"Please tell Mrs. Mayhew how helpful I was."

"Of course," I said, putting my hand on the doorknob.

"And Miss Davish," she said, still grinning, as I opened the
door to leave, "if you are ever in need of a position, my door's
always open for you, my dear." I nodded but fled her office as
fast as I could. God help me if I was ever in need of going
through her door again!

The address Mrs. Peck had given me, the Perry House
Hotel, was a respectable four-story stone building with sec-
ond- and third-story balconies and a predominant square
cupola, attached to the Opera House on Washington Square. I
inquired at the desk and was directed to a room on the hotel's
top floor. I knocked. I waited a few moments and knocked

again. No answer. I pressed my ear to the door and heard movement inside.

"Mrs. Crankshaw, it's Hattie Davish. May I speak to you?"

No response. "Please, Mrs. Crankshaw. I need to speak to you." I was poised to knock again when the door opened slightly.

"What's all the fuss?" the housekeeper hissed through the crack in the door. "I don't take well to someone pounding on my door."

"I'm sorry, Mrs. Crankshaw," I said. "I didn't mean to disturb you."

"What are you doing here?"

"May I come in?"

"Why?"

"Because you've done nothing more terrible than slice up some linen," I said. "Please."

"You're right," she said. "I never spoke of striking. As you know, I don't take well to people who complain, especially when there's nothing to complain about. We earned a good, respectable living working for the Mayhews. Not one of my staff had reason to mutter the word *strike*. Mr. Mayhew was wrong to dismiss me. I never encouraged Lester to come here. That was all his doing. I told Lester—"

"And you didn't kill him either," I said, interrupting her.

The door flew open. I gasped. The room behind the former housekeeper, simply furnished with a single iron bed, a walnut dresser with a thin white lace runner, a small side table, and a chair, was dark and in shambles. The curtains were pulled shut, the counterpane was crumpled at the end of the bed, the table was covered with dirty coffee cups, plates of partially eaten food, and a bottle of whiskey more than half-empty, and pages of a newspaper were scattered across the floor. But that didn't compare to the state of the woman before me. Her eyes were bloodshot, most of her hair had fallen from its bun and

lay haphazard about her shoulders, and she was still wearing
her housekeeper's uniform, now wrinkled and covered with
dark stains. From the scent emanating from her, both the uniform and the woman had not been washed in days.

"Who says I did?" Mrs. Crankshaw demanded.

"You were seen threatening him."

She nodded. "Yes, I cursed him and spit on him, but I didn't
kill that idiot Lester, rest his soul. Plenty of enough others
wanted to see that done. My poor sister will miss him, of
course, but I think in the end she might be better off. Lester
wasn't much of a provider and he was always making trouble.
No, I didn't wish him well, but I certainly didn't kill him.
James, on the other hand, that was my fault. I did get James discharged. That was wrong of me. I see that now."

"And James already has a new, respectable position," I said,
taking advantage of her pause for breath. *Astounding,* I thought.
Even in her condition Mrs. Crankshaw was wont to talk inter-
minably. "You need not fret on his account."

"He has?" she said with a slight sense of hope in her voice.

"Yes. May I come in?"

"You still haven't told me why you're here."

"I need your help in solving your brother-in-law's murder."

"You?" She started to laugh, a strangled cackle deep in her
throat.

Her reaction alarmed me. I'd never heard Mrs. Crankshaw
laugh before. Was she intoxicated? Was she of sound mind?
Was she truly as hopeless as she seemed?

"Yes."

"But why you?"

"Mrs. Mayhew has charged me with assisting the police," I
said.

Mrs. Crankshaw turned to stare at the drawn drapes as if
she could see the view. "Because the truth may be too close to
Rose Mont?" she said cryptically.

"Yes, something like that," I said.

"How can I help?" The former housekeeper held up a hand to stop me from saying anything. "Before you ask, I'm only answering your questions because I don't want anyone to think I killed Lester. I wouldn't take well to people gossiping about me and saying I killed him when I didn't. Lester was a troublemaker, stirring up a hornet's nest for no good reason, but I can't say he got what he deserved. His heart was in the right place. But he went about it the wrong way. And my sister would be alone in the world now without me and of course I couldn't give satisfaction to those who think ill of me already."

"When was the last time you saw your brother-in-law?"

"After that fool disrupted Mrs. Mayhew's ball," she said, shaking her head. "What did she do without linen, by the way?"

"She borrowed some from Mrs. Whitwell."

Mrs. Crankshaw nodded in approval. "Right! Good thinking. That lady won't be using it for months. I'm surprised Mrs. Mayhew thought of it, though." I didn't enlighten her of the truth. She sighed. "I let my temper get the best of me there."

"Yes, you could say that," I said.

"What? Are you implying something?" My attempt to lighten the mood was ineffective. Mrs. Crankshaw was defensive and unpredictable. I returned to my task of getting answers.

"No, Mrs. Crankshaw. I was simply agreeing with you. Could you tell me where you were the night and morning after your brother-in-law was killed?" I asked.

"I was here," she said absentmindedly.

"Alone? Or can someone corroborate your whereabouts?" She didn't seem to hear me.

"I've always wanted to be a housekeeper," she said. "You should be able to understand, if you're as good at your job as they say." I nearly blushed hearing this unexpected compliment. "I wanted to be the best. And I was. I worked for one of the richest, most powerful families in America. I ran two households, never complaining, never demanding anything more than loyalty, respect, and a hard day's work from my girls. And now . . ." Her voice trailed off as she stared at the door. "And now I'm branded a troublemaker, an anarchist, when the truth is that I don't take well to rule breakers and troublemakers."

"I don't know about those labels, Mrs. Crankshaw, but I may be able to eliminate 'killer' from the list, if you'll let me." She looked at me. "Will you answer a few more questions?"

"Right," she said, focusing once again. "I didn't kill him."

"I believe you," I said, not knowing why I did, but I did. "Were you here alone?"

She chuckled. "If I had had a man in my bed, I wouldn't have to worry where my next meal is going to come from."

I blushed again. "I didn't mean to imply . . ." She smiled for the first time. I was relieved, even if it was at my expense. "Did anyone see you?"

"No, I haven't left the room since I saw Lester after the ball."

"Would you mind if I inspected your clothes?" I said, indicating her housekeeper's dress, a separate skirt and bodice of plain black cotton. She frowned.

"Why?"

"Please?"

She looked down at herself. "I haven't had a chance to launder it yet," she said quietly.

"That's a good thing," I said, stepping closer. I walked around her, inspecting the dress as she watched me with suspicion.

"What are you looking for?"

"Evidence that will convict Lester's killer," I said.

"And?"

"And I didn't find anything."

"Right! Now what?"

"Maybe now you can find a way back to your sister in Queens and start over? She needs you now as much as you need her." The former housekeeper nodded and then burst into tears. I was speechless.

"Get out of here," she said, suddenly shooing me away from the door with her hands. "I don't take well to people who gawk at those less fortunate. You'll not get satisfaction from pitying me." Her comment stung. We were two workingwomen who could relate to each other's plight. I thought we had made a connection. Somehow I had expected more.

"Good-bye, Mrs. Crankshaw," I said cheerlessly. "I wish you the best of luck."

"Right!" she said, slamming the door in my face.

"He's no longer in Newport. I sent a wire to the Pinkerton detective agency. I'm waiting for the reply. Maybe then we'll know whom he's working for and why he was in Newport."

After leaving Mrs. Crankshaw to her own devices, I went to the police station to find Chief Preble. As I entered, he slapped a large fish onto the newspaper he had spread across his desk. With filet knife in hand, he began cleaning the fish as we talked. Unable to stomach the bloody entrails he pulled from the fish and dropped on the newspaper, I stared down at the plank wooden floor as I told him what I'd learned about James and Mrs. Crankshaw, including how I believed neither of them had killed Lester Sibley. Silas Doubleday was another story.

"You didn't have to send a telegram to find that out," I said. "I'm certain Doubleday was working for Mr. Mayhew."

"Why? Why did Gideon Mayhew have need of a Pinkerton man?"

"To rid him of Lester Sibley." I relayed every encounter I'd had with Silas Doubleday from the incident on the boat before we arrived to the conversation I overheard between Gideon

Mayhew and Silas Doubleday the morning I found Lester Sibley's body.

"From what you tell me, Silas Doubleday is our prime suspect."

"I didn't kill anyone," the man himself declared as he was led into the room in front of another police officer.

"Well, Collins, this is unexpected," Chief Preble said, speaking to his fellow officer but watching the detective. He rolled the newspaper up, fish, blood, guts, and all, and pushed it aside. "I thought you were in Providence on the Shackleton case. I've been waiting for Ballard to bring me back news of the man, and here you have the man himself."

"I was as surprised as you, sir. I'd gotten your wire to keep a lookout but didn't expect to see the man. I'd finished up that Shackleton business and was waiting for the train to come back. What luck, sir, I must say, to see Doubleday getting off the train at the time as I was getting on!"

"I didn't kill him," Doubleday said again as Patrolman Collins pushed down on his shoulder, forcing him to sit. "Lester Sibley was still alive when I left him. You can ask anybody at Condon's Saloon on Long Wharf."

"Okay, Doubleday," Preble said. "Tell me your story. Start with the party."

"I hauled Sibley away from Rose Mont after he interrupted the Mayhews' ball. Some crazy woman jumped out of the bushes at us, spitting at him."

"That would be Mrs. Crankshaw," I said. Chief Preble nodded, remembering my version of these events.

"Yeah, well, whoever she was," Doubleday said, "we left her at the gate, and went down Bellevue. At least two carriages drove by. One was a cab. I'm sure you could find the drivers." I relayed the chambermaid Annie's account of seeing Doubleday from her cab to the policemen.

"Okay," the chief said, "and then what happened?"

"I took him to his rooms on Spring Street," Doubleday said. "The landlady let us in. It was late and she wasn't shy about letting us know just how late."

"So the landlady can verify when you brought him back?"

"Yeah, the exact time too, because she kept glancing at her clock."

"And then what?"

"We went up to his room, I watched him pack and then I escorted him to the wharf. I even gave him enough money for a one-way ticket out of Newport. I told him to be gone by morning."

"And then you left?"

"Yes, I went straight to Condon's for a drink or two and then to the Ale and Oyster House. They have the best oysters in town." I cringed at the thought. The one and only time I'd eaten oysters, someone died and I'd spent an extremely unpleasant night lying on the floor next to my chamber pot. "I was there until I caught the train this morning. Ask anyone there. Lots of people saw me."

Chief Preble motioned to one of the patrolmen. "Go speak to the landlady and then ask around at the saloon," the chief said. "Speak to William Rife, the proprietor, if he's there." The patrolman nodded, snatched up his hat, and left. "And Lester Sibley, he was still alive when you left him?" Chief Preble asked Doubleday.

"Yes, of course, though before I left I did . . ." The detective suddenly hesitated. He began to whistle "Ode to Joy" under his breath.

"Before you left you did what? Break both the man's arms?" Preble asked.

"Yeah, well, I admit to that. He had it coming, showing up at Mr. Mayhew's house after all."

"What else did you do, Doubleday?"

"I . . . ah. It was only talk. I was trying to frighten the guy into leaving, you know. He'd been stubborn before."

"If it was only talk, what did you say to him, Doubleday?"

"I warned him what would happen if he didn't get on that boat and leave."

"What could you possibly say that would further prove your point? You'd already broken both the man's arms." Detective Doubleday dropped his head on his chest, refusing to speak. Preble grabbed the Pinkerton man's chin and jerked his head upright. "So what did you tell him would happen?"

"I told him he was a dead man."

CHAPTER 33

After a taxing day and a half it was a relief to sit at my typewriter, feel the comfort of the keys beneath my fingertips, and work. Mrs. Mayhew had requested an account of how I'd spent my time, as she would say, "keeping the police away from Rose Mont." As I pulled the second sheet of paper from my typewriter, I glanced at the suspect list I'd created yesterday. Taking up my pen, I crossed out Mrs. Crankshaw and James. And then I reluctantly crossed out Detective Doubleday. Before I'd left the police station, the patrolman sent to speak to Lester Sibley's landlady and the proprietor of the alehouse returned, verifying Doubleday's account. That only left the Mayhews and the surviving Whitwells. I shook my head.

This can't be. There has to be someone else. I looked at the list again. What was I thinking? Suspecting any one of these people would not do me one bit of good. In fact, the list's very existence put me at risk of losing my position. I had to destroy it.

Before I could question what I was doing, I pushed back from the desk, stood up, and grabbed the list of suspects. I strode over to the fireplace, retrieved a match from the mantel, and lit a candle. I placed the corner of the paper in the flame. The moment the paper caught, I threw it into the cold fireplace. The flame grew as the paper shriveled up, turned brown and then black. I jabbed the paper several times with a poker, certain to reduce it to ashes.

I returned to my desk, put another piece of paper into the typewriter, and began to make a new list of who else might have killed Lester Sibley.

1.

I sat with my fingers poised over the keys, but nothing came to my mind except the image of Jane Whitwell trying to run Lester Sibley down in the street with her son's car and Nick Whitwell threatening Sibley at the police station and again at the ball. At least I'd never seen Eugenie threaten the man, I thought. Could the mother and son have been in it together? But why? To protect Harland Whitwell's reputation by deflecting blame elsewhere? Or did they believe Lester Sibley and his threats of strike drove Mr. Whitwell to take his own life?

I stared at the blank list until the rattle of my doorknob startled me out of my reverie.

"Who is it?" I asked, glancing at the fireplace.

"It's me, Hattie. I have your dinner."

"Oh, do come in, Britta," I said, sighing in relief. But who did I think it was?

The parlormaid, with Bonaparte at her heels, came in with a tray. Britta wasn't in the mood for talking. She smiled as she set down the tray but left the moment I thanked her. I wasn't much in the mood for eating. I sipped some coffee, took nibbles of the sponge cake, and absently fed Bonaparte bits of the fried codfish in sauce tartare as I stared at the ashes growing cold in the fireplace. I might have destroyed the evidence of my suspicion, but I couldn't shake the feeling that I was right: Someone on that list was responsible for Lester Sibley's death.

"I don't need you for the rest of the morning," Mrs. Mayhew said. "As long as you keep me informed as you have been, you may do what you will."

I'd spent another restless night, but having fallen asleep in the early morning hours, I nearly overslept and missed Britta bringing in my breakfast. Mrs. Mayhew rang for me as I was finishing my cold coffee and toast. To my relief, we slipped into the quiet routine of her approving menus and bills to be paid and dictating responses for over three dozen invitations she'd received the day before. Miss Lucy had been right. Now that she had gained Mrs. Astor's approval and had firsthand knowledge of a murdered man, Mrs. Mayhew was very likely the most popular guest in Newport.

I was disappointed to be dismissed. I needed the distraction. On another day I might have relished the chance to go hiking or finally visit Easton Beach and go swimming, but today my thoughts were preoccupied with ways to prove one of the Whitwells killed Lester Sibley. How I would accomplish this without the police's help and without jeopardizing my position I had no idea. It was an insurmountable task. I decided to take a hike anyway and headed back down Ocean Avenue. An easy seaside stroll might put my mind at rest.

I made the right decision. The solitude was a boon, allowing my mind to empty of all my cares: death, secrets, and Walter's mother. Only twice did a carriage pass by, interrupting my repose. As I strolled along, I concentrated on the gentle sounds of the wind rustling through the brush and the quiet lapping of the water. I found a large, flat stone on a tranquil sandy beach and sat there for over an hour watching the black cormorants preen and sun themselves, with outstretched wings, on the rock outcrops jutting up through the water. The reality in which one family attended balls, dinner parties, and lawn tennis tournaments while their neighbor suffered from the ill effects of gossip and suicide felt a world away.

It felt a world away, that is, until I saw Eugenie Whitwell and Cora Mayhew leaving Bailey's Beach on my return toward Rose Mont. I couldn't help but scan the area to see if Walter was with them. I hadn't seen Walter since Tuesday night and couldn't help wondering if he'd been with Eugenie again. But the girls were alone. I tried to pass unseen, but without luck.

"Miss Davish," Cora Mayhew said, "what are you doing here?"

"Your mother gave me the morning off. I was enjoying a stroll on this beautiful day."

"Well, you always seem to be where you shouldn't," Euge-nie Whitwell said, picking at the black lace about her collar. "This is a private beach."

"I was just passing," I said, biting my tongue, trying to stay professional. What I wanted to say was, with her father dead less than a week, that it was she who had been where she shouldn't. I resolved for a less petty reply. "And I am in the road, not on the beach."

Eugenie rolled her eyes. "All the same," she said.

"I've heard you've been asking around about that man who was murdered," Cora said.

"Yes, your mother asked me to."

"Mother? I knew she was a gossip, but honestly, Miss Davish, that's going too far."

"She hopes to avoid another visit from the police," I explained.

"Oh, yes, now that sounds like Mother."

"May I ask you a question?" I said, having no better way to broach this subject than to ask directly. "About Mr. Nicholas Whitwell?"

"Absolutely not," his sister said.

"Eugenie," Cora said, putting her hand on her friend's arm. "You and I both know that Nick is not above suspicion. You were there. He threatened the man, for goodness' sake. Miss Davish isn't going to say or do anything that my mother doesn't approve first. Isn't it best that she ask the questions, rather than the police?" Eugenie shrugged. "You may ask your question, Miss Davish, though I don't know what I could tell you."

"Do either of you know where Mr. Whitwell went after he left the ball? Or where he was the next morning?"

"See," Eugenie said, pointing her finger at me while looking at her friend. "She suspects Nick. First my father and now this!"

"That's the trouble, Miss Davish," Cora said, ignoring her friend's outburst. "No one knows where Nick went. And he's not talking."

"Next you'll want to know how he hurt himself," Eugenie said snidely.

"Yes, it would be good to clear that up," I said.

The loud roar of a motorcar engine rumbled a few moments before the machine was in view. Nick Whitwell drove around the bend and headed right for us, swerving and skidding to a stop on the sandy road. We all leaped several feet backward to avoid our feet being run over.

"Oh, Nick!" Cora yelled. "You frighten me every time with that thingamajig."

"And you love it," he said. Cora smiled. Nick pushed open the door and jumped out. The only sign of his mourning was a black band of crape around his arm and straw hat.

Astonishing, I thought.

"We were just talking about you, Nick," Eugenie said. She sneered when she pointed at me. "The social secretary turned policeman has a few questions for you." Nick stomped over to me and stood far too close for my comfort. Unlike when the incident in the house took place, I didn't have a wall behind me. I took a step back.

"What are you asking about?" he demanded.

"Everyone's wondering where you went after the ball," Cora said.

"Whose business is it anyway?" he said, thankfully turning away from me and confronting Cora.

"Please tell us where you were, Nick. Otherwise it makes it seem like you have something to hide," Cora said.

"I was on the yacht, okay?" Nick said, heading back toward his car. "I was drunk and didn't want my mother to see me. Is that a crime?"

"No, of course not," his sister said.

"So why not just say so before?" Cora asked. He ignored her.

"Satisfied?" he said to me.

"Is the yacht anchored by the Lime Rock Lighthouse?" I asked.

"No, it's in Brenton Cove. Why?"

"Lester Sibley was found dead in a stand of bushes in sight of the Lime Rock Lighthouse."

"So? You think I killed him?" He stormed back toward me.

Cora stepped between us and put her hand on his arm. "It's not just her, Nick. I heard you tried to run him down with your car." Nick laughed. Cora frowned. "This is serious, Nick. Is it true?"

"Who told you that? Believe me, if I wanted to run him down, he would've been dead in the street, not hidden in some bushes."

I knew Nick was telling the truth, at least about the incident with the car. But I'd been sworn to secrecy by his mother. Could Jane Whitwell have killed Lester Sibley? She'd been on my suspect list, but I'd never seriously considered her before. After failing to kill him with the car, did she shoot him with her husband's gun? Had she taken revenge out on Lester Sibley, killing him the same way her husband had died? Or was Nick lying about being on his father's yacht?

Nick walked to the car and opened the passenger side door. "Come on, ladies, Mother's waiting." Cora and Eugenie climbed in. "How about you?" he said, looking at me. Eugenie glared at him.

"Me?" From my brief inspection of the car, I saw several places where the paint had been scraped away and the front fender was bent. The way he drove, it was a wonder there wasn't more damage. No, I was not about to get into a motorized carriage with a reckless driver, let alone a possible murderer.

"There's room, so I must insist," he said.

"That's kind of you, but I'll walk."

"I insist."

"She said no, Nick," Eugenie said. She didn't want me in the car any more than I did.

"I don't care. I've been the gentleman and offered her a ride. She's not going to turn me down. Are you, Miss Davish?" he said, spitting out my name like a piece of rotten fruit.

"Please get in, Miss Davish," Cora said, rolling her eyes at the bickering siblings.

Between Nick's veiled threat and Cora's insistence, I had no choice. I clambered in, squeezing my way into the back with Eugenie. She glared at me but said nothing.

"By the way," Cora said, gently touching the bandage on Nick's cheek. "You did say you got this falling in the driveway, right?"

"Oh, you know," Nick said, smirking.

The motor revved and we lurched forward with a jerk. The sound was so deafening as to put an end to all conversation. I grabbed ahold of my hat as Nick Whitwell took every opportunity to cut corners close or to swerve violently around carriages, startling the horses. Cora screamed in delight. Nick's driving reminded me of Walter's but with an ill intent. When we finally reached Glen Park, I didn't know who was happier to get out of the car, me or Eugenie. Yet I still had to wait for everyone else to get out before I was able to extricate myself from the contraption.

I will never ride in one of these things again!

"Thank you, Mr. Whitwell," I said, biting my tongue. *Let him assume I mean for the ride and not for my arriving in one piece.*

"Sorry, but you had to know," he said. So he had driven recklessly, endangering all of our lives, to teach me a lesson.

"Un, deux, trois," I counted under my breath. "Had to know what, Mr. Whitwell?" I asked when I gained control of my temper.

"That if I had wanted to run Lester Sibley down, he'd be dead."

I already knew that! I nearly shouted, but refrained. I clenched my fists, dangerously close to losing my temper. *And my job,* I thought. I took a deep breath.

"But he is dead, Mr. Whitwell," I said, satisfied as the shock of either my words or the presumption of my behavior registered on everyone's face. Eugenie gasped. "And I intend to find out who killed him," I said before I turned on my heel and walked away.

With my head pounding and my ears still ringing from the jarring roar and racket of the motorcar's engine, I knocked at the servants' entrance of Glen Park again. I inquired of Mrs. Johnville, who opened the door, whether I could speak to the laundress. Without a word, Mrs. Johnville had one of the scullery maids show me the way down to the basement.

She'll be glad to see the back of me, I thought.

"Hey, Jesse," the scullery girl said. "Someone's here to see you." Then the maid turned and ran back up the stairs. Jesse looked up from wringing out a piece of black linen.

"Good morning, Jesse," I said as I approached the boiling vats of water. "I'm Hattie Davish, Mrs. Mayhew's secretary."

"Yeah?" the laundress said, putting her arm and whole shoulder into her task.

"I wondered if you've happened to come across beggar's-tick seeds on any of the clothes from the past few days."

"Beggar's-what?"

"Little seeds, about this big," I said, holding up my thumb and index finger to show her. "They stick to clothes and are bothersome to remove."

"Yeah, I have," she said, surprised to know what I was talking about.

My heart skipped a beat. "You have?" I tried to contain my excitement.

"Yeah, they were a bear to get out. I pricked my fingers." She held out a finger for my inspection. It was red and raw, like her whole hand. I didn't see any puncture marks, but I believed her. My heart was beating fast. I was about to discover who killed Lester Sibley. "Luckily there were only a few of them."

I frowned. A knot welled up in the pit of my stomach. *Only a few?* From my foray into the bushes where Lester Sibley lay dead I had over a hundred seeds stuck to my skirt. I would've thought the killer's pants or skirt would be likewise thickly covered.

"Why do you want to know?" she asked.

"I've been given permission by Mrs. Mayhew to help the police in their investigation of Lester Sibley's death," I said.

"Ah, you're the one that was asking around about old Mr. Whitwell too, aren't ya?"

"Yes, I'm afraid so. Now about the beggar's-tick seeds," I said, hoping she wouldn't ask me more about her master's demise and delay telling me who might've killed Lester Sibley. "Do you remember whose clothes they were on?"

"Sure, there's only one man in the house now," she said sadly.

So it's true, I thought. *Nicholas Whitwell killed Lester Sibley.*

"I won't be washing shirts for Mr. Whitwell anymore."

"Shirts?" I said. This didn't seem right either.

"Yeah, the prickly seeds were on the collar and sleeve of Master Nicholas's shirt."

"And you found nothing on any of his pants?"

The laundress shook her head. "No."

This didn't make any sense. If Nick had waded into that patch of bushes to either shoot Lester Sibley or hide his body, he must've gotten more than a few seeds stuck to his shirt. Could he have plucked most of them off, including all of those from his pants, while missing a few on collar and sleeve? Nick did not strike me as the methodical type. Maybe he simply got rid of the pants in question.

"Are all Nick's clothes accounted for?" I asked the laundress.

"Of course."

Could I've gotten it wrong? Could the killer have shot Lester Sibley and walked away with only a few or none of the sticky seeds? The police had cleared James and Mrs. Crankshaw in part because their clothes were seed free. Anyone could remove a few. What was I going to tell Chief Preble? Mrs. Mayhew? I'd been so sure.

"Even the pair he wore the night of the ball?" I asked.

"Especially that pair." The laundress snickered. "I don't want to say anything bad about the gentleman, but the man's a slob. I always have to clean coffee and wine stains from his pants. That pair even had grass stains on it! And now that I'm thinking about it, the shirt with the prickers had grass stains too. . . ." Jesse hesitated and squinted her eyes at me.

"What is it, Jesse?" I said.

"I didn't think much of it at the time, because like I said

Master Nick isn't known for his kind treatment of clothes." *Or anything or anyone else for that matter,* I thought.

"But?"

"But in light of why you're here asking me these questions, I've got to ask myself something."

"And what is that?"

"Why did the shirt, you know, the one with the beggar seeds on it, also have blood on it?"

"That's a good question, Jesse," I said, my hopes rising. "A very good question."

CHAPTER 34

"Once again I must apologize for intruding upon your grief, Mrs. Whitwell, but I wonder if you know where your son is?"

After speaking with the laundress, I immediately tried to find Nick Whitwell. Yet despite the fact that I had left him with Cora and Eugenie by his motorcar less than fifteen minutes ago, he was nowhere to be found.

"You are intruding," she said. "Please leave."

"I'd like to ask him a few questions."

"I will not ask you to leave again, Miss Davish. Now go on."

"Ma'am, right now, your son is the prime suspect in the murder of Lester Sibley."

"How can you possibly say that? Nick had no reason to kill that man."

"He must've had a reason," I said. "Maybe he blamed Lester Sibley, the harassment, the threat of strikes, for your husband's suicide? Or maybe he merely wanted it to look like your husband was murdered in order to collect the insurance money and avoid scandal?"

"How dare you accuse my son based on such flimsy speculation? I will not have you disparaging my son's good character with such lies."

"He did lash out at Lester Sibley at the ball. And he tried to choke the man at the police station."

"So?"

"Ma'am, the shirt your son was wearing at the ball had beggar's-tick seeds and blood on it. And he has no true alibi."

Mrs. Whitwell turned her head away. I thought I'd finally convinced her that her son was in serious trouble if what I suspected was true. Instead she surprised me with a dismissal. "And what if he did kill him?" she said. "Harland Whitwell, my husband and Nicholas and Eugenie's father, is dead. No one will blame Nick for lashing out at the man responsible. That labor man was nothing but a pest." My jaw dropped in utter astonishment. How could anyone have such a sense of superiority, a sense of living above the rules of a civilized society? Besides, we both knew Lester Sibley had nothing to do with her husband's death. Before I could respond, though I have no idea what I would've said, Weeks stepped in through the open doorway.

"You have visitors, ma'am." He held out a small tray with four calling cards, all with the bottom right corner bent, indicating a condolence call. "I told them you were in mourning. Shall I send them away?"

She glanced at the names on the cards. "No, send them up, Weeks," she said. "Miss Davish and I are finished." Thus the end of my interview.

"Certainly, ma'am. This way, Miss Davish," the butler said. I followed him out the door and down the steps. Weeks disappeared into a small receiving room off the entrance hall. "Mrs. Whitwell will see you now," Weeks said to those waiting as I passed by on my way out.

"Davish," Miss Lucy called. I looked in as Miss Lucy, Miss

Lizzie, Walter, and his mother were rising from their chairs. They were Mrs. Whitwell's visitors. I waited for them in the hall. "What brings you here?"

"I'm conveying my condolences as you are," I said, purposely vague. Miss Lucy frowned. Walter smiled at me. Mrs. Grice saw her son's reaction. Her countenance was blank.

"Follow me, please," Weeks said.

"Visit us when you can, dear," Miss Lizzie said, patting my cheek.

"Or sooner," her sister said. "You still have much to tell us."

"I'll try," I said, not anxious to spar with Miss Lucy over gossip and news I was honor bound not to reveal. Walter pressed my hand slightly as he passed. The three followed Weeks up the stairs. I turned to leave.

"Coming, Julia, dear?" Miss Lizzie said. I looked back. Mrs. Grice hadn't followed the group. Instead she was inspecting a hand-painted porcelain vase, displayed on a pedestal at the foot of the stairs, depicting the Greek goddess Gaia, half rising from the earth.

"Yes, I'll be but a moment," Julia Grice said.

"Mother?" Walter said, concerned.

"Go on, Walter. I'll follow you shortly."

Walter frowned but followed the elderly sisters up the stairs. I continued toward the door.

"Miss Davish, wait," Walter's mother said.

I knew a demand when I heard one. I turned again to see her staring at me. "Is there something I can do for you, Mrs. Grice?" I asked.

"Yes, Miss Davish, there is." And then she smiled at me for the first time. My heart raced and my fingertips started to go numb.

I liked it better when she was scowling, I thought. "And what is that, Mrs. Grice?" I forced myself to ask. I didn't want to know the answer.

"You can leave my son alone."

"Ma'am?"

"I can't say it any plainer, Miss Davish," she said, slowly walking toward me. "You will not see my son again. Is that understood?"

"Is that what Walter wants?"

"How dare you ask me that? I'm his mother. Who are you to question me?"

"I believe I'm the woman your son loves." I finally said it. I finally voiced what my heart wanted to believe, but the moment I did I wished I hadn't. Julia Grice's lips curled. I thought she was going to spit on me. Instead she did something worse. She laughed. And she looked so much like Walter, unbidden tears welled up in my eyes.

"You think Walter loves you? You, a working girl? Walter doesn't love you. He's amusing himself with you, that's all." I let out a gasp and a few tears rolled down my face. "Oh, dear, you poor girl." She stepped forward and gently put a hand on my cheek. I was so stunned, I couldn't move. I couldn't bring myself to shrug her hand off. She patted my face with her fingers. "I had nothing to fear from you after all, did I?"

"Why would you fear me?" I whispered.

"Because you could jeopardize everything. I have high expectations for Walter's future, and you, or any girl like you, have no place in it. After all I've done to educate him and support him in his dalliances, I'm entitled to nothing less." My shoulders shook as I fought the torrent of tears bubbling up from deep within me. I would not let this woman see how much her words hurt. "I pity you, Miss Davish. Walter has obviously been a naughty boy." She released her hand and started up the stairs.

"Oh, and Miss Davish," she said, turning and looking down at me. I didn't care what else she had to say. I didn't care if she told Mrs. Whitwell how impertinent I was. I didn't care if Mrs. Whitwell told Mrs. Mayhew that her secretary was dis-respectful to a guest. I didn't care if she revealed that she killed Lester Sibley. I wasn't going to hear another word from that woman's mouth. Before she could say more, I wiped my eyes with the back of my hand, picked up my skirts, and ran.

And nearly ran right into Mrs. Mayhew.

"Miss Davish!" the lady exclaimed.

"I'm so sorry, ma'am," I said.

"Why are you in such a rush?"

I couldn't tell her the truth, so I lied. I've tried repeatedly to curtail the habit but I slipped back into it too easily.

"I'd noticed the time, ma'am, and thought you'd be want-ing me back at Rose Mont."

"Well, that's conscientious of you, but I'm actually glad that you're here."

"Ma'am?"

"I have a task for you and I was dreading having to wait. Now you can go do it for me, posthaste." I brushed the front of my tan-and-yellow-striped day dress and straightened my hat with matching yellow silk roses. I'd thought I looked smart this morning. Now nothing mattered. I took a deep breath, banishing thoughts of Walter and his disagreeable mother.

"Yes, what is it you'd like me to do?"

"Search Gideon's yacht again."

Not that again, I thought, letting a sigh escape my lips. I looked immediately at Mrs. Mayhew to see if she noticed my reaction to her request. If she did, she didn't comment on it. I was lucky. She might've taken offense.

"Ma'am? Am I looking for something new?" Why would she send me back to search an empty yacht?

"No, with Mr. Mayhew in New York, I simply want you to look again." She obviously had her suspicions but wasn't going to share them with me.

"For evidence that someone is staying on the yacht?"

"Yes," she said, stopping as we both heard footsteps approaching. "I'd like you to do it right now, while I visit with Jane."

"Of course," I said as Nick Whitwell came into sight.

"Oh, Nick," Mrs. Mayhew said. "I'm so sorry about your father." Nick walked right past me without a word or glance, into Mrs. Mayhew's outstretched arms. She patted him on the back before he stepped away. "I'm going up to see your mother. Will you escort me?"

"Of course, Charlotte," he said.

"I'll be back at Rose Mont in an hour or so," Charlotte Mayhew said to me, placing her hand on Nick Whitwell's arm. *An hour?* That would barely be enough time for me to get to the yacht and back to Rose Mont. At least it would give me something else to think about. She began climbing the stairs, talking over her shoulder as she went. "I'd like a full report by then. It needn't be typed up. You can tell me what you found."

"Yes, Mrs. Mayhew," I said as Nick Whitwell looked down at me and sneered. "Be careful," I added but left unsaid, *You may be holding the arm of a killer.*

CHAPTER 35

"Mack, is that you?" I shouted.

No answer. The same boatman as before had been kind enough to row me back to Mr. Mayhew's yacht, no questions asked. But why would he come aboard? I called again. Still no answer.

I'd been aboard the *Invictus* a few minutes and saw nothing that indicated a woman had been here. Yet Mrs. Mayhew may have been partially right; someone had been here. A man's waistcoat and tie were tossed over a chair. An ashtray filled with the butts of several cigars, a dirty glass that smelled of port, and a pair of spectacles sat on a table in the yacht's small library. A small set of dumbbells lay in the middle of an unmade bed. Were members of the yacht crew living aboard the ship? I wondered. From the sound of footsteps I'd heard, whoever it was may have returned.

"Hello? Who's there?" No one answered my call. I climbed the stairs and peered around the deck. I saw no one. If a member of the yacht crew had returned, why weren't they answering my call?

"Mack?" I called again. I stepped onto the deck and looked down to where the boatman and the dinghy should be. They were nowhere in sight. A surge of fear and panic shot through my body.

Where did he go? How was I going to get back? And if Mack was gone, then whose footsteps had I heard? I grabbed hold of the railing and yelled, "Mack! Where are you? Mack!"

I heard no reply from the boatman but instead heard the quiet tap of footsteps merely feet away. I started to look back, but suddenly two hands twisted my head, snapping my face forward. The brim of my straw hat crunched loudly as it broke, blinding me.

"Help!" I screamed.

My attacker put a hand in the middle of my back and shoved me hard. I pitched forward, losing my grip, and tumbled over the railing. My hat flew off my head, but it was too late. I didn't see who pushed me. My hand smacked the side of the boat as I flailed in mid-air, desperate to stop my fall. And then I slammed into the water. I opened my mouth from the shock of the hit and water surged in. Gasping for breath, I forced my head above the surface, spitting water and gulping for air at the same time. I thrashed about, splashing my arms, trying to stay above the water, but the weight of my sodden dress, corset, and shoes conspired to pull me under. I went down a second time. I struggled to the surface again but could barely get my face out of the water. I gulped for air, desperate to breathe, to scream for help, but I gagged on the water filling my lungs before I slipped beneath the water again.

Splash!

The sound was muffled, but the dark blot above me, blocking the sun's rays as they reached their tendrils toward me in the deep, confirmed something or someone else had entered the water. *Have they come to finish me?* I struggled to swim away as the darkness drew closer, but I grew tired, light-headed, and my vision began to fade as I slipped farther and farther under the waves. I closed my eyes to the approaching darkness and floated weightless with the sun's sparkle dancing like stars around me. Suddenly I felt pressure again. I felt arms wrapping around me. I was moving upward, rushing toward the sun, toward the surface. I was forcibly propelled into the air and gasped once again.

"Walter," I said, sputtering. The doctor had one arm wrapped around my waist, pulling me along with him as he swam toward a rowboat bobbing on the water a few yards away. "Walter," I said again before everything went black.

"She gonna be okay?" a man said.

I came to abruptly, violently coughing up water. I rolled onto my side and then my knees. I was on the dock with Walter kneeling beside me.

"That a girl," Walter said, placing a hand on my back. "Get it all out."

"What happened?" I said.

"You were drowning, Hattie. Thank goodness, I got to you in time."

"How did I get onshore?"

"I helped him pull you from the water," the man said. "You're undeniably a landlubber, aren't ya, miss?"

"Mack?" I said, peering up at the boatman standing above me.

"Yup."

"Thank you," I said. "Thank you both."

Walter chuckled. "I told you I needed to chaperone you more." Then his smile disappeared as he helped me to sit up. He leaned forward and whispered, "To tell you the truth, you had me quite worried. Try to stay still and quiet for a moment." He pulled out his watch, placed his fingers on my wrist, and watched the hands tick. Walter dropped his hand from my wrist and then crawled behind me, placing his ear against my back. I blushed and gazed at the ground, the boatman looming over me, witness to one of the more intimate moments between me and Walter.

"Take a deep breath," the doctor said. I did as I was told. He moved his head slightly. "And another." He sat back on his heels. "It's hard to be sure without my stethoscope, but your lungs sound clear."

"I'm fine," I said, the words sounding as hollow to me as I knew they did to him. I wasn't fine. I'd almost drowned. Mother was right. People died on boats.

"I've heard that too many times from you to take your word for it, Miss Davish." He took a plain brown wool blanket offered by Mack and draped it over my shoulders. Then he wrapped his warm arm around me. I hadn't realized how cold I'd felt in my soaked clothes. "What happened?"

"I was on the yacht," I said, pointing to the *Invictus*. "I can't swim and . . ." I hesitated. My memory was a blur. I'd heard footsteps. My hat brim broke over my eyes. I remembered the feel of someone's hands on my back. "And someone pushed me."

"What? Someone pushed you into the water?"

I nodded. "I called for you, Mack. Where did you go?"

"I went back to the dock, remember?" In my panic, I'd forgotten we'd agreed for him to return in thirty minutes' time. "Thought I'd be back by the time you were ready to go."

"Yes, of course. I forgot. Did you see anyone on the yacht?"

The boatman shook his head. "No."

"Did you, Walter?"

"No."

"By the way, why were you here, Walter?" I said. Disappointed and confused, I spoke more harshly than I'd planned.

"I followed you. Mack and I were halfway to the yacht when we heard you scream."

"But why?"

"I heard what my mother said to you. I didn't want you to believe for one moment longer that our relationship means nothing to me." I looked into his eyes and wondered how I could've ever doubted him. He tried to pull me toward him, but I resisted. "What's wrong?"

"Having this conversation for a second time makes me wonder if your mother isn't right. It will never work between us, Walter."

"How can you say that?"

"We're only here for the summer. Then what? I'll get a new position and travel to who knows where and you will go back to Arkansas."

"We'll figure something out." I looked at him dubiously. He took both of my hands in his and kissed them. Mack suddenly found an extreme interest in a flock of seagulls soaring over the harbor. "I love you, Hattie," Walter whispered. "And I almost lost you just now. I can't even bear the thought of it."

"But—" Walter's mouth on mine as he kissed me cut short my feeble protest.

"If they weren't Mack's or Dr. Grice's footsteps you heard, who was on the yacht with you?" Chief Preble said.

"I don't know."

Walter had driven me back to Rose Mont to change into dry clothes and report back to Mrs. Mayhew. After the jarring ride with Nick Whitwell in the motorcar, I'd expected the swift jaunt in Walter's rented gig to feel familiar and tame. I was wrong. I bounced and lurched about until, no longer able to control myself, I leaned over the side and choked up water still in my lungs and stomach. Walter took pity on me, offering me his handkerchief and slowing the horse down to a walk.

Mrs. Mayhew was dismayed but not surprised by my news

of finding evidence that someone was staying on the yacht. She was dismissive, however, when I suggested a man, most likely a crew member, was aboard and not the mistress she suspected.

"Why would a crew member shove you into the water?" she'd said. She had a point. But whoever it was, he had wanted me off the boat in a hurry. Why?

When I told her of my near drowning, she relinquished me from all further duties for the day and encouraged me to continue working with the police. I suspect she was as hopeful of catching the phantom mistress as she was sympathetic to my plight. Walter, insisting on not leaving my side until he felt I was fully recovered, drove me, this time at a pace I could've kept up with had I walked.

He must care for me, indeed, I'd thought.

"But you suspect someone?" Chief Preble asked.

"I went there on Mrs. Mayhew's request. She had a suspicion someone was staying on the boat while Mr. Mayhew was in New York. That person may be who pushed me."

"Mrs. Mayhew suspected a vagrant of living on the Mayhew yacht?"

"No, a mistress."

"Ah," the policeman said. "I see. And that's who you think pushed you?"

"I don't know," I said. "It could be."

"Or?" Chief Preble said, hearing my hesitation.

"Or it could've been Nick Whitwell."

"Why Nick Whitwell?"

I told him of all the evidence against the man. "He said he was staying on his father's yacht, but maybe he's been living on the *Invictus* instead. He overheard Mrs. Mayhew instruct me about the yacht. In his motorcar he could've gotten there quite fast."

"Did you see Nick Whitwell or his motorcar, Dr. Grice?"

"No, I'm afraid I didn't see anyone, except the boatman. We arrived only to see Hattie go under the water."

"Whoever it was probably hid on the yacht while Dr. Grice and the boatman rescued me."

"And they could be long gone by now," Chief Preble said.

"Yes, probably," I admitted.

"So there's nothing we can do. I'm sorry, Miss Davish."

"At least you can do as Mrs. Mayhew wants and search the yacht?" Walter said.

"Without Mr. Mayhew's permission? No, we can't do that."

"But surely there's enough suspicion surrounding Nick Whitwell to investigate further?" Walter said.

"Never mind, Walter," I said with a sigh. "The police chief and I have already had this conversation."

Chief Preble glanced at me with raised eyebrows as he answered Walter's question.

"Without concrete proof, there's nothing more we can do."

"Can do or will do?" Walter said.

Sam Preble shrugged. "We're talking about the Whitwells, Dr. Grice. I'm not going to risk scandal and my job on mere speculation. Sorry."

"You did what?" Gideon Mayhew said, again dressed in his athletic clothes and towel around his neck, but at least now he wore a bathrobe to cover him.

"Don't deflect the blame elsewhere, Gideon. I'm the one who should be demanding answers."

I'd taken an early morning hike as usual, staying well away from the coastline, had a short but pleasant conversation introducing myself to Mrs. Broadbank, the new housekeeper, upon my return and then a simple breakfast of coffee, toast, and jam. When the bell rang for me, I went up to Mrs. Mayhew's drawing room, refreshed, relaxed, and eager to do something I was trained to do. Instead I was to be witness to an ambush. As soon as I arrived, Mrs. Mayhew told her husband what she had discovered, through me, about someone living on his yacht.

"Davish here can tell you," Mrs. Mayhew said, pointing to me without looking at me. "Who is she, Gideon?"

"What is your secretary doing here anyway, Charlotte?" Mr. Mayhew said, avoiding the question. I wondered the same thing. I'd much rather be attending to the pile of mail lying unopened upon her table than acting witness to a domestic squabble.

"Leave us, Miss Davish," Mr. Mayhew said. I turned to leave, happy to oblige. "By the way," he said as I put my hand on the doorknob, "you're fired." I froze. I didn't know how to react. I'd never been dismissed from any position before. *Can he do that?* I wondered. *I'm Mrs. Mayhew's secretary after all.* I looked at Mrs. Mayhew for direction.

"What?" his wife screamed. "How dare you! She's my secretary." I felt a flicker of hope.

"Get another one. I will not have a meddler in this house."

Meddler? I thought. I was only doing what I was told to do.

"First Mrs. Crankshaw and now this. I've had enough of you interfering in the domestic affairs of this house. I run this house, not you. I say Davish stays."

"But I pay your allowance. And I say she goes. And I'll not hear another word about it." He stared at me, his eyes boring into me, unblinking.

"Don't worry, Davish," she said, looking at me for the first time. "I won't let you go without an excellent reference." She glanced back at her husband. "You and I know what loyalty really means. Don't we, Davish?"

"Yes, ma'am," I said, breathing a sigh of relief.

"Now get out!" Gideon Mayhew said.

I promptly left the room but stayed just outside in the hall.

"I just got done hiring the new housekeeper," Mrs. May-hew said, sighing. "Do you have any idea what it will take for me to get another secretary? Let alone one as trustworthy and loyal as Davish." Despite my sudden dismissal, I beamed at Mrs. Mayhew's praise. With a good reference I shouldn't have trouble finding a new position. But what would Sir Arthur think?

"Everyone's replaceable, dear," her husband said. "They'll be lining up to work for you. I have to say promising that trouble-maker a reference is more than generous. I wouldn't have been so kind."

"Well, I wouldn't have discharged her in the first place."

"Then we are both satisfied. Now if you'll excuse me, I'm off to the club."

I scuttled down the hall, hiding in a darkened doorway, hoping he wouldn't catch me eavesdropping. *But what if he did?* I asked myself. *He's already fired me.* What more could he do? A shiver went down my spine at the thought. I held my breath. I didn't want to know the answer.

I heard him cross the threshold and step into the hall when Mrs. Mayhew said, "You never did have an answer for my ac-cusation, Gideon."

"Because your suspicions aren't worthy of you, my dear," her husband replied as he strode down the hall. "Tell Davies I won't be back for dinner."

CHAPTER 36

"Here's your key, Miss Culver," the desk clerk said. I'd been admiring the young woman's hat, an ecru fancy braid with lace edge and a very high front brim, trimmed with matching ecru satin bow and feathers, as I waited for my turn to register.

When I left Rose Mont, reference in hand, I considered where to go. Lady Phillippa, without Sir Arthur's influence, wouldn't have me back. Miss Lizzie and Miss Lucy might oblige me, but I couldn't fathom living under the same roof as Mrs. Grice. I'd decided to check into the Ocean House Hotel, where Walter was staying.

If I can't be with Walter, at least I can be close, I thought.

A young woman, very pretty with porcelain skin, wide blue eyes, and pale yellow hair, took the key. As she turned away, I noticed a single beggar's-tick seed attached to the front brim of her bonnet.

"Excuse me," I said. "Miss Culver?" Any other time, I would never have intruded into this stranger's personal affairs, but I couldn't ignore the coincidence.

"Yes?"

"I couldn't help but admire your beautiful hat. I saw one like it in the latest edition of *La Mode Illustrée*."

She put her hand to the side of the bonnet and stroked the plumes. "Yes, I got it at a Parisian shop at the World's Fair. I arrived back a few days ago."

"I also couldn't help noticing that you have a beggar's-tick seed stuck to the brim."

"A what?" She sounded quite alarmed.

"May I?" I said as I reached to remove the offending seed. She nodded and I plucked off the seed, showing her.

"What is that?" she said, leaning over to get a closer look. Suddenly she scowled. "Nick!" she muttered, shaking her head. "I thought I got rid of all of those nasty things."

"Excuse me?" I said, shocked at her utterance.

"Oh, it's just that I had an incident that left me covered in these nasty, prickly things. My maid swore she'd removed them all."

"An incident?" I said, well aware I was being nosy. "You're not a plant collector or hiker then?"

She laughed. Instead of questioning my motives, she was clearly enjoying our conversation. "Me, a hiker, a plant collector? My word, no. I'm not one for the outdoors at all, actually. Only the thrill of it got me to go to Bailey's Beach in the first place." I raised my eyebrows at her. Going to Bailey's Beach wasn't what I would consider thrilling. She glanced around to see if anyone else was listening. "At midnight," she said from behind her hand.

"Oh!" I said.

She grabbed my arm and pulled me to a corner of the lobby and set me down next to her on a settee. "Shocking, isn't it?" she said, smiling.

"Yes, it is."

"Well, what if I told you that we didn't have bathing clothes with us?" She stared at me with wide-eyed anticipation, waiting for me to grasp her implication. She giggled and clapped her hands when my face betrayed my shock. "Needless to say, my wine that night wasn't watered down."

"Of course," I said. "Now I see how a simple excursion to Bailey's Beach could be quite a thrill of a lifetime."

"Yes, quite," she said, squealing with delight. Suddenly her smile disappeared. "And I thought the ride in his motorcar would be too."

Motorcar? I knew of only one person in Newport with such a conveyance.

"You were with Nicholas Whitwell?" I said.

"Yes, can you believe it?" she said. "My mother would swoon knowing I was out at night alone with a Whitwell."

"What happened in his motorcar?" I asked, remembering my experience in the contraption.

She scowled and started playing with the feather plumes on her hat. "It was dreadful, simply dreadful. We were having such fun, driving down sidewalks, spooking horses, stirring up birds, taking curves on Ocean Drive, and then he had to go and crash into the bushes. Tipped it right over! We had to walk all the way back." I tried not to smile at her distaste for one of my favorite pastimes. "Dawn was breaking when I snuck into my room. Luckily Aunt Sarah is a deep sleeper." I could only imagine what "Aunt Sarah" would say if she knew her niece was cavorting alone with a man in the early morning hours. Fortunately, Miss Culver's impetuous and risky behavior and her aunt's reaction wasn't my concern. Her alibi for Nick Whitwell, on the other hand, was.

"And that's how you encountered the beggar's-tick seeds?"

"You can't imagine how simply awful it was." She shuddered. "My dress was dirty, my hands were scratched"—she showed me her hands, but any scratches were hidden by her gloves—"and I was covered with those nasty seeds, in my dress, my hair, and, as you noticed, my new bonnet."

"And Mr. Whitwell?" I asked, remembering the bandage on his cheek.

"Oh, besides a scrape on his face, he wasn't much worse for wear. He didn't fall into those bushes like I did."

"So you can say you were with Mr. Whitwell from around midnight until almost dawn?"

She frowned. The deep furrows between her brows weren't becoming on her youthful face. She probably was no more than sixteen or seventeen years old. "Yes, why?" Before I could answer, she said, "By the way, I don't think you introduced yourself, Miss . . . ?"

"Miss Davish," I said. "Hattie Davish."

"So why are you asking me all these questions, Miss Davish?"

Now you ask? I thought. She had already told me far too much. "I'm an acquaintance of the Whitwell family," I said.

"You are?" she said, slightly surprised.

I nodded. *That's stretching the truth,* I thought to myself. *Shame on you, Hattie.*

But Miss Culver took reassurance from it. "Then you know what a scoundrel Nick can be." Her beaming countenance belied her words. She didn't mind this scoundrel at all.

"What I know, Miss Culver, is that you have been a good friend to Mr. Whitwell today." Now I understood why Nick had been reticent about his injury and his whereabouts when Lester Sibley was killed. Nick hadn't killed the labor man but had compromised his engagement to Cora Mayhew. If word of his escapades with Miss Culver became common knowledge, it might put his relationship with Cora, his social status, and his future in jeopardy.

"Why do you say that, Miss Davish?" the young woman said.

"Because you've given him an alibi for murder." Her eyes widened and her hand flew to cover her gaping mouth. "But I would keep your midnight adventure to yourself. Rumors run rampant in Newport. You wouldn't want your aunt to find out."

She nodded. "No, I wouldn't. She'd ship me back to Newark, and Mother, without blinking an eye!" She stood and looked around the lobby. An extremely rotund older woman in a black floppy straw hat too large for her head waddled toward us. Miss Culver's reaction to seeing the old woman told me the woman's identity before she called her by name.

"Aunt Sarah, over here."

"Electra, where have you been? We'll be late for the concert at the Casino. We must be seen. You'll never marry well if you aren't seen."

"Oh, Aunt, you don't have to worry about me being seen. It's more a matter of who sees what." Electra Culver turned and winked at me. I blushed. But despite our differences and her scandalous behavior, I couldn't help but like her. I smiled back.

Her aunt glanced at me, squinting her eyes. She didn't understand Miss Culver's meaning and she didn't know who I was. She hadn't even asked. "Well, let's go," Aunt Sarah said.

"By all means," Electra Culver said. She watched her aunt waddle toward the door. "I can rely on your discretion, Miss Davish?" she said, lowering her voice.

"Of course," I said.

She smiled, stroked the plumes on her bonnet again, and followed her aunt out the door. I stared after her until a flash of gold in the street outside caught my attention.

If only I could sell the secrets I know, I thought as I watched Gideon Mayhew's trap, the family crest painted on the side in blazing gold leaf, go by. *I'd be as rich as Gideon Mayhew.*

Dismissing that thought, I returned to the registration desk to get a room for the night.

★ ★ ★

After unpacking a few things, I typed up a quick note to Chief Preble, informing him of what I'd learned from Electra Culver. Knowing the police weren't seriously considering Nick Whitwell as a suspect, I felt justified in not revealing that young lady's name. Let it be enough that Mr. Preble might have a clear conscience, knowing Nick Whitwell was innocent. I dropped the note into the hotel's mailbox. That done, I fruitlessly knocked on the door of Walter's room, two floors above mine. I longed for a sympathetic ear. His absence was fortunate. Instead of uselessly complaining to Walter, I focused on what I needed to do—get a new position. I returned to Peck's Employment Agency, much to Mrs. Peck's delight. With the inquiry made, I had nothing left to do but wait. I took advantage of the afternoon sunshine, returning to my room for a few specimen jars and heading back to the beach across from Gooseberry Island where I'd seen seabeach amaranth growing. After a couple of hours, and several plant specimens richer, I returned to the Ocean House Hotel via the harbor, drawn to the spot where Lester Sibley was killed. I looked around and noticed nothing new. Then I walked up the lane and found the path down to the water's edge. I found a large, flat boulder with a view of the harbor, Fort Adams in the distance to the west, the Lime Rock Lighthouse and the *Invictus,* Mr. Mayhew's yacht, just across. Without setting out to do so, I was in a prime location to notice who, if anyone, boarded the vessel.

Would I see the person who pushed me? I wondered. I set my bag of jars down, pulled out a pad and a pencil, and sat down.

Despite the leisure time, or maybe due to it, I felt restless. My abrupt departure from Rose Mont and my uncertain future were in part to blame. With Mrs. Mayhew's reference and thus no black spot on my record I felt certain I would secure a decent position soon. Yet I couldn't help wondering whether that position would take me away from Newport and Walter. And how would Sir Arthur react when he returned from England to learn the circumstances of my dismissal? But my restlessness was also in part due to the loose ends, the unanswered questions I still had. I made a list:

1. Who pushed me? Mr. Mayhew's possible mistress? A crew member? Why?
2. Who set fire to the bank? Why?
3. Who killed Lester Sibley?
4. Where will I be this time tomorrow?
5. What am I going to tell Walter?
6. What am I going to tell Sir Arthur?

When I looked up, I noticed a rowboat tied up beside Mr. Mayhew's yacht. Who was that? I wondered as I watched a person clamber over the side of the yacht, awkwardly carrying a large satchel tossed over their shoulder. And what was in the satchel?

I collected my things and sat watching and waiting as the dinghy made its slow progress toward the dock. I stood up as the person disembarked from the docked rowboat and lumbered closer.

It was Delia, the Mayhews' laundress.

Was she Mr. Mayhew's mistress? Could she have been the one who pushed me overboard? *Impossible,* I thought. Yet what was she doing here?

"Delia," I called out to her.

"Hattie," she said, smiling. "What are you doing here?"

"I could ask the same of you," I said.

She pointed to the load on her back. "What else, laundry."

"Of course," I said, relieved. "But do you always collect laundry from the yacht?"

"No," she said, laughing, "Mrs. Mayhew insisted I gather up

anything that needed washing. We all know how Mrs. Mayhew's been lately about her husband, if you get my meaning."

"I certainly do. She insisted I take a look around twice."

"Well, at least it wasn't a completely wasted trip." Delia indicated the laundry bag over her shoulder.

"So you don't think he has a mistress?"

The laundress shook her head. "Maybe you saw signs of a woman being onboard, but I certainly didn't." I had to admit I hadn't seen anything suspicious either. Except of course that someone had recently been aboard. It must've been a crew member returning early after all. But why would he push me overboard? I remembered Mack's jokes about me being a land-lubber. The crew member would have no way of knowing I couldn't swim. Could it all have been a joke? If so, I wasn't laughing.

"All I know is that the clothes I have in here are all Mr. Mayhew's," Delia said.

Mayhew's?

"Why would Mr. Mayhew's clothes be there? He's in New York," I wondered out loud.

Delia shrugged. "From the stink of these gym clothes, they may have been there for days." But I hadn't seen any dirty clothes onboard the first time. Where had they come from? And when? "Well, I better get these back," she said.

"Before you go, may I ask a favor?"

"Sure, what?"

"Remember when I asked you about the beggar's-tick seeds? If you had seen any on anyone's clothes?"

She nodded and then her eyes widened. She threw the laundry satchel to the ground and ripped it open. She yanked out a jacket, waistcoat, and pants. They were covered in beggar's-tick seeds. "Like this?"

"Yes, like that," I said.

"Then maybe you know why these were crumpled up in

the linen closet? I found them when I was retrieving the laundry satchel." I nodded. "What does it all mean then?"

I was speechless. The evidence before me was clear. Yet how did I tell Delia that the little sticky seeds implicated no one less than Gideon Mayhew, robber baron and one of the wealthiest men in the country, in the killing of Lester Sibley?

"Hattie," Delia said anxiously. "What does it mean?"

"Trouble."

CHAPTER 37

"What do you expect me to do?" Chief Preble said when I found him. Sergeant Ballard at the station had said the chief was "out on the dock." That wasn't very helpful. Newport has dozens of wharfs and docks stretching out into the bay. After following as close to the water as possible, hoping to catch a glimpse of the policeman among the boatmen, dockworkers, and commercial fishermen, I found him in the same place I'd found him before. He had several small fish on the dock at his feet. "Because the man had some seeds stuck to his pant leg? It's not enough to accuse him of murder."

"But why else would he have the seeds on him? He must've killed Lester Sibley." The policeman shook his head. "But he's a member of the same Newport shooting club as Harland Whitwell," I said, remembering seeing the directory for the club on the yacht. "Even if he never had access to Mr. Whitwell's gun, he must have one of his own."

"That may be, but we're talking about Gideon Mayhew here. Without absolute proof, I'm not about to risk everything by accusing one of the most powerful men in America of murder. And seeds are not proof."

"What would be?"

"A witness, maybe."

"What about a confession?"

"Of course, but Gideon Mayhew isn't about to walk into my station and offer up a confession."

"He might confess to someone."

"Like who?"

"Like me."

Chief Preble laughed. "That's ludicrous. And here I thought you had a logical mind, Miss Davish."

"It is not ridiculous," I said, bristling at his derision. The policeman could see it on my face.

"Okay, Miss Davish. Tell me why he would do such a thing?"

"For the same reason you aren't taking me seriously. I'm a servant and he believes servants don't count. So he might confess to me because he'll assume he won't be prosecuted."

"And he'd be right. If he made a confession to you and you alone, I still wouldn't be able to arrest him."

I balled up my fists in frustration. *"Un, deux, trois,"* I started counting under my breath to control my anger. "You're telling me, Chief Preble, that you'll only consider arresting Gideon Mayhew if he confesses to you directly or to someone of his own stature?"

"If he's actually guilty of what you accuse him of? Yes, basically."

"Then that's what he'll have to do." I left the dock with Sam Preble snagging a fish and shaking his head.

As I nervously stood at the back entrance of Rose Mont, waiting for the bell to be answered, I glanced up at the second-floor window of Mr. Mayhew's office. How had I missed noticing how much the gargoyles carved below the sill resembled the man himself? *Can I do this?* I wondered. Before I had a chance to reconsider, Mrs. Broadbank opened the door and welcomed me in. She sent word of my visit to my former employer.

"Thank you for seeing me, Mrs. Mayhew," I said when she called me up. She was dressed to go out.

"I received your note and am most curious. So you think my husband does have something to confess?"

"Yes, ma'am. I do."

"And you are willing to confront him in my stead?" I nodded. "All right then, he's in his study, but I don't know for how much longer. Let's go now."

I followed Mrs. Mayhew down the corridor. I passed Britta in the hall. Mrs. Mayhew ignored her presence, but Britta and I locked eyes. I couldn't stop and answer the question in her gaze. I hoped I'd be able to later. My former employer and I stopped in front of Mr. Mayhew's study.

"Remember," Mrs. Mayhew whispered, "I will be listening at the door. I'll hear everything he and you say. If he doesn't confess to having a mistress, I will deny playing any part in this scheme."

It was only fair. I'd already been discharged from my position, and with a reference in hand I had nothing to lose. Mrs. Mayhew had to live with this man. I suddenly felt guilty misleading Mrs. Mayhew about her husband's possible confession. Her life might forever be altered by the news.

And oh, how the rumor mill will run rampant after this day, I thought.

But would Mrs. Mayhew suffer from it? I wondered. No. Somehow, she would twist it to her benefit. I didn't have to worry about Mrs. Mayhew. She would be fine. Mrs. Mayhew, mistaking my reverie for hesitation, knocked.

"Come," a male voice from within said. Mrs. Mayhew

opened the door, careful to stay behind it, and nearly pushed me into the room.

Gideon Mayhew was standing at his desk, looking down at a ledger he held in his hands. He looked up when I entered. "You?" he said. I expected anger, insults, or accusations, but instead he laughed. "You have brass coming here, I'll give you that. What do you want?"

I took a deep breath, straightened my hat, pushed my shoulders back, and took a step forward. "I've come to ask you a question, Mr. Mayhew."

"Yes?" He looked down at his ledger again.

"Did you kill Lester Sibley?"

His head snapped up from his reading. I heard a gasp come from the other side of the door. Mrs. Mayhew now knew what confession I hoped to draw from her husband. I took it as a good sign that she didn't charge into the room to stop me.

Gideon Mayhew remained silent. No denial, no shouting, no slamming his ledger down. Instead what he did was even more frightening. He slowly set the ledger down and walked around his desk toward me. Instinctually I took a step back.

"And why would you ask that, Miss Davish?" he said, the tone of his voice steady. Too steady.

"Because Delia, the laundress, found hundreds of beggar's-tick seeds on your clothes. Either you've developed an overnight penchant for wading through bushes or you killed Lester Sibley."

Gideon Mayhew stared at me for a moment, a moment too long. I took another step back.

"Get out of here, girl. You're trespassing." He turned his back on me.

Relief flooded through me as he walked back toward his desk. Until that moment, I hadn't realized how much I'd underestimated the physical danger I was putting myself in. But with every step that put distance between us my courage rallied.

"Or what, Mr. Mayhew? Will you shoot me as you did Lester Sibley?"

He turned, more annoyance than rage on his countenance. "If you continue to annoy me as he did, yes," he said. *There! He said it. He confessed.*

"So you did kill Lester Sibley?"

He raised his arm, pointing to the door. "Get out!" he shouted. His command spurred me toward the door, but it opened before I had a chance to reach it.

"Did you, Gideon?" Mrs. Mayhew said, standing in the doorway.

"Did I what, Charlotte?"

"Did you kill that labor man?"

"Have you been listening at the door? I always knew you had a penchant for gossip, but you've sunk to a new low if you feel you must eavesdrop on your own husband."

Mrs. Mayhew ignored him. "Answer my question, Gideon. Did you kill that man?"

"Yes, I did."

"Why?" his wife demanded.

"The man was a pest, a nuisance. What he preached was stirring up unrest and that's bad for business. You know what I'm talking about, Charlotte. Even you lost a good house-keeper to the opiate that man was peddling." I didn't remind him Mrs. Crankshaw never professed to believe her brother-in-law's message of better pay and shorter hours. I knew that even her family relation to the labor man would've been enough to get her discharged, whether she was innocent of believing his message or not.

"So you killed him?" Charlotte Mayhew asked.

"I tried to get rid of him many times. I had Doubleday dump his propaganda into the bay. I had Sibley implicated in the bank fires."

"You set the bank fire?" I said, astonished. I'd known about the trunk full of propaganda pamphlets, but I'd never discovered who'd started the fire.

"Doubleday did," he said casually. "The bank was failing anyway. Whitwell suggested it. Unfortunately the savings bank burned more than the Aquidneck National did. I can tell you because we won't be getting the insurance anyway."

"And Lester Sibley?" his wife insisted.

"The police arrested him for the fire, but when that didn't deter him I ordered Doubleday to beat some sense into the man. Nothing worked, Charlotte. Sibley refused to desist."

"So you killed him?" his wife repeated.

"What was I supposed to do? The man invaded my home. He had the audacity to step foot into my house and preach his message in front of my guests. He gave me no choice. He had to go."

"You encountered him on your way to your yacht, didn't you?" I said. "You said you didn't sleep in your own bed that night." Both Mayhews glared at me.

"How did you know that?" Mrs. Mayhew asked.

I ignored her. *Let that be my secret,* I thought.

"Lester Sibley hadn't heeded Doubleday's threat after all, had he, Mr. Mayhew? You encountered him walking from the depot. He had no intention of leaving. In fact, he was heading back toward Rose Mont, wasn't he? So you killed him." Mayhew glared at me. The hatred in his eyes told me I was right. "Do you keep your derringer on the yacht, Mr. Mayhew, or do you walk around with it in your pocket?"

"Are you still here?" he said. "I thought I told you to get out."

"Is that why the clothes, the books, and the other things were on your yacht? You were staying there?" his wife said, again ignoring his comments to me. "But you said you were in New York?"

"On occasion I stay on the yacht instead. But how did you know about that?"

"I thought you had a mistress, Gideon. You haven't been acting quite right. I suspected something was going on."

"So you spied on me?"

"All I did was have someone take a look around the yacht."

"You were snooping. Admit it."

"Yes, but—"

"Obviously, I've been too indulgent. Charlotte, I forbid you from indulging in this disgraceful behavior again. You got what you wanted—Mrs. Astor at the ball. Now it's got to stop. You'll have everyone talking about me and I won't stand for it." I was aghast that the man, who had confessed to killing someone, was admonishing his wife for snooping.

"So you don't have a mistress?" his wife said, again ignoring his commands.

"No, Charlotte. I don't have a mistress."

"Then why all the extra sessions in the gymnasium?"

"Fit body, fit mind, Charlotte," he said, shaking his head. "You should try it sometime." I looked at his round, plump wife and felt sorry for her. She was married to a horrible man. "Now let this be an end to this."

But then his wife smiled. How could she smile? Granted it must be a relief to know your husband wasn't committing adultery, but the man had admitted to committing murder. Wasn't that worse?

"You pushed me into the bay," I said, now knowing that no one else could've done it. "Why? Because I was working with the police?"

"You were trespassing," Mr. Mayhew said, looking back down at his ledger. "Now, Charlotte, get this woman out of here."

"I can't swim," I said. He ignored me, reading his ledger as if I'd already left. "I almost drowned!" I declared, shocked by his indifference.

Charlotte Mayhew grabbed my arm. Seeing my last chance slip away, I said, "Don't you worry the police will arrest you?"

"With what evidence? On whose say-so?" Gideon Mayhew said bluntly as his wife pulled me out of the open doorway.

"Be gone now, Miss Davish," Mrs. Mayhew said.

"But Mrs. Mayhew, you must go to the police. Your husband confessed to murdering a man."

"I'm surprised at you, Miss Davish. I thought you were a girl with a head on her shoulders. Didn't you hear what he said? My husband wasn't confessing to murder. He was talking about business. And you know we women aren't much for business."

I stared at her in shock, disappointment. My scheme had failed. Mrs. Mayhew had heard the same thing I had and she wasn't going to tell the police. I'd gotten someone of Mr. Mayhew's stature to witness his confession, someone I thought I could trust. But that had been my mistake. Gideon and Charlotte Mayhew were more alike than I ever would've thought. Her husband had insulted her, cheated on her, meddled in her running of the household, confessed to murdering a man, and she had still taken his side.

Only proves I should stick to what I was trained to do, I thought.

I was eager to leave Rose Mont and everything having to do with the Mayhews behind. Yet I'd never felt so powerless. Gideon Mayhew was going to get away with murder and I could do nothing about it. Or could I? If my time with Mrs. Mayhew had taught me anything it was that knowledge was power, and for once I wasn't obligated to keep her secret.

"I'm relying on you not to say a word of this, Miss Davish," Mrs. Mayhew said.

I cringed at her familiar phrase. "I'm sorry, Mrs. Mayhew," I said, "but I don't work for you anymore. And I know where your true loyalties lie. I came here on my own time and I will do what I will with what I heard today."

"How dare you!" she shouted at my back as I turned from her and descended the grand staircase and, for the first and only time, walked out the front door.

CHAPTER 38

I can't let him get away with this!

I left the Mayhews and Rose Mont almost physically ill knowing that Gideon Mayhew had committed a murder he would not be prosecuted for, at least not in a court of law. However, during the walk back to my hotel I recalled how many times the Mayhews and others in Newport's high society had mentioned not wanting to have that same society disparage them. In fact, even as he was admitting a crime Gideon Mayhew was admonishing his wife for making him look bad with her snooping. Public opinion mattered. The Mayhews understood, more than almost anyone in this resort town, that gossip and rumor could be as damaging as a police arrest.

But Mr. Mayhew wasn't concerned about confessing to me because he didn't see me as a threat. And rightfully so; word from me would be ignored by his peers and by the police. But what he didn't count on, and which Mrs. Mayhew was well aware of, was that I had connections. Connections whose insinuations would be listened to. That's why she insisted I stay silent. Her recently won acceptance into the highest levels of Newport society depended upon it.

I'm sorry, Mrs. Mayhew, I thought. *Not this time.*

As soon as I arrived at my hotel, I wrote a note to Miss Lucy and Miss Lizzy, suggesting I had some news to share and hoping to come for tea. While I waited for their reply, I typed up all I knew about Lester Sibley's death that I could tell the elderly Shaw sisters. I wanted to clarify in my mind what I could reveal and what I could not. I'd promised to keep several secrets in the past few days and wouldn't want to inadvertently go back on my word. When the time came their reply was swift, and when I arrived at Moffat Cottage I was surprised to see Lady Phillippa there already sipping her tea. Was I late? I glanced at the pendant watch pinned to my dress. No, I was here at the exact time Miss Lizzie indicated. So why was Lady Phillippa here?

"Ah, Miss Davish," Lady Phillippa said before Miss Lizzie or Miss Lucy could greet me. "Mrs. Fry said you'd be here." I looked to Miss Lucy.

"We saw Lady Phillippa at the Casino earlier, dear," Miss Lizzie answered instead. "We told her you were coming to tea with news."

"As I had news for you, I invited myself to tea," Lady Phillippa said.

"Yes, yes," Miss Lucy said, "everyone has news, but no one is saying a thing. On with it, I say. Sit down, Davish. You're making me antsy." I tried to hide my smile as I complied. My standing had nothing to do with Miss Lucy's restlessness.

Miss Lizzie handed me a cup of tea. "Milk, sugar?" she asked.

"No, thank you. This is fine," I said.

"Will you two stop talking about tea and tell me what the news is!" Miss Lucy's face was red.

"Well, Miss Lucy, if you are so eager," Lady Phillippa said, "and as I must get ready for dinner at Mrs. Ogden Goelet's, I will speak first." She set her cup down.

"Finally," Miss Lucy said, under her breath but loud enough for all to hear. I wondered if her hearing was failing. Lady Phillippa looked askance at her for a moment before turning to look at me.

"I've had a letter from Arthur."

I stopped drinking my tea mid-sip and placed it back on the saucer. Before I heard another word, I set the teacup and saucer on the table. I didn't trust myself not to spill it.

"He has arrived safely at his ancestral home and his father has recovered quite remarkably from his illness."

"That's good news," I said, wondering what it had to do with me. I glanced at Miss Lucy. From the glower on her face, she was wondering the same thing.

"Yes, it is. It means Arthur will be able to return to Newport before the end of the Season. He will be here for the horse show in September."

"I'm glad for you," I said, trying to hide my disappointment. Sir Arthur's early return did nothing to solve my current predicament as I'd hoped. Unless he sought to engage my services again, I was still unemployed.

"It is well for you too, Miss Davish, as he has requested that I secure your services again."

Thank you again, Sir Arthur, I thought. I recounted the numerous times Sir Arthur had procured me employment, working either for him or for one of his many distinguished acquaintances. Only once had his recommendation gone terribly wrong. I shuddered to remember Mrs. Trevelyan.

"Apparently Arthur and this American colonel spent the entire voyage to England discussing this new project." I'd missed some of what Lady Phillippa had said. It didn't matter. I'd soon find out all about it from Sir Arthur. "Knowing you are currently at leisure, I presume that you accept?"

It didn't surprise me that my dismissal from the Mayhew household had already reached Lady Phillippa's ears. It did surprise me that, knowing this, she would still engage me, even at Sir Arthur's request.

"Yes, of course," I said. "But is Sir Arthur aware of my dismissal?"

"No, not yet, but knowing Arthur, it won't matter. Mrs. Mayhew gave you an excellent reference, didn't she?" Again I was taken aback by the speed with which news spread over the grapevine.

"Yes, she did."

"Then it's settled. You can stay at Fairview. Where are you staying now?"

"The Ocean House."

"Hattie, dear," Miss Lizzie said. "You didn't have to do that. You should've come and stayed with us."

"Yes," Miss Lucy said, her arms folded under her sagging bosom. "Then we wouldn't have had to wait until now to hear your news. That is, if you ever get around to it."

"Oh, Lucy. That's not the only reason we enjoy Hattie's company."

"No, but right now it's the most important one," her sister said.

Lady Phillippa rose. I rose as well, but the elderly sisters stayed where they were.

"Well, I must be off. I'll arrange to have your belongings brought to Fairview tonight."

"Thank you, Lady Phillippa," I said. Mrs. Peck at the employment agency would be disappointed, but I couldn't be more relieved. To continue to work for Sir Arthur and not have to leave Newport, and Walter, so soon was more than I could've hoped for. My only concern now was earning my keep. "May I ask, ma'am, what I'll do while we wait for Sir Arthur's return?"

"Oh, didn't I tell you? A parcel, addressed to you, arrived with the letter. From the size of it, you should be kept quite busy indeed. Good day, ladies."

"Good day," Miss Lizzie said. Miss Lucy merely grunted.

"Good day, Lady Phillippa," Walter said as he passed Sir Arthur's wife leaving the room. "Miss Davish," he added, smiling as he walked toward me. His mother was a few steps behind him.

"Oh, bother," Miss Lucy sighed. "Now we'll never get to the good part."

"Lucy," Miss Lizzie hissed. "Be patient."

I leaned over to the old woman as Walter and his mother took their seats and Miss Lizzie poured them tea.

"Don't worry, Miss Lucy; the wait will be worth it." I smiled at her and she licked her lips in anticipation.

"Oh, very well," she grumbled, but I could see she was appeased.

"What will be worth the wait?" Walter asked.

"Walter," his mother admonished. "Prying is a most unbecoming habit." I noticed she still didn't look at me or acknowledge my presence. At least she hadn't objected to my being there. And fortunately so, for I think if Julia Grice had made an issue of it Miss Lucy would've breached all protocol and sided with me. She was desperate to hear my news.

"The news, Dr. Grice," Miss Lucy said, ignoring her houseguest's ironic comment, "that Davish has come to tell us. I think she knows who killed Harland Whitwell and Lester Sibley."

"Oh?" Julia Grice said, looking at me for the first time.

"Is this true, Miss Davish?" Walter said. "Have you solved another murder?"

"I haven't read any such thing in the papers," Mrs. Grice said.

"And you won't," I said.

"Why, dear?" Miss Lizzie said, slathering her crumpet with butter.

"Because Harland Whitwell's death will remain a mystery." I saw Miss Lucy's shoulders sag. "And the police won't prosecute who killed Lester Sibley."

Miss Lucy perked up immediately, sitting on the edge of her chair. "Why not?" she said.

"Because Gideon Mayhew did it."

Everyone gasped.

"Davish!" Miss Lucy said, clapping her hands. She was almost giggling. "Do you actually think Gideon Mayhew killed that labor man?"

"Yes, I do."

"How could you say such a thing?" Mrs. Grice demanded. "Without proof you are disparaging one of the most important, influential men in America and you're nothing but a secretary. If the police won't prosecute him, who are you to make such scandalous claims?"

"Because I have proof," I said. "He confessed to his wife, in my presence."

I glanced over to Miss Lucy. She'd closed her eyes. Her face was pale and her body had gone rigid. I thought she was going to faint. Instead a wide grin spread across her face. "By God, Davish, you were right," she said, opening her eyes wide. "Like the first dance at your debutante ball or the melted butter on your mother's biscuits after churning all day, it was worth the wait. Every agonizing minute! Now tell us everything he said."

Which I did. When I finished the room was silent for several moments as my revelation settled in.

"So he's going to get away with murder," Miss Lizzie said, aghast. "How horrible."

"Yes, horrible," Miss Lucy said. I could see in her eyes she was already tallying a list of her friends she was going to call on as soon as I left.

"Some people think they are better than everyone else," Mrs. Grice said, shaking her head. I looked at Walter to see if he caught the irony of his mother's words. He shrugged his shoulders slightly and smiled.

"You're right, Julia, dear," Miss Lizzie said. "Some people think the world is only here for their amusement and that they can get away with anything, even murder."

"I never did like Gideon Mayhew," Miss Lucy said.

"Me either," her sister agreed.

"Mrs. Mayhew seemed nice," Julia Grice conceded. "But I'm glad we didn't socialize much with the husband."

"Now, Miss Lucy, I must beg a favor."

"What is it, Davish?"

"I must ask everyone actually, if I may. If you decide to repeat what I've told you, please be so kind as to not use my name. As Mrs. Grice so kindly pointed out, I do work for my living and must maintain a certain level of integrity. Besides, I wouldn't want to embarrass Sir Arthur before he even returns."

"Yes, good thinking, Davish," Miss Lucy said, nodding her head vigorously. We both knew full well that the source of the rumor never mattered, only the probability that it could be true.

"Of course, dear," Miss Lizzie said. "You have our word." Walter and his mother nodded in agreement as well.

"Thank you," I said.

James, the footman turned butler, arrived then, bringing a fresh pot of tea. He caught my eye as he bent down to set it on the tea tray. A slight smile flitted across his lips. His eyes sparkled. I was glad to see him happy.

"Oh, Chase, dear," Miss Lizzie said, "would you bring more butter?"

"Of course, Miss Shaw," James said, a consummate professional again. We waited for him to leave before discussing Gideon Mayhew again.

"I guess that explains why I saw Gideon Mayhew's yacht sail out of the harbor a little while ago," Walter said. I wasn't surprised. Mrs. Mayhew must've convinced him to leave before the rumors spread. "He'll go back to New York, or even to Europe, until someone else's name is clouded in scandal."

"You did?" Miss Lucy said.

"Yes, I quite enjoyed getting out on the water yesterday," Walter said, winking at me. "So I decided to rent a skiff to get a better look around seaside. I saw him heading out to sea as I was docking."

"Well, that's what I would do too if I'd killed a man," Mrs. Grice said in disgust.

"The Sibley man was killed with a gun, wasn't he?" Miss Lucy asked. "One of those little pocket pistols?"

"Yes," I said, worried what she might say next.

"Then maybe Gideon killed Harland as well? They never did find Harland's gun."

"Oh, dear," Miss Lizzie said. "Do you think so?"

"Not necessarily," I said, knowing the full truth of Mr. Whitwell's tragic death. "Any one of the derringers the Newport Shooting Club members receive as a symbol of membership could've been used. Besides, Mr. Mayhew was in New York at the time."

"Either way, I'm disappointed in you, Davish," Miss Lucy said.

"Why, dear?" her sister asked before I could.

"She should've solved that murder too."

"Miss Davish is a secretary and not a policeman, Miss Lucy," Walter said, coming to my defense.

"I know that," Miss Lucy said peevishly. "But I wanted to know who did it!"

"Maybe his son did it? He's quite the disreputable young man," Julia Grice said, curiously joining the conjecture. Maybe knowing I was no threat to her plans, she was relaxing in my presence. "Like you said, that gun was never found."

"Yes, maybe Nick did it," Miss Lucy said hopefully.

I felt frustrated and helpless. I'd done my job; I'd uncovered the truth about Harland Whitwell's death. Yet I couldn't stop everyone from wondering. Nor could I stop whatever rumors they might spread about Nick Whitwell's involvement in his father's death. Maybe the gossip would force Jane Whitwell to reveal the truth. I could only hope so.

"That reminds me, dear," Miss Lizzie said. "I heard yesterday that Cora Mayhew called off the engagement."

"Well, that's not surprising," Miss Lucy said. "I should've known when Lady Phillippa mentioned her son escorted Cora to the polo match."

"Supposedly the name of one Miss Electra Culver, a young girl of seventeen, has been connected with him. From what I heard," Miss Lizzie said, "the two were spotted au naturel at Bailey's Beach."

Mrs. Grice gasped. Miss Lucy frowned.

"Lizzie, how long have you known this? And how did you know and I didn't?"

As the two sisters continued to argue, Walter said, "With all your investigating, have you had a chance to collect any plants?" His mother scowled as Walter turned from me to her. "Miss Davish here is an excellent amateur botanist."

"Yes, thank you for asking, Dr. Grice," I said, the words in my mouth sounding so formal. "Newport has proven a rich hunting ground for new specimens. I could show you sometime if you'd like."

"My son has no interest in your plant collection," Julia Grice said.

"You're wrong, Mother," Walter said. "Many medicines

have their basis in botanicals. Besides, I'm most interested in everything Miss Davish does."

"Walter!" his mother exclaimed. "Be careful what you say. Such a declaration could be misconstrued."

"Very well, then I must be more clear." Walter stood up and walked over to me. Miss Lizzie and Miss Lucy stopped their conversation and watched as he offered me his hand. I took it and he assisted me from my chair. He placed my hand on his arm and escorted me across the room to face his mother.

"Mother," he said. "I don't think you and Miss Davish have been properly introduced."

"Walter," his mother said, trying hard to avoid looking at anyone in the room. "This is most unbecoming. You are needlessly misleading this poor girl. Please sit down."

"Miss Davish, this is Mrs. Winston Grice, my mother," Walter said, ignoring his mother's reprimand. "And Mother," he said, gazing into my eyes and bringing my hand to his lips, "this is Miss Hattie Davish, the woman I love."

Miss Lizzie, dropping her second half-eaten crumpet into her lap, butter-side down, clapped her hands and giggled like a schoolgirl. "Oh, Walter, dear," she said. "I knew it."

"It's about time," Miss Lucy added.

"Is this true, Walter?"

"Yes, Mother, it is."

"Are you sure?"

"Yes, very sure."

"Very well," Mrs. Grice said. I didn't know what to say. Mrs. Grice took a deep breath and finally looked at me. She didn't offer her hand, she didn't smile, but suddenly I knew what Mrs. Mayhew must've felt when Mrs. Astor's calling card finally arrived when Walter's mother nodded slightly and said, "Then I'm pleased to make your acquaintance, Miss Davish."

"And I yours, Mrs. Grice." And I meant it. I'd never been more pleased in my life.

3 1170 00952 0838